Praise for TAMAR by Ann Chamberlin

"Thought-provoking and engrossing."

"Rich and subtle, woven of threads brilliant and dark, Ann Chamberlin's TAMAR is a story of dignity and courage in the face of outrageous betrayal, wisdom and selflessness in the midst of ignorance and greed, the triumph of what is best in us over what is worst—this is a big, beautiful, powerful book."

"Chamberlin brings to life the drama of the diminution of earth-based goddess worship before a male god that forbids any other deity. The tale of passion, loss, and fated retribution includes wonderful elements . . . and piquant details."

"A fascinating journey into history. . . . Ann Chamberlin brings the ancient realm of King David to startling, thrilling life in this tale of a time and place where God was called Goddess, and dwelled in the secret groves protected by the knowledge of women. TAMAR is a one-of-a-kind adventure of the mind and soul. Don't miss this."

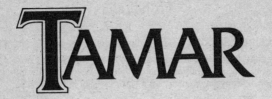

TAMAR

Ann Chamberlin

A TOM DOHERTY ASSOCIATES BOOK
NEW YORK

To Natalia

This is a work of fiction. All the characters and events portrayed in this book are fictitious, and any resemblance to real people or events is purely coincidental.

TAMAR

The excerpt appearing on page 150 is from *Thespis: Ritual Myth and Drama in the Ancient Near East* by T.H. Gaster. Copyright © 1975 by T.H. Gaster. Reprinted by permission of The Gordian Press.

The excerpt appearing on page 314 is from *The Sumerians* by Samuel Noah Kramer. Copyright © 1963 by Samuel Noah Kramer. Reprinted by permission of The University of Chicago Press.

Cover art by David Cherry
Maps by Ellisa Mitchell

A Tor Book
Published by Tom Doherty Associates, Inc.
175 Fifth Avenue
New York, N.Y. 10010

Tor® is a registered trademark of Tom Doherty Associates, Inc.

ISBN: 0-812-52370-9

First edition: March 1994
First mass market edition: December 1994

Printed in the United States of America

0 9 8 7 6 5 4 3 2 1

PEOPLE AND PLACES OF TAMAR

ABSALOM—Son of David and Maacah, younger brother of Tamar.

AHINOAM—Wife of David, mother of Amnon.

AMMON—The land and people east of the River Jordan. Their capital, Rabbath-Ammon, is present-day Amman, Jordan.

AMNON—Firstborn son of David. Ahinoam is his mother. Tamar's lover.

DAVID—King first of Judah, then the combined kingdom of Israel and Judah, then an ever-growing empire.

GESHUR—The land and people where Tamar and Maacah were born. It is the present-day southern Golan, bordering on the Sea of Galilee.

JEBUS—The land and people of a small kingdom surrounding the city, also called Jebus, which David conquered and renamed Jerusalem.

JONADAB—The son of an elder brother of David named Shimeah, hence the cousin of Amnon and Absalom.

MAACAH—Mother of Tamar and Absalom, wife of David.

MICHAL—The daughter of Saul, former king of Israel. David married her.

TAMAR—The narrator of the story, Snakesleeper, and heir to the throne of Geshur.

TOPHETH—The sacred shrine of the Jebusites to Goddess, in a valley at the foot of the mount where Jerusalem stands today.

David lived sometime between 1075 and 970 BCE (estimates vary). This story takes place during his lifetime.

In the Name of Goddess
Most-Merciful, All-Powerful, Mother of All Life,
I, Tamar, called Snakesleeper,
of the House of David, who is Israel's King,
Daughter of the High Priestess Maacah,
Daughter of Onekbaalat, also High Priestess,
Who was Sister and Wife to Talmai, the Son of Ammihud,
both Kings of Geshur,
do write this Testament with my own Hand.

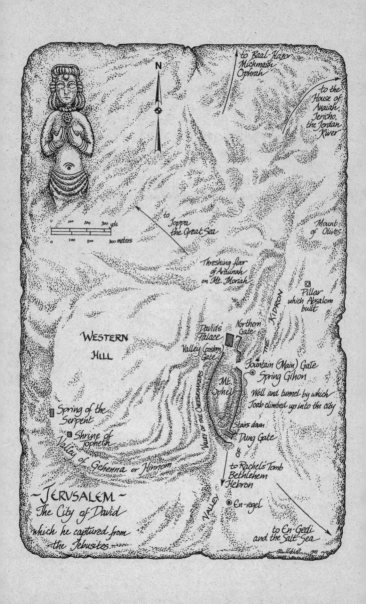

to Baal-Hazar
Michmash
Ophrah

to the
House of
Avaiah,
Jericho,
the Jordan
River

N

to Joppa
the Great Sea

Mount
of Olives

Threshing floor
of Avaunah
on Mt. Moriah

THE KIDRON

Pillar
which Absalom
built

WESTERN
HILL

David's Palace

Northern
Gate

Valley (Goshen)
Gate

MT.
Ophel

Fountain (Main) Gate
Spring Gihon

Well and tunnel by which
Joab climbed up into the city

Spring of the
Serpent

VALLEY OF THE CHEESEMAKERS

Stairs down

Dung Gate

Shrine of
Topheth

Valley of Gehenna or Hinnom

to Rachel's Tomb
Bethlehem
Hebron

VALLEY

En-rogel

~ JERUSALEM ~
The City of David
which he captured from
the Jebusites

to En-Gedi
and the Salt Sea

ONE

I

WHEN I WAS four years old, my father emasculated himself. He ran naked from the temple afterward, through the narrow streets of Aphek, with the ritual stone knife in one hand and his severed parts in the other. Blood flowed down his legs and dripped from his elbow. He threw his flesh into the open doorway of the wattle-and-daub hut of a local potter and then staggered back to the temple where he fell moaning and writhing with pain on the flagstones at my bare feet. That is my first memory of this world.

The potter's family came and brought the clothes: a woman's robe, mantle, and veil, which my father would wear the rest of his days. And my mother came, tall and cool from the temple interior, stepping between the light and dark made by columns twenty cubits high with their mushroom-shaped capitals. She took me by the hand and led me away.

"So he will never be unfaithful to me or to Goddess," Mother explained my father's actions to me at the time and afterward, whenever I woke crying and in a cold sweat from blood-drenched nightmares. "He has submitted to Her will in the deepest, most reverent way a man can. Goddess give us the strength as women to equal his strength as a man."

That very day we left Aphek—my mother never to return—and began our descent from the heights of Geshur south to the hills of Judah, to the city of Hebron. The oracle had spoken, or my mother, who was her interpreter, thought she had. The sanctity of former ties was outweighed by the conceit of a destiny beyond that her mothers had known. The bride-price was paid, and my mother was to marry David the king.

It was spring. I remember the date palms and the pomegranate orchards about the Sea of the Lyre in bloom. Over our heads the white sprays of date blossom (like showers of falling stars) filled the air with the sweetest scent on earth.

"You were named Tamar," my mother told me. "That means the Palm, and for this blooming beauty and promise of abundance we render annual praise to Goddess."

Mother had the litter stopped so she could gather some of the lower pomegranate blossoms to put in her hair beneath her high-priestess's veil. Then we rode on, taking a curve so we could no longer see from whence we had come. A twinge of pain came over my mother's face. She caught me by the shoulders and pressed me to her so tightly it hurt, forcing tears from my eyes. I closed them, but I could not block out everything. To this day, I can close my eyes and smell, very clearly, the scent of bruised pomegranate blossoms finally purging the smell of blood from my nostrils.

I remember the excitement of fording the Jordan River.

"Truly, aren't there easier fords than this?" my mother asked.

"You've no need to be afraid, Lady." This was how the interpreter translated what Joab, the commander, said. The commander himself spoke in a voice one uses to children, a voice that did not inspire confidence.

"I am no coward," Mother said.

The commander smiled, humoring her.

"My presence on this journey should be testimony to that. But look now, two of the first three pack animals have already lost their footing and their burdens," Mother said.

"We are rescuing your belongings," Joab said. They were, bedraggled bits and pieces of them. It seemed a terrible waste.

"Why ford here, where the waters are so dark and swift and where the overgrowth hampers every maneuver on the banks? I myself could show you several more hospitable places nearer Aphek. They are well known and praised by all travelers. My officers are wont to collect duty at these places."

"If they are known to every traveler," the commander replied, "they are surely known to the Israelites as well, who will have their archers stationed at such places just looking for us."

"What? And must I, High Priestess of Geshur with the neutrality of religion worn about my person like my veil— must I, then, go creeping about Goddess's world like a smuggler? Or worse, like a fugitive with blood on his hands?"

Joab did not stop to consider that the sort of smirk with which he regarded my mother as the meaning of her words came to him could be transmitted without intermediary. Joab. The name means "God (*the* God, the Unnameable One, God of Abraham, Isaac, and Jacob, the Jealous One who allows no other), *He* is my father." Very little translation should have been necessary for my mother to make a character assessment of a man with a name like that.

How like his belief did that man look! Short, almost stunted, but powerful to the point of obscenity: a chest like a bull's, biceps like an ordinary man's thighs, and thighs of mythical proportion. His face was broad and flat, pierced by a dagger of a nose and compressed by a heavy, beetling brow around which, even when it was hidden by a helmet, he always wore a band of cloth. At four years old, I pitied him, thinking he must suffer from perpetual headaches and they were what caused him to be so rough and gruff. From where I sit today, I suspect he liked to be the way he was and wore the band to catch his sweat, to show he sweat a lot. He liked to sweat, liked to work up to a sweat, liked to smell like a man when he sweat, and if there were no battles to be fought, no wells to be dug, no friends to oblige him with a wrestle, then he would put on full armor, tie 'round that band, and run up hills and down in the heat of the afternoon just to sweat.

What should such a man think, looking at my mother? She was taller than he was by almost a head, and not very beautiful, at least in the way such a man would count women's beauty. She had the broad, heavy cheekbones of our family from which a firm mouth hung, lean from exercise and unused to being a closed, soft buffer to much of men's foolishness. In many ways her features paralleled his: powerful, thick, though set on a taller and lighter frame. That must have been disconcerting to a man who looked to his women for complement, not competition. Worst of all was that veil around her face, that unabashed declaration that she was who she was, high priestess of the she-demon most of Joab's emotional if not physical energy had gone into eradicating. Man that he was, I cannot believe Joab had never tried to defeat Goddess with what hung between his hips as well as with that which dangled from the left hip alone. And I know nothing of the ways of Goddess if I am too far off the mark when I suspect that all his previous bouts with veiled ones had left him feeling vanquished. Anyone who does not come to Her mysteries in humility, willing to lose himself totally to Her power of renewal, is bound to feel lessened. Rather than having to think himself weak or unclean, Joab must put the blame on the other party, which could only increase his loathing.

So I doubt very much that in Joab's smirk there was any envy of David as far as my mother was concerned. He must have been aware, of course, that my mother was more than just another prize for David's bed. Though he would have condemned it soundly as a heathen practice, Joab could not escape the weight of the tradition of my ancestors that put inheritance of our kingdom in her person as the firstborn female. But Joab was more than David's commander in chief. He was also his nephew, and the tribe of Judah has family traditions of honor, too, traditions that stated clearly even to Joab's action-greedy mind: What is good for my mother's baby brother's ambition is also good for mine. He had little thought other than getting "the goods"—my mother—down to Hebron as quickly but also as safely as possible.

Joab broke off their interview at this point as the fourth donkey began to balk at the prospect of entering the water where his colleagues had fared so ill. The animal needed a good shove from behind and a flick or two of Joab's whip to get him going, but whether these could not have been provided equally well by one of the other men standing around arguing in their strange tongue at the top of their lungs with wide-flung gestures, I am not now in a position to say. Mother, I know, always felt it otherwise: that a choice of attention had been possible and had been deliberately made—in favor of the donkey over herself.

Mother stood and watched the progress with the animal, her heart as murky as the stream in which the little hooves thrashed wildly. Of course she had known the ways of Judah were not hers. But it had never really struck her before what the jealousy of a god that demanded exclusivity might mean. Her policy had always been to let others worship what they would as long as Earth was held inviolate. But when you were no longer in the position of magnanimous sovereign, and when that other worship did not return the favor, when it condemned your faith and along with it even your sex, to the position of life-and-death opponent on the battle-field—well, she had been unprepared for its destructive force on her sense of wholeness and of self.

But the oracle had said—! She herself had interpreted it—Ah, there was the catch. Anyone who interprets divine will knows the translation can never be perfect. Otherwise any common mortal could pick out the pieces for himself. One can only hope to be as clean a filter as possible. Mother could not have helped but wonder then if she had come to this oracle with some impurities of self-ambition that sullied the very nature of the transmission. But she was already doubting herself too much under the influence of Joab's smirk that seemed to say: "Silly woman. Just keep quiet and leave me in charge. I'll handle everything."

"Am I to keep quiet, then," she thought, "and see myself and my child as well as our belongings swept away by this current?" She mentally shook herself of her doubt. "I am Maacah, High Priestess of Geshur. I don't care what your barbaric god would have you believe, but only this: I will not let you believe I am of no account."

The next moment that opportunity presented itself, she made the interpreter persist. "But what have we to fear from the Israelites more than from this water? What have we to fear that we must go creeping around their territory like thieves in the night? David's great enemy, Saul, the King of Israel, is dead."

A flash of Joab's eyes at her from under those massive brows and that rag smeared with grime and sweat made her mistrust herself again.

"So I was given to believe," she apologized.

"The man has heirs," Joab said.

"His son Ishbaal?"

"Ish*boseth*," Joab said.

Men of Judah, we would come to understand, thought it a profanation to speak the word *baal*—"lord"—even in the context of another man's given name. This was because it was used too liberally by all of their neighbors to address their gods. They still allow their women use of the word; on Hebrew women's tongues it means "husband." In Joab's version of Saul's son's name, "Man of Baal" became "Man of a Shameful Thing." But the name he next gave to the son of Saul with a ball of spittle in the dust obviously defied the translator's skill, for he wouldn't translate and only grew red.

"I understood," my mother said, "that Ishbaal had to flee across the river and was only able to make a feeble attempt to rule under Saul's old general, Abner, from Mahanaim, far in the eastern desert."

"And it is true." It seemed as difficult for Joab's tongue to form such a concession to a woman as it was for him to say "Baal." "Ishboseth refuses to give up the title to his father's kingdom even when all he controls is the King's

Highway. The King's Highway, of course, would have been our first choice of route but, it is at present impossible."

"Still, I don't see why—" Mother gestured to the river, where the shouts and struggles of men and animals finished the sentence for her.

"Most of the backbone, as you said, is Abner's, not that son of Saul's. Reduced as they are, Abner *will* continue to fight—a war for jackals, hit and run, by night, never a decent, out-and-out battle like honorable men. They know we would win. We can never tell where they will strike next, and you may be sure there is no target they would rather hit than this one, this one that will put Israel in such a tight vise between your Geshur in the north and our Judah in the south. We do have two full days' crossing of Israel—what is nominally Israel—to make before we reach the land of the Philistines and can let down our guard and ford where we will. Until then—the land is wild and roving with packs of Abner's wolves."

"David—?"

"Yes, David would soon bring order to Israel," Joab said.

"Why doesn't he do so, if they are just a rabble?"

"Lady, that is easier said than done, even for a David."

Mother realized then that much she had been led to believe about Judah's king would have to be pared down to match reality. True, there had been other, more sober voices in Geshur's councils, but she had not believed them—she had not wanted to believe them. And had she then, she who knew Goddess's awful power, had she been swayed by romantic tales and songs—"and David has beautiful eyes. . . . a shepherd among the lilies"—and fallen in love with the name of David like some silly girl? Goddess forbid!

She closed her eyes against the thought. What did she see against the black, then, that made her open them so quickly, ready to face the dissolution of her dreams, come what may? My father's blood in the streets of Aphek . . . ?

"Very well," she said to Joab, consenting to climb into the litter once more and to hand me over to the strongest swimmer leading the tallest donkey. "I see that your plan is best."

Joab smirked. Of course it was. God was his father, after all.

▣ II ▣

WE WENT BY the Way of the Sea, and by the Road to the Land of the Philistines. It may surprise you to learn that David and the Philistines were allies, for the tales they will have taught you from your youth will have emphasized how David freed his land from these People of the Sea: killing their giants and hearing his god whisper the battle cry, "Attack Philistia at dawn" in the rustling of a terebinth tree. Yet at the time we left Aphek, David still paid tribute to Achish, a king of the Philistines, to whom he had fled for protection from Saul's jealous wrath. Only later did he gain the courage first to let the tribute slide and then to take up arms against his former lord.

"Remember our three little puppies at home?" Mother asked.

I did, and wept with homesickness. Mother had sickness of another sort brewing in her heart.

"I am reminded of those three puppies with a rag between them," she said. "One may snatch it away from the others in their tug-of-war, but never for long. These three puppies are the Israelites, the sons of Judah, and the Philistines.

They are all newcomers to this land they fight over so; it is a newfound toy to them. We who have been here since Goddess gave breath to the Earth, we have grown too old for such games. And we realize, too, that the land is not of our making, but of Hers."

The escort David had sent for us was about half sons of Judah and half Philistine mercenaries. At night we watched these two "puppies" playing knucklebones by the red glow of the fire, kept low so as not to attract a third group, the Israelites. Their snarls of triumph or deep-throated growls suspecting cheats had none of the innocence of puppy play. "They look more like Abner's wolves," I suggested to Mother. She breathed a sleepy reply and did not satisfy my hunger for active conversation.

You see, anxious as I was not to miss a thing on the journey, the rocking of our litter tended to put me to sleep for a good portion of each day's ride. That was just as well for my mother during the day, who did not then have to keep me entertained or put up with my squirming from one side to the other. But it meant that when evening came, and she could not wait for supper to be over so she could find her bed, I came alive in the cool and the dark.

Next day, in an attempt to keep me awake so I could sleep at night, Mother went against her prejudices of rough men of war. The men of Judah had prejudices of their own and thought it beneath their dignity to tend children, but one of the Philistines was willing to take me into his saddle with him. It worked well for a while because we were beginning to catch glimpses of the Great Sea now, with which I was much impressed. It had the look of smooth, well-tanned leather dyed a brilliant blue.

"It is not like our Sea at home," I told my saddle companion. "It does not end in a far shore, but seems to go on to the edge of the world."

"The world is much greater than that," my Philistine friend assured me. "My ancestors came out of that Sea from a land days' and days' journey beyond sight."

Then we saw something that impressed me even more: a group of men, laborers, faces darkened with trepidation, had paused by the side of the road to watch us pass. "It is the red plumes on our helmets," my friend the Philistine explained. "They never fail to cause a sensation in all the seaside towns where we are masters."

My friend did not say anymore, but the concern in the faces of the laborers was eloquent enough. Though the People of the Sea were sprinkled among them like salt most sparingly, when they did put in an appearance, things did not bode well for the mass of folk that is the true meat of the land. They could expect taxation, looting, conscription, a few rapes at least. Fortunately, David had seen to it that this group was well enough paid that, though they might kill their own grandmothers at his orders, they would try the luxury of brothels instead since they could afford it. But this group of men we passed could have no way of knowing that.

Still, I was even more concerned about them than they were about us: their bare legs were dark purple clear up to the knees.

"Canaanites." The Philistine was surprised at my question. "Surely that shouldn't startle you. They are natives in the land, like you."

"No," I insisted. "No one in Aphek has purple legs."

I grew impatient with our conversation, for though this man knew some little of our language, he was not up to explaining this present mystery, and I demanded to go back to my mother to learn the truth of the matter.

"The Philistine is mistaken," she said, "as are many others who call all of us who have lived here since time began 'Canaanites.' 'Canaan' is the name of the mollusk from which the royal color is extracted. Those men belong to a true Canaanite clan. There are whole tribes purple to the knees from the vats where they dye fabric in that color for a livelihood."

"The Queen's color, the Queen of Heaven."

"That's right. And the color of kings. It is a good living, but such tribes are few and proud. And they are isolated because they can only settle where they can get the shellfish needed to make their dye and yet where the swamps will not swallow them. There are many peoples, many accents, many livelihoods—and many gods from 'Dan unto Beersheva.' "

"Some child in a land far away—when he thinks about me, he thinks my skin and hair must be the color of a wine-taster's tongue."

"Yes." Mother smiled. "That's how misleading a general name can be. It is best not to generalize about people—Philistine, Canaanite, or son of Judah—but learn to know each one separately if you can."

With such deep musings in my small mind on the warmth of my mother's knee, I was soon rocked sound asleep again. Even today, though David may no longer serve the Philistines as he did then, he is still far from bringing unity to the land, perhaps for the very fact that his god loves to generalize so.

On any summer's day after our arrival in Judah, when the heat became intense, when the flowers that all the women picked at dawn to hold in their laps and sniff at to keep away evil vapors were withered before noon, when the slaves sat too listless to wave a fan, and even a swim took too much energy, my mother used to always sigh and murmur, "O Goddess, but isn't it as hot as the Way of the Sea today?" The Way cannot have been any more humid than what we knew at Aphek, but heat is harder to bear when all the rest of one's life is in tenuous disarray. And Mother was always sensitive to such things. She liked thick walls, cool fruit juice, awnings and fans.

I don't remember the heat the way she does, for one's tolerance for such things is greater when one is young. But two things I do remember mark that journey as the most important change of my life.

The first change began when I wandered away from our tent one night. The nursemaid had put me to bed as usual, offered water and trips out behind the tent, stories, sweets, and toys to hug. To no avail. She called my mother and my mother offered me the breast again and again until I was too full to do more than bite and get a smack for it. Then I dutifully closed my eyes and tried to sleep.

But I really wasn't tired. And even in the dark, I knew there was a whole new world out there to be explored. Other nights, when I'd crept out, I'd gotten no farther than the tent door before the universe, Goddess's jewel box, struck me with such awe that I was rooted to the spot until someone noticed I was gone and took me back to bed. I cannot remember what it was, but this night something drew me out beyond the awe . . .

The whole camp was out of their tents hunting for me. Even the Philistine guard was not sure of this land—their Dagon was not god here. They knew the general lay from well to well and town to town, but they could not tell if there were cliffs or quicksand or wild beasts or demons ten lance-throws or only ten steps away. Rituals to tame such wilderness were not part of their religion.

They didn't find me until light came and they could trail my footprints. They tracked me to an outcrop of yellow sandstone where I had made my bed—fulfilling all their worst fears—curled up to sleep with a viper as big around as a man's arm. It was as yellow and tawny—khaki, almost—as the stone on which we slept, with many dark brown bands and black stripes at the stubby head. Goddess keeps such Snakes in the caves beneath Her temple as Her servants and emissaries, but my mother had never seen one of such a size.

The best marksman among the escort raised his bow to sight again and again, but always lowered it in the end. "I don't dare shoot," he whispered with dread. "They are so entangled, the child and snake. I can't be certain the arrow would hit the snake and not her."

"No man could," a companion comforted him. "And suppose you hit the brute? There's bound to be life left in it, even as only a reflex, to sink enough of its poison into that little breast to kill ten men."

"No, I won't be responsible for the death of one of David's household we're being paid so well to guard."

Meanwhile, walking a fine line between haste and caution, my mother set about to work the charm that was the only hope. She caught one of the mounts, milked her, and brought the warm milk to the outcrop. Then she took a branch of the sacred fig she had carried with her from

Aphek, set it on fire, and fumigated the place, calling on
Goddess to be with her and hers. Then she handed the
branch to Joab who stood dumbly by, all his sweat to no
avail, and, while she made music for the Snake with the
shimmer of her sistrum, he played the part of incensor,
which I don't think another man has done before or since,
and certainly no man of Joab's temperament.

The viper awoke and shook itself. It raised its head on a
foot of body and prodded the air with its tongue. Then it
slowly disentangled itself from me (still soundly sleeping)
and slid forward. Our escorts were so amazed they did not
even think to shoot until its head was buried in the bowl of
milk.

I knew nothing of this until much later, for when I awoke,
my mother had fainted in a trance and the snake was dead.
But already the men were calling me Snakesleeper, the name
I carry to this day. Of course I was heiress to the throne of
Geshur and to the station of High Priestess, celebrant of the
Great Bed Mystery, from the moment I was born, simply by
virtue of my lineage. But those who know the Snakes, oracles, pythonesses—those who can read Goddess's will and
speak in Her Name—we are called by Goddess's hand, not
born. Only very, very rarely are both powers combined in
one.

Mother was not well at all that day. She had the Philistine
take me into his saddle so she could have the litter to herself
and stretch out. When I had had enough of the guard and
his clumsy ways and yearned to ride in the litter again,
Mother was still weak and insisted, in spite of my screams,
that I stay away for the entire day. Perhaps it was the fear
that exhausted her, perhaps the use of too much magic, or
else it was the deeply felt loss of a sacred Serpent soul. I
know she often wished the Snake could have been taken
alive. "You and she might have shared the greatest secrets
as you once so prettily shared a bed," she often sighed.
Naturally Joab would hear nothing of a live Viper joining
our company. And Mother herself was not so secure with
the Legless Ones that she would attempt it. She was only
High Priestess, after all. She did keep the skin and had it

cured, nonetheless—like dull brass on copper, the patterned picked out in scales as carefully as knots in a carpet. I would always wear it on sacred occasions.

"Snakesleeper." My mother said it with more reverence than the others, even of those who were there. She knew that one who has slept with vipers will have the gift of prophecy, of poetry, and the ability to understand the tongues of animals and birds and hear the words of Goddess in the passing wind. Had we stayed in Aphek, my gift would have been immediately acknowledged by everyone and carefully nurtured. Of course, had we stayed in Aphek, I never would have met my Snake. It is difficult to tell what Goddess intended. No doubt She intended exactly all that happened, for She is Queen of Heaven and Stringer of Stars.

But we were no longer in Aphek, and the great burden of all this nurturing among strangers hit my mother to the marrow. Probably this was the main reason for her great exhaustion. Since her talk with Joab, she had been stricken by a sense of treachery and unworthiness even to be her own sacred self. And now to be responsible for the heavy magic of one such as I—it was more than she could bear. All that day she struggled with the burden, wanted to refuse it, wanted to escape it to the warm safety of Goddess's arms in death, or to send me safely there before her, while she lived out the punishment she now felt she deserved.

In the end she was strong—or else very, very weak. She did not kill her body, but in that struggle, I do fear she finally killed her will. The second thing from our journey that marked great change was an emblem of this. It happened upon our arrival.

◉ III ◉

THERE WAS TIME to rest and change our travel-worn clothes before our presentation to David. Our rooms were small and dark, the bland clay walls unalleviated by any color. But they were cool, and my mother sank gratefully upon the low bed without complaint.

"O Goddess," she sighed. "I shall sleep an entire circuit of Your moon."

I think she fully intended to keep this vow, but she had not taken into account the lack of privacy the harem in Hebron allowed. All of David's other wives with their servants and their many red-haired children crowded in our doorway to catch a glimpse of the new wife: their new companion and rival, and one of "them," a Canaanitess and a worshiper of false gods, besides. I, too, did not escape their scrutiny. A child by another man, a mockery to David's supreme lordship. What complications would I bring to their uniform lives?

Mother waved her girls to go let down the drapes before the doorway and to keep stray gusts of wind from making peepholes. But this hardly discouraged the women. Though we could no longer see their plain, pasty faces and their dark, simple, homespun veils, we could hear them just outside, where they'd set up gossip shop for the day. One voice bubbled in the dialect we understood only enough to know that we were the subject. Then a lively chorus of high-pitched laughter responded. This exchange had a vigor that said they could keep it up all day.

It soon became apparent that we were to have no sleep at all that afternoon. And if one could not sleep, what use was there in putting off the audience any longer? Mother sent a girl ahead to warn the king that we would see him as soon as we were dressed. The Hebrew women were not total strangers to the niceties of bathing as we at first believed, but they indulged only once a visit of Goddess (or "visit of the demon," as they call their monthly courses). At that point, our command of the language was such that we couldn't grasp the ritual. We contented ourselves with a sponge and a jug of water instead.

I wore light wool the color of a sunset. It made a nice contrast with my dark skin. My mother wore blue of such a shade that it cooled the wearer as well as the eye of the beholder. Her dress was of Egyptian linen, narrowly pleated and so finely spun and woven that where it fit tightly, at the points of her breasts and across the hips in back, her flesh showed through and turned the fabric violet. Such fabric was rare in those days, what with the political disruptions in Egypt. But if one had to choose one body to single out for the glory of such a costume, I thought, none could be found more deserving than my mother's, still young and flawlessly firm. Mother painted her thin lips the color of pomegranate skin and tried to give them that fruit's roundness. She worked to dilute the strength of her eyes with quantities of kohl.

"O Mother!" I cried, clapping my hands with joy. "You're so beautiful!"

Mother tossed a brief smile in my direction. I was still a child, and there was much in the world I had yet to see before she would consider me an unbiased judge. Then she signaled to the maid to carry the fan before—we were ready.

"Wait, Mother! Your veil!" I said. I had never seen my mother go out in public without an elaborate Goddess veil covering a good portion of her lower face as well as every hint of her hair, rich with braids and curls. This veil was a sign that she was High Priestess and that no man could own her beauty, even with but his eyes, unless she and Goddess willed it. Anxiety, I thought, must have made her forget to finish this part of her dress, for she had no more on her head than a gold circlet and a wisp of Israelitess veil she had improvised from other garments.

"Mother, you forgot your veil," I said again, for she showed no sign of having heard me.

I tugged on her dress to tell her a third time, and her hand came down in a quick, hard slap.

"I am not going to wear that veil in David's land," she said in a fierce whisper. "Don't ever mention it again."

I held my stinging hand, too hurt and surprised to whimper. All I could think was that David must have some awesome power to make such a change in my mother, a power that must rival Heaven. I followed my mother dumbly out of the room, amazed at her bare head and what it might mean. I was much too amazed to get any satisfaction from the dead silence that fell over the gossiping wives when they saw just what wealth of costume if not beauty they were up against.

Now I realize that I had little to fear from King David. It was barely two years before our arrival that even his own tribe of Judah had anointed him with that title, and I would be fully eleven before he took Jerusalem and made it his capital over the united tribes. For us, having journeyed from a land where dynasties are measured in centuries, that was infantile indeed. Once he married my mother, however, David was, in name at least, King of Geshur, and even before that he had had a very clear notion—god-calling, perhaps—about how he would proceed, jumping kingdom after kingdom until all the land from Egypt to the Euphrates would know him.

My mother hated Hebron from the first: the flies, the barrenness, the language, the people, our barracklike quar-

ters—one small square room after another around the open
courtyard, where what little shade there was came from
mats and tattered awnings, not breathing trees and plants.
The dust and the dryness made her skin rough and sagging
and her hair dull before their time. No doubt this was ag-
gravated by her feeling that she deserved punishment and
this was it. She cried before David on their wedding night,
and it wasn't because she was a frightened virgin. I am proof
of that.

I do not mean to suggest that David wasn't kind to my
mother. He was, in his come-and-go fashion. But she was his
third wife, after all. If you count Michal, the daughter of
Saul, who had been taken from David and given to another
man, she was his fourth; fifth if you counted Haggith (he did
not), who had still only given him a daughter; and sixth or
seventh or eighth if you counted the various concubines.

I adjusted to the change much more readily than my
mother did. Children have that talent. I found the high, dry
air invigorating. And suddenly, I was surrounded by play-
mates. When I first arrived to take my place among them,
David's children included a daughter older than me, a son
and two daughters younger, and another son, the firstborn
Amnon, about my age.

Amnon and I . . . But more of that later.

If David wanted to be sure no one in the world would ever
forget his name, he was well on the way to success. He will
be remembered for sheer numbers of descendants carrying
his patronym, if not for any virtues he ever took time to pass
on to them.

Perhaps because monarchy is still a new experience for
them, I have found the princes of Judah and Israel naively
confident in their own immortality. Even on their dying day,
they awaken with a sort of wonder at themselves—"What
great thing shall I do today that the world will be even more
amazed?" They tend to let their children raise themselves—
they are too busy (and have too many children) to be as
carefully pruning and nurturing as my mother and her people are. Geshur is, after all, a land so ancient that heredity
goes back over all the ages to she to whom Goddess first

gave the breath of life. With the weight of all those generations on your head, you learn to be more humble. At least
you realize there is little either you or your children can do
that hasn't been done before. You are neither creating nor
utterly destroying (Goddess willing!) anything—just passing
it on. Such a humble attitude makes parents and children
much closer, less competitive. I think it is why my grandfather capitulated to David so soon, after so little struggle,
and gave his voice of encouragement to his daughter's final
decision. Only those in precarious, fresh, not-quite-legal po-
sitions struggle or give their lives to causes. My grandfather
knew, even as he let my mother go, that he had bequeathed
enough of Geshur to her that she would not forget. And the
spirit of Geshur would continue to live in her—and in me
and my descendants—forever.

It was great fun for me, who had lived all my life 'til then
in the temple where one had to be reverent and grown-up
from the day one was born, to suddenly become a child with
other children to inspire me and to split the blame with
afterward. Within a month, I had learned Hebrew as well as
I knew Geshuri, and even before then, I had no trouble
communicating. To this day my mother addresses me in her
native tongue. Whatever David had her brought to his
rooms for, it was not for conversation. Her Hebrew would
always be limited to pleasantries of the table and a few
orders for the slaves. It must have been lonely for her. It
must have been hell those first few years as she lost me,
hardly in the same way, but no less permanently, than she
had lost her first husband, the love of her youth. . . . But it
was she who had read the oracle, after all.

I dwell on this so heavily here at the beginning for you
must understand that there was no tie of blood between
David and me. That must be clear. I was born far away from
him, far from Judah, in Geshur in the temple of Aphek, the
daughter and heiress to the High Priestess Maacah, daughter of the High Priestess Onekbaalat and her husband King
Talmai. In my land, blood goes through the woman, as is
only natural. It is a matter of their different personalities, of
course, but usually her consort undertakes most of the oner-

ous day-to-day business of ruling, conferring and deferring
in the heavy matters; the soul of the land is hers. My father
was a fine, tall, handsome hero of the people, the one my
grandfather felt was worthy to stand at his divine daughter's
side. What, exactly, it was that my mother felt was missing
between them I cannot say. No doubt from her first conversation with Joab she realized that love in the hand is worth
twenty in a strange land, bright though the glint of sun may
appear on them from a distance. I don't even know what my
father's manhood name was. And of course, any who did
know are forbidden now to speak it.

Sometimes, along with all my "brothers" and "sisters," I
would fall into the habit of calling David "Father" as he
wanted me to. But always, come spring, I smelled the
pomegranates and the dates in bloom again and I remembered. . . .

▪ IV ▪

And David has beautiful eyes;
Fair and ruddy,
He is a shepherd among the lilies.

THIS VERSE IS engraved now upon the people's minds, carved there as wagon ruts in the roads are carved by pilgrims in the spring and by carts in the fall at the time of the vintage Booths. It was sung by women in their maidenhoods who are now become matrons, and it is recited by old men into their beards when their dried brains can think of nothing else of all they have seen in the world.

I do not mean to imply that you should not count these verses when you try to compose an image of the son of Jesse in your mind. I do not mean, either, that you should wink and say, as one does of a bridegroom, "Any king is handsome." I will simply say that I do not know. I never looked at David with eyes like that. It wasn't that he was so much my elder; he has charmed and continues to charm girls my age and younger. But maybe it's only the title "King" and the hope for a few jewels to stick in their ears that charm them. In that case, he is for them what he has always been for me: a symbol, featureless, the man hidden behind the state and the ambition, the anointed of his god. He is like some great mystical stone that stands in the middle of a valley. Barren women go and rub themselves on it to get children—not for the stone's sake, but for their own, for the magic in a symbol of power.

"She pleases me," he said, seeing from her costume that my mother must indeed be the High Priestess of Geshur. With that, he married her.

Hebron is not like Geshur where, if the high priestess ceases to be pleased, it is the consort who must choose between death or castration and anonymous burial among the attendant eunuchs. Perhaps not even her own heart asked itself whether or not David pleased her. All I know is that Mother suddenly came to the realization that she needed a child—a male—by David to secure her position in Judah. It was a thing she had never considered before. Because I, her firstborn, had proven to be female, hale and without blemish, the necessary heir to her station in Geshur, she had kept me at the breast even until we arrived in Hebron. But the minute she made her discovery, I was quickly and rudely weaned. Mother painted wormwood on her nipples and its bitter taste, like stomach bile in the back of my throat, came between us. When, only two months after our arrival, I was told we should soon have a baby, Goddess willing, I was still feeling the hurt. I warned them (to myself), "Very well. Do this thing. But nothing good will come of it, you may be sure of that."

David, for his part, was very pleased. The third (or fourth) wife Haggith discovered she was with child so shortly after my mother that they might have been seeded in the same night, and that was a feat worth his remarking. As far as I could see, though, there were three babies in the family already. Babies were as common as loaves of bread in the court of David and as easy, I imagined, to come by, for I had never known famine. Neither had I tried my own hand at the bread baking.

I did not notice when my mother's swelling belly gave me

less and less to climb into, for the change from day to day was imperceptible and how things were a month or even just a week before was ancient and forgotten history to a child for whom there was eternity in a day. But I remember well the day she approached Abigail, the head wife.

"Where is the shrine?" my mother asked. She had taken great pains to learn this phrase in the Hebrew, but her tongue was clumsy with it nonetheless.

Abigail was passing her son Daniel back and forth to Haggith, trying to teach him to walk. Daniel was "not quite right," even his mother had to admit. At nearly two years old he could only take a step or two from his mother's arms before tumbling into Haggith's. The child was tall for his age and pudgy from always being carried, and it was not easy to carry such a big boy. Both women were large, Haggith with child, Abigail just with being Abigail, and the task was wearing them out.

"Hmmm?" Abigail clapped her hands, forced a smile of hope toward her son, and did not hear.

Mother repeated her question: "Where is the closest shrine?" Her accent grew worse with the effort.

"Shrine? What do you mean, *shrine?*" Abigail asked, distracted.

Mother looked helplessly at me. She had no words in Hebrew to answer such a complicated theological question.

"Mother means," I said quickly, "that she needs to get the knots tied so we can have our new baby." I looked up at Mother and she nodded. As far as she could tell I had made a very good literal translation of the Geshuri temple cant.

"Get the knots tied?" Abigail repeated. "Get the knots tied? Child, I never heard of such a thing." She seemed somewhat relieved to discover that her Daniel wasn't the only child who babbled incoherently.

"Maybe she means . . ." Haggith began a suggestion and finished it with a look. Whatever dark message moved across the young woman's heavy-lidded eyes, it made Abigail snatch her son up even before he tumbled and hold him to her with a sign against evil.

" 'I am the Lord your God and I will destroy your high places and cut down your images and cast your carcasses upon the carcasses of your idols, and my soul shall abhor you.' " The head wife's jowls burned and her temples were wet with sweat.

My mother understood enough to know that this was some sort of curse. She threw her arms protectively about her belly and was silent and afraid until time let her become hurt and then, bitterly defensive. "No wonder Abigail's son is not right," she said to me in our language and she lifted herself up with dignity as we strode away from the two women. "She obviously did not have Goddess with her from the first."

"Jerusalem." A hushed voice called us from the court to the rooms of Ahinoam. The second wife had her new baby daughter at her breast and her two older children at her feet.

"I'm sorry. I do not understand," my mother said. But there was none of the tedium in her voice with which she usually said this, her most-used phrase in Hebrew society.

"Hush," Ahinoam said as she peeked out into the courtyard at the other two wives and then drew us into privacy.

In a corner of the room, Ahinoam's Amnon and his older sister Hannah were playing at stork, posing on one leg with their arms tucked up like wings. Amnon had much better balance than either of us girls and really could make his slender body look like a stork's. He always was very good on his feet and had already begun to perform the swaggering men's dances of the desert with a kitchen knife instead of a ceremonial sword to the delight of us all. Hannah soon lost interest in a game at which her little brother constantly beat her, and she went to practice the spinning of wool, which her mother was teaching her. That was something in which she need fear no competition. My delight, however, was in Amnon, and I stayed with him, even when I had to bow to his skill and become a dove instead, going on two feet and singing instead of posing on the rooftops.

Meanwhile a maidservant was called to act as translator between the mothers. Mother did not trust the girl to be faithful to her policies and would have preferred me, but what they were to speak about was beyond my vocabulary in either language. I was glad, for I wanted to forget about babies for a while.

Though the child's world of make-believe interested me more than the grown-ups' affairs, I remember something of what passed between my mother and Ahinoam. I have always had a mind for liturgy, and perhaps it was the relation-translation, call-and-response way in which their dialogue progressed that helped it stick in my mind. Every line was repeated twice, after all, once in Hebrew, once in Geshuri, and I understood both as one.

"Where is the closest shrine, that I may knot this new life safely within me?"

"Jerusalem. There is a shrine in Jerusalem."

"What is Jerusalem?"

"A fortress. In the height of the hills. There is a town. The sons of Jebus have lived there as long as any remember."

"The sons of Jebus. We of Geshur have an ancient friendship with the sons of Jebus."

"But beware. David has fresh hatred against them."

"Let David fight his own wars."

"Sister, David is our lord and master."

"Forgive me, Sister. But tell me, how shall I come to Jerusalem?"

"It is forbidden."

"Is it forbidden just to tell?"

"I have never been. I have only heard. It is a long way— two days, maybe more."

"Tell me all you have heard."

"Topheth is the name of the shrine," Ahinoam began in her light and gentle Hebrew. "It is so called for the music of the sacred drums that accompanies the sacrifices. It lies in a grove in a deep, lush cleavage in the land just south and west of the fortress of Jebus. In ancient times it was the home of the sons of Hinnom, and it is sometimes called after their name, too. My people, who worship only the God of our Fathers, call it 'Gehenna' between clenched teeth. That is our word for the Netherworld. Our priests declare that the cloud of smoke and incense that hangs perpetually over

Topheth is unhealthy. The earth, they say, molders with death like a swamp because of all the heathen sacrifices buried there."

My mother stopped listening to the translator halfway through this speech.

"She was obviously making up that last part of the translation," Mother told me later—years later—when we discussed the scene together. "She went on and on—much longer than Ahinoam's speech had gone. Didn't you notice?"

I had not.

"I could not believe Ahinoam herself could say those things," Mother said.

"She is a Judahitess like the others. Even if she is Amnon's mother."

"But she looked the very incarnation of Goddess—may She favor us—that day."

"What, thin, gray little Ahinoam?"

"You were obviously too busy playing to notice such things. She was still swollen with the fertility of her pregnancy—that youngest girl was born just after we arrived in Hebron and couldn't have been over six weeks old at the time. Ahinoam was still in her impurity, anyway, and nursing. Nursing has that effect on some women more than others, Ahinoam more than most. Even her cheeks were plump and joyful at the new little life at her breast. 'No wonder Ahinoam is blessed with three such pretty children,' I said to myself that day. 'She has a profound respect for Goddess.' "

To this day I don't believe Ahinoam was any less a Judahitess than the other wives. "Ahinoam"—that very name, "my brother is good," shows how little her parents cared for the feminine and let her know every time they called her that they would rather have had a son.

"And you know the rumors about her," I told my mother. "About how she was raped . . ."

"Tsst! If you weren't so grown-up, I'd turn you over my knee for using such language, girl." I'd used the Hebrew figure of speech that was bandied about among soldiers in the court like no more than the word for "bread." But "rape" is such a profanation that Geshuri tongues will not say it.

"Rumors! They are the bane of any harem," my mother said. "I'm often glad I cannot speak Hebrew."

Ahinoam was a remarkable woman, even I had to admit, in that all this naming and gossip that might have made her the very picture of fear and hence of hatred and close-mindedness had instead made her more tolerant of human desires: she put them before those of Heaven. Very few women named for their preferred brothers are able to name their own first child Hannah—"a gracious thing"—when it, too, is a daughter. And it was not mere coincidence that Abigail ran the harem as first wife though Ahinoam had borne David his first son. To a woman with a character like Abigail's, one could not offer greater charity; Ahinoam was of such substance that she could afford to be that generous, day in and day out.

As soon as Mother could after her interview with Ahinoam, she asked David's permission to go to Topheth until the child was born. David refused. Flatly. He was praying to his god for a son, he said, a son who might be a leader among his god-fearing people.

"Can more prayers hurt?" my mother pleaded. "I, too, want a son."

"Prayers to a she-demon would only cancel out what good my priests have done," was David's quick reply.

He would not even let her carry out the necessary rituals under his roof. So we did it all by night, in secret. No doubt this had some effect on the quality of the fruit.

Mother would awaken me when all the rest were asleep. Her first word would be "Hush," and we would make our way to the deserted courtyard without a lamp. There she would hold my hands up to the moon in an attitude of prayer and together we would recite the ancient formulas. We did this naked, our skin almost white in the moonlight and my small body so different from my mother's round-ness that, for all I knew, we might have been different sexes.

With incense and offerings, stones and feathers, she drew and cast the fortune of the child within her and, with a knife, symbolically cut the pain and danger to herself. I helped feel the responses by placing my hands on her bare belly and waiting for a kick. Unfortunately, I hadn't always the patience to wait it out. Once I felt the life, I got too excited and full of wonder to wait for the next movement—whether it came on the right side and meant a boy, or on the left and meant a girl. But I was proud and learned, too, the humility of reverence by being called on to participate so young.

· V ·

OF COURSE STAYING awake at night meant we slept late in the morning. This did not go unnoticed by the others; in spite of her condition, they accused Mother of laziness and—worse—unfriendliness because she wasn't around to help get a new piece started on Haggith's loom. Haggith had a fairly fine fabric in mind, and setting the hundreds of threads in the wool at just the right tension would take many hands and the better part of a day interspersed with chatter and the traditional date-palm pudding that made loom-making something of a sacred ritual.

"God willing, I shall make wraps, blankets, and swaddling for my little one," Haggith said. Then cattily, "Can't that one from Geshur have the good grace to allow me a child as well without turning sullen with envy?"

And I found myself a latecomer to the children's games.

On this particular day, Amnon, with whom I really would have rather played, was long gone into the fields or other exciting places. I didn't yet have the courage to hunt for him alone. His sister Hannah was all I could find. She had started out to help the women, for she was a helper, but they

must have reached a point where she was more of a nuisance
instead and sent her to play on her own in another corner
of the yard. She did that obediently, too. She was playing a
sort of skipping game on a figure scratched in the courtyard
dust.

My four-year-old heart skipped faster than her feet as I
approached and saw what the figure was. It was Mother's
magic star, an eight-pointed Goddess star. With a wedged
stick on a lump of clay, we could make it with four quick
strokes: a cross superimposed by another cross set at an
angle. In Geshur we work this star on our banners, on our
amulets, on our robes of state. This one drawn in the dust
Mother had enclosed in a circle and burned a different
magic herb at every point, mandrakes in the middle. You
could still see the ash. No one could mistake it for David's
six-pointed star. I've heard it said that in David's star the
triangle on the top is the man, the one on the bottom
the woman, and when he flies it on his flags, that's what he
means. Whether that's true or not, I can't say.

Now, if such an eight-pointed sign had been found in the
temple of Aphek, the finder, if she had not known a pregnancy was in the confines, would reverently circumvent the
place, praise Goddess, and run at once to find the artist and
rejoice with her. Mother knew better than to hope for such
things here, and she had meant to scuff it out before we left
that night, but the moon had set by then and she couldn't
see how thorough a job she was doing. Obviously there had
been enough of the outline left to appeal to Hannah's imagination to resketch it and to make up a game.

"You want to play?" she asked. She was meticulous—
uncomfortably so—about always inviting me to join her. I
can imagine what her mother must have told her—"Yes, I
know she's younger than you and her ways are strange. But
God wants you to help her get over her strange ways and
embrace ours. . . ."

"I . . . I don't think we should be playing on that," I said.

"It isn't hard. Don't be shy. I made it up by myself. I'll
teach you."

Still I hung back, stammering. Tears filled my eyes, and at

that I was angry, for I hated Hannah to see me cry. She
would not tease me. It would be worse. She would feel sorry
and try to mother me. Although I could not define them at
the time, they were tears in the face of sacrilege; Mother's
devotion had become my own.

"It's for the baby," I said with fierce courage to cover my
tears.

"What is?"

"That." I couldn't profane it with the Hebrew word for
star, which, in my mind, was nothing like it at all.

"What baby?"

"*Our* baby. The one in my mother's womb."

"Don't say dirty words."

"What dirty words?"

"What you just said."

"Baby?"

"No, the other one."

"W—?"

"Ugh! Don't say it. I'll plug my ears."

She did and so I waited, confused, until she chose to
unplug them and start skipping again.

"Hannah. Don't do it. It's for our baby."

"I don't know what you're talking about."

"My mama's going to have a baby and that's going to
help her."

"Everyone knows your mother's going to have a baby.
But God doesn't need any help making babies."

Carefully feminizing the divinity in my mind, I could
agree, "Yes, I know. But it's hard for the woman as well.
And it's dangerous if certain . . ."

"Nonsense. You don't know what you're talking about."

"Yes, I do. My mother—"

"My mother told me all about it. When the time comes,
your mother will go out and find her new baby under a fig
tree."

"What?"

"Under a fig tree. That's where babies come from. Don't
you know anything?"

"No—"

"Of course. That's where I came from. And Amnon and our new baby sister. My mother has had more children than yours and I'm the oldest, so I guess I should know."

"Well, maybe that's how they come here, but in Geshur—"

"Well, God knows how you do it in Geshur. But if your mother wants a God-fearing son for my father David, she had better get him the way we do it here. We want no devils here."

My mother had kept no secrets from me. It was only my youth that had me in confusion. Heaven knows, Ahinoam probably avoided the—to her—unpleasant subject until the very wedding night caught up with her daughter. That is, at the base, men's doing. It makes them feel more like men to have something to frighten, to hurt and to take by force from ignorance. That is the doing of the gods. They are making up for lost time, for all the ages when there was no god but Goddess, when women kept the flocks and seeds and with them the secrets of life and birth, and men were regulated, kept to the sterile hunt, and allowed into the secret precincts to sow only with Goddess's blessing and Her oblivion.

Sometimes Mother did talk to me as if men had nothing whatsoever to do with babies. Women used to tell their men this to keep them mystified and reverent. It is still common in temple parlance and it may, I suppose, in the wrong hands, cause as much confusion as the fig tree tale. Of course no one is obliged to believe it anymore. It is just the traditional metaphor that everyone understands means a temple upbringing.

Even today, in the oldest temples, in their dark back niches, you may find Goddess figures from that primordial time. They are huge women, swollen in the last stages of pregnancy, rather like the rude, round charms peasant women still cling to during their time and not at all like the slim, seductive figurines that are made by popular demand for the sanctuaries and private niches nowadays. A woman with child and a nubile girl both epitomize womanhood, I suppose. But as I stood and prayed beside my mother in her expectation and many times since, that pregnancy, for all its bloat, discomfort, and awkwardness, was much more deeply and anciently feminine than a slim waist and painted lips. And much less male-induced than a harlot's beauty, too, for all that the myth of woman as sole creator has been dispelled.

"It was Roeh the Shepherd," so my mother told me, "who stole the secret of how babies are made from the temple and spread it to the rest of mankind. For his sacrilege, Goddess turned him into a scorpion. All scorpions you may find behind your water jug in the morning are his descendants, fruitlessly trying to stick you with their protest. Such creatures one may kill with impunity and without the holy words. It is no sin. But no more than one can collect back into the teat milk that has been spilled could even Goddess pick all men's minds clean of that sacred, powerful knowledge once it had been whispered to the wind. Given a part in life, men grabbed for it all. That was the beginning of 'God.' "

And of men like David.

At the time, I could only protest lamely to Hannah, "We are not devils in Geshur."

Now our debate disintegrated into "Are so," "Are not," until the only way I could see left to make my point was with teeth and nails. Hannah was older than I, but I was nearly as tall and she was handicapped by her perpetual fretting to keep her dress clean. Our almost-equality made the fight last much longer and be more destructive than most children's spats. Though we were both blinded by tears and hurt in several places, neither would disintegrate into a surrender until we were forcibly torn apart by the women who'd had to drop the precious tension in their yarns to do it and were therefore furious.

"She wouldn't let me play my game on my nice drawing there," Hannah gave the first coherent explanation of our fight.

But the look on Abigail's face when she saw the "star" threw that coherence into chaos and our tears into utter insignificance. The other women followed the head wife's eyes and then her face into horror, but only Abigail dared to speak the word all of them immediately thought. *"Witch-craft."*

The community of eyes moved slowly around the circle looking for the culprit, the commandment ringing in every head, "Thou shalt not suffer a witch to live." Directly in front of Abigail stood the curtained door to my mother's room, behind which she still slept. And here the eyes lingered longest of all.

"But little Tamar was afraid of *it* first and tried to keep my Hannah from it," Ahinoam protested. "God shield my child." She was not subtle enough to see how close of kin are fear and reverence, and the others accepted that protest, at least until the exorcist should be called.

And the exorcist came and worked his magics over the spot, a mirror's reflection of my mother's work with feathers and incense, with the addition of a pitiful squawk from the sin offering as the head was wrung off and the blood splattered around. All the harem—even my mother did not dare absent herself although she had to look away from the sacrilege and wear a band of amulets under her robes to protect her unborn child—stood around and watched soberly, considering the pigeon's throat as their own. All were impressed. I must wonder, however, why men are ever expected to read the secrets of women with any authority.

Abigail's sharp gaze toward my mother's door had had more understanding in it than this fellow's gray eye that could see the situation only as a man sees. The wife from Geshur was pregnant by her master, the exorcist's eyes seemed to say. What reason should she have to be discontent or wish to jeopardize the child by dealing with the black arts? On the other hand, Abigail shrewdly discerned, what desire should David have to jeopardize his relationship with Geshur by such an accusation? No, the exorcist had to say it was unclear whose hand had drawn the sign. It was, after all, obscured by the fact that Hannah had traced over it herself. All that could be done was to daub the little girl with blood, singe her hair, and give her an amulet to wear lest, unwittingly, she be the handmaid of the evil one.

"Send for me if this evil should recur," the man said, picking up his share of the sacrifice to go home. "We may have better clues next time."

You may be certain Mother never gave him a next time.

In due time, Mother went down to labor and the child, a son, came forth with a healthy cry. He was small, but determined to live, and we understood that David's god had answered his prayers. My brother plainly out-ranked Haggith's son Adonijah, who wasn't born until a month later. Because Daniel would never be right enough to rule, that left only Amnon between us and the throne. I think this fact made a change in my mother, very subtle at first, but I saw it in how she smiled as she gave her son his first suck and I was led in to welcome him. Holding him, she felt herself holding a kind of power she had never held before and she rather liked the sensation. She did not say, but clearly the thought had not escaped her, how little it would take to make her son heir. One need not even consider Amnon if this one at her breast were strong and blessed enough. Was not David himself the youngest of eight sons? I wonder how that thought flavored the milk on the little boy's tongue.

David was very pleased. He refused to enter the birthing room because of the impurity, but he stood outside the door and sent the message in: "Wife, beloved of me and of my God. Ask whatever boon you will, and it shall be granted."

David did not wait for her answer, but left in a high good humor to run a raid on some unprotected corner of Israel like a thief in the night.

And Mother did not bother to ask. She took the chance when it was offered, albeit she had only just been delivered and the salt the midwife had rubbed into the little boy's skin to toughen it was hardly dry. She packed us up, my brother and me and a single trusted slave, and left that very night to ride to Topheth and to the House of Goddess.

◨ VI ◨

AT TOPHETH AND at five years old, I first came to an understanding of the law of sacrifice. Of course, I have known since I knew anything that it was something that was done, and that is as much as most people ever learn: in fall one sows, in spring one reaps, and in the heat and anxiety of summer, one makes sacrifice. Or they explain it in a boorish manner—"The gods, like men, get hungry and must be given food." I understood that much at five, but there was more to learn. Time has given me ritually sophisticated words to describe what I discovered, but even at such an early age and without the words, I gained the feeling of it. I was born for Her service, you see, however the times have inhibited me.

A young kid had been my constant companion since our first arrival in David's household. By the time cuteness was no longer in his favor, he was become one of the family to such a degree that looks were not considered at all. When we looked at him, there was only a jumble of emotions and memories registered in our minds and by these we recognized and held out our hands to him, not because of certain physical features.

I say *we* recognized the goat like this, for I had always assumed Mother shared my feelings. She had let me feed him chunks of bread from the plate and even let him sleep with us, though more at first than later. He had grown until the tripping of his little cloven hooves over our bodies was no longer ticklish but indeed dangerous. He was something of our own there among the blood of strangers. Mother enjoyed speaking a most familiar Geshuri to him, which he seemed to understand. For when she would counsel with him about the obvious, almost pathetic way in which Haggith paraded about the courtyard every day to show off her condition, the kid (we always addressed him by a Geshuri term meaning "the Sage") would demonstrate his wise understanding of my mother's words by mincing on tiptoes into the courtyard after the hapless Haggith, at which we would laugh until the tears rolled, and Haggith never suspected the mirth we had at her expense by way of our goat. She might have accused us of evil-eyeing her had she ever come to know.

But when we stole off by night toward Topheth and Mother made certain that Sage was strapped onto the donkey along with her infant's cradle, I knew full well he was not *that* much a member of the family. Neither was he a milking nanny she might take to sustain life along the road. I now felt heartlessly betrayed by all the times when David had sent his man into the courtyard to pick among the flocks for a sacrifice to his god and my mother had stood firm and refused Sage to the knife in no uncertain terms (Hebrew or no). I knew he was meant to be our offering in Topheth.

From Hebron (a cradle in the hills where David was spending the infancy of his kingship), all roads are downward tracks. But the terrain one must cross to reach the shrine of Topheth is so steep and wild that even those who have no reverence for the sacredness of the spot are forced to say "Go up to Jebus, go up to Topheth." In those days, too, Jebus was enemy territory—enemy to David, I mean. Geshur had always had good friends among the Jebusites and I believe there had even been exchange between our two shrines. Mother little feared for our reception once we got into the sacred precincts. But that past history did not make the way any easier for present members of David's household. We had to worry about attack from the home side, too, for full well my mother knew that what she was attempting by the dark of night David would view as if she'd deserted him on the very fields of battle. The land we had to cross was kept as a wilderness, a no-man's-land between the antagonists. The way was known but by hearsay to us and, though we feared the night, we feared the day all the more. It took us two full days of almost constant travel to arrive. I was thrilled by the adventure, but that did not rub out the fact that Sage was making his final journey.

It was late winter and the night air harsh and chill. But, because of the season and because we had enjoyed some rains in the hills, the landscape was not as tedious or unpleasant as it might have been. At most seasons (or maybe they are the seasons that only seem the longest) the hills are like the face of some old woman whose paint the glare has melted off. What few blotches of freshness still remain in between the wrinkles and cracks are rendered pathetic and ugly by comparison to the great, dusty, carbuncled and scarred expanses of wasteland.

Our slave had no easy task driving the animals, even with just two of them, for when they grew tired, the donkeys wanted to stop right where they were, however exposed the spot might be. And when she got them aroused, they could only think of going off the trail and into the wonderful grass to feast. Sometimes she was behind, pushing and beating, and sometimes she was ahead, braking, and more than once, the poor weary thing could think of no more to do than to sit down on the ground and weep.

Surely Goddess was with my mother, for riding all night donkeyback less than a day after giving birth would have been the death of many another woman. The slave babbled of birthing fever and of evil spirits that stole infants and of the thrashing she was going to get when her part in the matter was discovered, and she wept all the more until she was useless. Then my mother's faith was like a warrior's blade. She walked and led the animals herself—the peril of present pain was nothing to the eternity of dreaded unknown possible if she did not immediately get divine sanction for herself and for the fruit of her womb. Goddess heard her prayers and she endured and gave courage to us all.

Knowing and trusting her faith only made it more difficult for me to accept what must become of our Sage as a result. I felt wicked, yet I could not help wanting him to be allowed to live. I became sick in my stomach and liver as I saw visions of sacrifice with my pet in the major role. At a most difficult and dangerous descent, when the slave was sobbing and wiping her eyes, my little brother yelling healthily for food, and my mother moaning a bit at every bounce down the rugged hillside, my confused emotions and five-year-old loneliness got the better of me and I, too, began to cry.

"Now what, for the love of God, is wrong with you?" the slave cried, at her wit's end with fear and exhaustion. "Isn't it enough that we must be chasing after demons in the wilderness? Isn't it enough that, between a sick woman and two children, I'm left with all the work? Isn't it enough that David will burn us alive when he finds what we've done? By God, I'll teach you to cry, girl!" And, having found that her stick made no impression on the donkeys, she raised it to me.

Mother was there before I could sob again. She wrenched the stick out of the girl's hand and stood, not wielding it as the girl had done, but holding it like a scepter. I shall never forget how regal she looked. It was very dark, but time has made the picture clear in my mind. Others might have set to and beaten the slave, but that was beneath my mother's dignity. Others might have tried to argue with her fears, but Mother did not mention what were only reasonable concerns, concerns we all shared. She also did not mention the difference in status as others would have. The way she stood was proof enough.

"Never," my mother said, very quietly and yet with a voice one was yanked up by the ears to hear, "never call on David's god when we are about Her business. Never."

"No, Mistress." She never did again.

I'd forgotten I was crying in my awe, but when my mother tried to rearrange our mounts and put me on the rear so she could ride with my brother to hush him, I refused to be parted from the goat and clung so fiercely to him that he protested and kicked the donkey carrying us. Neither would I let Mother take my brother back with her, but clung to her, to her faith and beauty, which were strong and good and which must be made merciful by my tears. At last, my mother, calm and dignified as ever, gave the baby to the slave, told her to ride with him on the rear donkey and give him a finger to suck for a while. She herself would walk and lead.

"See how our Sage looks about him," she said, after we had walked in silence for some time.

"Except when he sleeps," I said.

"Do you think he dreams when he sleeps?" she asked me.

She knew the proper answer and smiled when I said definitely, "Yes."

We talked about the goat for some time, caressing the details of his unblemished body with our hands and words, and he rubbed the crown of his head, where the hair came out in a spiral, against us when he could, which was the best response he could make, strapped to the baggage as he was.

"And you, my little Sleeper with the Snakes. What is it that you have dreamed this night?"

She was not humoring me, or beguiling me with baby talk. She had great reverence for that night when I felt the Serpent's breath upon my face. She knew by what power I was still alive and what that power had given me. I was not afraid to tell her then about my feelings for the goat.

She nodded with interest and concern. "Should we not offer the Sage then?"

I found myself answering my own question and believing it. "We must. It is Her will. But . . ."

"But . . ." Mother said, and she smiled when I did not finish my sentence. She helped us over a great seam of rock and when the easy plodding resumed once more, she said, "Little Snakesleeper, are you afraid to die?"

I could not think what to answer, so she said what I would have said had I been old enough to have formed such words. "No, no. At five years old, one cannot have seen enough of life to have a fear of death. But you are afraid to be alone, away from those you love and those you need. Even your little brother knows that fear." We could hear him behind us. The finger was not enough, but let the slave worry about that for now.

"Death is . . ." my mother began again.

"Bad! Bad!" I sobbed, taking the tone I had often heard scolding me, as if death were a naughty child. The careful attention my sorrow was receiving made it worse.

"Is it bad when David kills his enemies? You love to dance when there is a triumphant return. Those enemies would otherwise kill him and us. Is that bad? Is it bad to kill a scorpion, a son of Roeh one finds sunning himself on the bake oven? Or even a sacred Viper when the proper words have been said—when she threatens the life of one's child?"

"I want to live," I said simply.

"And I want you to live. I sang one of the great Legless Ones to her death for your sake."

"It is good to live."

"But for us to live, things must die."

"No."

"You like a feast—when there are platters of good flesh steaming, when you can dip your crust in the grease left in the platter for breakfast in the morning."

I could not see clearly where this reasoning was leading us, but I could tell my mother would—not trick me, exactly, but in her wisdom make me see something I did not want to have to acknowledge. I did not reply.

"Well? Do you like such feasts?"

"Yes?" I doubted not my answer, but the reply it would in turn receive.

"Are you not then taking the life of some sheep or goat into your life? Did not someone have to say the words of sacrifice over that creature, holding its head toward the east with one hand and the blade in the other?"

"But not Sage."

"No, not Sage. But his kin. His sire, his dam, his brothers and sisters."

"He doesn't care about them."

"Doesn't he?"

"He has us."

My mother chuckled, then her voice took on the quality it has after many hours of chanting: sonorous and unreal. "In a faraway land there are a people who keep no flocks."

I exclaimed my disbelief that there could be such barbarians—even the sons of Amalek who know no houses of clay, nor any gods but the wind and rain, even they have flocks. My mother's smile assured me that it was a time for imagination.

"They never know the joy of an animal's companionship. They never know the sorrow of losing it."

"How can they live?"

"There are the poor in Hebron who taste of meat but once or twice a year at festival time. There are grains and fruits provided for them."

"But even the poor have their milk. They could not work their fields without the strength of curds and cheese."

"Very well, let us say these people far away have no flocks, but their god provides them with all the milk and flesh they desire, fully prepared so they need never let the blood of any creature, nor see any creature die. They never even notice as it turns upon the spit how like their own the muscles are, and how the fat and bones encase them. Would you like to live there with those people?"

"Yes," I said, enchanted through my tears.

"Ah, but powerful as this god is, he cannot stop death. His people beg him to, but he cannot. Even Baal cannot defeat dark Mot but for half the year. When death does come to them or to those they love, these people are confused and afraid. They have not seen the wolf among the flocks or the lion upon the gazelle. They have not learned through daily example that death is the way of flesh. They blame one another for this curse and turn with swords, each one upon his neighbor, to cause more death, more confusion, which brings about more death again, until each man has borne the sins of the land a hundredfold—like the scape-goat. Or they blame their god, perhaps, call him powerless or dead, and after such blasphemy, what must this god do?"

"He must strike them down," I responded ritually.

"So indeed he must. Death is neither good nor is it bad. It is needful in its season. And it is awe-full. And praised be She who calls us to learn from our earliest infancy to face it with due reverence, to know whence comes our meat, our strength, our life, our death."

"So be it," I said.

"Now, our Sage," and she laid her hand gently between his horns where the spiraling hair made the shape of a star about the bare flesh, "has been hearing our conversation. The priestess will speak holy, soothing words to him, beg-ging his pardon for any pain she may unwittingly cause him, and commend his spirit in smoke to Goddess, his flesh to the use of those who serve Her. He shares our blood and life, so we help him to understand death, as he helps us to under-stand and accept it, as best we can. We cannot be kinder to our animals than that. Earth is no kinder to us."

And so we talked softly to Sage as we stumbled over the path. Mother spoke of how even the Earth beneath our feet must die, in its time, once a year when all cooling breath of life is still in the barren summer. I do believe our animal participated in the talk as well as that behind his dark eyes was capable of. Those eyes seemed moistened with tears as he looked at us, but there was neither hatred nor misunder-standing there. Soon I lay down across the donkey's back, my head pillowed on the goat. The last thing I remember seeing was the infinite swarming of stars, Goddess's abode, overhead.

Whatever differences time has tossed like boulders from a landslide between us, I have always been grateful to my mother for all she taught me of Earth and Heaven. I was not raised in a place where daily ritual could bring these things to my understanding without my ever knowing I was learn-ing something and without any effort on her part. Those who have had these mysteries infused in them like daily bread may say my knowledge is too objective and therefore artificial. But they cannot argue against the burning force with which such learning can enter the mind on a fugitive night, when only She is audience.

When the sacred grove was opened to the public the next day, when I'd been draped in new purple and belted with my serpent's skin (it went 'round me four times in those days instead of only twice as now), I was required to be maintainer, the one who holds the animal while the knife is drawn. Actually, it was only a ritual in my case, for I could not keep my eyes open for my tears, and Mother had to hold my other hand. Sage did not struggle—he was not afraid with me there—and no one was counting on a five-year-old at her first maintenance being able to bear the full responsibility. It was only required that I be there, reach out and touch death. I had to feel how it was when Goddess took him completely into Her possession, how his whole being shook like one spelled, then how being was no more and he grew still. The convulsions passed to my sorrow and added to my tears. I learned a great lesson from this, even though others did the real job of holding for me.

Mother held my hand later, too, when I had to watch and see that shank I knew so well become divine as it was prepared for the fire. The reedlike leg was thrust stiffly, bizarrely upward and the shaggy hair fell away from it against the way it had grown, down toward the altar. Mother held my hand as I partook of a small but ritually important portion of his flesh and held it by sheer force of will in my stomach.

Throughout all this I felt miserably weak, but from that weakness I gained strength. It was I who held my mother's hand in my own small one when the word came from the oracle.

The oracle stepped like one newly materialized out of the smoke, her bloody hands leaving their prints on the bowl that contained Sage's liver, wherein she had read the future.

"Your son—your brother—" the oracle said, "can be given no name."

"No!" my mother cried. One hand went to her mouth, the other squeezed mine until I feared my bones would break.

She was allowed to cry, but the oracle continued without blinking: "The readings are unequivocal. His tiny body is so full of discordant being that Goddess cannot sanction him. He must be given to the great fiery kingdom to which, for all the magic in the world, he belongs. His life would be, if allowed to pass, a greater sorrow than his death."

I felt my mother's hand, cold and shrunken thin until the gems of her rings slipped of their own weight to the palm side. But she bowed her head and spoke: "I accept Heaven's will."

▫ VII ▫

"Topheth lies in a grove in a deep, lush cleavage in the land." I remembered the words of Ahinoam. David and his people, who have no patience with any but his god, condemn it. His priests declare that the cloud of smoke and incense that hangs perpetually over Topheth, stretched between the sacred trees, looking like fine cobwebs from above on the walls of Jebus (what is called today Jerusalem), is unhealthy. "The earth," Ahinoam said, "molders like swamp with all the sacrifices buried there." Don't these superstitious people know all the sacrifices are burned first with pure fire and then sealed in jars before being committed to the earth? Granted, worshipers sometimes do fall ill, but that can always be explained by some impiety on their own part. No one is denying that this valley is a place of awesome, yes, dangerous power. But to condemn it as an abomination is either mere ignorance, or weakness and fear to face this great power. So is it to take one of its names, Gehenna, as they do, for the place where those who deny their god will endure ceaseless torment after death.

I loved Topheth from first sight: the lush green of terebinths, figs, and tamarisks beneath a ridge of sheer white rock, deep, sheltered, and quiet. The birds loved it, too: Her holy doves and hoarse gray ravens acrobated over the open air, singing for joy. Yellow flowers were sprinkled like gold dust over the green hillside, and streaks of blood-red anemone ran down to the Holy Place. I remember the sight of a broken bird's shell, white and pure upon the gray dust of the forecourt. The cloud of smoke and incense stretched between the sacred trees looked like a fine, soft coverlet to me, not the unhealthy fog David's priests described. From the lowest point of the valley springs a well and it accompanies all human sounds with music of Goddess's own making. David's god likes to be worshiped in high places, brazen and exposed. I prefer Her hidden places and the mysteries of Woman.

At Topheth I first heard an oracle's voice, and my future was intoned in more ways than one. The voice declared my brother's fate. And it was emblematic of my own. The voice came from the heart of the sanctuary and grated with harshness yet with strength on the encircling sacred stones as if they were too snugly placed, as if the voice were living flesh dragged across their rough-hewn faces with violence until it was raw and curling with blood. For a long time, it was impossible to tell what was making the sound, and, even when I did see her, stepping forward with her proofs in the bloody bowl, I could not believe that such thunder could come from such a slight body.

This was not a high priestess, not like my mother, not like the kindly matron who had been ushering us through the rites until now, whose knife had killed the Sage. This creature was hardly human. She was thin—one could count her ribs and see the two bones in her forearm, which the white skin seemed to suffer pain in covering. Her hair was irregular in length, texture, and color, browns, blacks, grays. It seemed thin and transparent, as if she'd never grown more hair than a two-year-old. Her eyes were sunken, shielded, and circled thickly with blue-black as if with kohl, but there was no paint on her face. Her breasts were bare, tiny and flat, hardly more than a man's, and twisted below and up between them she wore the glossy skin of a spotted Viper. I do not remember who had been the Snake One in Geshur; even if I had, it would have meant nothing to me at that early time. This was, then, my first experience with one who, like myself, had been called to be familiar with the Snakes.

It wasn't until the body, but most especially the voice, of this Snake-Entwisted One forced itself into my mind that I first had an inkling of what my future might be. This lack of a sense of things to come in one who is now so consumed by it may surprise you. It does me, looking back. But I had been told over and over that in her childhood, Mother had been like me and that, when I grew up, I should be like her. I had great respect for my mother and thought her the most beautiful of Goddess's beautiful creatures. But she was High Priestess in Geshur and I guess I knew with another sense that one who has slept with the Snake is never the same as anyone else, even if that someone else is her mother.

Topheth's oracle spoke her verses and I listened not so much to their meaning as Mother did (for they declared the awesome future of her son) but to their being and their expansion forward and backward in time to the very roots of all the fruit of Goddess's all-creating Womb. My little goat was forgotten, but I knew his sacrifice helped prepare me, purify me, to hear and see what I was meant to.

I am not explaining very well what it was that struck me. But then, it is something not to be explained, a mystery between us who wear the skin and She who beads the night with stars. Suffice it to say that it is the power behind any verse of prophecy that makes it true. The words vary each time and are for the worshipers. The power is eternally the same and is for us alone—no more than two or three in a generation.

I soon forgot my mother's cold hand and my little brother whose fate was sealed. I had eyes only for the Snake-Entwisted One and she, as soon as the most difficult and consuming part of the ecstasy was past, only for me. I know that under the possession one must be blind to most of the world because if one were to let it enter with the force and clarity with which She comes in at that time, it could very well mean death.

But the Snake-Entwisted One blinked the glaze from her eyes enough to see me and she held her hand out to me. Her painfully thin arm was tracked with tiny marks in various states of heal—white, red, blue, or black—marks of the fangs of the sacred Snakes. The marks were on her breasts, too, like the sooty tattoos of certain wild tribes of Amalek, like the scars left by red-hot iron, like flecks of lapis lazuli growing beneath her translucent skin. I dropped my mother's hand and took the stranger's.

"So you are a friend to the Snakes?" she asked me. Only so close could one see that she was really very young— young even to five-year-old eyes. From a distance the gauze of her hair had seemed dull, if not gray, and the wrinkles put into her face by the exertion had made her seem older than the matron.

"I am Snakesleeper," I said simply, with little understanding.

"Ah! And so young?"

"I am five," I protested. That did not seem so young to me.

She smiled and did not scold me for tempting Death with mention of my age as Mother would have. Mother was overwhelmed with the rites that must be performed over my brother and was not heeding me then.

"Then this belongs to you," she said and handed me a small round stone the size and color of a sheep's eye.

"A bezoar?" I knew what it was, but I was awed.

"Yes. I found it in the intestines of your little goat."

"He gave it to me."

"Yes, I think he did. You will find it useful if you are called to work with the Legless Ones. I have one myself."

She showed me a similar stone she wore about her neck in an amulet. I decided right then that is how I would wear mine.

"This is the stone to which I owe my life," she said.

Then the Snake-Entwisted One began to speak in verse. One cannot always help it when one is entranced. She told how she had come to wear the skin. She had been born to simple peasants and had never been to the shrine at all until her eighth year. Then one summer's night when the heat made her restless, she left her mat and went down beneath the stairs to help herself to a ladle of water. One of Goddess's dark Messengers was there before her, cooling its skin in the water sweating from the jug and curling about the base in such a way that she couldn't tell it from moon-shadow until it was too late.

Her parents assumed their daughter lost, but her grandmother, a pious old woman who remembered well the days before King Saul when Goddess was unquestioned everywhere, said they must not call in the mourners until they had carried the child down to the holy place. Prayers were cheaper than mourners and a grave. More to pacify the old woman than with hope to save their child, the parents did as she asked. They were poor people, had five other daughters and great worries to marry off even those.

From full to new moon, the girl lay in the shrine knocking at the gates of the Netherworld, swollen and black with poison, senseless and in fever. Since none had seen the Snake that bit her—it was not one of those kept in the caves beneath the sanctuary—and none could tell even so much as the sex, there was very little in the way of exorcism that could be carried out over her. They applied the bezoar and prayed.

The fangs had but grazed the surface, or it was a very weak Snake, or, most likely, Goddess had called the girl to Herself in the thirst that had brought her down from the roof that night, for she lived through the bite. Then, of course, there was no returning to her parents' house. Goddess had laid claim to her forever.

The skin she wore was not her Snake's. It had belonged to her predecessor. And to hers and to hers, shed from one to the next in a mirror image of how the Snake renews its skin eternally. It is extremely rare that the skin and the body are so closely one as they are in my case. Divining is hard on one who must constantly descend into the pit and let the Serpents give them their sacred knowledge and their words in the form of their poison. Women of the Pit age and die young. This Snake-Entwisted One, I came to know, had shed her skin and not been replaced before I turned eleven, for she was not in the place when David took it. That would make hers a calling of less than fifteen years. I thank Goddess, Who gave me such unity with my oracle that only rarely must I induce the trance, only rarely is the task of prophecy so demanding on me.

All this knowledge of technique and responsibility was still far from me. All I understood was the power, and it so moved my soul as the Snake-Entwisted One spoke that I was quite prepared to descend into the pit with her and press fangs to both my inner arms right then and there. I did not want to be bothered with any caution or thought of antidote in my haste to be about my work, about my Holy Mother's work.

The Snake-Entwisted One spoke of poetry and I listened. It was from her that I first learned to call the holy Bridegroom "Dod," as in the chorus "My Beloved is mine and I am His . . . ." And to Goddess (or to the high priestess who takes on Her divinity) she gave the epithet "Shulamite" for the Peace brought to the world when She has worked Her yearly magic. When David renamed Jebus, I don't think he realized this was the peace meant in Jerusalem, the City of Peace. She taught me other such pretty phrases that I love to use today.

Goddess forgive me if I have divulged too many of Her secrets. I think I have not, but it is matter of a most sacred nature that I have been discussing here and not to be taken lightly, nor passed along unauthorized to anyone. I know She has Her own deadly ways of dealing with those who would try Her secrets and who are not fully initiated into Her wisdom. She will protect Herself if I have spoken amiss.

The great brazier was stoked and roaring. The dancers circled it with sympathetic leaps and body-waves of skill and beauty. The Snake-Entwisted One sang. The High Priestess held my little brother in her arms and he, oblivious to his fate, slept from his final suck. My mother was herself a High Priestess in another temple and had performed the same service to others' children. She stood, gray like slate, held her swollen breasts, and, with great strength and dignity, submitted to the sacrifice.

But I, like my brother, was suckled into oblivion by milk of another sort and saw none of this. It was all a warm blur of things-as-they-ought-to-be-at-last all around us as we sat, we two who were really one, holding hands and our Snake skins whispering to one another when the scales touched. Pythoness, as the Philistines call us, is a lonely calling, and our times of union are so rare and precious that those about us allowed us the time together without comment. They had to wait for the evening star to rise before the final act of sacrifice, and so there was no need for haste.

· VIII ·

IT WAS HOURS, days, years, perhaps, before I came to understand clearly what it was that put an end to that warm, comforting blur with the intoxicating power and yet the softness of new wine. Slowly, like the growing ache of a rotten tooth, I came to realize that the edge of my well-being was being disturbed by chaos. Hard iron and confusion, men's smells and voices in the women's sanctuary. Before it had been well-frayed parchment, like soft, warm wool to the touch. Now a skin, newly cured and prepared, glossy and stiff, the edge could draw blood with a careless pass of the hand. Already the prophecy concerning my little brother was being fulfilled.

David had had to come in disguise through the land of the Jebusites, for he was not powerful enough to incite them to battle yet. Besides, he realized that as soon as he was told of our flight, there was no time for drawing up either battle lines or negotiations for peaceful passage.

His figure did seem familiar to me, but he wore pilgrim's garb and I did not recognize him. And the contradiction of a pilgrim armed and flanked by surly soldiers refused to explain itself to me, as did the contradiction of men-of-war where there ought to have been only women's peace.

"Up on the platform there!" David ordered his men. "Save that child!"

The High Priestess suspended my little brother, naked and squirming, over the brazier halfway between Heaven and Earth. David's men hesitated at the fearsome sight. They knew it would be sacrilege to mount the platform, and their hesitation gave the woman time to overcome her shock and rattle off the prescribed liturgy:

> Great Lady of the Fearsome Eye,
> To You we offer this child.
> Take him to the midst of your burning heart
> And there, sanctify him,
> Make of his life, abundant life for those—

She almost laid my brother into the fire.

Almost, but not quite. David himself defiled the platform, snatched the child, and knocked the High Priestess over the brazier instead. It was nearly molten with the heat by then. It burned right through her robes and left nearly half of her body, after the oozing blisters and angry scabs, pasty white like fresh-kneaded bread. Years later I would meet the High Priestess of Topheth again, an old, shriveled woman. Such a deformed state—brought on by too intimate a contact with the divine—excluded her from ever officiating before Heaven again until her dying day.

I remember the wild drumming, the shrieking, the running. The Snake-Entwisted One who'd been sitting by my side to watch the sacrifice got to her feet. I did, too, and looked this way and that in a helpless search for a way out of the confusion. Then she by my side raised her awesome voice and began to call down the curses of Heaven upon the defilers of the day. I opened my mouth and echoed her in an infantile voice:

> As the Queen of Heaven lives,
> In Her holy Name do I curse you.

Cursed be you in the city,
And cursed be you in the field.
Cursed be your basket and your store.
Cursed be the fruit of your body
And the fruit of your land . . .

Then, as we continued and I grew more secure, for the first
time, it happened. Though my eyes remained open, the
trance came over me. Another voice entered me with a
shudder. It took up the refrain and then began to counter-
point her with fearful words of its own:

Cursed be the increase of your cattle,
And the flocks of your sheep.
Cursed be you when you come in
And cursed be you when you go out.

So we stood, side by side, hand in hand, and cursed like
a double volley of arrows.

I have the impression that we cursed for a very long time.
But then, I was unused to the suspension of time that occurs
when one is prophesying. Even if the men were dumbstruck
when they first heard us, that spell could not have lasted
very long. Time weighed heavily on their minds.

"Stop those drums!" David shouted. "They'll rouse the
men of Jebus. Quickly, we must be on the road to Hebron
before the Jebusite men-at-arms come down from the
mountain height."

A direct confrontation would have meant their end, as it
does for the raiding fox of the desert.

Sooner or later, whichever it was, I found myself sprawled
on the ground. Though I hadn't felt it at the moment, I
knew David had knocked me to my everyday senses with the
metal studs of his wristbands. I heard my little brother
howling.

"Don't stand there like a fool who never held a baby
before! Give him to his mother!"

I began to cry, too, feeling like the defenseless little girl I
was, feeling the blow after the fact. A soldier picked me up

and tossed me roughly onto a donkey. A second soldier led
Mother by on another donkey. At a jarring trot we rose out
of the Valley. As they passed I could see that Mother had
wrapped my brother's Goddess nakedness in her shawl and
was giving him her breast. She did not even look back at the
shrine, but hushed him with a little lullaby. "Hush, child,
hush," she said to me when her driver brought me alongside.
But I could not be comforted. At least, she was not the one
to be my comforter any longer.

When Jebus was out of sight behind a hill, David, who
had been covering our retreat, goaded his animal up across
the wild and rocky growth on either side of the narrow path
until he rode parallel to my mother.

"Good God, woman," he exploded, "good God, what
did you think you were doing, giving our child into the
hands of that witch?"

My mother didn't understand his Hebrew, and the bewildered half smile she fixed him with seemed to convince him
of his next words.

"You people aren't human. Killing your own children!"
said the man who had killed many another man's son. "By
God, a donkey doesn't do that."

She understood the emotion of his words even if she
didn't understand their meaning. She bowed her head and
murmured something.

David sputtered with impatience and was about to prod
his animal off to the end of the line again when I spoke up.

"Goddess has rejected this child," I said, as surprised at
the sound of my own voice as I had been to hear it prophesy.

David looked at me sharply.

"That's what my mother said," I told him. "Goddess has
rejected him from life and claims him as Her own."

"Rejected him? Rejected my son?" David railed. "Why,
I've never seen such a healthy boy. By God, didn't you hear
him yell at the shrine? If those drums don't draw the Jebusites on our tail, his yelling will. Stupid, stupid woman. I
ought to knock some sense in you. I will the minute we're
out of Jebus."

"Physical strength alone does not fit a person for-life," I

translated my mother's next murmur. "Men cannot understand these things."

In spite of the insult in the words—especially the ungracious way I interpreted them—David was silent for a moment. Perhaps he remembered the words of his own prophet Samuel when he had anointed the young son of Jesse from among all his older, stronger brothers: "Look not on the height of his stature, for the Lord sees not as a man sees. For a man looks on the outward appearance, but the Lord . . ."

This wisdom he shook from himself, however, and said: "Look, woman, look. Can you get it through your head? All this land, as far as the eye can see—all this land will be for our son and his brothers, from Dan in the north to Beersheva in the south. The God of my Fathers has promised it to us."

My mother said nothing, but looked down at my sucking brother instead. So I spoke without prompting: "This land belongs to Shulamite, Goddess of the Jebusites."

"Ours," David said, not having realized in his passion that Mother hadn't spoken, that he was arguing with a child. He repeated, "Ours. If we are righteous, if we forsake false gods, if we refuse to give our children to Moloch. If we are righteous, my household and I, we will win all this for ourselves with the help of God. We will live in houses we did not build, eat from trees we did not plant. That's the promise, from the mouth of the God of my Fathers, if we're righteous."

"That doesn't sound very righteous, to eat of another's labor."

"Just look at this land," David continued.

He had hardly heard me as he waved his hand over the hills around us, sloughing rocks like goats their hair in spring. We were already in wilderness by then, the small patches of regular green where wheat had been sown becoming more and more infrequent, and now all behind us. We had to squint to tell sheep from stones at the edge of sight. The fortress of Jebus at our backs looked just like the rock it grew from and, when recognized, lent an element of surprise to the scenery that set the heart pounding with trepidation. Then the fortress was behind a hill and there were only the lengthening shadows of scrubby acacias and stone-strewn grass flecked with wildflowers that tried to grow in the chalky, grayish soil. The grass grew, like a beard of two days' mourning, on the east and north sides of the hills only, burned off the others. The land was all more wild and a little frightening with Goddess's presence than pretty.

"It's all going to waste. When we move in, we'll show them how to use it. We'll show them that this place can be made to bloom as a rose."

"Like a rose in an enclosed garden, pruned and strangled against a wall."

"The child is talking nonsense," David declared.

Mother shot me a glance that told me to hush. It was just as well because I couldn't find the words to explain about a wilderness. Goddess kept it to Herself and prohibited the rich man from putting a wall around it and watering his vines there by the labor of his slaves. She did this to keep a place for the poor to run their few goats, for the widow to gather wild herbs for her pot, for the initiate to gather mandrakes for her sacred rites, for the partridge to have her nest and raise her little ones undisturbed.

Just then, my brother turned his face from the breast, looked up at the gruff red hair and beard peering at him, and gave what both parents took to be the first bloom of a toothless smile.

"Just look at that," David exclaimed. "How could anyone want to burn that? He knows his papa."

Again, a glance of warning from my mother; again, I bit my tongue. Again, I sensed but couldn't explain as a five-year-old how every mother finds it difficult to obey Heaven's will. And David had just made it too easy for Maacah of Geshur to play deaf. Even as an adult, I wouldn't want to try to explain it to the youngest of eight sons as David was. As the youngest son of an estate that must be divided eight ways, expansion seems the only answer. That's what makes a conqueror.

"It was promised to my Fathers," David said, "that our

offspring would be as numerous as the stars in the sky. God knows what He's about."

"And how shall we number the stars in the sky," I said, "if the campfires of all your descendants dull the heavens?"

Those weren't my words, they were Goddess words, and David spat at them with a fury. He raised his arm; my face still bore the imprint of those brass stubs on his wrist. My mother gave a little cry and he lowered his arm.

"You watch yourself, girl," he said instead. "Just watch yourself. I am lenient this time because my God is a God of mercy. But He has also said: 'Rebellion is like the sin of the witch.' And again, 'You shall not suffer a witch to live.' The fire you prepared for this innocent babe, we can also prepare for you. Your mother and you are strangers to our ways; I try to be sympathetic. But my God is a jealous God and, with His help, I try to rule as He has commanded. I will not be so merciful next time."

David reached a leathern hand and lifted my mother's face to him more roughly than tenderly. "Tell that to the mother of my son so she can understand it in that pretty head of hers."

My mother gazed back at him with a face that seemed to say, "Please, please. I'm so grateful you saved my son. I'll do anything you say. But forgive me. You must save me from myself."

Then David let her chin drop and kicked the flanks of his mount. He rode yelling to the end of our company, his infamous slingshot at the ready. A small party of vengeful Jebusites had just appeared in the evening glow at our tail.

"Run! Run the beasts!" he instructed his men. "God willing, we can outrun them."

By the time we reached the safety of Hebron, the Goddess-given strength of the past two or three days faded and the pangs of birth caught up with my mother. Perhaps David had brought the pangs to Topheth hidden under his false pilgrim's robes along with his sword. There were times in the next month or so when the other wives feared for Mother's life and soundly condemned her foolhardiness. I think she came to believe them. As her gratitude made her submissive to David, she grew submissive to my little brother, as well. I never took precedence over him again.

The Hebrews admit that Heaven has special claim upon the firstborn son of a woman. They remember that truth from their ancient and more god-fearing past and tell a story of their times in Egypt when the hand of Heaven proved this in a mighty way. But these days they shy away from the true offering—all life placed on the altar, to be accepted or rejected as Heaven wills. David trusted in the watery and once-upon-a-time-efficacious blood of a ram to redeem this brother of mine at the end of a month.

David named his son at this ceremony. The name he chose was Absalom—"Father of Peace." That had nothing to do with Shulamite. It was to publicly proclaim the peaceful reunion of my mother and himself. In spite of his attitude toward Goddess, David always spoke in high terms of peace, set it up like some idol on a pedestal. In times of upheaval such as those were, people long for peace as they long for the presence of a god and will follow anyone who promises it to them, even if he takes everything else from them and leads them through a thousand battles to get it.

Absalom. Such a name for one who should have been laid nameless upon the brazier! His future was dark and full of wrath, just as the prophecy had said; we'd seen its beginnings. One should not try to give a contentious spirit any name at all, especially not a name that is a blatant and self-deceiving lie.

I was the daughter, not the precious son, and my opinion was not asked in the matter. But I had seen and felt the trance. I thought more strongly than I had before: "Very well. Do this thing. But nothing good will come of it, you may be sure of that."

Two

▪ IX ▪

I HAVE BEEN confronted all my life by those who dismiss my Serpent gifts with gentle smiles as if I were still only four or five years old and trying out the limits of the world with my fantasies. Is there not the proof of my poetry? I say in defense. That is hardly an idle child's fantasy. "Yes," they nod and say. "But you are David's daughter. Did he not compose great psalms? Should one expect less from a child of his?"

But, you see, I was not David's daughter. I never got a chance at his glowing ruddiness or his thick red hair which, since all the other princes and princesses came by it naturally, was the height of fashion. Like any rich man's daughter, I could have squandered for paints and dyes if I'd wanted to, crushed carnelian, hot pepper paste, and henna, and not have had to content myself with constant cheek-pinching like the poor.

There were times, as I was growing up, that I felt Heaven had cheated me, for none of my mother's beautiful traits had fallen to my inheritance, either. Though I had Mother's dark hair, I had none of its texture, and the olive coloring of my skin seemed grafted from a different tree entirely. Mother's skin was pale and lucid; mine was very dark. In olives, the darker ones give more oil. But such is not the prophesied harvest of that shade in a little girl.

Absalom was heir to the double portion of good looks in our rooms. His hair was thick and, like David's, the color of just-hulled chestnuts. Like Mother's, it fell naturally into the plump curls that others spend all their time and energy trying to achieve, only to have it turn into a limp imitation as the feast wears on. Absalom had Mother's eyes, too, which seemed even larger on a boy than on a woman. His lids were dark with protective kohl, with lashes so thick that if you were not completely entranced by them, you could not help wondering at the effort it must take to hold them open.

Jealousy would have been understandable—justified, even—when I had to stand by and watch how women—and men, all the way up to David—found my brother's hair and a flutter of his eyes irresistible. But no. Jealousy was not how these things affected me. I found the cooing and fawning all too silly in people who ought to have been old enough to know better. I was not jealous, but sometimes I could not help being afraid. His beauty would have been described as "good" and "a blessing" by anyone asked, and they would make signs against evil lest too much praise should harm him. To them my fear would have been like a child's demands for water at bedtime when what she really wants is not to be left alone in the dark. But I could see very well how the sharpness of a blade would sometimes appear in the innocent twinkle of my brother's eyes. He knew what he was doing. All the time, manipulating. He knew full well.

Absalom not only got everything he wanted with a flash of his eyes and a toss of his curls. I could have lived with that. But he also played the people of the household off one another as they all contended to be close to that beauty. He set maid against maid until there was nothing but bickering, and our rooms became a byword for contention in the court. I learned to comb and braid my own plain hair at an early age just to be left out of it.

Mother would come and try to make peace, but she would only make matters worse. She was jealous of his attentions herself. She got rid of slave after slave and then felt pangs of guilt later when she found that the next was more spellbound than the last. Always the mischief was, at the base, my brother's doing. He knew it and I knew it, but no one else would admit it. He set Mother against David and all the other wives in her jealous protection of what she had created and had never regained the courage to destroy. I forgot all the words to the Snake-Entwisted One's song, but the feeling always came back to me. The All-Seeing One, She was right about Absalom.

So I inherited none of David's good looks. Those who insist that so much time under his roof must have bestowed something on me would give me his poetry instead. Indeed, of all the children of the King of Israel and Judah, it's a wonder that I alone should have been touched. Solomon, they say, has some flair for words, but from those verses I have heard attributed to him, I can tell you none of them is original. He rehashes his father's old psalms to leach them of honest emotion and put more generally palatable sentimentality there. I've been told that he claims some of my verses as his own, too, but I shall curse the fellow that first recites his version to me. Still, all this is as much as saying that, whereas a man may give blushing cheeks, red hair, or beautiful eyes as a legacy to the fruit of his loins, the quick and true Serpent tongue is a gift of the gods alone.

It did me no harm, of course, to grow up in a household whose air David decorated with music as another man might have the walls painted or the doorways hung with fine Babylonian tapestries. Even when his prosperity and self-flattery made the song pretentious and garish, the product of wealth rather than the soul, they still had their effect on me. When Goddess has blessed one with the true sense and Serpent-licked ears, bad taste is as good at giving one things to oppose as good taste is at giving one things to champion. And in the earlier, humbler days in Hebron, when David still let his soul lie open to his god on a night, I cannot deny that there was great power in his verse.

There was so much power, in fact, that I was somewhat afraid of poetry and prophecy, my very own calling, in those days. Those who would laugh at this nonsense, saying they have heard poetry all their lives and never felt it frightening, they are those who could listen forever and never be sensitive to the least bit of its true power. I actually avoided it when I could, as one who must think clearly—a soldier before battle or a priestess before sacrifice—avoids the effect of strong wine.

But as my little brother grew, there was less space for my soul to expand in my mother's rooms, and the courtyard drew me. I went out on my own especially at evening, for not only had the ritual of coaxing, bribing, tantalizing Absalom to sleep each night grown unnaturally like the response to blackmail, but it was then that the best music was made in the king's hall. I never went directly to the hall, however, for I was afraid of the same power that tempted me, afraid of what people might say.

The most-worn path in the courtyard was that between my mother's door and that of Ahinoam the Jezreelitess. Ahinoam's son, Amnon, David's firstborn, was my best playmate, and my feet loved that path between our doors warmed by daylight. But in the cool of evening, when I could endure my brother no longer, the tapestry of Jezreelitish handiwork would be drawn across Ahinoam's door and I would hear that little family within, a family at their supper: the clink of platters and the low, pleasant chatter as food satisfied their hunger. I would pause outside in the growing dark just long enough to hear my little friend, as the man of the room, intone the blessing. The Jezreelites are a people who fear David's god and Ahinoam was known as a very pious woman even among them. The sense of her piety, though it was not the same as mine, joined with the singsong prayer of my dear companion and was good comfort.

Being thus instructed in the power holy verses could have when used properly, I would gain more courage to go on to listen in at the greater things being recited in the king's hall.

There is one evening in particular I remember eavesdrop-

ping. It was the night David, King of Judah, sat bargaining
with Abner, general of Israel. It was in the spring of my
tenth year.

Many another spy would have paid dearly from many a
public treasury to know of the spot I had found to listen in
on this meeting of the king and kingmaker. It was beneath
an ancient olive tree where I could lean my cheek against the
eastern wall of the hall. That wall still held the warmth of
the morning sun after dark. Here I could hear everything as
if I'd been in the very room, a slave waving a fan over the
king's head, my tongue cut out so I could not gossip.

What deals David and Abner were striking at this meeting
that evening had great import for the history of the two
kingdoms. Indeed, that meeting has been called a wellspring
of treason, murder, and conquest. I do remember them
mentioning Michal.

"King Saul's daughter," Abner described her, "God rest
the old man's moldering soul."

This caught my interest because it was female.

"My wife, the wife of my youth, my first beloved," David
waxed poetical.

Abner sniffed skeptically. "Anyway, I've brought her here
now, you've got her under your roof—"

"And tonight, tonight I shall take such pleasure—!"

"Taking more pleasure because your majesty knows this
pleasure makes him King of Israel."

"Exactly. At last the God of my Fathers smiles—"

"In return for which, having brought her here against the
will of Israel, against the will of her brother, against her
own—"

"Damn the will of her brother."

"My sentiments exactly."

"Tonight, such pleasure—!"

"In return for which, my lord, I must claim my pleasure."

"Your pleasure?"

"We have a bargain made, my lord—"

But the rest was not what I had come to the wall to hear.
I drowsed, the mutterings of politics wasted on me.

Suddenly I wakened to full attention, for I knew that

David had called for his lyre and was tuning it to sing. I knew that, though he was more astonishing in his psalm singing than in any other skill his god had blessed him with, David did not like to sing in public except when ritual or pleasant evenings with close companions prompted it. He especially refrained from singing when his military status called for a harsh and rigid bearing. The two attitudes were incompatible. Yet here was David, King of Judah, singing and playing for Abner, Israel's kingmaker. Their dealings must have been very satisfactory indeed.

I silently praised David for his choice of verse. It was proud, yet not too slow, sifting like dust from the slits of the high hall windows, down through the last of the setting sunlight into the court.

> My heart is indicting a good matter,
> My tongue is the pen of a ready scribe.
> You are fairer than the children of men,
> Grace is poured into your lips.
> Therefore God has blessed you for ever.
> Your arrows are sharp in the heart of the king's
>   enemies
> Whereby the people fall under you . . .

"I am honored," was all Abner could think of to say. He was, too.

I closed my eyes; I needed no eyes for what I saw. Neither were they closed from weariness, for I remained very alert. I began to sing myself. I knew no words but those of David's psalm, so I sang them, over and over again. But my inflection and the hollow intonation I effected came from what I had learned from the other Snake One, half my young lifetime away.

◙ X ◙

"WELL, LITTLE ONE," a voice from the present startled me. "Your tongue tells me you are a child of David, but your face tells me other things. Whose child are you?"

"I am Snakesleeper," I said. I had forgotten for the moment that I had other parentage.

"But who is your mother?"

"Maacah of Geshur." I remembered myself before the sternly practical face that confronted me.

"Ah," she nodded. "Little Absalom's sister." Everyone knew Absalom.

The woman was heavily veiled, even for a nighttime stroll, in mourning black, yet she had drawn the veils back to speak with me and I saw her features: thin lips, small, irregular nose, receding chin—her coloring pinched and pale as if she suffered chronically from the cold. In time I would come to know these features as a mark of the house of Saul, features which, ill as they become a woman, become a man even less. At the time I could not imagine who this stranger in our court might be.

"Do you know who I am?" she asked.

Her asking had a certain note of taunting in it that made me suddenly remember all the gossip of the past few days and realize, "You are Michal, the daughter of Saul."

It took me some moments of silent staring at that rather homely face before I could believe what I had said and believe that this was the woman who made my mother feel so threatened. But then I remembered that what I was to Geshur, she was to Israel, and I said bluntly, "It's through you David wants to make sons to be kings for Israel."

My words confounded her for a moment and they brought another figure, a second woman in ash-covered veils, a maidservant, out of the shadows. "Off with you, wicked child. My mistress cannot bear the chatter of silly children."

"It's all right, Zipporah." Saul's daughter had recovered her voice and spared me. "I cannot go all my life avoiding other women's children."

Turning to me, she asked, "Have you already had your supper?" with a motherly condescension that was almost as frustrating as being torn away from my east wall.

"No," I said.

"Well, where's your mother?" she asked. "Or were you naughty and sent to bed without?"

"Mother's with my brother," I said.

"Oh, I see." Her voice seemed suddenly ten years more adult. "Will you come to my rooms? I'm sure Zipporah can find us something to eat." She stretched out a hand toward me. "Come on." Finally I took her hand.

I expected to be painfully uncomfortable in her rooms. I expected my breaths to seem years apart and never to come evenly or unconsciously. I expected I would sit keeping the soles of my feet on the floor so I could get up and leave as soon as I could. I expected the rooms to be proper and gray and badly lit and clumsily trying to be pretty in bad taste and in spite of mourning, just as their mistress was. I was surprised by what greeted me as I crossed the threshold. It wasn't an unpleasant surprise and I felt at home at once.

When David kept his court in Hebron, the wives' rooms were all pretty much alike. A new door was simply pierced

through the courtyard wall, bricks baked and mortar mixed
and a new square apartment, air-vented near the top but
otherwise windowless, could be ready off of it in a matter of
days. The plaster was still cool and damp to the touch on
Michal's walls, and its smell permeated everything. Not all
of her belongings were out of their road-dusty bundles and
boxes; they clustered in a heap of impermanence in the
center of the room, yet to be flung to the walls with the swing
of settled living.

Nonetheless, I felt welcomed and at home, for against the
pinkish plaster of her western wall (it was too large to fit in
a niche) stood an image. It was the first thing to be unpacked. The image was breasted and full-hipped but otherwise featureless, little more than an Ashtoreth stump. David
and those who follow his god would call such things teraphim, "disgraceful things." Under the pressure of such
terminology, Mother had "put such things from her"—
wrapped them in old rags and placed them in her inlaid
chest. Mother had grown ashamed to have those clay eyes
looking down on her as she went about without her veil, as
she gave the breast to the child that really belonged to them.
Their loss made Mother even more dependent on David and
Absalom for her inner strength. It is never good to put away
Her from Whom life truly springs.

"Fie! I knew bringing this child here was ill-omened," the
maid said, noticing how I gazed at the figure. She mistook
my reverence for a stare of condemnation.

But Michal scolded her. "Leave the child be, Zipporah."
Then to me she said, "You needn't tell tales about my
image, child. David knows all about Her. And another one
I have here, behind this curtain."

"And he allows it?" I asked.

Saul's daughter laughed a laugh with shades of her father's madness in it. As if she needed David's permission for
anything. "My image," she said, "once saved David's life.
He had better allow it, or *he* won't be allowed."

I was surprised to find myself seated as comfortably as if
I'd been in my mother's rooms. Michal's furnishings obviously did not expect the arrival of careless children. Her

bright rugs were unprotected by coarser matting; the fine crockery, painted in two or even three colors with birds, lozenges, and other fanciful shapes, was displayed on knee-high tables. Perhaps the display was a little blatant. An older woman whose children are grown and who has no grand-children moving underfoot may be glad that she can now bring down her treasures, but she is very self-conscious and sobered about it all the same. So it was with Saul's daughter. I might well have spent time worrying about my clumsiness. But there was too much else to stimulate my mind to be fretting about my body then.

Michal had fallen into a melancholic silence for a mo-ment, which Zipporah tried to lighten with gossip as she prepared a little food. "What do you make of this Abigail, child?"

I shrugged. "Abigail is the first wife—"

At this Michal left off her silence and laughed bitterly. "They call Abigail David's first wife. Don't they know *I'm* the first one? *I* had David's virginity . . . and he had mine."

It seemed the only thing that could rouse Michal from her melancholy was to remember the past. Seeing my interest, this she proceeded to do with set inflections and phrases that let me know she recited it often and whenever she could, probably to her maids, or simply to herself when no one else would listen.

"I loved David from the moment I first saw him, so fair and ruddy, playing and singing for my father the king. At first my father determined to take such a fine specimen as a son-in-law and offered to give him my sister Merab. Well, she was the eldest and the prettiest—"

Zipporah spat against evil. "Goddess hears when you say such things."

"Well, Merab was the most fortunate, anyway. But then David began to make a name for himself. They'd come home from a campaign and it was David the maidens looked for with their baskets of flowers and their palm branches, not my father. 'Saul has killed his thousands and David his ten thousands,' they would sing—within my father's hearing. So my father married Merab to another. She is the happy one."

"Your envy will do her no good," Zipporah remarked.

"But you said you were married to David—before, before Abigail," I urged.

"So I was. David was ambitious, you see. I think he liked Merab more, but either one of us would do, so long as she was Saul's daughter. Myself, I gave David more encouragement than was modest. I wasn't initiated yet, I didn't understand. I believed the Goddess stories. I didn't understand that they are stories for the Great Bed, for ritual, to take our humanity from us from time to time, not for real life—"

"What did your father the king say to all of this?" I pressed on for the Goddess details of the story.

"My father wanted David dead. So—he hit upon a plan, straight from the tales. 'The only bride-price I demand for my daughter,' he announced in the hearing of all, particularly David, who was always listening, 'is one hundred foreskins of the uncircumcised Philistines.'

"Now, you know it's against the religion of the Philistines to mutilate their bodies in any way, particularly not with the sign of a covenant with my father's god. To get those foreskins, you would have to kill them first, circumcise them afterward. This, my father thought, would surely be the end of anyone who tried it. No one would be so foolhardy as to attempt it."

"It looked like you were destined to die an old maid," Zipporah clicked.

"No one dared—no one but David. And he did it, just like in the story where the monster is slain and the princess delivered."

"He had help," Zipporah scoffed.

"I suppose he did have help, from his band of young men."

"A couple of them died for those foreskins."

"I suppose they did," Michal said, "but I was there, sitting on a cushion at my father's feet, when David strode in, a sack the size of four melons on his shoulder."

" 'O Anointed One of Israel,' " Zipporah said, mimicking

David's voice and courtly tones until we all giggled. " 'I've come to purchase me a bride.' "

"And then he spilled the sack right there on the rug at our feet," Michal said, clapping her hands with pleasure and surprise, just as she must have done when the event was really happening. "All these little, squirmy, hardening rings of bloody flesh, like insects, like a sack of locusts. Not one hundred, but two hundred Philistine foreskins."

"Two hundred, hah!" Zipporah said. "What did you do, count them?"

"Goodness, no! It wouldn't be seemly for a woman—"

"The men, then? Did your father have all his doddering, nearsighted scribes sit down in a circle around this heap and add them up on their tablets? 'What do you think, Noah? Is this a whole one or just a part?' 'It looks like here's another piece that fits onto that one.' "

Michal doubled over with laughter. "I imagine maybe they did," she said when she could speak again. "I did see them shooing the dogs away from taking their supper there."

" 'Off with you, Gib,' " Zipporah mimicked again, slapping at an imaginary hound. " 'That's the princess's dowry.' "

"I was too busy—getting married."

"You said David had your maidenhead," I asked, "not Goddess?"

"Well, my father's god, you know. Fool that I was! I was just a girl. I hadn't even come to the bleeding mystery yet. But David was in a hurry—"

"Always in a hurry." Zipporah shook her head.

"—and his haste was intoxicating. If I'd been initiated first, I'd have known to treat these stories as they are meant to be, not as a promise of happy-ever-after."

"What did your father the king say to all of this? Didn't he want to go back on his word?"

"I suppose he did. But he was king, Goddess rest him, and didn't."

"Besides," suggested Zipporah, "with them married, he'd have a good idea where David slept every night, not like

when he was a bachelor shepherd boy, camping one night
here, the next night there."

"I knew when I saw one-eyed Avram lurking in the street
outside our door what my father had in mind."

"Avram was Saul's assassin," Zipporah explained.
"Keener with one eye than most are with two."

Michal sighed. "I was still not initiated. I was still young
and in love. I told David what I'd seen, then I let him down
from our bedroom with cords."

"Now comes the part about the teraphim," Zipporah
said.

"My sacred household image, yes. To give him more time
to escape, I dressed up the male image and put it in bed with
me."

"Do you want to see how it looked?" Zipporah looked at
me keenly, as if she had Avram's one eye.

"Zipporah," Michal scolded. "She's just a child. Nowhere near initiation yet."

"So she shouldn't come to initiation too late, as you did."

"I'd like to see," I pleaded.

So they drew back the curtains and I was face to face with
a life-size statue made of wood, complete with a large and
erect penis to grant fertility to any household in which it
stood.

"This one's circumcised," Zipporah assured me.

"Just like David." Michal giggled.

"Well, come, Lady, let's show her how it was."

So the two women bustled about amongst the half-
unpacked luggage until they'd found a fuzzy pillow of goat
hair dyed bright red, which they set on the image's head.
Then they wrapped the image in a blanket like a man just
called from bed.

"Very like David, wouldn't you say?"

"Yes." I giggled as Zipporah gave another quick tug on
the blanket to keep the figure modest.

"Well, it was good enough to keep Avram fooled for an
hour or so," Michal said. "By the time he burst in with his
sword slashing—"

"Look at the head of this poor teraphim," Zipporah

clucked, lifting the pillow to show me what I had missed in my fascination over the other part of the body. Half of the head was missing.

"—by that time David was safely out of my father's reach. That was the last time I saw him," Michal sighed, "vanishing into the dark at the bottom of those cords. Did he care what happened to me at all? I went to the baths regularly for a full nine months before I could believe it. Not even a red-haired child to remember him by."

Zipporah was putting away their playthings. She spoke with her chin on her chest, holding an edge of the blanket and looking back wistfully at the red-mopped statue. "You must have felt just fine the next morning after sleeping with that one, Lady."

"Well, I must confess a night spent alone with the statue did set me to seek out Zipporah and the Women's Mysteries—after those nine months were up. And they helped me to see Phalti for the good, good man he was—is. He still is," Michal insisted firmly, "he still is the best of men."

"Who's Phalti?" I asked.

"The son of Laish of Gallim."

I had to admit that still didn't mean anything to me.

"A nobody," Zipporah said.

"My father gave me to Phalti when David ran away and became an outlaw."

"Ah."

"One might have hoped for a better match for a king's daughter," Zipporah clucked.

"But that's exactly what recommended him to my father. He had no ambition to steal the king's victory songs."

"When a king's daughter has lost her virginity"—Zipporah said it directly to me as a warning—"even her value comes down a notch or two."

"That's exactly what attracted me to him, too. Still does." Saul's daughter began to weep into her lap as she remembered.

"Phalti is not a man for whom one feels passion."

"He's a simple man. He's a man who enjoys sitting quietly beneath his own laden vines and olive trees on a summer's evening and, from that vantage, surveying no farther than his own boundary stones. The things he husbands do not grow over-lush, for he wields a firm hand with the pruning hook, but they do grow fruitful."

"You have children by him, then?"

I heard Michal say "Five," but it was Zipporah who had to carry on: "One every other year as apples bear: the little boys so like their father, the little girls that played so prettily at this same image's feet."

"Phalti doesn't mind teraphim, then?"

"Father outlawed images after they aided David's escape."

"Let women keep their religion in conformity with the powers that be," said Zipporah.

Michal said, "I kept this image—"

"As a doll for the girls, perhaps?" suggested Zipporah.

"Stricter Israelites condemn figures even as patterns on pottery, but Phalti is not one like that."

" 'Twas that strictness and image-hating that brought an end upon the king your father," Zipporah the maid commented with the settling of self-satisfaction in her face.

"I no longer care to argue the matter with you, Zipporah," Michal said.

"You know I'm right," Zipporah said firmly.

· XI ·

IT WAS OBVIOUS by now that Zipporah was more than just a maid. She was a small, sharp woman whose features reminded me of the thin, needlelike beak and talons and the erect crest of a hoopoe bird as it pries here and there for ants and grubs. I have met other women who became more livid when their anger was raised, but never any who were perpetually so foul-tempered as Zipporah. Even feast days failed to rouse her spirits. If anything, she found that chores were more wearisome and more could go dismally wrong on such days than normal. The trick in dealing with Zipporah was to take glumness as a joke and ire as her form of entertainment. I learned this trick only later, once when I could not help laughing at the absurdity of one of her outbursts. My nervous laughter brought a thin, sharp smile to her lips, which, though it quickly faded, helped me to piece together all the fragments I'd learned of her up until then. She was protecting herself with a stern exterior and was as happy as a king secure behind a great bastion.

"Zipporah is from the town of Manasseh called En-Dor. Do you know it?" Michal asked me.

"Of course she doesn't know it," Zipporah said.

"I do," I protested. " 'The witch of En-Dor,' I've heard of that."

"Witch!" Zipporah exclaimed. "Oh, I like that!"

"En-Dor has no holy place but a cave without so much as a woven mat door to keep the sanctuary," Michal explained. "Nevertheless, it draws pilgrims from much larger sites, and the reason for this is a race of Seers inhabiting the cave. Zipporah is a younger daughter of this famous clan."

"So she acts as your Seer, Lady," I said, triumphant at having figured that much out and hoping to redeem myself for having used David's unflattering word *witch*.

"My Seer along my dark-spirited road. That's only part of the reason. Zipporah is the last person still on earth today to see my father alive. It was at the battle of Gilboa."

"Do you know of the battle of Gilboa, child?"

"Saul and the Israelites camped against Achish and the Philistines of all five cities," I recited.

Michal nodded, then continued, "Surveying the opposite host, my father's heart failed his breast. Samuel, his prophet, was several years in the grave and Israel was cursed with the silence of Heaven."

"It was in an attempt to break that awful silence from the mortals' side that Saul had outlawed the worship of any other deity than the one he wanted to hear," Zipporah continued the story. "With these gods went all the images by which one could tell their oracles, the practice of priestesscraft, and the use of holy caves and their rites. Such fools men are!"

"It is true, alas!" Michal confessed. "Such measures had done more harm than good, for there, on the battlefield of Gilboa, when the fate of Israel dangled before the iron spears of Philistia, even Nature drew her veil before her face and sent neither flight of cranes nor wind in the acacias to take an omen by. The Israelites could only stand and count the fast chariots and iron weapons of the enemy and compare them with the brief tally of their own armaments. Only ill omens could be read from that inquiry."

"An ill-omened day indeed," Zipporah said. "And no light to see it by."

"Unable to sleep with an unknown morrow before him, my father came to the cave of En-Dor. Three years of outlawry had not diminished the name Zipporah had inherited from her many illustrious forebears."

"I knew the king at once," Zipporah said, "even though he was dressed as a common foot soldier. I was afraid he had heard I'd been breaking his laws and was come to incriminate me.

"Of course I'd been practicing the craft all the time of the prohibition," Zipporah snapped as if someone had pointed an accusing finger at her between her last speech and this, though no one had even thought of doing so. "Of course. Sometimes the law was an excuse to turn away when they couldn't pay enough, but even a king—even your father, mistress—cannot keep the spirits still when they want to speak."

They had risen that night at her command. Or rather, it was the single spirit, the shade of Samuel the Prophet, that Saul had wanted to see.

"He was a tough one." Zipporah clicked her tongue. "All his life he'd served a god who did not approve of the dead returning, and even in the Netherworld he could not be made to change his views. He came nonetheless. I have ways. And he told the king what it was he wanted to know. It was not good news, I'm afraid, and that was that. Well, I happened to have a goat in the cave that some shepherd had brought me. I'd second-sighted half a dozen of his flock and led them home for him by magic. Your father paid me well in gold, so I could afford it. Besides, I had compassion on him. He had been fasting all that day in fear. I killed the goat and roasted it for him. I dare say, if old Samuel spoke the truth—and a spirit, even a perverse one, has no reason to lie—that was the last meat he ever tasted, mistress. It was well flavored, as I recall. Plenty of garlic."

You might find this way of speaking to an orphan cruel. I did at the time. But that was Zipporah's way, and Michal seemed to thrive on it. All these years later, it is Zipporah I remember with most reverence—yes, even fondness. For all her stern and cynical exterior, I found more of worth within her than in her mistress, whose kind and languid face hid confusion and the sprouting seeds of madness. Yet if she shared her father's dangerous state of mind, Michal was also wise enough to seek with him the cure. She did not flinch at the pain Zipporah caused because the vision the witch conjured up was as true as it was vivid.

Because her tears were already flowing, Michal did not hesitate now to describe a further pain, and one much fresher. "So my father fell," she said, "and all my brothers, and . . . And Abner, whom my father trusted, he has sold me thus to David. In return for me, David has taken Abner on his side, the winning side. Back I come to David, whom the quiet love of Phalti has taught me now to hate."

"Phalti is still alive then?" I asked.

"Of course he's still alive," Zipporah snapped because Michal was now speechless with grief. "No divorce, no return of the bride-price, no nothing."

"And your children—?"

"Oh, child, if you'd seen him." Michal spoke now over sobs. "If only you'd seen him—"

"Abner's dragging her off, can you imagine? She's kicking and screaming, he's using four men to keep her on the donkey, even though he has her hands tied behind her . . ."

Michal rubbed her wrists in anguish as if the bonds were still there. "Phalti followed after. All the way he followed after, carrying our youngest on his shoulder and weeping openly into the corner of his torn cloak. They turned him back at sword point at Bahurim."

"Lest the sight of him offend David and spoil the plot."

" 'Turn back or we'll drag that child off your shoulder and run him through.' I heard them say it. Ah, what the house of Saul must suffer! Ah, my good husband! Ah, my babies—they still need a mother's milk! And the older ones, too! Sarai, my girl, the eldest. Such a comfort she is, such a help. She is more than a daughter. She's a sister, a friend!" Michal wailed as if at a funeral.

Mistress and maid wept, and I watched uncomfortably until finally I learned to shed tears of sympathy. We wept until our tears had cooled the infected sorrow somewhat, then both women sighed helplessly and wiped their eyes. I mimicked them in this, but I could not then turn with their relish to the tray of herbs, scallions, parsley, and such that we had meanwhile been served. These green things demand an adult tongue, inured by years of sharp, pungent flavors and bitter sorrows. They waken up dulled appetites and palates and bring onion tears to eyes wrinkles have wrung dry. Children who feel everything new and to the quick can eat but little of these things with the strong spring tastes. I even noticed something on the tray that mother had been eating a lot of lately, too. It was the cooling leaves and slices of root of mandrake. I knew such things were definitely not for children, being somewhat violent in their side effects. They were to help a woman against sister wives. My stomach rumbled.

"Come, Zipporah," Saul's daughter said. "Haven't we any sweets for the child?"

"No, mistress."

"Oh, I'm sure we must. I know. Of course. We have the last of the Ashtoreth cakes."

"But, mistress . . ."

"Zipporah, she's just a child. She has no compunction against Ashtoreth cakes."

Compunction? Hardly. It was all I could do to keep from squealing with delight at the suggestion. Mother had given up making these offerings to Goddess this year because getting the maids to carry out her instructions over the language barrier was no longer worth the trouble to her. The fine cedar and soapstone molds that had been her mother's and her mother's mother's had joined the teraphim at the bottom of her chest.

To be sure, every woman in the court baked to greet the spring with water-mellowed honey and almonds and the other good gifts we have to thank Her for, whether they actually did thank Her in ritual or not. That wonderful smell was as much a part of the best-of-all seasons as the smell of asphodel on the hillside. But it took great skill to make these cakes in their proper Goddess-shape and, since Mother no longer tried, there was no one in the court at all who cared to do it properly. The dough tasted fine as stars or moons or flowers or whatever other delicate shapes the women molded it into, and you might say (though you got a slap from the most pious god-worshipers if you did) that in these shapes, too, they were celebrating Her creations. But there is no substitute for the true shape, formed in a temple-blessed mold with devout prayers of thanksgiving. Nothing tastes so good, though all the ingredients be the same. Spring would come to Hebron at last and after all, I sang to myself.

"I know, Zipporah, you would rather we dispose of them properly and break them up on the roof for the little birds to come and eat. But did we not find this little one like a bird under an olive tree? Fetch her a cake, Zipporah."

The cake was rather stale. Michal must have baked it at home in the north and brought it with her. All that time the cake had lain beneath a cloth to one side of the idol. In the heat, the honey stuck to the cloth and I had to brush off woolen fibers before I ate it. Nevertheless, I can't think when I have relished anything more before or since. The dough was evenly and lightly browned, making the little figures seem truly made of sweet, divine flesh and not of man's stone-ground flour. I nibbled carefully around the hips in a sort of ritual I'd long ago devised to make the cake last as long as possible. I ate the legs whole, first the right and then the left as one steps into a ritual bath. When I bit into the breasts, I found that even all that time and distance had not made their centers lose their softness.

Michal watched my delight and caught some of her own from me. I did not think at the time, but I realize now what complicated emotions that woman was called upon to bear. She had been taken by force from her husband of ten years, from her children (the only children she was to ever have)— all this after her father's and her brothers' deaths and her betrayal to David the enemy by her only remaining kin. No wonder she had kept her seclusion—and kept all of us in the court gossiping. No wonder the mind of the king's daughter often took infantile flights of fantasy and allowed the presence of images and Ashtoreth cakes to comfort her with childhood memories. At the time I could only lick the crumbs off my lips, suck the last sweet flavor off my teeth and the inside of my cheeks, and smile up at my hostess.

"Now you shall sing for us," Michal declared.

"Me?" I asked.

"Of course. I heard you out by the wall."

"That was a song of David," I replied.

"So? A daughter of David shall sing us one of his famous psalms."

"I am not a daughter of David," I sulked. "I am Snakesleeper."

"I see," Michal said, raising thin gray-black brows. She shot a glance at her maid, but Zipporah was too busy sizing me up with sharp black eyes to return it.

"Go tell it in Gath," the maid said, playing with the words of a lamentation David had written that had become proverbial. I had not thought how my relationship with the Snake might threaten her spiritual powers. "There's much to Seeing you've never dreamt of, girl. Never in a twelve-month of snow."

"Still, she can sing. I have heard her. Sing for us, child."

"Of course I can sing," I said, confidence coming to me suddenly as it does when one is about to be inspired. At the time I did not know where it came from, but I said, "Any Snakesleeper can sing."

And so I sang. I began with words of David I had heard earlier that evening, but then went on with words of my own that had never been spoken to human ears before since time began. Now, of course, all the verses are sung together and are sung as David's "A Song of Loves." Scribes try to reconcile the differences in style and try to make it fit with other works of David's religious moods. How many questions it would answer—but problems in propaganda it would raise—if they knew the truth. The truth is that I composed it at the age of ten—using his cadence, I'll

admit—but with Ashtoreth cake on my lips and to celebrate
Michal's arrival in the court. I have done much better since.

> All your garments smell of myrrh
> and aloes and cassia,
> out of the ivory palaces
> whereby they have made you glad.

> Listen, O daughter, and consider
> and incline your ear.
> Forget also your own people
> and your father's house.

> So shall the king greatly desire your beauty,
> for he is your lord,
> and worship him.

> The king's daughter is all glorious within
> Her clothing is of wrought gold.

> She shall be brought unto the king
> in raiment of needlework.
> The virgins, her companions that follow her,
> shall be brought unto you.

> With gladness and rejoicing
> shall they be brought.
> They shall enter into the king's palace.

> Instead of your fathers shall be your children,
> Whom you may make princes in all the earth.

I might have continued, and the young scribes would have
more to memorize for their lessons today. But Michal had
buried her face in her skirt and was sobbing so loudly that
I didn't dare.

"Tell it not in Gath!" Zipporah said. "Wicked child, to
make the king's daughter cry, reminding her of her sorry
fate. Off with you. You should never have come here in the
first place."

Later I was to come to understand that such a reaction from En-Dor's Seer meant only that she had been very impressed and did not want to admit it. I had felt the power of these words while I was speaking them. It was glorious and my audience's reaction was painful and confusing. It was physically as well as mentally painful, for Zipporah grabbed me fiercely by the arm to usher me to the door.

"Wait! Wait!" Michal cried after us. The sobs in her throat entangled the words and made them come out shredded and ugly. She stood, wiped her eyes on her veils, and tried to catch her breath for a moment before continuing. "Little one."

"Yes, Lady?" I was on the verge of tears myself.

"Ah, little one," Saul's daughter said with a gesture of helpless struggle against the world. "Someday you, too, must know what sorrow it is to be the daughter of a king. Then the songs you make will have different tunes." She clutched my arm then as if she would snap it in two. "As Goddess is my witness, and you, too, child. I will die rather than have a child by this redheaded son of Jesse."

I left her rooms.

"And where have you been, daughter?" Mother even handed Absalom to a maid to confront me.

"At Michal's," I said quickly, with innocence that is more difficult to feign at ten when the difference between innocence and sophistication is only just coming to one's awareness.

"Michal's?"

"Michal the daughter of Saul. The new wife." Then I added with an even greater stretch of innocence, "She has Ashtoreth cakes."

Mother looked at me hard for a moment, such a long moment that my innocence was almost driven away. But my mind called out silently to Goddess, and She and I prevailed. Mother turned from me without a word and reclaimed Absalom. Then I was allowed to go to bed without supper. Early in the morning Amnon came over to play and I was glad I could excuse myself from our rooms.

Up to this point I have not written much of Amnon, at least not as much as his influence on me should warrant. Perhaps this is because we were so much together that day fades into day and soul into soul. There is no sudden appearance on the scene to remember him by, as there was with Michal. It seems he was always there, a part of me. We played often enough with the other children, but they came and went, got bored or quarreled or found their own games, and sooner or later it was just Amnon and I again.

The older girls were domineering and always got their own way. For instance, sometimes we mimicked the king at his feasting. The older girls would stand by David's ceremony, unwavering and unimaginative as the adults, and have only the men sit down to eat. They found much more pleasure in competing with one another as our mothers did, to see who could send in the fanciest mudcake stuck with twigs and leaves, or pebble sweetmeats sprinkled with dust and served on a bit of broken crockery. The boys never had the patience to sit drinking tempered mud and talking while all the preparations went on. They were either shrewed into miserably sticking it out—"Talk war and men's business like Father does!"—or they escaped and ruined the game.

At this time Amnon still wore little girls' dresses and lapis lazuli beads in his hair to preserve him from the evil spirits that covet male children. There's much truth in the saying "Little boys are born at ten; until then they are but girls." Sometimes the youngest boys got confused and used feminine forms of their verbs and adjectives when speaking of themselves, for they heard little else. Of course, the day Amnon was removed from the company of women and sent to learn to be a man was not far off. But we were blissfully unaware of it at the time.

We played at chariot and driver that morning. There was always some lively discussion as who should be driver and who should be horse.

"You always get to be the horse," Amnon protested.

This was true, but I didn't care to admit it. I stood holding the reins and scuffing the dirt.

"I'm a good horse," Amnon continued, and he demonstrated. His horse was very graceful, his galloping very dancelike.

I scuffed dirt. "But David's favorite horse is a mare," I pointed out, and that, too, was irrefutable. "He likes her for her endurance."

Then I had to demonstrate that no one was better at neighing and tossing her mane and pawing the earth than I.

"All right, you may be the horse again," Amnon admitted with a good grace.

And he led me to our "stall," an unused corner in the grown-up stables, brought me water and sweet grass, and curried me using the real brushes that tickled.

Amnon held the reins, but he let me have them free and I led the way. I went up by the eastern wall of the king's great hall. Then we sat and talked, or, then again, we said nothing and simply sat in the sun that was still spring-low enough to enjoy.

"Shall I sing you a song I made up?" Playing by the eastern wall reminded me of the song I had composed the night before for Michal (one does not forget such things).

"You made up a song?"

"I'll show you." Reins and grass behind me, I sang for my friend.

"You made it for Michal?"

We were both serious enough then to understand why it had made her weep—the references to her father's house, left behind forever, and to children. Such things flatter other brides, but not Saul's unfortunate daughter.

"I like it very much," Amnon said.

"I'll compose something for you," I promised him.

"When? Now?" he asked.

"No. No," I said. I had not done much composing yet in my short life, but what I had done was enough to know that the feeling there with us at the moment was not the sort that produces poetry. "But sometime," I promised. "I shall compose for you the greatest poem ever made."

"And I . . . I . . ." He could not at first think what to promise in return. Then he said, "I shall marry you."

"Marry me?" I grew hot and angry. "I promise you a

poem and all you can promise in return is to make me as miserable as Michal?"

"I—I wouldn't make you miserable," Amnon stammered. "I would make you happy."

"I don't want to be *made* happy," I said. "I want to *be* happy from my own self."

Amnon fell into a frustrated silence, unable to explain further what he meant. In time I was able to see that he had meant to promise the greatest thing he could think of to offer a girl and that I should have been flattered. I should, indeed, have even accepted graciously, in childish delight and imagination. But our play for the day was spoiled and there was no remedy. And in spite of the misunderstanding, assumptions had been put into words and they sat like that in the back of our minds from that day forward.

· XII ·

IT WAS NOT until early autumn of my tenth year that David felt himself secure enough on the treacherously won throne of Israel to turn his attention to lands never held by any of the Hebrew tribes. He and his men marched against the Jebusites. He took only the very faithful troops of Judah and his Philistine mercenaries and laid the siege with them, planning to wear the enemy out during the winter, then call muster of all Israel to take the city in the spring.

As the campaign progressed, David found that siege tactics wore on his men as much as or more than on the enemy. The Jebusites' god, even the Most High as he is called, had fortified the city with walls so imposing that the generals had to guess where the sheer cliffs of divine creation ended and the great stones set there by ancient giants began. Besides this, the god inspired a sorcerer to rain such curses down upon David and his men that some few died of faint hearts without ever having come an arrow's distance from the foe. What is told of these taunting words is only as soldier minds have remembered them. Soldiers' pride makes them out to be only some sort of shieldbearer's taunts—"The blind and

the lame can defend these walls alone"—but there must
have been true power in them, whatever was said. I would
have liked to have met that sorcerer and heard those words
from his own lips, to learn something of his skill. But of
course he was the first to be put to death when the city fell.

The siege of Jebus dragged on before those mighty walls
for almost an entire year. In his frustration, David made a
good many lavish promises to the man who should find a
way to breach those walls. Finally, Joab, the son of Zeruiah,
our onetime guide and David's nephew, found the city's
water source, carefully hidden by rocks and shrubs outside
the walls. One moonless and fateful night, Joab climbed the
secret, treacherous shaft to penetrate the very heart of Jebus
with a handful of men.

By dawn, they had opened gates; before noon, David held
Jerusalem. He did it—Joab did it—without Israel, which
brought their tribes up from the north in awe, not in be-
grudged submission, which might have been fatal to David's
cause. Jebus became truly the City of David, for there were
not even the tombs of his reverend ancestors there to make
prior claim to honor. For Joab's part in the victory, David
made good his promises. The king made his nephew general
of all Israel and Judah and betrothed him to Hannah,
Amnon's sister, David's firstborn daughter. Hannah was
nearly thirteen years old.

My memory stirred when it heard the gossip of "Jebus,
Jerusalem."

"I've been to Jebus," I murmured to a group of children.
Suddenly I had their attention. "So, what's it like?"

These many years my memory had clung to the image of
the Topheth I'd seen as a child: "There is blissful peace and
righteousness in the sacred grove beneath Mount Jebus.
And the heavenly intoxication of the smoke of sacrifice is
caught within the valley walls." I found a captive audience
as if I were an ancient and honored spinner of fables.

"It's wicked to honor foreign demons," warned sensible
Hannah, who was nearly thirteen and betrothed. And most
of the children chose to follow her example.

But Amnon heard my longings out in full, and one of my longings became to share with him that holy experience.

The harem stayed in Hebron 'til the passing of midsummer, and then we journeyed to join David in what was to be his new and unique capital, which he chose to call, above the dust and ruin of its defeat, one of its little-known Goddess names, Jerusalem, the City of Peace. His rhetoric still proclaimed the eternal wish as it had at my brother's naming. Greater power made the myth seem more possible, but it did not give it any more actual reality.

We spent one night underway at Bethlehem, the tiny town of David's patrimony where Saul's men had discovered him, full of promise, a shepherd boy. Here we were quite royally entertained, considering the small size of the place and the fact that every homeowner in town was kin to David: uncles, cousins, and brothers. If David's kin did not nurse jealousies that Heaven had passed them by and favored the youngest over their heads, they at least were not greatly impressed by princes they could address familiarly as "sons."

Amnon especially had a difficult time holding his own. After having been soundly beaten by his older and more vigorous cousins at both footraces and wrestling, he finally resorted to bragging to them about our move to the Jebusite city.

"There is blissful peace and righteousness in the sacred grove beneath Mount Jebus," Amnon said, cheeks blazing, "and my father's going to be king there."

"Peace and righteousness in Jebus?" the cousins scoffed.

"Yes. And the heavenly intoxication of the smoke of sacrifice is caught within the valley walls."

"The smoke of pillage and the fires of defeat is more like it."

"Have you been to Jebus?" demanded another cousin.

"No, but I know someone who has." Amnon stood by his defense.

"Who is this someone?"

"Yes, who is this fool and blind man?"

"Any shepherd lad can drive his flock to Jerusalem and back to Bethlehem in a single day."

"I myself have done it twice."

"And didn't we all at one time or another make that short journey as messengers to older brothers in the Judean army?"

"Who even needed that excuse? One could run up to watch the battle for an afternoon or so."

"Out of idle curiosity!"

It was at this point that Amnon brought them all over to me for confirmation of his tale. It was by my mother's campfire; there was room for the three first wives and their families in the ancestral home, and the rest of us were camping under the stars.

"I can't understand why you're wasting your time with such fellows," I told him and turned away.

"I have to be gracious to kin," he whispered hoarsely, following and pleading after me.

I answered his plea and turned to his defense for a moment. But the discussion, though loud, never progressed beyond "Is so," "Is not," "Is so."

"You call this graciousness?" I walked farther into the night. Away from the smear of torch- and firelight, it was a beautiful night on the hillsides of Bethlehem. The sky was filled with double the usual magic. "Must you waste such magic to yap like dogs over a cubit's worth of honor?" I asked my stepbrother.

The eldest cousin pulled his most devious and underhanded weapon into play and said again, "Aw, but she's just a stupid girl."

Amnon's fists clenched in a reflex to protect me against such slander. But his training overcame the reflex. He was old enough to have been taught that boys get more attention than girls, and so what occupied boys' minds must be more important than what occupied my own. And what older boys worry about must be the worries of the world.

"Stupid girl," he echoed the cousin and left me to worship Night alone.

This little episode in Bethlehem was of so little consequence that I would have ignored it entirely were it not for the leader of the cousins. His name was Jonadab. I cannot ignore that because of what happened later.

"Better is coming," I promised both Amnon and myself under Goddess's spilled jewel box in the sky. "Just wait and see."

David provided all his wives' daughters with new matching dresses to add to the pageantry of the procession into Jerusalem. This was the origin of our multicolored garments ("As Israel robed his favorite son, so I my many daughters"), by which the virgin princesses are still known today.

I was dressed and on my donkey before the tents were struck in the morning and I had to be dragged off to attend respectfully to the morning prayer and sacrifice. I did not have to share my mount with Absalom's cradle as on my earlier journey to Jebus, but I wished I could. I wished I could ride ahead with the boys to see things first and to talk with Amnon about them. I wished we would only hurry and get to the city, to Jebus—and to Topheth.

Passing the Potters' Field, my hopes were high, heightened to a pitch by my impatience. I did not pause to see how dry the field was—too dry to delve for clay in the last few weeks of five or six long months without rain. Dust demons rose threateningly from the desolation, but I could not stop to heed their warnings. It was coming, Jebus was coming, it was . . . it was before us.

My heart grew sick within me at what I saw.

Directly against us rose the bosom of the Central Valley. In late winter, as I remembered it, it was a pleasant place, filled with the tents of the cheesemakers and with their newborn flocks. Now it was abandoned, bared so one could see the rapacious work of the quarrymen on the smooth curves of the earth. The Jebusites had had to make improvements in the fortifications when David marched against them, and they had been completed with careless haste. No rains had yet come to ease the white limestone wounds with fresh green.

Jebusites were in their orchards and fields, concerned with the harvest, but the twisted olive trees with their fruits heavy and shiny with oil could not cheer them. The harvest was now for masters, no longer for themselves. The Jebusites had not known such a burden since the Egyptians were in the land. With heartless boredom they watched us pass, counting in our great numbers no glory, only the many more foreign mouths their labor had to feed before their own. I looked away in shame for their shame and thought perhaps sometimes it is better to die than to sue for terms, a thing I had never considered before.

Depression and defeat hung over the city like the heat, trying one's faith. People endure drought calmly in its season, but not when the rains are long looked for, when the cisterns are low and muddy, when even the tamarisk grows pale yellow and brittle. If I had thought to be greeted by joyful faces who would welcome me as one come home and bid me join in Her worship with them, it was the wishful delusion of a child. As we passed by the holy place, the Valley of Topheth, I saw that Her sacred well had been the only source of water for David's men during their siege, for River Kidron's channel was marked only by muddy pools during the dry season. The soldiers had not toppled any of the standing stones, nor had they cut down any of Her trees for their fires. I should have been grateful for little mercies, because other sacrilege had not stayed their hands. Clan signs of Judah had been carved and scribbled in charcoal on the altar. The figures were gone, stolen for the gold and jewels, to receive worship of a different, baser kind. And all Goddess's maidservants had fled, not wishing to share the secrets of the Great Bed with a lustful and bored army holding siege. Fifty men, no matter how reverent they are, cannot pass through a place as softly nor quench their thirst with as little disruption as a single barefooted priestess can, and these men had not had reverence on their minds. The veils of smoke had blown aside and all that was secret and sacred, all I had looked forward to worshiping in private, lay exposed and barren, without remarkable features, without mystery.

As the long caravan passed in review up the flanks of the Kidron and into the shadow of the city walls, Amnon was able to turn in his saddle and look down and back at me. He made signals—"Have we passed it yet? Where is the sacred spot you told me about?"

I signaled, "No. There is nothing," and looked away from him, as shamed that day as any Jebusite.

Cousin Joab moved up and down the line with a conqueror's air, making sure all went smoothly, lashing slaves and animals when it did not, letting himself be seen as the hero of the day. About this business, he paused again and again to match his pace to Hannah's. I was fully aware of how often. I could avoid Amnon, the ruined sanctuary, and the sullen Jebusite faces that lined our path, but unless I closed my eyes, I could not help but see the donkey directly in front of me on which Hannah rode. Joab might court her openly now, for they were betrothed by David's own word. Hannah blushed and hung her head and generally made him feel the lord and master. She enjoyed the prospect. She was her father's daughter, and a daughter learns different things than a son.

Though the sky was perfectly clear, it was of a gray cast, thinner than usual, like finely hammered Philistine iron. As we climbed up and approached the shadow of Jerusalem's walls, I shivered. The shadow of responsibility, of adulthood, of marriage, of children was likewise stretching down into the sunlight of my childhood, touching already Hannah's feet, now her waist; now she was all gone from this, our generation, which I had once thought would stay young and carefree and wise forever.

I held my mount back from the shadow of the walls until Joab looked back and saw me, with the rest of the caravan coming up behind, stumbling and pressing on my tail. He cursed the perversity of asses in general, of little-girl riders in particular, and gave the poor creature such a lash that I could not hold it any longer and it leapt forward with a squeal.

So it was that we entered Jebus, Jerusalem, the city of the Most High God, the City of David, the city of unbreachable walls and of deep shadows in the afternoon.

· XIII ·

FOR NEARLY FIFTY years the seat of David's god had been in Gibeah of Kiriath-jearim. For the Israelites, the most proper and solemn title of this coffer is "The Ark of the Covenant of Yahweh of Hosts Who is Enthroned upon the Cherubim." But I have heard it called a score of different names and after nearly so many gods. I have heard it called after Reshef, the plague-bringer, and after great Mot, Death, by some who remember what havoc it wrought among the Philistines.

For most of those fifty years, the Philistines had been lords of Kiriath-jearim.

"The time is now ripe," I heard David declare from my seat by his new eastern wall, "to throw Philistia back toward the sea."

"But aren't the Philistines our allies?" someone in the council asked.

I thought at first the voice belonged to Joab, but it must have been one of the other cousins, for Joab was not so naive. Now Joab spoke, explaining patiently, as if the betrayal should have been obvious policy from the beginning.

"Now that the throne of Israel, in the person of Princess Michal, is firmly in our king's grasp, David no longer needs Philistine help against the northern tribes."

David concurred with his general's assessment. "The northern tribes are most particularly devoted to this Ark. In order to win Israel's favor, we will free Kiriath-jearim."

Within a month, the Philistines had decided keeping the rocky lands of dark, superstitious people was not worth the trouble and they had retreated to the coast. It greatly gratified David when the northern tribes came to Gibeah in their hordes. It was the first month of pilgrimage they had enjoyed since the death of Saul. David took their numbers as a sign of their devotion and thankfulness to him for being the Ark's deliverer. But then reports were brought to him that this congregation was used by Israel as an excuse to bring disparate and festering conspiracies against himself and the unity of his kingdom to a unified head.

When the pilgrimage was over, David went down to Gibeah to pick up the pieces. Abital, Sephatiah's mother, the wife chosen to accompany him on this journey, told us about what they'd found there.

"Our master cursed himself that he had not been there in person during the pilgrimage to show the northern tribes that his faith was one with theirs," she said.

"He might curse himself, too, for not having considered the power in that Ark," commented Ahinoam, who was usually a gentler soul, but she was, after all, from Jezreel.

"If such ferment is brewed when the Ark is honored, what should happen if It were displeased?" fretted Haggith.

"Yes, what should happen if, God forbid, the Ark should be carried into battle against our husband?" asked Abigail.

"God forbid," echoed Abital piously. "In any case, David has sworn by the God of our Fathers that that will be the first and last pilgrimage to Gibeah as long as he lives—or to any place, for that matter, where the Holy is not firmly in his grasp."

"Thank God for that," the wives concurred.

"Where he is the one to put the food in the priests' mouths," my mother commented to me in our own language, "and thereby insure that what came out of their mouths again in preachment or prophecy would be faithful to him."

You may well imagine what dust of scandal was raised when, shortly afterward, a move from Kiriath-jearim was proposed.

"A man, even a king, does not tell God where He is to dwell," said Ahinoam.

"Certainly not this God," said Abigail, somewhat more ecumenically, "the God of our Fathers, Whose long history of travels and deeds is known and feared even by those who do not revere Him. He and His Ark were in Shiloh for generations."

"Until, like a great-grandfather past work," Mother said privately, "he seemed to become an old, half-forgotten fixture delegated to a dark corner and tossed the leftovers after the priests' meals. A mortal in this situation sighs and grumbles toothlessly in his beard, knowing no other home or life but this he inherited from his father before him. He escapes into another childhood and so passes the time until he can die and save his daughter-in-law further trouble."

But it was not so with this god.

"When at length He lost all patience with this maltreatment," Abigail continued the tale, "God of our Fathers and of the Ark rose up and brought the Philistines down upon Shiloh, destroying the town and all the priests' household. With rejoicing the Philistines brought the Ark to their land and housed it in their best and highest temple, the house of Dagon, and tried to make the Ark, the great Power that had willed to aid them now, at home with baskets of grain and their finest Dagon dances. But the Lord of the Ark soon let them know that their uncircumcised best would not suit Him."

"Like a child in a fit of temper, only with plague and destruction to work with," Mother editorialized.

"Oracles were consulted, and at last it was determined to load the Ark upon a cart drawn by two milch cows and let the Lord drive Himself whithersoever He wanted to go. The cattle finally halted and knelt down in the fields of Beth-Shemesh, over the border in the land of Gibeah.''

"Their calves and full udders completely forgotten," marveled Ahinoam.

"But even here, when the people were too preoccupied with their own shameful temple to the sun to do more than sacrifice the animals the Lord Himself had brought with Him, the Philistine plague of rats and flies and boils was sent again. It was not until the high sanctity and cleanliness of the priestly house of Gibeah—"

"Always cautious and pure." Ahinoam again.

"—was brought that the dying ceased and the Ark made Itself at home in peace."

"And now our master David," fretted Haggith, "even with such a history as example, wants to undertake to move this Object?"

"It suits his ambitions," said Mother aside.

"He has decided to move It when even dumb cattle bow themselves to the knife when God is pleased?"

"And when even the sacrifice of little children is not enough when He is not?"

"Sisters, it is not our place as women to question our husband's decisions," concluded Abigail. "It is our duty only to begin preparations to receive our God, as David has asked us."

The wives were not oracles, but then it did not take an oracle to read the outcome of this move.

"It was not too far out of Kiriath-jearim."

"So I heard as well."

"A bolt of lightning came out of a blue sky and struck one of the porters dead as he stretched a hand to steady the Ark."

"Such impiety!"

"Gashed and dusty with mourning and further infected with rage, the second man—"

"Can you blame him? He was brother to the first."

"—he refused to continue."

"Nor will he carry the Ark back to Kiriath-jearim."

"Condemned prisoners, promised their lives, cannot be induced into service."

"They prefer an executioner limited by the boundaries of this life over the unknown horrors both here and beyond that the Lord can call up."

"So the Ark stays where it is?"

"Under the care of the man on whose property it happened to stop."

"A Levite of Gath-rimmon."

"The Lord knows what He wants."

"Hapless and quivering man of Gath-rimmon!"

And we, who were waiting in Jerusalem, put away our new festive dresses and our tambourines, breathed easier to find the air still wholesome, and went back to our normal round of duties.

It was just after this anticlimax that my mother, consumed as usual by Absalom, asked me why I didn't run off and visit Michal. "Michal gets David all night. She can answer your whys all day. He'll have none of the rest of us until she's conceived. He has six sons living already," she said, fondling Absalom's curls as if just that one should be enough. "Why must it be she?"

Her question was mere rhetoric, I knew. If David could get one male child from Michal, it would take precedence over even twelve-year-old Amnon because of its mother's father. To father a son on the daughter of Saul the King of Israel would make David's own claim to kingship undeniable, for all that was left of the decimated house of Israel were crippled sons of sons and the unclaimed sons of concubines.

"It would counter all the ill effects of attempting to move the Ark," I suggested as the only reason that hadn't been worried into the ground.

"You are so smart," Mother snapped. "Go on, let Michal put up with your tongue for a while."

I would have gone gladly. On days when Michal did not have fits, she herself would throw open the tapestry when she heard my step, invite me in like her own long-lost child, chide me for not visiting sooner, and burden me with her mothering. Then she would look on proudly as Zipporah taught me to sing, and the sun swept quickly down to the horizon. But this was not one of those days.

"I can't," I explained simply to my mother. "She's going to have a baby."

Mother grew pale and flushed by turns and demanded how I could be sure. "Have you heard idle rumors?"

"No rumors, Mother. But I'm certain. You know how Michal has fits all day when David has been with her all night."

"Serves her right."

"Zipporah growls and snaps at me and flings the hanging down in my face when Michal has fits. Today she is having another fit."

"So she has fits. It's the weak mind of her family."

"It means David was with her last night—again. It is over a month now since she went to the baths. She is not having her time of uncleanliness—and, as she would say, 'blessed rest from David.' Doesn't that mean she is with child?"

Mother made quick calculations. In such a close household, everyone's cycle was close to the same and easy to keep track of. Then Mother grew solidly pale and closed her lips tight. She didn't say a word to me or anyone else, but soon enough it was commonly known. The entire harem went about with tightly closed lips, fondled their male children even more than they were wont, began to count months anxiously and to make all sorts of vows and sacrifices.

I could only make silent, vague prayers for the health of my friend behind the closed hanging because I knew that what she felt about her own condition was giving her fits. Later I understood how she had done all one can do with wads of wool and seed-killing poisons to prevent conception. Small discomfort was tolerated to spare her from a greater misery. Such measures had worked long and well until David began to fear that, after five children by another man, the daughter of Saul might have grown barren. But they did not work quite well enough.

In spite of, or maybe because of, his wife's ominous behavior, David was lifted up in his heart by the news. He was legitimate upon his throne. The blood of Israel was growing and swelling again under the rain of his seed. The god of the Ark had blessed him. The god couldn't be angry after all. The high holy days were past, those days when David's god scowls down from his heavens and his people fast and beat their breasts in fear and trembling before him. To have those days behind him without major cataclysm gave David the courage to try once more.

We were all out in the fields in our flimsy little Booths. The Booths are a rite even David cannot do without. He says living in Booths reminds him that his fathers roamed the desert. It seems to me Booths have more to do with the sown land; every hand is needed for a week or so during that season out in the fields and vineyards for the harvest. Even one of the house of Judah might as well decorate his little lean-to with myrtle bows and sheaves of wheat and feast and drink new wine to make a little party of it. But the ritual where everyone stands and sings, willow wand in one hand, citron or pinecone in the other (we of the Goddess prefer the pinecone as it is more originally Her fruit) should make the meaning clear enough. Nine months of rains after bringing those two disparate objects together, one prays that a new crop may fill the fields and burden the vines again.

The first rain had fallen on us in our Booths that year, but most of David's household was not about to give up the festivity for the sake of a little mud. Absalom, for one, loved the mud, and played in it outside the Booths by the hour. Perhaps the assurance that even the rains were normal again convinced David all would be well if he moved the Ark. But I still think it was Michal's conception that did it most of all.

▣ XIV ▣

IT WAS NEAR the end of our stay in the Booths that Amnon the firstborn brought us word: "The Ark has begun to move. At the sixth step, a sacrifice was made and accepted. All seems well. It should be in Jerusalem the day after tomorrow."

"It's not so far, surely, from Obed-edom's," said Abigail. "Why, we can almost see it from here."

Some went out to see and brought back the report: "Yes, we can see them, a column of smoke mixed with dust on the northern horizon like God leading His people through the wilderness. There must be a great host with them."

"Why should it take so long?" Abigail persisted.

"They must continue to sacrifice every six steps of six different sorts: flowers, fruit, oil, wine, fowl, and flesh," Amnon explained.

"That accounts for the smoke," said those who watched the horizon.

"The priests will grow fat on that," was my mother's comment in Geshuri when I translated for her.

"I'm sure I wouldn't dare to be anywhere near it when they move it," said Haggith, the fourth wife.

"Have the oracles been consulted about this move?" asked Ahinoam.

"Abiathar has consulted his seer stones and declared if only Levites are allowed to touch the Ark, all will be well," reported Amnon.

"Abiathar would say that," Mother commented to me in Geshuri, "being a Levite himself. That leaves a fine legacy for his tribe."

Ahinoam didn't understand my mother's words, but she did understand the tone. "Let's not be skeptical. Abiathar has been our husband's source of heavenly guidance since his earliest days in the wilderness."

"I would have asked Gad the Prophet myself," said Abigail.

"Gad has been asked and he approved," Amnon assured her.

"I'm still anxious."

"He's sent to Zadok the priest, priest of the high place of the Sun Standing Still."

"And Zadok says?"

"He has come to pad the move with such rites as he used to protect his people throughout the Ark's stay in Gibeah."

"How about Obed-edom?"

"My father the king has taken augury from how that man and his household fared during the months the Ark has been on his threshing floor."

"And—?"

"And never could one imagine a servant of Edom prospering so well."

"It's all the offerings pilgrims visiting the Ark have left at his doorstep," Abigail assured us.

"David wants such prosperity at *his* doorstep," commented my mother.

"I thought of making the pilgrimage myself," said Abigail. "Thank God, now I won't have to." A Sabbath's journey or two, no more, was quite enough pilgrimaging for Abigail's bulk. A donkey couldn't carry her farther; certainly her swollen legs couldn't.

"My father the king has also sent to Philistia for a liver

reading," Amnon said, "to Ammon for a casting of lots in the name of Milcom, and north to Shiloh to recall the practices that once pacified the Lord in that place."

"Heathen practices?" Ahinoam asked.

"Abiathar and the Levites are upset by this," Amnon admitted.

"They are far too selfish of Heaven for my taste," Mother commented to me in our own language.

"But my father in his wisdom has decided it is better to be safe than sorry for being too narrow-minded. He is king now over an empire with many people in it," Amnon said. "Although our God is a jealous God, He may reserve place for some of the wisdom of others. Abiathar and the Levites, for all their dark words, have not refused to shoulder the Ark because of this."

"As long as they have the final say over each rite and their share of the sacrifices, they won't," Mother concluded.

"Now, that's what I'm sent to tell you," Amnon said. "Lady Abigail, my father wants you to be in charge of the baking."

"By the God of my Fathers, there's baking to be done?"

"For a multitude. My father's invited them from every tribe, from every corner of the kingdom. They've already begun to congregate under Jerusalem's walls."

"I hope I get plenty of help, that's all I can say." Abigail looked at us all threateningly as she heaved her bulk to her feet to begin the trek up to the palace ovens. "What does he want? The usual flat loaves, I suppose. They'll want meat, too, but if the priests provide it, each man can cook his own."

"There's something else, Lady."

"Well, Amnon?"

"He wants you to make raisin cakes."

"Raisin cakes?" Abigail repeated, stopping in midswing and staring at her stepson. Nobody said anything for a beat until Abigail herself said, "You mean like cakes 'for a shameful thing'?"

"Yes. My father said with the Ark festival he would bring all things under his sway."

"But not shameful things, surely."

There was a bit of discussion here while everyone said why one should or shouldn't make cakes for the Queen of Heaven.

"Not shameful things—"

"But if the king our master said—"

"It's the wrong time of year," Mother declared. "My husband knows nothing. Goddess cakes are for spring."

Abigail didn't wait for a translation. "You must have gotten the orders wrong," she asserted to Amnon. "David should know better than to send a child on such an errand."

"Amnon is a good boy," his mother stood up for him. "You're thinking of your son, how *he* couldn't carry the message that the palace was on fire, God forbid."

Amnon stood for this scrutiny uncomfortably but insisted stoutly, when they let him get a word in: "By the God of my Fathers, that's the message he told me to tell you."

"Our husband sent my son for the very reason we wouldn't believe him otherwise," said Ahinoam.

Abigail sniffed at these words and sat back down. "Well, the simple fact is, I don't know how to bake raisin cakes. I'm proud to say it, yes, I've never dirtied my hands with such a task."

Another quick babble ensued in which it was determined who could and who could not. My mother was the only one who knew, that was the result of this debate.

"And it's the wrong time of year," she insisted.

"And nobody can understand a word she says," said Abigail.

"Michal knows how," I piped up then. "And her maid, Zipporah."

The mere mention of Saul's daughter caused a grim silence and exchange of glances all 'round.

"Michal," somebody said at last, like a pinprick in a dam that started the flood of a liturgy.

"Michal's too good to come to the Booths with us."

"Had to have a Booth built for her on the roof of the palace, of all things."

"You didn't see me pampering myself like this when I was with child."

"And the time I had with my first one! Why, I couldn't—"

"We know all about your difficulties, Haggith, thank you."

"It's the fits."

"Yes, she has them."

"Her father did, too."

"It runs in the family."

"Only a madman would think the throne belonged with them."

"Perhaps this child she carries will—" The woman stopped herself in midsentence, but she made no attempt to counteract her envy with a blessing.

"I could ask Michal about the cakes." I nearly shouted to make myself heard. Now everyone looked at me—and was silent.

It was at that moment that Absalom decided he had had enough of Amnon and his news being the center of attention. Cramming both fists as full of mud as he could, he dumped them both into the hair of Ahinoam's youngest. There wasn't much scolding; Absalom was never scolded. But when the shrieking and scrubbing and laughing and crying were over, Abigail had decided to send a handmaiden off to David at his place with the Ark to confirm Amnon's orders. It was nearly nightfall then; the girl was allowed to wait for morning, and it was nearly nightfall again before the word came. When it came, it was so unequivocal that it was decided we had to pack up and return to the city right then to make up for time lost in disbelief.

"I don't know how to make raisin cakes," Abigail fussed, still not settled into the task, "but I imagine we'll need raisins."

This was the logic behind her giving both Amnon and me a large basket of vine-dried grapes still on their shriveled branches that had been collected between songs and dances in the Booths. There was a basket for Absalom, too, but it would have to be returned for. Absalom never carried anything.

"This will hardly do," Mother muttered. "Doesn't the first wife see that these aren't really dry enough yet? Do you see why they are springtime food? Don't these people pay any attention to the world around them?"

But I didn't bother to translate. I was pleased to hoist my basket to my head and begin to hike after the others. A weight on my head made me feel graceful. I imagine we made quite a procession, all the daughters in their multicolored gowns David liked us to wear—probably so he could tell daughter from handmaid and not shame himself with any serious mistakes at bedtime. The cut he favored for us, the daughters, was very blousy in front—to further remove temptation—and lifting my arms up to steady a load made it not quite so. It also helped to show off my Snakeskin—not part of the uniform—which pinched in my waist attractively.

By my side, Amnon was not so fortunate. He had insisted on taking the heaviest basket, but being a boy, he couldn't put it on his head. He tried one hip, then the other, but he had always been quite hipless. It really was a struggle, either knocking on his legs or numbing his arms and crushing his chest if he held it up. Still, he persisted in trying to demonstrate that he could set the pace. I think he was greedy for someone to congratulate him on how he had brought the message from his father, but I didn't.

As we neared the walls, we became aware of more tents and fires than just the watch; many more. They winked from every rock and even on the dangerous slopes.

"What's that?" I asked no one in particular.

It was Amnon who showed off his knowledge. "The beginning of my father's multitude to welcome the Ark."

"Will you dance with them when the Ark arrives?" I asked.

"No!" Amnon said as if I'd suggested they might use him for sacrifice.

"You dance very well—so I remember." I relented a little and gave him that praise.

He did not take it as a compliment. "Women dance. Only women and men of the desert. I'm a man. Father would not be pleased," Amnon declared stoutly, as if I were ignorant, but banging the basket most painfully against first one shin and then the other as he did so.

What strange forms they made by firelight, all the multitude practicing a cacophony of rites. There were young shepherds from Benjamin with movements like the wild trills of their flutes. The priesthood from Gibeah and from Jebus were there, clad in animal skins complete with claws and teeth; David's mercenaries from Philistia, who danced with sheaves of wheat; Ammonites with timbrel; Moabites with sheep and goats, dance partners now, offerings later; prophets, ambassadors, and fortune-seekers from all four corners of the Land. I smelled fire, sweat, and the winter's first mud returning to dust beneath all those milling, prancing, whirling feet. I couldn't help but stop and stare, and Amnon set down his basket gratefully beside me to watch the sight. The sight, however, was all Abigail needed to convince her of the magnitude of her task.

"Let's keep moving," she shouted down the line from her perch on a donkey at the head. "As the Lord lives, these will never all be fed. Not from my oven. Not without a miracle. Not if you don't hurry along."

So I turned to move on, but as I did, I felt my skirt plucked, my king's daughter's skirt.

I turned to see a girl about my age, no older, dressed as one of the virgins who dance for Goddess. A flimsy skirt swung from a belt so low on her hips that pubic hair would have showed—if she'd been old enough to have any. Both belt and a skimpy bodice were hung with bits of shells and metal that would make a pleasing sound when she danced. Now she folded her arms in front of her, embarrassed. Well, that's something in her favor, I thought. She at least knows it's sacrilege to appear like that away from the sanctuary. Then a wild leap of flame as some rite behind us splashed a campfire with oil illuminated her face and I felt true pity for her. She was so heavily made up as to be almost comical. It would have been comical, if those red, red lips and cheeks, and black, black eyes had not been such an obvious mask.

"Excuse me," she said, her voice hardly more than a whisper. "Are you of the house of David?"

"Are you blind as well as blasphemous?" I wanted to ask. But I didn't. I'd heard the hissing accent of the northern tribes in her speech, so I knew she must not be familiar with David's house. I replied gently that we were as if breaking bad news, all from the gate until we vanished into the coming night, all David's wives, daughter, sons, and handmaids.

"But I don't see Michal, Saul's daughter," the girl said.

"No, Michal stayed in the city. She's going to have a baby."

And then I stopped short. Another fire sacrifice of oil and I could see, under the mask of makeup and the accents of the voice, something so familiar that I almost shouted it. "Are you her daughter?"

She was. Her name was Sarai. "Please," she said, hugging her arms even tighter about her bare midriff in what was becoming a chilly autumn night, "Please, tell my mother I am here. Outside. Among the virgins who must dance . . ."

"Yes. I'll tell her."

"She won't be pleased I came in such a debasing fashion. I know it. But it was the only way I could think of. I had to come. We miss her so. I'd . . . I'd like to see her."

"That might be possible."

"I have so much news to tell her about us all. Little Rechab's talking so bravely now—she should hear him!—and Rachel's lost a tooth. I made certain she buried it carefully so the new one would come in straight. And Ishbaal said to tell her he's—"

"Come on, Tamar," Abigail yelled down the line. "We need those raisins."

"I'll tell her you're here," I promised and hurried on.

When a god returns to other high places, the women leave off their weeping, wash their faces of dried blood and ash, and put on new garments. But David's god, much as the king tried to replace the one with the other, is called neither the Son, nor is he called Tammuz, and his rites are not the same. David sought to bring joy to his household along with the Ark. He brought tragedy instead.

· XV ·

IT WAS THE middle of the next day before I got to carry my message to Michal. I'd been so exhausted when we'd returned that I'd fallen asleep without thinking even to wash the dust from my feet. And Abigail, who threw herself into her labors without any sleep at all, had a job for everyone in the harem the minute she stirred. The head wife had come up with some sort of recipe for Ashtoreth cakes without the help of Mother or Michal; she couldn't be expected to admit they knew something about the kitchen she did not. I think it must have been her Passover honey cake with a little leavening and raisins thrown in haphazardly. They were alternating out of the ovens with loaves of plain bread, and sometimes it was hard to tell the difference. Some handmaids who lent a hand to it had a flair, but most were strict Israelites, happy to model their dough into what looked like swaddled infants rather than nubile women in all their glory. Perhaps infants and women are much the same in their minds. There weren't nearly enough raisins and—

"Quit your complaining and take a turn at a grinding stone," was all the apology I got from Abigail.

There's nothing like a stint at the grinding stone to recall to mind all your unfulfilled promises. As soon as I could without arousing criticism, I pleaded a need to relieve myself and hurried toward Michal's apartment instead. When I arrived, Zipporah was pacing back and forth in front of the drawn curtain, wringing her hands. That could mean only one thing: David was in there with her mistress. What? Taking his pleasure at this time of morning? And on the day when the Ark was to arrive as well? I thought all sons of Israel and Judah were under the ban not to come near their women 'til the Ark was installed . . .

"I won't do it!" Michal screamed at the top of her voice from behind the curtain.

Zipporah saw me then and, with a finger to her lips, bade me make no sound. But she didn't send me away, which was a good sign. We listened together. If David had come for pleasure, he had a long way to go.

"You have a lot of nerve, asking me this thing." Michal again.

"I thought you'd want it." That was David for sure.

"Then you haven't the faintest idea what I want in this world."

"It's for your God, resplendent on His throne."

"His throne that you have taken captive. You expect me to rejoice for that?"

"I just thought it would satisfy everyone's feelings for the Holy if you and I made the Great Bed . . ."

Zipporah caught my eye with a look that said, "The man is in desperate straits if he must think 'Great Bed' to win over Israel, isn't he?"

Michal scoffed, "The Great Bed there on the roof in that little harvest Booth in the view of all Israel."

"Exactly."

"You will rape me there as you raped my land and all our ten tribes. Because that's what you'll have to do, son of Jesse. You've had your way with me here in this room. You've filled my womb and I hardly whimpered, though, by God, if I could tear this mite from me, I—"

"God cleave your tongue for such a saying, woman."

"I mean it, by God. And by that same God, if you take me on the roof in front of all those men who served and loved my father, I'll put up such a fight and caterwaul, you'll have to knock me out to do the deed and then you'll see how pacified Israel is with your rule. I'll do it, I swear."

"All right, all right. You win. No Great Bed. Though I thought it might please you, you with your teraphim and all."

"You think I like having my people, my God and my Goddess humiliated and put to your purposes?"

"Won't you at least come and lead the dancing?"

"You understand nothing of what I've just said, do you? Why don't *you* lead the dancing if it means so much to you?"

"I?"

"You, son of Jesse."

"Men don't dance."

"I know men who do. The best men. Prophets do."

"Let me qualify that then: men only dance when God possesses them."

"And women know what it means to be possessed all the time. Is that what you're saying?"

"Yes—"

"My father danced when his God was with him."

"Your father again? How many times have I told you not to mention—?"

"Not up to my father, are you, son of Jesse?"

"Quiet, woman, or—"

"Perhaps if you learned what it was like to be possessed—"

David suddenly burst from the room without hearing her, without giving Zipporah and me time to find some innocent occupation. Fortunately, he did not notice us. He flashed with gold, with purple, with iron and bronze, his robes of state for the celebration, and was gone.

Zipporah and I hurried into the room while the curtain still swung. We comforted Saul's daughter, Zipporah with her arms and her curses against David and David's god.

And I with what I thought would be a comfort, news of her daughter's presence among the dancing virgins.

Michal grew pale, then nauseated at my words.

"It's all right. It's just morning sickness," Zipporah said, bustling after her lady with bowls, jugs, and damp cloths, anything Michal might need before she knew the need herself. But Zipporah didn't seem to believe her own words.

An infusion of ginger root seemed to restore calm somewhat. As soon as she was able, Michal threw a veil over her head and we went out to the parapet to see what we could see. Unfortunately, the Ark and the dancing were both at hand. We heard the drums before anything, the rattles and then the bray of the rams' horns. They with the drums and rattles made dances of their music. At every six steps the priests sacrificed. In the midst of it all, in a sort of clumsy, halting progress, came the great golden coffer, borne on the shoulders of the Levites.

And David danced before the Lord. All his gold and purple he had stripped off and danced with nothing but a seamless linen ephod about his loins. Among the Benjaminite shepherds he danced, among the whirlers in ribbons of colored wool and the prancers in lion skins, among the sheaves of wheat.

And David danced among the maids of Israel, the maids who danced in the open dances meant for the sacred groves. David's ephod was too little to hide what he found attractive of the proceedings, even from our distance: it was clear he was not dancing with the god, but before the god. Every step was calculated, as calculated as his bartering when Abner sold Israel south, as calculated as an ambush in the Judean hills. Only that beneath his ephod was beyond the control of his calculation. It betrayed inside him still the young shepherd who hung his head, ashamed of his weakness before those worldly wise about him, whose crowns and armbands he wore, whose well-built homes of luxury he retired to, whose cultured daughters he took to wife. He trusted the wisdom of these others and feared his own simplicity.

The maidens danced with limping steps, their hair loose

and swirling, their belts and bodices rattling, their fingers
tapping small cymbals, their midriffs, the site of their bud-
ding Goddess power, moving most of all. Among them
David moved, not possessed, but possessing. And when he
approached the girl I recognized as Sarai, Michal gave a
little cry and fainted dead away.

I helped Zipporah get her back to her rooms, but I didn't
stay. We had passed Abigail—red-faced, bustling, and everywhere at once—who in spite of the obvious distress of
Saul's daughter muttered loud enough for all to hear, "Well,
some of us pull our own weight around here."

I left Michal with Zipporah and went and joined the rest
of the royal women, sweating and dusty with flour as much
as any slaves. My task, I remember, was to sort and clean
the raisins. There was hardly time for my fingers to become
sticky and clumsy and next to useless with the task, even
with constant licking, before I saw my brother reenter the
baking court. He'd been shooed away just about the time I
settled to my raisins, but now he was back, and in his hand
he held a clay trap such as is used for catching mice. As I
watched in horror, Absalom stood his full height in the
middle of the kitchen and dropped the trap. It was full of
mice. He did it on purpose. I saw his eyes. The little creatures, frightened by the shattering crockery and sudden light
and starved by their captivity, ran everywhere there was
flour or grease or raisins or darkness.

In the thick of the shrieking and scolding and running
about with brooms that let flour billow up like a dust storm,
Zipporah, the "witch" of En-Dor, entered the court. This
added to the confusion and surprise, and Absalom gloated.
He couldn't have asked for more gratifying chaos.

Zipporah sidestepped a mouse as if it weren't even there,
but she was as white as if her sharp bones had cut through
her own flesh and were pressing just below the skin. Wordlessly, she crossed the room to where I was trying to gather
up the spilled raisins with sticky fingers and she began to
usher me out with her.

"By your leave . . . Mistress needs you," Zipporah said,

but not before I had cried out with the pain of her grip on my arm.

Mother was glad for an excuse to spare Absalom the beating he deserved and for some diversion from the general cursing of her son's wickedness.

"No," she said firmly, grabbing my other arm. I was the only one who understood her exact words, but everyone could catch their sense. "My daughter will not be calling on Michal any more today. Some people have time to sit nursing their less-than-glorious pregnancies with wine and fans in the heat of the afternoon. But most people, including my daughter, have work to do here in the baking court. Zipporah, you can very well tell your mistress . . ."

"Mistress is dying," Zipporah said, her voice as thin and sharp as her fingers that cut me like knives. And the baking court forgot all about the mice and stopped to listen. "I thought when she asked for the beast she only wanted it as a pet, as a protecting spirit, to offer dainties to—you know, as pregnant women do." Zipporah's heavy breath seemed more important to her than her words. "Was I to know she wouldn't be content to feed it through the safety door? I never would have sent to Topheth for it had I guessed. Never!" There was no shadow of her usual relishing in misfortune. Between gasps for breath on her part as well as that of her audience, she continued: "A serpent has struck my mistress. I need the Snakesleeper."

◙ XVI ◙

AFTER THE HEAT of the baking, Michal's rooms were cool and clammy. The air was stale and lifeless and, hanging over all like some dancer's transparent veil, I could smell the smell of Serpent. Toppled over on the floor lay a small gilt casket. I nearly tripped over it as my eyes strained in the unaccustomed darkness. The casket lay open and the inside was neatly lined with fig leaves, smooth underside up. That careful preparation spoke of someone who knew Goddess, and who tendered great reverence for Her swift and deadly Messengers.

I grew used to the light and I was able to see the Messenger itself, half out, but still half in, and still curled up in that soft bed of leaves. It was a young female with fine, subtle patterning as if she were a belt embroidered for a wedding and then left forgotten, hanging and bleaching in the sun. I knew at once that she was a different breed than the one who had given me my serpent skin and my name—one from the desert rather than the seaside—and the thought made nervous energy tingle to the ends of my fingers. The poison of such a one might not respond as readily to my work.

I was not intimidated by the task before me. I was only taking account of the difficulties, weighing them against my inexperience and calling up powers of another sort to even out the balance. I had not seen my patient as yet. It is usually best to learn all one can of the Snake first, for the patient is surely going nowhere but, Goddess forbid, the grave. The Snake, if it is still alive, is as frightened as anyone and will slip away if it can.

There was no chance of this one gliding any farther out of its nest of fig leaves though. Zipporah, when she had seen what it was doing to her mistress, had beaten it to death, flattening its head and that part of its body out of the casket against the floor. Brain and venom had been forced up through the viper's eyes and nostrils.

Energy tingled again in my hands and shoulders. It is easier to work if the Snake is left alive, but there are few with the courage or presence of mind at such a time to allow it to happen. As it is with Goddess's other domain, passion, so it is with Serpents. One strives to control them and turn them to the good they can effect. Yet all the time we understand the power is there and that mortals have no way of controlling it but through Her.

Mother stood between me and the couch where Michal lay as if shielding either me or the patient. It was Saul's daughter herself who finally called me to her side.

"So, little one," she said. Her voice was not weak, but it came with pain. She had been bitten on her breast and arm, and the poison was already spreading to her face. She was losing vision and had to squint to see me. "You think you can save me?" she asked.

"Goddess willing," I replied.

"Ah, little one." Michal slowly shook her head on a swollen neck. "That scaly Messenger put enough of its drug in me to kill three men. I made sure of that. How easy, then, to kill one old woman and the half-formed child that shares her blood."

A murmur went through the crowd, floured to the elbows, that pressed at the doorway. Energy throbbed at my wrists and temples. She wanted to die. My friend Michal wanted to die. It would make my work even more difficult, that the patient could bring no will or hope of her own to the task.

Indeed, there are those who would say that even if I had had all the experience in the world, this cure would have been impossible. You must understand that I had never cured a soul before, nor had I even seen it done. Sometimes, when Mother was not paying enough attention to me, I used to hang on her skirts and demand of her, "What am I, Mother?"

"Snakesleeper. I've told you that a hundred times if I've told you once."

"And what can I do?"

"I've told you that, too."

"Tell me again."

"Later."

There was no "later" for me when Absalom was around. I knew that. So I insisted. "Can I understand the language of birds and the meaning of signs?"

"Yes."

"Can I walk in a pit of Serpents and fear no death?"

"Goddess willing."

"And can I heal those bitten by Snakes?"

"With faith."

"How can I do that?"

"I don't know."

"But how shall I learn?"

"It is not my gift, I'm afraid."

"But tell me. Tell me how it is done."

And she would summarize the healings she had witnessed in Geshur, briefly or in more detail, depending on her mood. I had everything she knew memorized by the time I was five and could tell when she left out so much as a quiver of the healer's little finger. But it was one thing to have her reminisce how the healer in Geshur worked, quite another to turn as I did now to the crowd at the door and say in a voice, high-pitched, which I could not control, "No one must speak the name of this Beast from now until the cure is accomplished. Please, as you fear Heaven, use only such words as 'Legless One,' 'Spotted Girdle,' or simply 'Messenger.'"

The crowd I addressed rarely took me seriously, even when I was only one of the children. I was not one of "the" children, not one of David's, after all. They were sober, listening to my words, but hardly ready to conform to such a request. Still, I knew this was my task, even if they did not.

Mother came out of the crowd and put her hand on my shoulder. I was glad to have her there, for I thought she would give my words more credence. I should have known that all faith in a Snakesleeper must be roused by Herself or it will not be roused at all.

"Come away, Daughter," my mother said.

"No." I did not understand.

"Come back to our rooms now."

"No." I grew certain I had heard her right the first time, but still I did not understand.

"There is nothing we can do."

"But . . . but I must heal her."

"No one can heal her, Daughter."

"I can."

"Child, you have never done it . . ."

"I can try."

"Saul's daughter is past hope. She wants to die. Let her go in peace."

"But am I not Snakesleeper?"

Someone in the audience chuckled and it spread like plague. Mother did not deign to give her responses to our little liturgy right then and there. She began to draw me off.

"No!" I said. I broke away and burst back into the sickroom.

Though the poison was already affecting Michal's eyesight, it was also allowing her to sense things as a Pythoness can. They say one's sight is never quite the same after such an accident, even if one isn't called to the oracular service as a result. Some things she saw even clearer than I could at the time and to my childish clamoring she said calmly, "Go with your mother, little one. She doesn't want me to live any more than I myself want to. Leave me in peace."

Having my attention thus called to it, beneath the thin mask my mother wore I could see a face to whom it was fiendishly important that I not make a scene in front of all the rest of the harem. And beneath even that was a face more deadly than any viper's, a face full of ambition for Absalom her son.

Mother was by no means alone in this. Many that crowded about the door nursed similar ambition for sons present or as yet unborn, many much more openly than my mother who was, after all, a Queen of Geshur and not like some rude princess from the desert. To them all, the snake-bite was like the very touch of the hand of their god, whatever deity it was that they had spent their most fervent prayers on for the last two months. Let only that child of Michal's die and the throne of David would remain so much closer to their own hands.

Mother blushed. She knew I'd found her out. She reached out a hand to take me again, but I ducked and, as I did, I snatched up the crushed body of Goddess's Messenger from its casket. When I rose again, I seemed to add an extra cubit to my height and I dangled the Serpent as a shield before me. Everyone knows it is death to touch a Snake even until sundown on the day it has been killed. Though dead, the poison remains fatal, for the creature is divine. People have been known to die from the graze of a fang in a head several hours decapitated. Mother and Zipporah fell back at bay. The faces at the door disappeared with short, involuntary screams and fled to see to the burning loaves.

"Now," I said to Michal. "Now, Saul's daughter, now I am the Snakesleeper. Now, tell me, do you want to die in truth? Think how you are on the brink of the endless abyss, of the land where there is always hunger and naught but mud to quench one's thirst. Think of the chill of night's shades in the desert. Do you want to die?"

"Little one, I . . ."

I kissed the broken head of the Serpent as if it were yet alive and I were beginning to trance. Then I began to smear the venom and brain that had been crushed out of the skull onto my face. "Do you want to die?" I insisted.

Michal started to sob and my confidence grew. Already my power was showing itself able to bring forth truth from an iron-barred door, extremely well and painfully guarded.

"No, no," she sobbed. "I am afraid. I do not want to die. But I . . . I do not want this child within me. Oh, Maacah of Geshur and to all the other wives, too. I don't want your David's seed. If I could, I would cut it from me and give it to you to bear, since you crave it so jealously. God of my Fathers, I would like to see her, Sarai, my own little one. I would like to touch her fine, soft hair again before I die. I pray for that."

"You shall see her!" I cried.

"No, no, little one. Better that she should mourn a mother dead than that she should know how I've betrayed her father and herself and all her brothers and sisters. She expects me dead already and has mourned enough these past two years. Let her put on her festival dress and dance before the Ark. And let her learn later, when she is older and stronger, of the sorrows a king's daughter must bear."

Michal closed her eyes and all was silent but her belabored breath. I felt the Serpent's brain glowing on my cheeks and on my temples like the flush of a fever and my mind was inspired.

"Daughter of Saul," I said. "My mother has powers, too, though they are of a different sort than mine. Barren women she can cause to be fruitful. And fruitful women she can cause to close and never open again. If she swears now to perform her magic upon you, will you accept and hope in mine?"

My words took a long time to find their way through the poison clogging her mind. When at last they touched, she opened her eyes with new, clear sight as if the cure were already taking effect. "Goddess bless you," she said, and to my mother, too.

"Swear," I ordered my mother, thrusting the Viper's body at her. She swore, touching the tail with the merest tip of a finger. Some say the tail can sting, too, like a scorpion's, and she was afraid.

But she had no hesitation to fulfill the oath, nor to help me carry out my work.

· XVII ·

MOTHER WENT AT once to fetch my skin from the bottom of her chest. Absalom whined and tried to keep her with him when she entered our apartments. She told me later she had slapped him, promised him more when she got back for his prank with the mice, and instructed the maids in no uncertain terms that they were to keep him out of the way. What she was doing was for his sake more than any fondling she might ever give him.

But I think there was compassion in her at this time as well as her ambition. I watched her hands at their work and admired them as ever in their knowledge and understanding of the way of life and of women. One cannot work such cures and not have compassion for sacred Goddesshood as manifest in each and every woman.

As for myself, once Mother had run from the room to get our nostrums, I bowed my head and spat three times on the broken head I held within my hands. One should spit between the Serpent's fangs to effect the cure, but there were really no fangs left in that battered mess. I took what brain was left in the mass and scooped it into a mortar Zipporah handed me. Then I curled the rest of the body gently up among the leaves of its nest and closed the casket lid.

Mother returned. We decided it was most important to get the poison stabilized first, for Michal's eyelids were already drooping stupidly and her mouth opened as she struggled with each breath. Even though as long as the child was still in her, Michal would not set her full mind on the cure, I began to chant. I girded my loins with my Snakeskin, then I knelt beside the stricken one. I slashed the swelling punctures with a flint knife and sucked at them for all I was worth. The fluid I withdrew I spat into the mortar with the brains. I mixed the lot with dried fig leaves, chanting all the while, moistened it with a bit of wine, and asked my patient to eat. She didn't get more than a morsel down. She began to vomit, which was not a good sign. A flood of inspiration filled my mind, and I decided to try what was left of the mess as a poultice instead. I smeared it on the wounds, then took the bezoar stone from my neck and bound it first on the breast, which seemed to be the worst bite. Later I would move it to the arm. Now there remained nothing for me but to sing and trance and watch the labored breathing. It was Mother's turn.

The fetus was dead before Mother started to withdraw it. Naturally, something so small cannot endure having so much poison pumped through it more than once or twice. That it was dead eased Mother's work physically as well as spiritually. She began by using a flint knife, to sharpen an olive twig which she then topped with a bit of sea sponge and inserted in the neck of the womb. This had to remain while she soaked the trimmings from an ironworks in wine, infused mustard, cedar resin, and wallflower seed, then gave it to Michal to drink between poison-swollen lips. Michal did manage to keep this down, and called for more wine, which was good. Zipporah gave her as much as she could. Then the twig was replaced by a heavy copper needle, which eased the way for a ball of carpet wool soaked in a mixture of laurel, pepper, and goat musk. Within an hour, the pains began. Mother encouraged them by extinguishing, then relighting lamps into which she had dropped lumps of donkey dung. It was a powerful magic smell. We were all a bit nauseated by the time Michal was pushing and screaming.

It was a male child, one could already tell. We laid it, too, in the casket, between the coils of that which brought about its death. Later and alone, I performed rites of burial for the two in the Valley of Topheth. Both in the selfsame casket they lie: the bodies of one of the holy Messengers and the little man-child, union of the houses of Saul and David, that might have spared the united kingdom all the grief, separation, strife, and rebellious claimants to the throne it must now endure. Sometimes I wonder what virtue there is in the acts I perform. To save one woman so dear to me, was it worthwhile to condemn all the population to such strife? Well, the baby was dead anyway. All my magic could not have saved him, so the people must look elsewhere for their savior than half a cubit beneath the soil of Topheth.

But if it were not Goddess's will, my hands and lips would not have been blessed as they drew out the poison. I might even have died myself for touching the carcass. Yet I suffered no more than a small blister on my lips and, of course, a slight prophetic headiness as the poison sank into my skin. Such things only helped the cure and prepared me for the many, many things yet to come in my work with the Serpents. Am I not the Snakesleeper?

Our work took a day and a night and a day together. It was very hard for one who had never been allowed to stay up past the setting of the second watch even on a feast night to stay alert through all of it, but Mother supported me. Yet she did not baby me or tell me what to do unless I asked for suggestions. When our work was done, she hugged me, as one woman hugs another, not as mother and daughter, and kissed me on the cheek. Then I fell weeping from exhaustion into her arms and she allowed me to be a child again. She picked me up, Snakeskin and all, and carried me back to our rooms. Absalom can never come between us and that moment.

Through all of this, David was feasting and dancing with his god. As he did, the thought came to his mind that he should perform the Great Bed anyway, that he should demonstrate who was king by taking another bride or two from Israel. His choice fell on one of the dancers.

"Stop your blubbering," said the guard who ushered the girl into the royal tent hung with woolen pomegranates and golden almonds. "The king does you great honor."

It was Sarai, the daughter of Michal, he shoved to the floor at David's feet.

"Please, my lord, don't do this thing," the girl wept, throwing her arms around the king's bare knees. "It was wrong of me to come, I know that now. A fool's errand. But don't do this thing that would be an abomination for both our houses."

David waved the guard away. The weeping, the pleading, the shell-covered breasts as yet unripe against his legs, all this aroused the linen ephod in a moment. He pressed his knees forward 'til they hit the ground and the girl was wriggling there desperately under him. Just as desperately he threw off the ephod, just as desperately he plunged the belt the little way farther down it had to go and saw the pudendum, as hairless as a greengage plum.

And then the words hit his brain. "I'm Sarai. Your Majesty, no! By the God of my Fathers, I'm Michal's daughter!"

And David looked and he saw beneath the mask of makeup the weak jaw he hated so much in his enemy's family, and he knew that it was true. With a bellow of rage, he smashed that jaw. He took the time to throw a robe on, no more, before he called for the guard to return.

"She is a spy from the house of Saul," he said. "A witch. Burn her."

Sarai was mercifully unconscious as they carried her to the place of her execution.

David the king stood in battle dress at the front center post of his long black tent and watched the building of the witch's pyre in the distance. He didn't wish to appear too dependent on Heaven, but from time to time he couldn't stop himself from touching the talismans that hung there: his youthful slingshot and a bloody lock of Goliath's hair; several Philistine foreskins; a purple pouch worked in gold with the first letter of his god's ineffable name—what was in the pouch I never learned. Relief was on the son of Jesse's face when he turned from the tent post to an approaching messenger.

"Well, is the pyre ready yet? I know a lot of fuel has been used for all the sacrifices of the past few days, but surely by now—"

The messenger had caught his breath and quickly disabused him: "Your wife—"

"Which wife?"

"Saul's daughter—"

"God, not Michal!"

"She's snake-bitten."

"Ah, God! Ah, God!" And when he could say more than that: "This is punishment for my sins," David groaned, as violent in his remorse as he had been in his anger. "Behold, I was shaped in iniquity and in sin did my mother conceive me."

A woman's screams competed with his from outside the tent. "Can that be Saul's daughter? So stricken that I can hear her from here?"

"Not Saul's daughter but his granddaughter," said the messenger, for the girl had regained her senses in time to see her pyre going up.

"Stop the execution," David ordered when he recalled his deed.

"My lord?"

"Stop it, I say. It may be that the sight of her daughter will save my wife and the mother of my child."

By the time Sarai was brought to her, Michal was able to sit up a little and embrace her.

"Alas, poor child!" she wept. "What's happened to your jaw?"

Sarai told her between tears.

"How glorious is the King of Israel," Michal said, looking over her daughter's head on her chest at David in the doorway. "How glorious when he uncovered himself in the eyes of the handmaids of his servants, as one of the vain

fellows shamelessly uncovers himself!" All over the court
you could hear the venom of her sarcasm.

"It was before the Lord, who chose me before your
wretched father and before all his house, to appoint me
ruler . . ." David blustered.

Then he learned that the baby was gone and that Michal
could never conceive again.

"By the God of my Fathers," said David, "I'll have that
little bitch of Phalti's sacrificed! I'll have her sent so far
away—! Or—or she can dance forever as a public harlot—!"

But Michal stood facing him without flinching, her precious daughter shielded in her arms. In the face of her firmness, David soon realized his threats were the tantrum of a
spoiled child. There was nothing he could do but storm out
of the room, ripping the hanging down as he went and
calling on the god of the Ark to curse the houses of Phalti
and of Saul and to curse the dark secrets of Goddess that
had worked such magic. So much for his reign of tolerance.

Sarai stayed with us about a week, but then she had to
return to her brothers and sisters to escape David's wrath,
and Michal never saw any of them again. David never entered Saul's daughter's rooms again and the chronicler will
say that her judgment was of the god, that she never had
children until she died. But that is David's reading of the
events, as to who gets counted as a child and what entails a
curse.

As for my mother, she was in royal disgrace for the better
part of a year for her share in the matter. But of course
nothing could touch David's love for my brother, and she
was content with that love by proxy.

• XVIII •

I WAS FIFTEEN years old and working among the terraces of Mount Moriah with the vinedressers. I was the only one from the household there. No one else took an interest in these rites—"For peasants," they said. Or, if they did take an interest, for the god's sake they did not show it.

Mother did not oppose my going. She would have gone herself, never mind whose wife she was, for she missed the rites and seasons by which Goddess fructifies the earth. No matter how wealthy she is, nor how surrounded by slaves, a Geshuri wishes for communion with the land she lives in, from whence she gets her daily nourishment. But Absalom, whom we had given up to join the men, was returned to our care for the moment because he was running a bit of a fever, and Mother dared not or cared not to leave him. Promising to bring home some ripe fresh citrons if any of the farmers had a surplus, I was allowed to attend the festivity with only the company of a single slave named Marah.

Marah was not much thrilled by the prospect. She, too, wanted to be home fetching cool water for my brother. A day on the terraces was to her only asking for drudgery, and life was full enough of that. To me, it was a welcome, healthy change. On a festival day, with the liturgy and ritual to help her already fertile mind, a fifteen-year-old girl can find plenty of romance in playing at peasant. There was comfort and stability in the rhythm of the work that those who do not live by it tend to call tedium instead.

The black and winter-shriveled grapes and the dried canes fell as the youths sang:

> As lord and master sat he enthroned,
> In his one hand the scepter of childlessness,
> In his other, that of widowhood.

And we maids responded:

> Yet see, they now prune him who prune the vine,
> Smite him who smite the vine.
> Make his rotten grapes to fall as from a vine.

with a hearty slash at every *vine*.

A lusty breeze came at us, tugging at our skirts, reminding us that, for all that it was a lovely day, it wasn't much past midwinter, and we should be grateful. Nearby was the threshing floor of Araunah. It was a simple open space in those days, set where the winnow fans might catch the breeze. The men had made the sacrifice there and were seething the young kids in milk as prescribed in the songs they sang:

> Behold, the breast, the breast divine.
> Over the fire seven times . . .

and so on, refrains and verses.

David's god is appalled that a newborn kid should be taken from the teat and boiled at once in what was so shortly before nourishment, warm from its own mother's body. A tragic image, granted, but that is what makes it so vivid. The rich, peculiar smell remains with one from one vinedressing to the next, as a reminder of the way of all the earth. It is only at this time that this sacrifice is asked of us. And if those of David's household would once leave their warm, overstuffed rooms on a vinedressing day and come out among the vines with the wind blowing that cooking fragrance into stomachs getting more and more aware and empty with the work, then they would not be so scornful.

When the last vine was cut and shaped neatly as if darned to its trellis, the men brought the great platters steaming up to us. Some dumped pitchers over their heads to cool off, for the work had been strenuous enough to bring on a sweat in spite of the wind. Others made proper ablutions, but neither could thoroughly clean our work-grimed and -scraped hands. We dug into the scalding, greasy mass of meat nonetheless, and wished all a good vintage, "Goddess willing."

"Goddess willing, indeed!" Voices from the road below echoed up to us and we turned to see half a score of riders. Of course, the men immediately invited the riders up. It is a misdeed not to give invitations to all at vinedressing time, and there was more than enough—even for the visitors' hounds.

There was much fluttering and giggling as we maids gathered up cast-off veils and shawls, shooed away the younger children, and gave our already-picked-at platter over to the newcomers. As the young riders left their mounts and climbed the vine terraces toward us, the local men suddenly wished they had moved aside from their platter as well. For our guests, beneath their muddied riding cloaks, wore purple on their garments and armbands and pectorals of gold and copper. But it was too late. Hospitality from the men and boys was now graciously but firmly refused and only ours accepted. Such insult can hardly be lived down, and the men spent the rest of what might otherwise have been a carefree feast fumbling with awkward, over-polite conversation. Meanwhile, with us girls who had shown immediate and true hospitality, the guests spent the feast bent knee to bent knee as if they'd been our brothers.

"Envoy to David, King of Israel and Judah," we learned their purpose, "from Joppa by the Sea." Indeed, one could smell the Great Sea and the tar of ships and sand and fish when they bent their heads and beards toward us to whisper bawdy jokes calculated to make the vines grow fruitful and us giggle and blush prettily.

"I know David has just returned from a successful campaign against Joppa," I said to them. "I hope he didn't do as much damage as he says he did."

The young men were not going to let anything dampen their festivity. They laughed out loud at my keen knowledge that what kings say and what they do are two different things. "Yes, David burned and plundered certain suburbs," they replied. "But the more fool he, an inland man who understands nothing of the Sea and only fears it."

"He might have given himself a fine harbor on the Yarkon River," one of the guests said. "Instead, he only destroyed the quays and warehouses there."

"And sent the merchants and their ships to crowd into our main harbor," added another. "We still get all the tariffs and business. The Yarkon settlement was only for overflow. David will never storm the walls of Joppa proper, and now he has done himself out of a seaport. Well, his loss is our gain."

One of the elders of the Jebusites tried to make some prideful remark about David's strength—he, after all, was David's servant, and if one cannot be strong oneself, one doesn't like to serve a weak man. The men from Joppa by the Sea brushed it aside with laughter as if it were a drunken jester's humor at the very end of the evening. "One who burns wharves and ships," they said, and made me believe their reasoning, "has no idea where true strength lies."

"Like crows that eat the grain," said one, the youngest of them. "So they are a nuisance. But what makes man man is that he, with Heaven's help, knows the secret to growing more grain again, which crows will never learn, and so they will always remain scavenger crows."

I had been wanting to brag that I was from David's household, but now I kept silent on the point and showed off with some witty remark of my own instead. I did not feel as cautious as the other maids did, for what was a prince to me but an equal and a brother? Soon I learned that the greatest among these visitors—and it was he who was the youngest, with a soft, round face that could not yet support a beard—was no heir apparent, but rather the lesser son of a lesser wife of Joppa's king. His companions, though they never failed to treat him like a prince, still did not refrain from teasing him when his voice failed to stay true for him. They ruffled his thick, dark curls where they escaped his golden filet and called him some pet name that, put broadly in their sea-drenched dialect, I could understand no more of than that honor was not its major implication. Perhaps it was the name of a fish I was not familiar with. At any rate, I felt no need to show him any deference by being coy.

There was no doubt that the men of Joppa got the best and the most when wine was brought. The Jebusites could not afford to let themselves lose control in drunkenness in the presence of such guests. They hardly took more than was needed to perform the libation at the vine roots, to add strength from last year's vintage for next year's. The men from Joppa, on the other hand, carelessly drank all that was given them. When at length the dregs were reached, it was clear they would have welcomed ten more jars and the alibi of total drunkenness.

The wine gave its color to the young prince's cheeks and I blushed myself to see how well it became him. His eyes grew clear and shiny as he spoke with a loosened tongue of the wonders of the Sea and of his home that embraced it with its wharves and quays. His gestures were caressing and wavelike, yet flamboyant and princely.

I mentioned that I had once been by the Sea—"When I was very young."

"Glorious, isn't it?" he asked, but did not inquire into the circumstances of my visit. Perhaps he thought, in my work-worn clothes, that I had been there as a slave and did not want to gray our conversation with clouds.

"In the middle of our harbor," he said, "is a great, fierce rock on which nests the spirit of the Sea called Yam, a flying monster, sort of half god, half demon, with serpent shape."

I showed interest in the Serpent shape.

"He must be propitiated yearly. That is our main religion in Joppa. Though we can appreciate the rites of the vine, there is not much use for them. What vines some few do grow without our walls were burned this year by David."

"I'm sorry."

"I'm not. They only made peasant quality—like this. No, worse than this. The best wine comes from the Sea."

"The Sea? How do grapes grow in the Sea?"

"From far lands across the Sea. From Alasiya and Crete. Our vinedressers are much better employed as longshoremen and sailors. Still, I am glad we got here to Jerusalem in time to celebrate the vinedressing with you."

"How so?"

"Well, it's nice to see you are not complete barbarians." I laughed. "Are we barbarians?"

"I mean, the tales one hears about David."

"What tales?"

"Oh, that he is such a barbarian that he can't even tell his smiths what sort of form to make the image of his god in. That he is ignorant of the power of other gods—and worse than that, that he doesn't care to improve upon his ignorance. That he is so narrow-minded he can't even think that each place on earth might have its own god and its own way of serving whatever stones or springs there might be. That he would ignore our Yam, for example. In fact, from what we'd heard, we fully imagined he would have done away with the rites of vinedressing and hoped—like some crow or wild fox—that the vines would produce of their own accord if he but pissed on them. Oh. Sorry. I haven't offended you, have I?"

"No offense," I said.

"Good. I didn't mean to. It's only the tales one hears."

"There is always some kernel of truth in such tales," I assured him.

"No doubt. But now I do not loathe having to meet the man."

"By what rites do your people propitiate your god called Yam?"

"Oh, there are hymns and sacrifices for every season," he said. "Our priests earn their keep, you may be sure."

"Well, what are women called upon to do?" I asked to encourage his tale.

"What? Young girls such as yourself?"

"Well, maybe a little older," I said to acknowledge my youth.

"Would that it were night."

"How so?" I laughed at what seemed to me a further skirting of my question.

"Men of the Sea are much controlled by the movements of the stars."

"So are we all," I said, remembering my mother's lessons to me on how to forecast earthly events by the heavenly.

He took encouragement from my sympathetic answer. "There is a constellation," he said, "that touches the meridian at the time of the Scorpion."

"There are three," I elaborated, "that form one great figure. A woman, her husband, between them their daughter. Their daughter is called 'The Young Woman in Chains.'"

"So is she called with us!" the prince exclaimed and we laughed heartily together to have found our stars in common.

"You understand, of course," he continued, "that these three arrive at the meridian along with the sign that rules over the fishes of the deep."

"Yes, that's true," I said.

"And that this is the beginning of winter, when all who venture into open seas risk being snapped by the great waves of Yam as only so much kindling wood."

"I didn't know that about the season," I admitted.

"If He is not calmed and soothed by great and supreme sacrifices, His wrath may continue thus forever."

"So what does one do?"

"The priests select by lot a certain household to provide the sacrifice."

"What is the sacrifice?"

"It is the same with Yam as when any man from peasant to prince sues for peace within his court. He needs a . . ."

"A wife?" I prompted him, for something in his own words had made him think of some personal trouble beyond our conversation.

"Yes. A wife. A woman. So they, the father, mother, and chosen daughter, are rowed out to Yam's rock. There are chains and manacles of such age that they stain the rock with rust like blood. The girl is fastened into these and, after hymns and offerings, the priests and parents row back to the shore and she is left."

"Alone?" I shivered.

"Alone but for Yam. She must serve there as His mistress until the calm of spring returns and He is satisfied and lets our ships out once again."

"Does she . . . does she live so long?" I asked.

"If she does not, it is a sign that Yam was not pleased with her. Then, even on the stillest days of summer, the sailors fear and pray and spill gold upon Yam's back before they dare go out. Fishermen, merchants, dyers, everyone suffers in those years."

"But then, some years she must . . . she must survive all those months . . . alone?"

"Actually, she is usually alive when they row out again in spring. I only remember one year when the girl did not return, and that was a year of plague, when death found its way into every corner of Joppa."

"But how—?" I did not mean disrespect, but this was not the way of the gods I knew and I could not take the business at face value as one who'd been brought up from childhood with its rites and jargon might.

The prince shifted and smiled like some eight-year-old who has just been told Roeh's secret of how babies are made but who hasn't had a chance to try it out yet. We were sitting side by side on a terrace wall, but now he got down and moved to stand in front of me with his back shielding what passed between us from the rest of the party. His breath was quite intoxicating on my face with its sweet, fermented smell, and he remained as close to me as leaning on the wall, a hand on either side of my hips, would allow him.

"On still nights when the tide is low," he said, "you can hear her sobs across the waves in town. But sometimes you can hear her laughter and, as they say, Yam sports with her.

"Young men"—and the prince lowered his voice even more—"young men sometimes swim all that distance out to her rock at night. Sometimes they do not make it. Sometimes Yam is jealous and their bodies wash up days later, beaten to death by His waves. But sometimes God is elsewhere. Or sometimes the young men trick Him. And they arrive on her rock with wine and dainties strapped upon their backs. With these they ply the maid and ask that she intercede with her Husband for them for such and such favors, for a prosperous year, for safe journeys, for sons, for love. I myself asked for such a favor, this year, when I first learned I must come up to Jerusalem . . ." The prince smiled distantly at the memory.

"And . . . and then?" I whispered.

The prince came out of his reverie with loud and rapid speech. "Well, then she comes back in spring, safe and sound and usually with child. That is a sign of special favor. The child is Yam's, of course, and is raised in the temple as such. If it is a daughter, she may follow her mother out to Yam's rock when she comes of age."

"I see," I said solemnly.

"Do you think you would like to live in Joppa?" he asked recklessly.

"I am certain I am not worthy to be Yam's bride," I said.

"No. That is a great honor—an honor and a God-calling one cannot aspire to except by Heaven's will. Still, that is not what I meant. What I meant was . . ."

But I never learned what it was he meant, for a cry went up among the prince's companions. They were all calling him by his pet name and teasing, "Here comes your mama. Behave yourself, now."

I was startled back into society, startled back to realize how naturally and unaccountably the prince and I had separated ourselves from the others. The other young people had likewise paired with the sleight-of-hand swiftness that comes over any shuffling of maids and men together like the dealing of broken-pottery lots where the hand of Goddess is present. It puts them, one and one together, in such a way that, even if there were days and months of mingling, better matches could not be made: the clown was with the comedienne, the poet with the songstress, and with the brazen braggart was the shy one who posed no threat and only gave the ears and pleasant smiles he longed for.

As if dazzled by the sudden light of the world and general company, I rubbed my eyes. Then I, too, could look down along the road and see a caravan of litters and slow-moving pack animals bearing Joppa's women and gifts to David. I wondered briefly which, if any, of those gifts would filter down to me, but I couldn't expect much, so I thought of other things. Our guests quickly took their leave and hurried rather sheepishly down the hill to ride on into town in proper and sedate form with their women.

All the other couples had made arrangements to tryst that evening. "The empty palace granary," Marah reminded her young man. She was not so sorry to have come with me after all. I knew the granary well. There was a high loft window where the moon came in and where young and unsympathetic boys (and I, too, on occasion) could climb and hoot at or drop pebbles down on the unsuspecting lovers below.

I did not know how to propose such a meeting and wanted to only because I had so enjoyed this young prince's company. So I stood silent while he gathered up his cloak and tried to sort his curls out from the garland of dried grapevines I'd crowned him with. He, too, was suddenly sober, awkward and shy as he turned to go.

"Look here," he said rather roughly as he tried to regain control of himself. "Look here, my name's Ahiram."

"Ahiram," I said, memorizing it and his features.

"I'm the prince of Joppa," he said.

"I know," I said.

"Now, look here, if you . . . if you want . . ."

I suddenly realized that he wanted me to trust him with

my name and status in return. "Snakesleeper," I said quickly and abruptly.

"Hey, handsome prince," his friends continued to torment. "Mama's watching you."

Then I said, "I mean, my name's Tamar. I mean, I'm the daughter of Maacah, David's wife. But everyone calls me Snakesleeper. I mean . . ."

"Tamar! My God!" The prince began to roar with laughter as he ran backward down the hill, plowing through vines and taking the top course off the terraces, making the farmers curse royalty in general under their breath.

"My God! My God, old Yam, you sly old bastard!" he shouted up. "Tamar, the daughter of David. I've come here to marry you!"

· XIX ·

AFTER HANNAH AND Joab were married, she continued to spend a great deal of her time with us. In fact, David was having a room built for her in his new palace. Hannah will always hold a special place in the king's heart because she was the first of all his seed. A disappointment, granted, in that she was not the son he wanted, but she was his, and until she was toddling and prattling "Papa," she was all he had to prove his manhood by. For this he will always remember her name and know her voice when all that come after are lost in the crowd. There were often tears when Joab came home from his campaigns and ordered his wife to his bed again. I overheard Hannah swearing by her god that she could not wait to conceive from all of Joab's attentions, for when she was pregnant and she had borne a son, she could come home to her mother and be David's child permanently.

Seeing that Hannah was less than two years older than me, just turned seventeen, I ought to have been more concerned about my own plight. I was the next female in the crowd that David had to worry about placing. But I had thought nothing of it until that day of vinedressing.

David was not worth the heir of Joppa, who'd long ago fetched in princesses from all the islands of the Sea. But keeping the hinterlands quiet so the sea trade could go on apace was worth sending up Ahiram and enough presents to buy a wife from among David's daughters. It was all fully arranged that I should go with the prince to Joppa, the city by the Sea, overlooking the harbor where Yam's rock is, and this within the month. In my innocence, I had not noticed what festivities were already in preparation about me in the palace. The proposal was indeed a surprise. But I was excited all the same. What I had seen so far of Joppa pleased me more than I could have hoped for. There was only one problem, something no one had stopped to consider. There was Jezebel, Ahiram's mother.

She must have been very young when she bore this son of hers, hardly more than child herself, the lust of a king in his old age, for she was still a beautiful woman. Perhaps she was only just now reaching the full ripeness of her beauty. Beauty, yes, but it was the hard, cold beauty of polished marble that makes men worship but which is of little comfort in bed on a winter's eve.

You will know the type. There's one in every harem. My mother might have been the one in ours, but that Absalom maintained such a check on her. Jezebel was rather more like Abigail (the fire those two struck simply passing in the hall was something to see), or like Abigail would have been had her son had wit at all to add to her own ambitions. What Jezebel was like to her son would compare favorably to how Bathsheba is now to Solomon. But at the time, Bathsheba was not even thought of in our home, much less Solomon, and we had built up no sure defenses against such behavior.

Mother was quietly entertaining Jezebel in her apartment when I burst in from the vinedressing. She audibly gasped with horror.

Mother had carefully bundled me up against the commonizing elements before I left, but one simply can't prune vines swaddled like a baby and veiled like an old widow, even on the coldest day of the year, and it was warm for winter. "Dark as a slave in the date groves during the harvest," Mother later said I was, and "looking nothing so much as like a long-dead rat fished out of the well."

The princes of Joppa had left us with the rites half finished, and as soon as they had disappeared into the walls of the town it had started to rain. We had gone on to dance nonetheless as the clouds rolled in like riders coming up from the Sea on gray and dappled mounts. It was so light a rain, and we found it so complimentary to our dance—an answer to our prayers, or as if the sky itself were setting down dainty feet in rhythm to the drum—that we stayed on much past what the ritual required and danced and danced with such a wet but gracious partner.

I danced longest and most joyfully of all. My mind was full of sea monsters and fanciful love. I craved motion lest, like a misburdened scale, the weight of my imagination might undo the equilibrium of my physical body balanced against my mind. Probably others would have rushed back to the palace to join their bridegroom-to-be. But I knew David and decorum would keep the embassy of Joppa occupied 'til evening and I could not bear to be cooped up in the harem, waiting, with an exhilaration of mind that my body was hard-pressed to keep up with. And the milk-boiled kid sat as heavily in my belly as my thoughts did in my mind and I must dance them out, both of them. I reveled in the rain until the sun perched white and weak and cloud-smeared and made ready to slip off the horizon.

Under the dripping, great smudges of sweated-on dirt still grimed up my face, my legs, and my arms. Under that, in an earlier layer, there was the tint that proved I had allowed the sun to look upon my already dark skin with a wintery yet keen gaze as only those who cannot afford the luxury of servants and veils do. I was wearing little clothing to be out in public—no more than one does on first rising, disheveled in the morning—and made Marah carry the rest. It was only too clear how filthy and how completely sun-exposed I was when I burst in on Mother and her guest.

Jezebel might have survived all this as my future mother-

in-law. But then I showed manners equal to my appearance.
Well, so did she.

"By Yam," she exclaimed even before an introduction,
"that is the ugliest girl I've ever seen."

"And you are the rudest woman I've ever seen," I replied.
Then I flopped down in a corner to sulk. It is too hard to
come in from the expanse of the open vineyards and to
suddenly try and fit into some narrow apartments. Outside,
the infinite mercy of Heaven winks at all in you for it is like
Itself. To go from that suddenly to the scrutiny of one who
would be unsatisfied with an oracle if the priestess failed to
drape her robes just so—it is too hard. I tingled so much
from the touch of the son—his and the rain's were like
repercussions in my mind of the same tingling tenderness—
that I was numb to the cold, hard slap of the mother—until
it was too late.

"Disobedient and self-willed besides!" Those were the last
words I heard Jezebel say as she rose quickly to leave.

Absalom was whining with fever in the next room. He'd
set his voice to just the droning pitch that makes one squirm
with pity. It was the sound a wounded cat beyond all help
makes, and one is irresistibly drawn to the misery all the
same. Even as an adult, Absalom was flawless in reaching
that pitch in simple, everyday statements. You had to go to
him. Mother watched Jezebel flounce out. Then she got up
and went to see her son without a word.

Later, when my indignation wore off, when realization,
remorse, and a broken heart came, I did not know what
pitch to strike to find relief or sympathy for myself. Mother
could only say that she was glad, not that I had shamed her,
but that I would not be taken from her so young. She was
sorry to have thwarted David's designs, but she had thought
all along that fifteen years old was much too young for a girl
to be taken from her mother, especially a girl uninitiated,
and "especially by a woman like that." It did not help at the
time to be told I was too young. I had felt so grown-up with
the prince of Joppa on the terraces.

We saw each other once again, Ahiram and I, at a grand,
general audience. But his mother had already spoken her

word and he dared not look at me. He was not the man that he had seemed to be among the vines. I think he was ashamed that he could not gainsay his mother. Of the gifts they'd brought, I think it was he who made certain I got one: a small yet precious silver ring in the form of a Snake grasping its own tail in its mouth. It had ruby eyes. What a disappointment it was to me that it was too big for any of my fingers. Some years later when I came across it in the bottom of my things and found it fit, it was not nearly so important to me.

But, Goddess, at the time, how I drowned You with my tears and prayers! Goddess, I hatched a hundred plots to worm my way to Joppa. Sleeping and awake, my mind crawled with the plots of brief little dramas where I would suddenly appear, radiant and graceful of speech and manners, white as milk, with a tongue like honey, and I would charm Jezebel into a tearful and humble submission. Or Ahiram would burst in, like some great hero come to save the maiden in chains, and carry me, trailing Egyptian linen veils of see-through white, past his mother and off to . . . to somewhere far away and very wonderful.

And I plotted how it would be to arrive in Joppa some time later (not much more than four or five months later—I could not endure a wait longer than that, even in my mind)—as the second, but much more cherished wife and produce sons in twins and triplets while *she* remained barren. For you see, when he could not have me, Ahiram sealed the treaty with Haggith's daughter instead. She was less than a year younger then me, more legitimately David's daughter, and ten times more obliging. Jezebel promised to raise her as her own until she should reach a proper age.

Haggith's girl is such a prudish Israelite, I thought bitterly. To be married to a man so strong in his watery religion! Can you imagine her reaction to the maidens of Yam's rock? Drowning out the weeping—and the later laughter in the dark—with David's psalms sung with all the force of her feeble, toneless voice? Can you imagine *her* chained to that rock? She would swoon away like pale curd in the sun before the bridegroom ever licked her manacles with his serpent tongue.

I spent so much time with angry, scornful thoughts like these that it wasn't until much later that there was room to consider the other hand. On the other hand, can you imagine me in the same room with that woman? In the same house? Our wills would collide into shattering chaos at every step. It was the mother who was important in that match, not her curly-haired, purple-clad, pink-cheeked son. And I suppose she made of Haggith's pasty girl just exactly what she was looking for in a daughter-in-law. I could not have made Ahiram the man he ought to have become against such odds. I can only hope he found many, many reasons to swim across the winter water of the harbor to set petitions before the Sea's paramour.

Nine months later, Marah the maidservant had a son for her temerity in the empty granary. There seemed to be the blue of Joppa's Sea in the whites of his eyes, but that was all the father left to him. Marah was whipped for it, of course, but that child saved David buying a new stable boy. About the same time as that birth we got another bride-hunting envoy, this time from Tyre. At Tyre was more Sea, more great shipping, more rites to Yam. But this time it was David who opposed sending me and promised them Amnon's younger sister instead. Tyre is too close to Geshur. If he sent me, there would be every reason to unite the two kingdoms in my sons and thereby effectively choke anything north of the Galilee and Dan out of David's hands. After that, whenever David counted daughters, he seemed to forget about me. Either that, or he left me to the end and sought husbands for his two-year-olds before he thought of me.

"I am glad for that," Amnon said.

I thought he was teasing me without mercy and purposely dumped a pot of soaked beans on his foot. It was only in time, when I stopped minding the whole affair at all, that I wanted to hug him for such words. Mother said I was much too young, and more age has assured me of the wisdom of her perspective. Goddess meant me to wait for my proper initiation and so I did.

· XX ·

A BROKEN HEART heals fast enough, especially when one is only fifteen and when the whole romance has no more substance to it than minstrels' ditties. What I did not recover from so rapidly was the realization that Goddess had put limits on my life. I'd never considered that possibility before. Now I saw I could not have and be everything. Jezebel's stinging condemnation of my skin and my looks— it gnawed at my insides and left a dull and bitter ache. It was true, I realized. I would never be a beauty. I could not take comfort that there were other things I would be allowed that few if any other women enjoy. They did not seem real to me at the time, and beauty was all that mattered to those I had as examples about me. You must realize that a king's harem attracts, demands, retains the most beautiful women the kingdom allows. Beauty—and, later, sons. But how was one to get the sons without the beauty to attract their father first? That was the constant worry.

I could bear being limited when I was alone. Then something of the Infinite came in the quiet and touched me and told me that my limitations, like the vinedressers' hook, were to give me the strength I needed to grow on the trellis She had prepared for me. I should not waste my energy growing full and sideward when it was my calling to shoot upward to the sun. But company always made me lose sight of this wisdom.

It was worst at the parties.

The ram's horn sounded, far away on the city walls, announcing that the new moon had risen. Immediately voices filled the halls, the rapid, piercing voices of women just come from an eventful day into the freedom of their rooms and the time marked "feast" where at last they could discuss it. The voices were somehow terrifying, like the war cries of battle, the volleys riddled with the rapid clatter of sandals loose on their feet like chariot steeds charging. The way their approach echoed ahead of them down the smooth plastered halls sent shivers down my back such as one feels before plunging into the cool pool of an oasis.

All the women gave parties, but Abigail's were, by all accounts, the best. It is not that she herself gave life to things. When she tried her tongue at wit, at singing, or at storytelling, the life of any party, she always aborted in either incredible poor taste or in childish simplicity until it made one squirm with discomfort to hear her. But this shortcoming was more than compensated for by the security of her voice at giving orders: those who could cover for her failings were ordered to attend.

One never asked if she should accept an invitation from Abigail. If she were invited, she counted herself lucky. If not, she could not hold her head up in court for weeks.

Abigail's rooms smelled of women when I entered, heavily of myrrh and astringently of rose water. As each woman entered, the fragrances swelled, as if the warmth of their bodies were the ember to spark a pool of oil, as a bundle of clothes gains form and life when worn. It was as if the smell were buoying up the ceiling, great cedar beams and all.

I ducked my head—took the plunge, I might say—and entered, too, trying to get past Abigail's bulk. She'd bound her hips with a brilliant red sash, and she ground those hips

about with enthusiasm as she pressed creamed smoked eggplant on each of us as we entered. I did not escape.

"Come, come, darling, you must eat! No man will ever
look twice at you, skin and bones as you are."

"Thank you," I said and took a blob on a triangle of flat
bread. I had to confess, Abigail could coax more olive oil
into an eggplant than any other I knew. Her cream was
always delightful, with just the right nip of garlic on the
tongue.

"Like the playful nip of a lover," sighed Haggith, "in the
smother of his kisses."

The room in general joined her sigh, for they had all, at
one time or another, known that same lover's nip.

"Well, so—!" laughed Abigail with another lash of her
red sash. "Have some more, child, so you, too, may be
nipped."

And I did—because I like eggplant cream, not because I
wanted to be nipped. I was beginning to wonder if this
concern for my marital status would be the main topic of
conversation this evening. Would it pursue me around the
room, be on every tongue, with every scoop of eggplant,
with every nutshell spat upon the rug? Would every shake of
Abigail's ponderous hips be a signal to ask it again? Was
that all people thought when they looked at me?

"Aha! It's just as I thought!" Abigail exclaimed.

I had bent my head close enough to her tray that she
could yank up my right-front braid with her free hand and
observe my earlobe.

"No wonder the prince of Tyre didn't want her. Her ears
aren't pierced yet."

Here was getting married, but now it was mixed with
something else again. In places where Goddess holds sway,
this business, like the piercing of the hymen, is part of a
serious and sacred ceremony. The jewelry is blessed and
hung there to protect the divinity exposed to the harshness
of the world there in one's face.

"No," I said.

"Abigail, you were right," Haggith congratulated.

"Whatever can Maacah be thinking?" Ahinoam asked,

looking across the room with concern at my mother, whose thoughts none of them could ever fathom.

I couldn't very well reply, "Mother put off the ceremony for me, not having easy access to the proper rites." So I said nothing and tried to get past the bright red sash again.

"Ritzpah, a needle and thread here!" Abigail ordered. "We must remedy this situation at once."

The night's entertainment was determined.

I realize that Judean girls by the thousands have their ears done under similar circumstances and suffer no ill effects. And Mother, as soon as we got back to our own rooms, would say the proper formulas over me. But she did not try to stop them then, when they grabbed me, when from fear I was crying long before the pain began. She made no attempt to explain to them as she did so carefully to me that whatever beauty I might attain to had been dedicated from my first yell to the caretaking of Goddess alone.

"So now I've done you a favor and you're in my debt," Abigail declared over my sobs and throbbing head. "But no need to thank me now. Some day you will. And here—"

She took the lavish rings out of her own ears to stop up the holes. "There's more for you, love."

The earrings were cold and clammy from her own white flesh against my hot, throbbing, blood-filled lobes and actually much too heavy with bits of carnelian and real gold to be placed in new raw holes. But it was more for general aesthetic pleasure that I was given them than to stop my crying or to add to my dowry.

"How nice the gold looks on such dark skin!" Ahinoam said.

"If Ahiram of Joppa could see her now, he would forget all about Haggith's girl," said Abital.

Haggith laughed loudest of all.

"Now there are favors for everyone!" shrieked Abigail with glee, tossing the hair back from the sagging, dead, and empty holes in her ears.

Her slaves brought out palettes with antimony and new brushes. The children were given strings of noisemaking beads for their entertainment, but I again became a victim of Abigail's great flattery. I was deemed old enough to receive a small palette of my own.

"Perhaps now you can catch a man," someone said—again.

And again it made my tears start up. I felt like some ancient, dusty image that receives new paint and garments on the holy day so the people can feel virtuous and that they have made amends for a year of neglect. I fingered the cool soapstone palette in my damp palms. The feel was refreshing and attractive enough that I looked down and studied the network of carved flowers. I found it lovely for its own sake and so I gave in and allowed it to give me some of its attributes. I allowed my eyes to be painted, but only once and thinly. The rest of the paint I let Mother have when sweat began to destroy her makeup.

It was hot, incredibly so. Even in the middle of winter in a rainstorm, a party heated up Abigail's close rooms. But now, in summer, it was unbearable. I gazed longingly at the door, where the drape was thrown back to announce our frivolity to the calm and sober new-moon night. Mother sent a sharp warning at me from under her painted lids. I was not to even think of so offending our hostess. I gazed at the windows, but they were too high and narrow to catch a breath at. Abigail packed them in like grapes which, when they bloom fresh and tiny in the spring, feel there is room to spare on the stalk. But when every fruit swells to splitting in the warm, ripening end-of-year, they are pressed together into shapes more square than the natural round.

Abigail, gleaming with sweat through her oils and unguents like a basted roast, shifted to loosen the Philistine bindings that were making great rolling creases in her flesh as she passed a tray of sweets. "Come, take another," she encouraged me. "Nobody likes a skinny girl. Besides, a girl who's just had her ears done gets three or four."

Her voice maintained the order-giving pitch she had extended all day in preparations. I didn't dare refuse. The honey dripped from the pastry and encircled my wrist. It was really too sweet to be swallowed all at once, certainly not without water, but it had to be done before the honey found its way to my elbow.

I was glad when her commands were turned against a young concubine. "Come! We'll see you dance."

"Yes, let's see what's kept David so occupied at night these past few months," said one wife to another without bothering to whisper.

"Be nice to her," responded Ahinoam. "It's her first party here."

"Yes, but it won't be her last."

"Now that the gifts have stopped and another, younger, has taken her place, she'll be with us forever."

"Hush, not so loud. She'll start crying again."

"Come, give her some room to dance," ordered Abigail. Hers was a great voice of sympathy when it came to the painful initiation into the true harem, the harem where a man was never seen. After all, Abigail had been the first to be discarded.

The circle widened as best it could.

"Why don't you pop on up into that niche?" Mother suggested. "You'll be out of the way and able to see better." She popped me up there.

In one corner, Ahinoam and Eglah began to drum. Those in the other corners were allowed time to finish their conversations. Until then their laughter shimmered like timbrel— one could have danced to its rhythm.

The concubine danced shyly, plucking her limbs back to herself time and time again like a mother will her toddler playing around a dangerous well, before they got away from her. "That's the best I can do," she soon said and sat down. Others were called up to take her place.

"It's a shame Amnon isn't here to dance for us," I mentioned to Haggith, who happened to be standing near me. I hoped if I could engage her in conversation she would reach me up a drink of wine. But another woman's son was not the best way to spark her interest. Alas that Ahinoam was drumming clear across the room. Did only she and I remember how Amnon had moved to touch our hearts? He was gone now, his parties with the men.

The niche was making my bottom numb. It also lifted me right into the thick of the heat and sickening sweet perfumes that hung like smoke and made escape even less likely than before. A better view of the same tired dancers was hardly compensation. From ear to ear straight through my head I began to feel stabbing pains like lightning from cloud to cloud.

"You must dance some more," Abigail said to the concubine with an effort to sound joyful. "We are hardly satisfied as David must have been."

The concubine got up, trying to match the fabricated joy. It was then I knew I was going to be sick.

I tried to tell my mother.

"Just a minute," she said.

The earrings weighted down my head and gave the fever no place to escape. The sweets I had eaten too quickly curled their sticky honey back up into my throat and pressed upon my tongue. But worst of all were the faces I had seen too much of until, like bright light, I could not shake their images from my eyes even when they were closed. Their faces glanced up into my niche and, without thinking, used my homeliness, my dark complexion, my trouble with the ear piercers, with Ahiram of Joppa, with all the things other girls found so easy and second nature, as similes and by-words to their gossip, as comfort in their own untenable situations. Their words throbbed in my fever. "Blessed be God," they said, "things could be worse."

"Mama . . ." I tried once more, but it was already too late. My insides came up and then fell down, and I tumbled limply after.

"Oh, the little wretch!"

"The inconsiderate brat. Just look at my hair!"

"And I had a shekel's worth of perfume in my braids. It'll all have to be washed out, wasted!"

The concubine said nothing, but held hands full of kohl running from her large round weeping eyes up to me against what she took, in her tender condition, to be a personal insult.

I remember how relieved my stomach felt to be empty, how pure and absolutely scentless the water Mother washed me with was, how wonderful the bed, and how welcome sleep.

▣ XXI ▣

IT SEEMED I slept forever, my rest was so deep, but I awoke before any other soul. The rest of the harem would not wake until the heat of the day was already dwindling into night; it took time to sleep off Abigail's wine.

The evil memories of my sickness and shame came flooding back all at once and I got out of bed to escape them. I took the earrings out of my ears so quickly it hurt, and my anger at the pain made me fling them against the wall. I got dressed in the plainest thing I had, reaction against the night before, forgot to brush my hair, which was still damp and unbound from the unscheduled washing, and never bothered to replace the gold and carnelian with the plain silver hoops Mother had provided for me. "Let them grow together," I said under my breath as I left the room. "And damn whoever tried to pierce them again."

The great house seemed deserted, for the men were long up and about their business while the women slept. Across the way, there was great activity as space for David's new palace was being cleared. The clouds of dust stifled the noise but caused discomforts of their own. No one of royal blood would be there unless he had to be and then he would be too busy for me. I headed in that direction.

Then, to the west, across the central Valley of the Cheese-makers, I saw where the men and boys were passing their time. Beyond the walls in the open and deserted spaces of the western ridge, the garden green ended with the abruptness of cliffs in the wilderness. There the men and boys were practicing their military skills. I set off toward them, toward the fresh breeze blowing across the stagnant town, clearing my head of the stuffy, close heat of the night before, my throat and lungs of the sting of vomit.

The late rains had brought great expanses of flowers, as bright and neat as if Goddess Herself with Her infinite patience had embroidered them on the hillside with a fine ivory needle. But summer had been upon us for three full months already and the heat was oppressive on the unshaded hillside. Now these same expanses (these same plants, in fact) were turned to sharp and brittle tangles against the heat and drought, and they caught my skirt and wounded my legs at every step. The dust was packed and hard as Mother's linen sheath the moment our Egyptian laundress took the ironing stones off its pleats, and the entire hillside was as hospitable as her room when she was ironing and in a foul mood from the heat. Yet I had come so far. It was a matter of pride that I went on; that, and the memory of the night behind me.

"Now, the sling—"

It was Joab's voice and it startled me.

Concentrating on the effort it took to climb the western slope in the heat, I had come much more abruptly and closer among the soldiers than I had intended. I was close enough that a few of the boys on the edge of the gathering yanked my unbound hair and hissed at my naked ears, teasing me to prove themselves men.

"Here is Maacah's daughter," said one.

"She is too ugly to be a wife," said another.

"Perhaps she will try her hand at soldiering instead," laughed the third.

"Gentlemen," said Joab, "your attention, please."

The sternness in his voice was emphasized by the sudden

arrival on the field of David in the armor everyone knew he
had taken off the dead Goliath and had cut down to size.
Under its weight and the weight of the sun, he was sweating,
but sweating manfully. My tormentors were instantly awed
into forgetting all about me, giving me a chance to retreat
to a nearby garden wall, which I climbed. From the wall I
was able to pick Amnon out of the crowd. He was no longer
so easy for me to recognize because I rarely saw him and had
not had time to get accustomed to him in a boy's short tunic
rather than a skirt. He was growing tall, too, though he still
did not stand out on the hillside among all of David's sons
and nephews and nephews' sons.

Amnon seemed particularly anxious when the sun glinted
off his father's breastplate and into his eyes. "God of my
Father," his dazzled eyes seemed to say, "how great You are
to have given me such a father. God, make me worthy of
him. God, be my God, too."

Absalom I didn't see. He must have been in the stables
with the grooms and the chariots, his favorite occupation
because it was so regal.

As I climbed from the wall up into the shade of an old fig
tree—the figs of a late variety, unripe, tiny, green, and
hard—I heard David begin to speak.

"So what are we practicing today?"

"We're starting with the slings, my lord," answered Joab.

"By God, you need to teach a boy how to use a sling?"

"That is the plan, my lord."

"My sons? Haven't my sons been given slingshots as infants instead of rattles?"

"Yes, my lord. But their technique is not always the best."

"Slinging is second nature. Why, I was no bigger than this
little lad here when I killed a lion after my father's sheep.
Have I ever told you that one? How I was all alone one
evening—"

"Evening?" repeated one lad close to me to his neighbor.
His irreverence and his accent told me he was a hostage boy
from another kingdom. "I heard it was early morning."

"They always told me it was the heat of the afternoon,"
countered the other.

"There I was, playing my harp and eating the dry crusts that were all my food for a fortnight, when suddenly, from behind a mound of tawny rocks just to my left—"

"I heard on the right," and "I heard over his shoulder," muttered the two skeptics below me.

"The great black shadow of a massive lion in midspring flew across my sight . . ."

We heard that story to the end, which Joab tried to hasten with only a cough or two. "Thank you, sir," he said when it was done. "We are all indebted to you for your fine example. But not all of us here have had the privilege of herding sheep—"

"I curse myself that I don't send all of my sons out with their own flocks."

"It's hardly necessary, sir, now that you are king."

"I am king, yes, but it's still necessary. When they come to their first battle, they'll see just how necessary it is."

"That is why we have training, sir."

"Who needs training when you've got a flock of mindless sheep and a wilderness full of predators? Those were the good old days."

"Yes, my lord. But the Egyptians train their young men. I understand it is the favorite pastime of the princes."

This statement brought a conceding grunt from David. "Good. And our empire will rival Egypt's. We will train our lads better than they ever dreamed of."

"God willing, my lord."

"Perhaps we may even have them making our bricks someday, eh?"

This suggestion brought the universal but mindless cheer men like to give for mutual encouragement. When it was over, Joab reached his sling toward David. "Sir, would you care to demonstrate?"

It was clear there was nothing David would like more. He took the sling, then rejected a handful of stones until he found one to his liking. "See?" He held it up for the class. "Round, smooth," he tossed it lightly in the air. "About this weight."

He fitted it in the sling. "The top right leaf of that fig

tree," he said and began to whirl the sling, slowly at first and then faster until it whipped and sang in the air.

He did make a glorious sight, whirling that sling in his Philistine armor. But that was not what made my heart stop. I realized it was *my* fig tree he was aiming for. I shouldn't have worried. Not without reason is David's slinging legendary; he could hit a single feather on a hawk in flight even in old age. The stone whistled as it flew past and the single leaf with no more than a finger's breadth of twig fluttered down to the ground below me. The audience whooped and applauded. Worship is the only word for what I saw in Amnon's eyes.

"Thank you, sir," said Joab. "Now, men, who can tell me when the use of the sling is strategically important? Prince Amnon?"

"In the hands of the skilled slinger," Amnon recited, "it has a range greater than most bows."

"Good. What else? Yes, Amnon?"

"It is especially useful for siege work."

"Why?"

"Because of its great accuracy when shooting uphill."

"Good. Anything else? Amnon again."

"Always Amnon," quipped the boy near my feet.

"Certainly we mustn't forget economy of ammunition," Amnon replied.

David laid a proud hand on his firstborn son's shoulder, and Amnon glowed. "I'm glad you mentioned that last part," the king said. "It puts me in mind of the time I faced Goliath . . ."

Now we were all obliged to hear that one again. However great the feat of shepherd boy against giant with an iron spear like a beam, after hearing it in all its detail standing on a hillside in the heat of the day, Amnon alone could still fix his father with unadulterated awe in his gaze.

"Thank you, sir," Joab said more than once before the tale was done. After he said it for the last time, he continued: "Well, men, shall we give it a try?"

Soon the hillside before me was cleared and the dry clumps of grass to my right shivered and shattered with the

impact of many flying stones. For all his command of theory, Amnon's practice was far from brilliant. At his first try,
the stone dropped from the pouch and hit him on the shoulder. An older boy stopped to give him instruction. From the
pointing and stopped activity on the part of the others, I
could tell that this was the cause for mirth. No doubt this
flaw was simply a matter of tension in the presence of his
father, for I had often seen my stepbrother sling, not out-
standingly perhaps, but adequately. Amnon picked up the
offending stone and moved off away from the taunting and
out of my view to the other side of the ridge to try again.

The next time I saw my stepbrother, his father had him by
the shoulder. "Now when I was your age . . ." I heard. Then,
"That's how true men are made."

As soon as he was able, Amnon escaped from his father's
heavy hand to the rear of the troops. I saw a violent red glow
in his cheeks.

Now Joab called for practice with shield and spear. "As
soon as the rains make water holes and war possible once
more," he said, "our king plans to move out into the desert
against the Amalekites. Though slings may be useful for
causing long-range confusion in the enemy hordes, the
Amalekites build no walled cities and most of the fighting
will be hand-to-hand in the open plains."

The spear master stepped forward. He was a son of Naphtali with legs like cedar and arms like giant bundles of
spears. I truly feared he might snap some of the boys' thin,
wiry arms as he positioned them properly with the patience
of a wrestler moving his opponent.

David did not set much store by trainers, particularly
spear trainers. "War comes naturally to a healthy boy," he
said. "When I was a boy, every stick was a sword. They
couldn't keep me from hacking and stabbing everything in
sight. A few good lashings from the old man and then
defense, too, is second nature. They ought to be sent out
with the flocks to see how naturally . . ."

While we listened to this lecture, I noticed Amnon's face.
The glow in his cheeks was still brilliant, only now in desperate excitement rather than shame. He liked this form of

practice. He liked the control of specific instructions one could follow for each minute movement. He liked the art, how like dancing it was. It suited well the lithe, slim body he had from his mother and he knew it—at least, he could sense it much as a young girl may sense that she is beautiful.

Most of the boys were older than my stepbrother and had been handling spears much longer—some had even killed men with them. But of them all, Amnon was the only one the Naphtali master could pass with a nod or sometimes even as much as a smile. The others had to have their arms and legs wrenched into proper position.

I could see by the direction of Amnon's poses and his feints that he hoped more than anything that David would recognize his skill and take away the shame of the slinging. But this pretense at warfare was growing tedious for David. "Yes, but spears are what Goliath had. Yes, but can they hit the mark with all this fancy footwork? Can they kill their man? That's what I want to know." The king gave some orders and sent a pair of runners for something to liven the games.

For David's satisfaction, the training moved from posing to throwing at a mark and at this, too, under the nodding of the great bull head of the son of Naphtali, Amnon was not the worst. He did not have the strength others could put behind their volleys, and the weapon fell short, but his movements were graceful and true. I settled back into the shrinking shade of the fig tree to watch him with pleasure.

Yet David was only too relieved when his men returned. He said aloud how glad he was to be spared further shame as he watched his firstborn son, the beginning of his strength, miss the mark repeatedly. Between them, David's men brought two other men with them, prisoners stumbling with their elbows fiercely bound in thongs behind their backs. And then I could see what diversion David planned.

The two prisoners were tied squatting back to back beneath the target standard so that their heads were a little lower than the mark, but not much, less than two cubits.

David addressed the recruits who stood, holding their

weapons gingerly in their hands. "Now, these prisoners are two Israelites."

"Which tribe?" asked one of the hostage boys warily.

"Well, we can't really tell, can we? Since their beards and heads have been shaved in disgrace and they wear nothing but a grimy loincloth."

"What's their crime?"

"Rebellion."

"Rebellion?"

"Suspicion of rebellion, shall we say? There's unfortunately not enough evidence to condemn them outright, but there is enough suspicion."

"To use them for target practice, sir?" Joab asked.

"The object is, of course, to miss the men and hit the target above them. This will get the boys used to facing other, living men in battle and to make their aim stronger. Then, too, as a sidelight, the game might put a little of the fear of our God into the would-be rebels before they're set free for want of evidence."

Twice I saw Amnon slip a few places back in the line of boys that advanced. Each took his turn and proved, if not his grace to the consternation of the son of Naphtali, at least his unflinching accuracy. It was not just more shame for himself that Amnon feared. It was a sense of some impending doom that not he, that no one could do anything to prevent. I sensed the helplessness myself, and, in an unconscious gesture, I began to rip leaves off the fig tree and to roll them nervously between my fingers. But this was a gesture of my own impotence, like Amnon's slipping back in line. No permanent escape was to be found.

Then there was nothing for the firstborn son to do but to advance toward the mark. His cheeks burned to me like signal beacons, a cry for aid that must go unanswered. His lips between those cheeks were white, drained of blood, his eyes alive with tears. He posed, he trotted forward, all in perfect form. But as he reached the volley point, he saw his father's eyes on him.

The missile flew. Its flight seemed interminable. There was time to observe, to think, to wish, to regret. And there was time for the prisoner to shout one or two words of prayer to his god. But there was no time to stop it then, when everyone could see, as clearly as Amnon and I had been seeing since first the exercise was proposed, where the spear would hit. I closed my eyes against the impact. But then I had to look and see how one of the Israelites slumped dead without a whisper and hung like some old rag from the spear transfixed through his left eye to the target standard.

All stood breathless, voiceless, like lifeless rags themselves, waiting for a sign to tell their bewildered souls how to react. While we all waited thus in indecision, Goddess decided our reaction for us. From out of a rock at the very feet of the dead man, She called Her Messenger, a great long Snake. I breathed at once with more ease because to me this was a sign that, as the Snake brings new, rich life from its dead lifeless skin, so by a proper movement, a proper word, life and new courage might be taken from this tragedy. The crown prince had, after all, not shrunk from killing his first man, and that was generally a time of encouragement and rejoicing. If proper sacrifices of both goods and personal pride were made at once, Goddess let me know that this sorry event could be in some way salvaged.

Alas for fortune, David did not read it this way. "By God, what an evil omen!" he exclaimed, making signs against that evil.

"Kill it! Kill the devil!" cried the men and they began to pelt the creature with their slings.

"No! Stop!" I scrambled from the wall and ran to the center of the action, oblivious of either stones or Serpent.

"He must be taken alive." I was by now so close to the poison fangs, the fangs grown angry by the raining stones and startling noises, that one strike would finish me. The men's activity was suspended once again.

"A jug! Something to put him in!" I called. I could not wait to see if my order was obeyed, for the Snake had raised up a quarter of his length and was swaying, dancing, testing my distance with his tongue. He swayed and I stepped as he swayed, fixing my eyes like fishhooks into his. He swayed and I stepped again, taking his movement into my body until it became mine and I felt myself become the controller. Then I began to sing the high, soft song of the Snake Charm. High and soft in ancient words I did not understand but that came to me. I could not now write out for you the syllables I sang, so high and soft in the language of Serpents, but they always come to me again whenever I need them. High and soft, high and soft I sang. With the words came the Serpent's name. He was called Father of Shadows. I called him by that secret name in my song and so gained complete control of the dance. Then, still swaying and singing, I stepped closer and closer. Slowly, carefully, I swayed down to his level and kissed his cool, hard head.

Flash, flash. The singing and swaying ceased. His great tail, almost black with his watered spots, thrashed like a whip against my legs and I caught my breath at the pain. But still I held him tightly. In my hands, well covered with fig-leaf stains, I held him just behind the head, so tightly that his jaws were opened and drops of poison forced from his needlelike fangs. He panted until the fig juice soothed him of his terror.

Then at last I could look up and around for the jug. Someone had emptied a great pitcher of his drinking water and Father of Shadows slipped almost gratefully into that cool, dark, moist interior. I stopped the hole with a stone and then walked straight off the hill and back into town without a word.

I might have taken that moment of triumph to say some few words to my captive audience. Some words of warning to those who would carelessly murder Messengers of Life, as carelessly as they murder men, some word of consolation to Amnon. But though I was Snakesleeper, to those eyes that saw evil in a Serpent, I was at best only David's stepdaughter and at worst a witch. Let them recover their pride on their own and decide what best to do with a day so darkened by ill omen. They did not need me and my Snake in a jar to tell them how to pay their blood money nor to bury the dead.

▣ XXII ▣

ABIGAIL WAS LIVID and it made her seem fatter than ever. David had sent her to discipline the harem, me in particular. My mother met her at the door.

"I don't care," Abigail said, "if you let your daughter run wild and get blacker than she already is. I don't care if her running loose is scandal from Dan to Beersheba. I don't even care if the crown prince killed a hundred men— Ahinoam's scrawny Amnon, though, I doubt it. All I want to know is, does that girl of yours have a snake in here? A snake in my harem, I won't have it. Remember what happened to Michal."

"I remember," my mother said when I'd translated for her.

"Does she have a snake? I'm asking you."

"I didn't want her to bring it here." My mother spoke the truth—she had insisted I get rid of him. She was afraid of stirring up just such trouble with the first wife. So far I had managed to cling to the water jug with profuse tears and pleading, but Abigail's coming made me cower with my treasure beneath a rug.

"I don't want to know what you think or don't think of it. I know what I think of your daughter and all I want to know is, does she have that snake in here now?"

"Come in and see for yourself." My mother stepped to one side.

Abigail was about to march in the room but then she stopped. The chances were too great that she would find what she was looking for, and she paled at the thought of snakebite. "Just tell me yes or no," she said.

"No," my mother said.

In the corner of the room where I huddled, cradling my great black Father of Shadows between my knees, my heart skipped for joy. I was going to be allowed to keep it. I even sent a polite but silent thank you to Abigail, for it was only her skittishness that retaught my mother what use there could be in keeping a Snake.

"Swear it," Abigail said. "Swear by the god of Isaac and Jacob."

"By the god of Isaac and Jacob," Mother swore without batting an eyelash. The words meant nothing to her. And seeing the great lady Abigail cowardly for once in her life brought conviction that what power I held could preserve her from the wrath of Isaac's jealous god.

Abigail snorted, her satisfaction puffed up with pride if nothing else. Then she stormed away and Mother turned to me with a finger raised in stern caution. She had lied for me over a very serious matter. I must not betray her by a too-boisterous joy.

"I'll get a hamper from the laundress to use as a cage," Mother said when the head wife was well gone, and that was the beginning of my menagerie.

From Michal and Zipporah I learned that my Snake needed daily water, a live mouse or bird every fortnight or so, that he liked the sun and air, and with this care, the great Snake thrived. Over the years, he gave me many an oracle, answered many a prayer for those who sought Goddess through me and him, and revitalized many a dying Serpent pit in long-neglected sanctuaries throughout the land. Often, when he was not too sluggish from a meal, we would sing and dance together, he and I, just for the fun of it. It was only last year that he died, full of years, and made his final message-journey to Heaven. I buried him in the sacred spot beneath Geshur's temple floor so a part of him could be with me forever.

One day when our companionship was yet very young, Amnon came and found me behind the latrine where I kept the Snake in a shadowy niche Abigail could never find. I was surprised but not a little pleased to see my stepbrother there in the harem. I had not seen him since that day he killed his first man, that day I won my first Serpent. Indeed, we had spoken maybe twenty words in all since coming to Jerusalem, since he had joined the men and could no longer play with girls and babies. Gossip told me how he fared, but of the effect of this faring on his mind I knew nothing.

"Hello," he said.

"Hello," I said. The pleasure in my voice fumbled in the nervous pause that followed.

"Well, here," Amnon said abruptly when there wasn't anything else to fill that pause. He shoved a jar at me.

I took the jar from him and started to open the lid.

"Careful," he stopped me. "They might get out."

"They?"

"Yes. Well, they're dormice, you see."

"Dormice?"

"Yes. Four of them. I found them in the stables."

Thus cautioned, I lifted the lid only a crack and, holding the jar up to the sunlight, saw the little family all curled up in one great knot of fur, sleeping through the day. Mother might make a good supper of them. "Thank you," I said politely.

"They're for your snake," he said, apologizing that my "Thank you" had not the joy in it he'd hoped for.

"Oh." I laughed with sudden brightness. "Oh, thank you!"

My mother had taught me to relish the delicacy. But Amnon's mother followed dietary laws for her god's sake and would not have taught her son so. I laughed again as I rehearsed how our communication had gone wrong. To him these little creatures we Geshurites fatten in jars in the kitchen were only food for cats and Snakes. It had taken us so long just to get over that one barrier between us that I fell silent again, fearing another.

"Do you think it'll like them?" Amnon asked.

"What?"

"It. Your snake. That is your snake in there, isn't it?"

"Who told you?"

"No one. I guessed. They told me you had to get rid of it, but I didn't believe them. I didn't want to believe that—not of you. I wanted to believe that nothing would make you give it up."

"It's a he," I said, still cautious.

"Oh. Sorry. Do you think *he* will like the dormice?"

It seemed a shame to waste a supper on the Snake when regular vermin suited him fine. But Amnon's guessing of my secret and his thoughtfulness pleased me. "Would you like to feed him one and see?" I asked.

"Oh, no," my stepbrother answered definitely.

"Don't worry. I won't let the Serpent bite you. You just have to drop the dormouse in quickly and close the lid. He'll be so interested in that food he won't even see your hand."

"You mean, alive? You drop it to him alive?"

"Yes. He won't eat a thing if it's already dead."

"No. I don't want to kill anything."

"You won't kill it. The Snake will, quickly. I've done it lots of times. There's nothing to it."

"But you're brave, Tamar."

"Not brave at all. Snakesleeper is my calling."

"You're lucky."

"Lucky?"

"To have a calling. All I've been told is that a prince must be the best. But we can't all be the best. So we must fight all the time among ourselves. And then I am . . ."

"Afraid?" I tried to supply for him.

He rejected my word fiercely. "Confused," he said. "Then I am confused."

When a child is born, until the mother knots the blue bead in the little boy's hair or hangs a charm of gold and carnelian about the little girl's neck, if it is well swaddled and padded about the hips, the stranger must ask, "Is it a boy or a girl?" That is always the first question. When a human is as yet neither good nor bad, slow nor clever, bold nor shy, cheerful nor morose, still we are either male or female. In our youth the difference is subdued as we play the same games together at our mothers' feet, dressed in similar clothes. Yet always there is that difference that is swaddled at the hips as if it were some great secret. Yet it is no secret. Though we are dressed the same, girls are dressed so because that is what girls wear. Boys are dressed so to fool the malicious spirits for whom, they are constantly told, their little lives are ten times more precious.

As Amnon's mother had taught him to think dormice no more food than if they had been stones while my mother had taught me twenty sauces one could serve with them, so his mother had taught him, in spite of the soft, round baby flesh and the little-girl clothes, to be a man, and my mother me, in spite of my dark, suntanned skin, to be a woman. The growing differences between our chests and what was still well hidden under our skirts assured me that our mothers had been right to train us so. They had been right to teach us, for how else were we to manage our womanhood and manhood creeping up on us, would we or no, if not by those rules? And yet there was a sadness in this, that two things, once so alike, as comfortable with one another as one might be with one's own reflection in an empty room, should now be so different. It was inevitable, sought for, and yet there was the sadness, as there is when all the million stars all so alike see one leave the likeness and shoot across the sky.

Is this what Amnon was saying to me? His words were confusing, from the man's world, but this is what they made me think. Perhaps, I sighed within me, there is no use we two trying to talk. We are grown too different.

"That is how things live," I told him, nonetheless. How like my mother I sound! I thought. How like a woman! I spoke again, but still my words were like ritual. "That is how things live. All things live by killing."

"I have had enough of killing. There—"

"Where?"

"On the northern hill. Where I killed— Where your pet came from—" He tried to look toward the basket, to say the name, but he could not.

I had forgotten the scene on the western hill except as the source of my pet. Amnon had not forgotten. He could not forget. The memory gnawed at him, did so day and night. The glow of humiliation returned to his cheeks, anguish stopped his words. I could say nothing.

"My sister's going to have a baby," he said after a long pause.

"Hannah? Yes, I know. David will be a grandfather. It's all the gossip."

There seemed to be some chain connecting this thought to the last in his mind, but I could not see what it might be. He did not elaborate, so I smiled encouragingly. "That's nice. She really wanted a baby."

"That's all she ever really wanted. All she ever hoped for. And now she is content."

"You'll be an uncle."

"But—"

"You'll be a father. Someday."

"But—" he repeated his single word with earnestness.

"You've only killed one man."

"But why does it even have to be one?"

"Because . . ." I said. "Because that's what men do. Boys become men, men become soldiers, and soldiers have to . . ."

"You sound just like Father," he said bitterly, and I did feel ashamed for having come up with no better reasoning than that.

"I am so tired of killing," he said again, a young lifetime full of tormented thought emphasizing each word. He began to mock his trainers in a stale and singsong voice. " 'The mace is for bludgeoning and stunning. The spear for piercing. The battle ax for splitting and cutting and hacking.' God of my Fathers! How can they talk like that? Those are men's skulls they're talking about. Men's bodies—flesh and blood like their own. And they speak so matter-of-factly about splitting and bludgeoning and hacking as if they were just so much underbrush. I can't do that."

We were different, Amnon and I. Very different. And yet I could see, like light reflected at the bottom of a deep well, something familiar and not so forbidding. "Have you told your father?" I asked him.

"You jest! Tell him that?"

"Your mother?"

"No, not her, either. She's so proud of me. Too proud of me. The firstborn son. At least, she tries very hard to be proud of me. I wish they'd both be proud of someone else for a change, Mother and Father, both of them. They're not very proud of Hannah at all. 'Well, it's about time,' they say. Having a baby, Hannah's just doing what she's supposed to do and it comes as naturally as breathing to her. To all women. I mean, Hannah is the real firstborn, after all. She was born before me. Not yet eighteen and giving her husband a child. You'd think that would be something to be proud of."

"Well, I don't know if *proud* is . . ."

"I was born and that was it. The only chance I'll ever have to be part of something . . . something that's not just a more efficient way to kill. Putting food on the platters every evening, making warm clothes for winter and drawing cool water in summer. Those are important things. Those are things that need to be done. When I was born, when I was at my mother's breast, it was all so selfish, all for me. And now I must do nothing but kill and kill until the end of the world is conquered for God and the glory of Judah. Or until I myself am killed by some other self-seeking man. I wish . . . Oh, God, how I wish . . ."

He could not speak that wish out loud. It was blasphemy. But with all my heart I understood and his tears begat tears of my own. He had never been taught it, as I had been from my birth. But with a sense deeper than learning, he had come to know Goddess's Mysteries, why it is we worship Her and why the Snakes—how She snatches life from death and holds it in Her womb with divine ferocity. That is being born again, that is springlike new life. He had felt it growing, swelling in him as I had, for men may love Her as well as women. But like some women, great with child, who think only to be attractive to their men, Amnon had tried to keep it bound tightly inside that he might be trim and comely to the world, not fruitful with the Divine.

◙ XXIII ◙

PERHAPS IF I gave him the words and the symbols, Amnon could understand the Mysteries more readily. We returned to my mother's room to sit more comfortably.

"Brother," I said, "has anyone ever told you the story of Roeh the Shepherd?"

"No."

"I thought not."

I stood up and fetched the dish of figs my mother always kept in our room. She kept them when they were in season, as now, soft and plump on the dish like women's behinds on a stone bench. She also picked them tiny and hard and kept them dried over the winter. "They keep away moths," she told the other women. "Their scent is attractive to men," she told me. "If David smells them, he will stay longer."

"Do you know this fruit?" I asked Amnon.

He couldn't have shrunk from me more if I'd brought Father of Shadows himself out of his hamper. David's people will eat figs dried, when they can't recognize them. And slowly, they're trying to take meaning from them so they can eat them ripe. But clearly, to Amnon, the meaning was still there.

"That's the fruit with which Eve tempted our Father Adam," he said.

"It's Goddess fruit."

"Fruit of the knowledge of good and evil."

"Yes."

"Please, Tamar, put it away."

"Don't you want to know good from evil?"

I had him there. He had to admit he wanted to be good. "But it's not always easy to tell."

"No, it's not."

"Like killing the prisoner."

"Like killing the prisoner. I don't know what's right or wrong there. Do you?"

Amnon shook his head.

"That's why Goddess sent Her Servant to me when he died."

"The Snake?"

"Will you eat a fig?"

"No, I don't think I'd better."

"Fine." I set the dish between us, took a fig for myself, and bit into the pink, seedy flesh. "Now, they tell a story of the beginning, when Goddess had made the world and—"

"God made the world. Men are the carpenters and the masons and the—"

"But when have you ever seen a man bring something forth of his own self?"

"What do you mean?"

"I mean, men have to have something outside themselves, wood or clay, something there to work with in order to make something. A woman creates from her own flesh and blood."

"I still don't understand."

Oh, but his god kept him ignorant! "I mean like a baby."

"Oh."

"So in the beginning, Goddess bore daughters and She and Her daughters . . ."

"Now, wait a minute. That's not true. God made the man first and then the woman to be a helper to him—from the man's rib, so you see, it was out of himself."

I thought about this for a moment. When we were younger this might have descended rapidly into a "Did not," "Did so" sort of argument. And it sounded just possible. So I asked, "Then do you have more ribs than I do?"

"Yes," Amnon said stoutly.

"Show me," I said.

Amnon was also old enough not to start a shouting match that began with "Abiathar the Levite told me so." We should have been old enough to be ashamed, but we weren't. We both rolled up our tunics and pulled in our stomach and counted each other's ribs. His hands were gentle but searching on my chest.

"See, they're the same," I said triumphantly.

"Well—I haven't been married yet."

"So when you become married, Abiathar the Levite will come and cut a rib out of you?"

"I . . . I don't think so." The idea was clearly not an attractive one to him. "No, that's not what happens at all. I've heard some of the older boys. They say . . . they say I'm to cut the bride like a knife."

"Well, I don't like the sound of that one," I said. I'd finished my fig and the discrepancies in our views were enough to keep him quiet while I continued the story.

"So the daughters of Goddess had daughters, and their daughters' daughters in the same fashion until one of them came to Her and said, 'Mother, can't you find something to liven our hours?'

"So Goddess sent the Serpent to whisper poetry and prophecy to Her daughters to enliven their hours. And Goddess made the Serpents so they could tickle the daughters between their legs and that gave them pleasure, too. And the daughters and their daughters were content for many generations. Then a daughter of Goddess came to Her again and said, 'Mother, can't You find a helper for me?'

" 'Helper?' said Goddess. 'I did it all without any help.'

" 'Yes, but You're immortal. You have all the time in the world. You can blow on the clouds when Your cucumbers are wilting and they will be watered with the rains of Heaven, whereas I have to carry water to mine. And I don't mind fighting off these lions You've created so much, but we are mortal and sometimes they do kill us. Besides, this Serpent You've sent us gives us such pleasure with his poetry and his songs, and his tickling. If I do all my work, I don't have time for my pleasure.'

" 'Ah, so that's it,' nodded Goddess wisely. So She went away and gave birth to the first man. Man was in the form of woman, but his breasts were always small and could give no milk. He was hairy, not soft, so the babies didn't like him. And he had no womb. Goddess taught Her daughters to make little men after this model and so the man and his sons were helpers for the daughters of Goddess. They carried the water for their cucumbers when they wilted and fought off the lions and got killed and so on. So that was fine, don't you see?"

"Not fine for the men," Amnon suggested.

"It was fine," I insisted, "until the first man went to Goddess and asked—"

"Men don't ask boons of a goddess."

"Of course they do. They do now in Geshur where I was born and they certainly did then, when there weren't any gods."

"How could there not be gods?"

"There weren't, that's all. The man went to Goddess and said, 'It isn't fair. You've given Your daughters wombs so all the children are theirs. You've given them breasts so they can feed their children and see themselves carrying on to eternity, whereas I cannot. You've given them the Snake for poetry and pleasure, and I have none. Have mercy, Mother, and treat Your children equally.'

"Well, so long and loud did he cry that if Goddess were to get any rest, She would have to answer his requests. She gave him a Serpent of his own and attached it to his body where a woman has a womb."

Amnon folded his hands in his lap when I said that.

"Now, Goddess was careful not to make this Serpent as good as the woman's. It couldn't give him poetry and it couldn't make him prophesy. It did not, like the Serpent, hold the key to life in his skin, death in his tooth. But the man could give the daughters of Goddess pleasure, although he could as yet take none for himself. And Goddess created gods for the man, lesser than Herself, but good enough. They are Her Helpers, lords of the seas and the rivers and the thunder and so on. These gods would give men their poetry and their prophecy.

" 'But,' She said to the man and the gods, 'I will not give you these figs to eat, for they are Our secret, My daughters and mine.'

"Then, one day, Goddess and Her daughters were sitting in the temple eating figs. Now, it was the figs that allowed the daughters to take pleasure and taught them the mysteries of bringing forth children. It was the leaves of the fig that allowed the daughters of Goddess to handle the Serpent for the life in his skin without suffering death from his bite. That is the secret of this fruit, and Goddess and Her daughters were laughing about it on this day and about men's ignorance. And Roeh the Shepherd, who had come into the temple courtyard to get a drink from the jug by the door, happened to overhear them. So when Goddess and Her daughters went off to dance and sing and play with their pretty babies in their groves, Roeh sneaked into the Holy of Holies and stole the fruit. When Goddess returned, She found Roeh dancing like a drunkard, like one of them, wearing an apron of fig leaves about his loins, so She knew what had happened. She was livid and changed Roeh into a scorpion. He may prick you by your water jug at night to this day, or when you play at shepherd in the fields. But for the figs, it was too late. Roeh had already eaten of them and shared them with his brothers. The minute the seeds cracked between their teeth, not only did they understand like women how children are made, but they gained a part in the creation. They also gained the pleasure. So it is to this day."

"That's not the story I heard," Amnon said. "That's not the story at all. I heard that the Lord 'put enmity between the woman and the Serpent.' "

"Yes, well, the other gods would like to take the sacred Messengers from us. But Goddess promised us as long as we keep our friendship, we will have the upper hand. If we let them take the Snakes, who will keep the men from taking their pleasure and then abandoning the daughters of Goddess with their children and all the work as well?"

"A man wants children," Amnon said "as much as a woman. A man can't be a king without sons."

"Perhaps, but he has the choice of which children to accept and which to reject. Without the Serpents, a womb has not such choice. As long as we have the Snakes, too, Goddess is with us in the Earth. You see, when Roeh stole the Secret, Goddess removed Herself to Heaven so men wouldn't try to take their pleasure on Her. Only once a year, She descends to the temple, makes a man a God, and then He can enjoy Her, and She Him. Then Their power goes out into all the fields of the land. In His brow, the rain clouds thunder. The grain grows from the head of Her hair, the trees bear fruit like Her Womb, the springs spill water like Her Breasts."

"You speak as if she is not just the Queen of Heaven but as if she were indeed the very soil beneath our feet."

"So She is. And the air we breathe and the water we drink."

"Then the God of my Fathers is master over her because he is 'the Lord of all the earth and the fullness thereof.' He is above dirt and dust and mud. Like a good wife, they all bend to his command. He may cut them, like a knife."

"That is what men say when they don't want to hear Goddess. That's what they say when they want to grab the Serpent for his Life."

"Our prophet Moses had a staff he could turn into a snake, then grab by the tail, and it would become a harmless staff again."

"Perhaps he knew Snake Secrets, then. But most men who reach for the strong life of the Serpent in the tail forget about how that life curls around and becomes the bite of death. Now, are you hungry?" I offered him the figs again.

My stepbrother touched the dish, then pulled back his hand. "I don't think I'd better."

"Why?"

"My father . . . my father wouldn't be pleased." There

was the high pink color in his cheeks I had seen on the
western hillside.

"You know, it is difficult for us when the Serpents are
ignored. But I think it is difficult for you as well."

"How do you mean?"

"Take me, for instance. When your father's god is setting
the standard, I am rejected because I am less fair than the
rest in his eyes—"

"You're not!" Amnon protested.

"The envoys from Joppa certainly thought so, when they
saw things through his eyes."

"I don't think you're so plain."

"Well, you're used to my looks. They've grown on you
over the years."

"No. It always pleases me to see how you are changing
and growing up and . . ."

"But imagine how it would be to be some foreign prince
come courting and to have David try and pass me off on
you."

"I don't think it would be so bad. For the prince. But it
would be for those of us left behind."

"You're kind. But obviously it's a chore David most tries
to avoid. My skin—I'm dark—"

"But comely," Amnon said, "as the tents of Kedar."

"I'm supposed to be the poet," I teased.

"Yes. And when are you going to compose a poem for
me? You promised, remember?"

"I remember. Someday. That's the first line of it right
there. 'I am dark but comely as the tents of Kedar.' I'll work
on it some more from there. But remember. You promised,
too. You said you'd marry me."

"You said you didn't want to get married."

"Well, I don't want to kill the lions on my own."

"You could, Tamar, you could. You could kill a man and
not flinch."

"So can you. You are your father's son."

"Is that a curse?"

"When I am a mother, I don't want to be killing. I don't

want to try to juggle the baby on one hip and a buckler on the other."

The image seemed so contradictory to him that he laughed and felt it no harm to promise, "Very well, if you become a mother, I'll fight your lions for you."

"And when I become a mother," I promised him, "you shall be a father. As I hold the child, so you shall hold me."

"You'll let me hold our child myself, won't you?" he asked, pleaded almost. "Don't shoo me away as Mother did Father."

"I shall be angry if you don't hold it. And feed it bits of fruit and bread when it has had my milk."

"Yes, well." He shrugged it all off with one movement of his shoulders. "I'm too young yet to marry."

"I'm not. They'll find some blind man who'll take me soon if—if you don't."

Amnon laughed nervously at his helplessness. He had not much more say in such things than I did. We came away knowing one thing, if only one thing, for sure. That is, that as Heaven created them, so we loved them, male and female. We wished we could be both at once, and now that we had learned that that could not be, we became both, each through the other.

We were young and full of new-polished hope.

I took Amnon then back to feed Father of Shadows and, as I had given the Snake nothing but water for nearly two weeks, he was brief with the little dormouse. We could even smile about it afterward and comment how the male snake looked pregnant with the great bulge of sustenance inside him.

Amnon and I, as anyone will, searched the night skies and caught our breath at the glory of a shooting star. But, nonetheless, we admired and were grateful for the monthly regularity of the moon.

That evening in our rooms I asked Mother if I might not be initiated that coming spring.

Mother looked away from something she was making for Absalom startled and blinked her eyes as if she had been so busy watching her son grow strong and healthy and handsome all this time that she had forgotten that her daughter, too, was growing.

"Well," she said. "We'll see. Goddess must choose you first. You may not choose Her. But perhaps She may come to you before next spring festival. Then, of course, you may become initiate."

"Thanks, Mama," I said, and I kissed her. Then she looked even more startled, for there was more than just "daughter" in my lips. She had felt—I had been unable to conceal the quivering—the taste of "lover" there.

◉ XXIV ◉

GODDESS DID VISIT me that winter and brought the Blood Mystery to me for the first time as I had known by a tenderness on my chest and a warmth in my heart that She would. Come the end of spring, however, Mother did not go with me to sponsor my initiation. Absalom again.

This time it was his hair. Actually, my brother's hair was frequently an excuse for trifling in our apartments. Mother loved nothing better than to comb and dress and oil and crimp and fondle his hair. She could sit thus engaged all day if one let her. Such a look of worshipful transport would come over her when he would lay that glorious head of his on her knee. She would take the thick, glossy curls one by one and caress them about a finger, all the while crooning to him in the gentle Geshuri tongue as if the blue bead of dependency and boyhood had, by some miracle that defied time, been allowed to stay knotted in his locks forever.

Absalom gave her this pleasure with the same gesture of reward with which women give their sons sweets for good behavior. He was fully aware of how well the simple act of combing kept her passion for him aroused beyond all sense

of motherly love, her soul curled about his own fingers as
surely as she curled his hair about hers. He also used the
ritual as a weapon against me, as a wedge between Mother
and myself whenever it occurred to him that we might be
growing too close. I knew this was true from the way he
watched me from the pillow of Mother's knee. His neck
would be loose, his eyelids heavy to give the impression that
he had been curried into total flaccidity. But always the eyes
beneath those lids were watching me with ferocity, prodding
for the slightest flush of jealousy with which to expose me.

I began to know I would go to this most important ceremony of a young girl's life without my mother only the day
before it actually took place when, with fancies of a painted
veneer, a false yet showy womanhood to come, I sat down
before Mother's cosmetic table. I looked in the mirror, gaz-
ing at the mystery of my face for a long time. Then I tried
a little red to make a pout of glamour with my lips. It did
not add to the mystery, so I tried a smudge of kohl as well.
The frame of my hair, hopelessly natural and limp, remained a disappointment. It was then that I found a very
small cruse I had never noticed before. It was lavishly decorated, set with precious stones and a silver filigree. But what
it contained was more valuable still. It was filled with gold
powdered as fine as air.

"Mother, what is this . . . ?" I began with delighted awe.

But before the visions of my possible own use grew at all
clear, I knew how I would be answered. "By Goddess,
Tamar. Don't breathe or you will puff it out all over."

I knew then that I should never have asked. I should never
have either hoped or assumed. This was a time of mourning
for those who served Goddess, when the only ornament one
permitted oneself was ash and mud upon the head. But for
those who worshiped David's god, it had become the fashion, set by the priests who had it as an ancient command
directly from Heaven, that this should be a time of great
vanity of headdress. Absalom, whose hair grew like weeds
around a well, boasted one year's growth down to his waist.
To this phenomenal weight he liked to have Mother add
unguents and a glittering layer of gold dust for the day of

polling, when men ritually cut their hair and presented its weight in offering to the god. None could make the show of matched offerings that Absalom could; by the time he was grown, the weight of his polled hair was two hundred shekels by the king's weight. I suddenly saw that because of my brother's vanity, I would not have my mother's company in Topheth for the days of my initiation.

The sun was setting to begin the first day of the fast. I shivered with nervousness, shifting from foot to foot, unable to sit for more than a few moments at once in anticipation of the opening rites to come. Mother seemed slow and distracted as she prepared a little packet of cakes and a jug of oil for me to take as an offering. I had wanted to be first at the shrine, but Mother knew that much of the effect of the first night comes from walking in the darkness into a mass of huddled, weeping forms that make it seem as if the stones, the hillside, the very air, all creation itself were mourning for the vanished Son. And she wasn't so negligent that she wanted me to miss this profound impression.

Soon enough she helped me tear my garments, undo my plain hair, and sprinkle it with ash instead of gold while she recited some short songs of mourning. I noticed as she bent to me that there were fine networks of wrinkles beneath her eyes. Even thick layers of kohl could not disguise them. She was getting older. I was supposed to be thinking of the death of Goddess's Son, but it was of my mother's death I thought, and of how I should be truly alone after that, suffering worse than in a famine, grown woman or not.

It was this thought more than anything that made me begin to weep. The rites of the groves are made for a divine purpose. They take the blurred images and emotions mortals struggle with from day to day and act them out plainly before our world-fogged eyes that we might see clearly what our lives are. I told myself with firm words to keep my upper lip from quivering, that I was come of age at last and that this is what it was supposed to be like, hard as it might seem. The divine, eternal Mystery of womanhood was blooming within me now, passed from Mother to me. I had to hold out my hand to others now, not fumble for the one so knotted up in Absalom's hair. I was indeed moving into the situation that Mother had held for so long. I could not hope to be the beautiful woman she had been. But then, neither could she be anymore in this life.

Mother patted me out the door, tears smearing her kohl and emphasizing the wrinkles all the more. She bade me say a prayer for my little brother. "And one, too, for me," she added as an afterthought.

I entered the Great Void. I'd been too excited to eat at noon and now I wished I had, for there were another three days of fasting ahead of me and the cakes staining my kerchief with their warm grease smelled very tempting. Knowing they were not for me made the scent graze my insides raw and leave me hollow as a water jug on its way to the well. It made me weep all the more.

Meeting Zipporah at the gate could not cheer me, for if there was a soul who relished wholeheartedly in mourning, it was hers. She was to be my sponsor in my mother's stead, but I could see I'd be given no comfort from her until the whole ordeal was over. Sobbing quietly together, we left the solace and light of the city setting itself down to supper and made our way (lampless, for lights are forbidden to mourners) around and down to the Valley of Topheth as if, in Goddess's footsteps, we were descending into the Netherworld.

The shrine in Topheth had been, to all intents and purposes, deserted since our arrival with David in Jerusalem. The gold and marble images were in David's treasury, and the priestesses and hierodules, those who give their bodies to help men to union with Goddess, lived now within the town walls for fear of David's soldiers. But even David couldn't keep the pilgrims away when the endless days of summer drought to come and cloudless winter days past put fear and trembling in the people's hearts. In twos and threes they came, women and girls leaving their homes, entering the bosom of the Earth. Men would bring the children later, for the joyous time, when God and Life returned. But the sorrow was for the women alone.

Zipporah and I were met underground by a living wall of worshipers that sobbed like some monster of darkness breathes with heavy, belabored breath. We sat down and became one of its stones, watching and wailing the whole moonless night for the young Hero that Death had snatched from his Mother's arms, leaving the earth dry and barren. We emulated his Mother, careless for Herself and for the plight of the mortals She sustains.

I may have slept against Zipporah's shoulder; the darkness and the drone of weeping lulled and confused my sense of time. But at dawn, all sleep was forgotten. The high priestess stood and made the secret sign by which all initiates, Zipporah among them, knew to rise and enter the inner sanctuary with her. I was left alone and the sun rose like hot grease poured over a night-chilled, iron-colored landscape. The wall of dehumanized mourning shattered with the spell-breaking light. We were meant to continue mourning, but it was different now that one could see that those all around one were women, farmwives and merchants' daughters, old widows and wine mistresses, and not disembodied spirits as night had led one to believe.

Then I was required to watch no longer. The high priestess with Zipporah at her side returned to view, their mourning rags exchanged for the first layer of their holy festive dress, white on black, Goddess colors, giving us a hint that some great resurrectional magic was being worked where we could not see it.

My name was called, and my secret name. I arose, left the hillside, and prostrated myself at the feet of the two women, speaking as I did the necessary words: "In the Name of Goddess, the Merciful, the Compassionate, I, a woman adrift in the world of men, beg admittance to Her holy Mysteries."

The high priestess stepped forward and lifted me up. "O Snakesleeper," she said in a voice that would not carry to the others watching on the hillside. "Rather should I ask to learn the Mysteries from you."

She bent and kissed the Serpent skin about my waist. I heard a murmur among the crowd as they wondered at her reverence.

"Do what must be done," I assured her. "My Snake Gifts

are small and weak while I remain a weak and uninitiated girl. What is the Mystery of the Snake to the Mystery of the Woman?"

The priestess was young and had not had time to gain the ease and self-confidence that comes with years at the post. Her predecessor's deposition had been untimely—when David had invaded the sanctuary and pushed her into the brazier. She herself had only just begun her training at the time. And since then there had been these several years when, for fear of David and his men, her duties had not been carried out daily, but only at the most important seasons. Her hierodules had retreated to the wine sellers', she to her sister's house in town, where she cared for the children and washed laundry most of the time. I could smell the ointment with which she had desperately—and in vain—tried to make her hands presentable for this ceremony.

I knew that if my presentation to Goddess were to have true effect, the priestess must be fearless and certain of what she did. I let her know that this was so, she realized it, and, with new command, she led me behind the brazier platform to the entrance to the Most Holy Place. There Zipporah threw a heavy veil over my head so I could see nothing this first time I stepped across the threshold and inside the very Womb of Great Earth.

I was the only one to receive initiation that year. Women were keeping their daughters from it for this and that reason, mostly because they feared that under David's new ways a girl's chances for marriage would be spoiled "if she knows too much."

> There are three things which are too wonderful for
>   me, yea, four which I know not:
> The way of an eagle in the air;
> The way of a Serpent upon a rock;
> The way of a ship in the midst of the sea;
>   And the way of a man with a maid.

Popular proverb makes these the greatest mysteries on earth and, naturally, these are what initiation before Goddess, in basic terms, deals with. Every child of four has been told in answer to his persistent "How?" and "Why?" the story of creation. He knows the story of the great battle against the chaos of the Sea that brought the world into being. And he knows the story of our first parents: how Goddess sent First Serpent as Messenger to the Man, who was too full of self-importance and would not listen, and then to the Woman, who was teachable and of listening ears. The Woman, our ancestress, it was who first ate of the sacred fruit of the fig tree and who learned to bring all there is of knowledge and wisdom and culture to our necessarily brief lives that would otherwise have been dismal and hopeless indeed. Or if the child doesn't know this version, at least he knows the story that David's priests recite, which is much the same but for the disparaging twist that would make the gaining of all this knowledge a crime against humanity.

In initiation we are given the powers of womanhood, a new secret woman's name, and symbols of our future. We are given certain rights, privileges, and duties that, yes, one can pass through life without and never notice she's missing. Life will not be any longer for me because I was initiated. I am not fooled into thinking that. (It may indeed be shorter if I should reveal too much of what I know.) Nor will I be wealthier because of it—wealth does not concern Our Lady. There are those who say I may expect more children than the uninitiated, or an easier time bearing them, or an easier life after death. Well, I have no proof of such miracles and they are not so important to me.

And yet, though they may never miss it in their lives, I have a sense that the uninitiated merely skim the surface of the great pool of life. On the surface are only green slime and insect eggs. To get pure water, and undefiled, one must let one's jug drop deep.

Granted, there is pain involved. A girl does not lose her girlhood without pain. Zipporah encouraged me at the time to yell as much as I needed to—none would think me amiss—and I'm sure my screams were heard out on the hill where the uninitiated sat in ignorance. They were told Serpents were biting me or some such nonsense. A Snakesleeper does not scream for Snakebite, you may be assured. One must either be pained in this way—killed to new life by women who understand, having suffered the same themselves—or one must be made to suffer later, on her wedding night, by a man who understands nothing but a love of his own power. This is blasphemy against the open giving of Goddess, who allows each woman to give or take as much control and pride in her own life as she would.

And then, at last, after three burial-like days, I was dressed in new robes, my hair done up plainly but fresh and anew, and my Serpent skin knotted proudly across my breast that could now by rights be given that term of fertility. I had become a woman and was allowed to behold the greatest Mystery of all, "The way of a man with a maid."

· XXV ·

Araunah King of the Jebusites had not been put to death when David had conquered his city from him. His position and his great furnished palace had been usurped and he now lived with what was left of his royal harem after David had picked it over in a compound that had once housed the overseer of his threshing floor. Now he served as David's overseer there instead.

Imagine what ill luck, what insult to Goddess, to have a man of such circumstances, defeated and dispossessed, continue to accomplish the shrine's spring sowing, its Sacred Marriage. Obviously, such a thing could not be. Yet David, who took over everything else, could not be induced to take his proper place as King in the Great Bed, particularly after what happened with Michal when the Ark was moved. And so Araunah's son, a young man full of promise and named Melchizedek, was chosen to come to his inheritance this one sacred time a year.

High priestesses are often allowed to get terribly old before they are retired from this duty to that of matron. But this one was still young and pretty and well matched to the

Groom, Araunah's son. It was the fourth year these two had come together. Two of those years had produced children and the priestess, when she had handed her robe embroidered with sheaves of wheat to Zipporah, displayed the sheaflike proofs of the stretch of her fertility across her belly. The Groom's robe was worked with stylized bolts of lightning and the hangings of the bed with all creatures and plants of the earth.

He was like a husband returning from a far journey, she like a wife on her first night after childbirth impurity. Reciting their beautiful call-and-response verses, the couple stepped away from the circle of initiates, up to the platform from opposite sides as if moving away from us, up and into the realm of Gods. One almost wished, as Melchizedek himself seemed to, that the priestess could be made his legitimate wife, the children his heirs and not assigned by necessity to Goddess's service. But such blasphemous thoughts were lost in the overwhelming joy of the moment.

The sacred union was accomplished, the secret, ritual words of blessing and thanksgiving spoken, and we initiates embraced one another. Then we hurried the Bride and Groom into their loose robes so they could make their triumphant appearance to the anxiously waiting mourners. I heard the cheers, the shouts of joy, what sounded like rain as the crowd opened their bundles of offerings and showered them down upon the couple. I waited anxiously for Zipporah to join me so that we could leave the confines of the shrine in our own festive garments together and go out and join the celebration. But something was detaining her. I looked back impatiently to see what it might be.

Across Zipporah's face like a smear of ash she had forgotten to wash off was a look of great evil. I followed her glance to the center of the Great Bed and likewise felt the evil sweep over me. The Bride had been unable to retain the seed. Like rain in evil years, it had fallen not on the plowed fields, but on dead stone and dust.

No one but we two noticed the calamity. Even the two major players had been so thrilled to be in each other's arms again that it mattered not to them if things did not go with orthodox perfection. Goddess feelings can so overwhelm one that rational accomplishment of what She requires becomes impossible. That is a problem mortals cannot ever completely conquer, and we must stand in fear and awe before Her because of this.

"Goddess shield us." Zipporah made some brief signs against evil and I copied her. Then she hurried out to try and stop the proceedings. It was too late. The ass had been brought and mounted. Beneath a canopy of waving palm fronds, the Groom had already begun to lead his Bride in the triumphant procession up into the city and then through the streets so that all might know of the victory that had been achieved that day. Everyone would know. Had the rite been completed, they might have been assured in their knowledge of Goddess's protection as they made their announcement. There had been this sign of warning given and it was going unheeded.

David, I thought. David and his jealous god would learn of this, of another's glory. With Serpent Sight I saw the danger clearly. In previous years, the procession had been contained by the people's fear. But this year the people had grown easy and comfortable with a lack of persecution. I heard no caution outside the shrine. This year it was their city and they would return to celebrating as they had always done, never thinking, as I did, that David was feasting a gold-dusted son of his own. He would little endure the triumph of the son of a rival.

"There's nothing for it, then. It will be as Goddess wills." Zipporah set her mouth firmly and grimly. She picked up a palm frond and, as was the prerogative of initiates, moved to the donkey carrying Tammuz the Bridegroom and his holy Bride. She walked with her hand resolutely on his flank while others, throwing off their weeds of mourning for the beast to trample, jostled with songs and danced to touch so much as the end of his fly-flicking tail to bring them good luck.

I did not have the lust for doom Zipporah had. I could not bear to follow and see in flesh the calamity I saw only too clearly in my mind's eye. I retreated back into the shrine.

I did what I could to dispel the evil, but repurification required the High Priestess herself, and I doubted I would ever see her alive again. I was shaking so much that I don't know whether what I managed to do was of any effect at all.

As soon as I could no longer hear the singing and shouting and there was room in my brain to think of something else, I decided to go and investigate the Snake pit. The air would be different there, cool, narcotic, and unearthly. There is always comfort for me among Goddess's Messengers, and I sought it now with a desperation.

I received no answer to my first song at the mouth of the pit. Well, perhaps they don't know my voice, I thought, and tried again. The season of the spring festival is the season of their lovemaking as it is of ours. One could expect knots of squirming infants hatched just last fall, no less deadly or wise for all that they look like no more than snipped ends of yarn on the floor of a weavers'. When I heard no signs of such activity below me, I pushed back the bar and opened the door. This should only be done by the temple's Snake oracle, but Topheth had no such woman now, and I am Snakesleeper and know all Snakes. I sang again and, when there was still no answer, I returned to the main part of the temple. I helped myself to a handful of protective fig leaves, then I trimmed a lamp and returned to the pit.

There had been a pit in Jerusalem since time began, yet the stairs were as if newly carved in the solid bedrock, for few had ever dared to use them. Ten broad, shallow steps brought me to the level of the gold and blue and crimson that made a floor of offerings at least another step deep— sandlike beads and rings, mostly, for they had to be small enough to drop between the grating that dappled the ceiling over my head and the floor at my feet with halflight. I could not stand up to my full height on that floor.

I could smell their droppings mixed with offered incense left over from a hundred ages, but I could see no Serpent. I tried the song once more and ended it in the middle with a sigh. The pit had been too long without a mistress, that was plain. Without human hands to bring them mice and water, without a voice to sing to them, the Snakes had left the place as only Serpents can—through solid stone, if need be—and gone to favor other spots. Or gone in all directions to haunt the farmer in his field, the maiden at the well, the child at his play, like the demon of the midday sun. If such things are not honored, they turn evil. So far had Goddess deserted Jerusalem for a lack of rulers who love Her.

As I turned to leave with a heart of lead, the swirl of my lamp sent the shadow of a giant Serpent dancing across the wall. I caught my breath, for the creature was in full striking pose, between me and the steps, and I hadn't the presence of mind for several breaths to begin to charm him. When at last I did, he didn't respond, but continued to pose, still the instant before a strike. He senses my fear, I thought desperately and, thinking that, I could do nothing to give myself courage. Instead of controlling my fear, it began to control me. To be struck in such a state could be deadly, even for a Snakesleeper, for the blood would course quickly to every limb without control. I stepped forward rigidly only to keep from stepping backward and allowing myself to become hopelessly cornered. Still no lightning flash of pain. I stepped forward again, and again. Now another step would put me in the center of the Serpent's tense coil. I stopped my song.

I took a deep breath and held it, knotting the air into the lowest part of my belly. I bent to kiss the reptile head in submission, my lips as cold and taut in anticipation of pain as pitched tenting. I let out my breath. The Snake crumbled to dust beneath that breath. He was dead, had been for a year or more. He had perished in that position, trying to strike at the source of his misery. Although it is true that Serpents hold the secret to immortality in their skins, it is also true that they do not always choose to employ it.

I recited some words of prayer for the Serpent's soul, but it was so long departed that I doubt they reached it. I covered his dust with a handful of gems and returned to the surface. Then I left the sanctuary for the first time in three days and stood alone in the clearing. The sun had set, but the western sky was smeared with light as if some great procession of timbrel and lamps were passing in the Netherworld, just below the horizon. What have they to celebrate in the Netherworld? I wondered. A still, breathless silence flung the same question back to me about David's Jerusalem. What did we ourselves have to celebrate on such an ill-omened day?

The rim of the clearing was set with the stones by which one can interpret the heavens and tell where Goddess's star will be morning and night. The moon was little more than new, but it was one of those rare nights when one could see the shadow of the entire disk just behind the lighted slip. Like a giantess, she peered over the massive walls of the city showing only so much of her face. But by the hang of her dark veil, one could tell that mourning had not eaten the beauties of her face away. In time she would return like a hierodule, full and shining, to society.

My sister devotees should have returned from the procession by now and lost their personalities of face behind anonymous veils. Throughout all that moon's month they should stand as hierodules at the shrine to receive the worship of the men. The men would come to gain their share of the fruitful magic we women had worked and kept to ourselves until then. Those women who did not draw partners after them as they passed through the town should have been standing like gilt statues in the clearing, letting the moonlight fall on the curve of their thighs or make twin infant moons of their exposed breasts. The circle of low, bedlike altars should have been steaming, sweating with use. But they were bare and cold. The evil was beyond repair and the only soul who ever returned that night was old Zipporah, stumbling down the path, for her eyes could not negotiate darkness anymore, hunting for me.

"Thank Goddess you're all right," and "A black curse on the son of Jesse," she said when she found me. Neither of us said more. I did not ask for an explanation of her curse and she did not offer one. She only threw a dark cloak over my shoulders—against the night air, or so the white of my initiate's robes would not be seen?—and took my arm to help her up the path.

Outside the gate I saw, rising like a spirit, a new pile of

stones among those crushing down on the bodies of traitors and blasphemers.

"The High Priestess," Zipporah said briefly, making a sign so her voice wouldn't call the young woman's shade up to haunt us. "For adultery."

I did not bother to protest, "But she wasn't even married." The time for logical defense and testimony was gone, if it had ever been allowed to come. I could remember the young woman's great joy earlier that day. I clung to that thought and to the memory of her humility and service and of how she had knelt to kiss my Snake's skin. She had transferred some of her power to me with that kiss and so would never really fade from my life. I never saw where or how Melchizedek fell and I did not ask.

Just before sleeping that night, I went out to see Father of Shadows and related to him all I had seen and heard that day. The thought came to me that he might well have been the prince of Topheth's pit in former days and I had been called to rescue him from a life of unsanctity, a death his striking poses would be useless against. Perhaps I was meant to return him to his proper place, but if so, the time was in a future I could not yet see.

Father of Shadows could not see that future, either, but he could tell me something of what was to come. I noticed that his water dish was empty, though I had only just filled it before I left for the rites. He was a desert snake, used to little water, who could soak up needed moisture from new fig leaves. It usually lasted him much longer than that. I filled the dish again and watched him drink it like a straw. When he could take no more through his mouth, I watched him slither into the dish and soak it up into his scales.

I poured him yet another dish and, as I set it before him, I sensed his message plainly. *Drought,* he said with a flick of his tongue. *This sacrilege will bring us drought.*

I closed the hamper lid and drank deeply from the jug, thirsty myself at the mere thought.

THREE

▣ XXVI ▣

I DON'T THINK David will ever finish his palace. New palaces, like new kingdoms, never let one be, never let one sit back and sigh contentedly: "I have finished the work God gave me to do." Once one has seen that he can build, that he can conquer, that he can take wilderness and put his stamp on it, he must forever look to the next addition, be it only a few rooms, or horizon to horizon of new land.

The new palace in Jerusalem is not like the palaces of Geshur, Joppa, or Tyre, though David did import his architects from these places and encouraged them to copy the best of what they knew. Old palaces of ancient families are hallowed in their antiquity, hallowed by the pits carved in the stairs by innumerable generations of feet, hallowed by the stains of innumerable jugs of wine being set and dripping in the exact same spot. One feels no desire to expand to the west in such a palace, for "the window to the west was always where my father stood and watched the Sea when state affairs were heavy on him." It would be anathema to fix the door in the southern hall that wobbles dangerously on its sockets because "It has always been that way. How should one know one was at home in the southern hall if it were not so?"

Just after I became a woman, David moved us from the old house of Araunah, leaving it to Cousin Joab, and established us in the new palace that he, having no feeling for the ancient alleyways, had torn down half the hovels in Jerusalem to build. The palace wasn't finished. It smelled strongly of wet plaster, and the threshold stones were slippery, fresh from the stonecutters' chisels. But we moved in all the same. David, suspecting nothing of the drought I knew was coming, and innocent as well of his own ceaseless drive to build and better and expand, promised that all would be completed by New Year and until then, there were roofs over our heads and we could very well step around the masons and their mortar.

The palace is of curious design. Women had complained to David that they needed more privacy, and privacy we got. No longer did evenly spaced and sized rooms open all onto a court so you could look across and see what Abigail was kneading up for her next party or how badly Haggith disciplined her children. No longer could the women congregate against the eastern wall in the morning and the western wall in the evening to talk about their difficulties until someone offered the bit of wool or the measure of flour or the word of sound advice that saw the problem through.

Our rooms opened on blank walls and halls, or on railings and empty air. The common court was often so far away that one did not have to be very sick or even very tired and listless to feel like keeping to one's own rooms and avoiding the succor of company altogether.

Such an arrangement turned the women dark and secretive, jealous and selfish. Since one's private rooms were now so important, it suddenly became crucial just what features those rooms had. Before one had been able to share the common room with contentment. Now women wrestled over things like a view, whitewash or ocher on the walls, noisy neighbors, an extra niche or two, and went to Abigail in droves to have the discrepancies made even. She evened them indeed, as she did everything, briefly and sharply, like a butcher dividing portions off a side of lamb with his cleaver. Those who could went beyond her to David himself, whose eye was not so mercilessly just and who promised things to a pretty leg and a tear he could not spare to Abigail's sense of the status of graying hair and years of devotion.

When Mother got an apartment within hearing of the common hall where all the young men slept, Absalom now among them, she refused to move, even when she was offered larger and airier rooms. Though Hannah got her own rooms for when she came to visit, which was often, I moved my couch in the same room with Mother, set at the same angle it had always been since we stopped sharing a bed when Absalom was born. When I was remembered at all, I was expected to be married out soon and so did not need a room of my own.

In the moving, Mother found a length of fabric.

"Oh, it's beautiful, Mama!"

"I've been saving it for years," she said, handing it to me to finger.

When I took it in my hands, I could smell the moth-killing herbs it had been pressed among.

"Years and years," she repeated with a sigh, "waiting for an opportunity worthy of its use and now, after so much waiting, its prime has come and gone for me."

"How is that possible? Just look at this wool, dyed such a rich red! Why, I'm certain there must be purple underneath."

"Yes, it came from the seaside vats of Sidon. Ah, but it bores me now. It makes me think of all the years gone by, wasted here, without its use, without an event worthy of such richness—"

"Mama—?"

"Would you like to have it, Tamar?"

"Thank you, Mama!"

She knew well how to divert me, and my youth made plans for it at once. "The date David has set to dedicate the palace is only a few weeks away."

The fabric's color said Amnon's name to me though why,

I'm not certain. He was never prone to such flashy colors; even his royal purples were more subdued. Perhaps it was that the shade was of such an unabashed purity that one kept staring at it long after the color "red" had impressed itself upon one's mind. It was a strenuous color, yet one looked to it to ease the eyes after so much duplicity and fraud in other fabrics.

Divided as the household was, I certainly did not think of Amnon at once because he and I had become such fast companions of late. And, since the tragedy of Tammuz—or rather, since my own death of girlhood to be born a woman—I had all but avoided him.

"Thank the God of our Fathers," David's other wives sighed and said, "she's finally learned some shame."

They may call it that if they care to. I describe it rather as fear—a good healthy respect such as one feels before any god—for the powerful Mysteries I had learned were part of my own body and which hung about me ever with my swelling breasts and new-grown hair like frankincense sanctifying the sacrifice. I retreated into an inner holy of holies and waited to see what use Goddess would make of me. Still, I could never feed or water Father of Shadows, nor even sit with him in the evening and whisper the secrets of my heart to him but that Amnon's name would rise from the well of my soul and be poured out in a cool and refreshing stream.

I prefer to embroider with linen because it gives greater control: it works up tighter and smoother and doesn't fuzz so much. But I knew Amnon wouldn't wear it if wool were worked with linen—part of the rules of his god. So when I was given my portion of wool from the shearing, I had the best of it sorted and sun-bleached and finely spun to a tight, long-stapled yarn as pure in white as the fabric was in red. It was to this bit of work I retired when the heat of the afternoon was too great, when the scuffle for favors among the wives was too fierce, when my quiet time of Mystery was on me.

Sometimes as I sat working the pattern that my Geshuri fingers could not keep from straying into vine leaves and doves, I could hear through the vents something of what passed in the neighboring boys' hall. I heard their versions of us all, from mothers and sisters to the latest concubine and slave. I heard their first attempts to make their own mark on the world of bartered kingdoms and treacherous battlefields. I winced at their jokes about what had become sacred to me. I learned to tell my brothers by voice. I learned what always hearing and seeing together may hide: that this one with a forceful presence had a voice as thin as reeds or as grating as slate on slate and that, hidden behind a pale, sickly exterior, this next one treasured words of deep thought and feeling.

It took me somewhat longer, but at length I learned to sense two major moods the hall could take on. The jokes and jibes were always the same, but something changed in the way they were said from one hour to the next. One was a mood of gentle good humor and the other, more brazen and open and rough and yet more tense, as if someone had come in and set all the swords blade-up on the ground and then bade the boys walk barefoot over them.

More careful listening to these moods taught me what made the difference: the one reigned when Amnon was in the room, the prince of the other, the setter-of-swords, was Absalom. Amnon as firstborn and his father's hope did manage to sheathe all swords, even when he and Absalom were in the hall together. Otherwise I think the boys would never have been able to sleep at night for the nervous jitters Absalom caused. I noticed with concern that the gentleness dwindled in frequency from week to week as Absalom's hold over the princes became greater and as Amnon spent less and less time in that atmosphere of backbiting and ugly lust it took all his strength to keep whitewashed.

Once I heard Amnon ask if he might not be spared a room of his own in this new palace, to which I also heard David's sharp reply. "No. Not until you're married," as if there was some doubt such luxury would be granted even then. "Is my son a woman, to hide away in her room like some rabbit in her hole? To grow pale and weak and a stranger to the men he must someday rule?"

I never learned where it was Amnon spent all his hours when he was not in the hall. I was only grateful he was able to find some other use for his energy besides maintaining his own against Absalom.

It was with these thoughts that I worked on the fabric. It was to be a light, sleeveless coat for ceremony on summer evenings. In a combination of care with over-haste, I once pricked my finger badly and had to add a star, a Goddess symbol, on the spot of blood just above the heart. But without further accident, I managed to finish by lamplight on the evening before the great dedication feast of David's palace.

As is the early fig among the trees,
So is my brother among the sons.

I gave the girl these words to say to Amnon that morning with the pressed and scented robe. Mother had had new sandals tooled for Absalom. She brought these out, too, and sent them over at the same time. Mother and I had to be out of our apartments very early that morning so workmen could come and excavate a grain pit for us. We rescued our best gowns from the dust and lime, dressed leisurely with Haggith next door, and went down to settle in our places for the feast even before the heat of the day was past.

On our way we passed through the courtyard where the meal was being prepared. Abigail, like one of her pots on the fire, was boiling merrily with a bounty of orders to give. We crossed on the very edge of the space, for we knew our presence was not called for. For such an important occasion all the food had to be prepared according to the strictest Israelite ritual and we knew what Abigail would say even before she said it: "I want no Geshuri hands here to make my feast impure! Hands that have offered flesh to idols, off with you!" She waved us on with the rag she used to wipe both dishes and her steaming forehead.

In former days Mother might have been frustrated by this. Now she calmly admitted that she was no longer a young wife to try and prove herself in the kitchen, nor a concubine to come parading in late so as to have more eyes upon her. Of course Mother took care with her appearance—more than ever, for her age was becoming difficult to camouflage. But the chains and rings that glared on younger women, competing with the glow of their features, and the paint and scent that were fresh, titillating experiments for them had become an inextricable part of Mother's being. A tree trunk, over time, will cover the stake that is hammered into its heart, incorporating the most irritating, the most unnatural corruption into its flesh until men can no longer pry out the stake without killing the tree.

David had caused the banqueting hall to be built in two sections. The smaller of these was roofed and partially screened off to keep the ladies decorous and yet still able to see and hear everything. The roof shaded us from the sun in the afternoon and at night from the moon, which might have had the harmful effect of madness or of interrupting our own monthly cycles by the force of its phases. The larger men's section was open to the sky so the sacrifices might rise unhindered to heaven. The banqueting hall wore its first coat of sweet-smelling reeds, donkey-packed up from the oasis of En-Gedi. When we crossed to our places, the reeds were still firm and glossy beneath our feet. When we left in the fullness of the night, they would be soft.

I sat with my cheek pressed against the smoothly carved cedar of the lattice that screened us from the men; a spiral would leave its red mark on my face when I looked up. I watched the armsbearers haggle over where to place the various standards. The golden Star of David, the tawny Lion of Judah, the blue Ark of the North, the white linen of the priests, all the rainbow of tribes, their colors like their interests clashed there, fluttering in the late afternoon wind. So would the men be when they came, unable to harmonize themselves.

The bearers, men of but humble station, were willing to go to blows to assure that their master's banner, a limp and willess proxy for the man himself, won the place that was his due. Those who had no pretensions at high rank found competition trying to outshine in humility: "No, truly. My

master is more deserving of this lowliest spot than yours,"
and "I insist" until I blocked it all out with cedar scent,
tranced, thinking on the approach of one whose banner
would be a white star on red, sealing a spot of my life's
blood between it and his heart.

As I sat, I was given another verse of the poem that would
be my poem of poems:

> He brought me to the banqueting house
> and his banner over me was love.
> Stay me with raisin cakes,
> Comfort me with figs,
> for lo! I am sick of love.

I might have been given more inspiration, but I was
forced from ecstasy with a start as incense and cymbals
announced the arrival of the king himself to begin the dedication sacrifices.

Gad the Prophet, David's seer, who was as deaf as the
Netherworld but who saw much with his eyes—like a pair of
tweezers—was there to pick through the entrails and take
readings for our fortunes. The readings were good enough,
but I for one was somewhat disturbed that this palace—a
place in which I should have to find my shelter for some time
longer at least—would be dedicated without the sacrifice of
a child. There is to this day no more beneath its floor than
a young kid, a seven-branched lamp, and a bowl of parched
grain to symbolize the life that ought to have fixed its pillars
forever. Surely a man with foresight could have found one
infant, lately born dead or one born crippled or idiot, or a
two-year-old just died of fever to lend the strength (greater
than one might think) of its sweet little life to an edifice of
such importance. Such substitutes can be used if one is
opposed to actually finding some widow or father of twelve
willing to sell their least little one to a king who is loathe to
offer one of his own as was done in ancient times.

I remembered back to my fifth year when David had
invaded Topheth and cheated Heaven of one little life that
was Heaven's due. Absalom was still not too old to make a

fitting plea to Heaven of David's wish that his house might continue forever. But I knew no such sacrifice would be offered to clear the air. It was not the way with the house nor with the god of David.

Throughout the preparations and first minor sacrifices, the princes, younger wives, concubines, and honorary guests made their arrivals, disrupting the ceremony with displays as grandiose as I had suspected they would be. Then, at the very last possible moment before the climactic knife was drawn, before the final "Hosanna" and "Amen," my handiwork stepped into the center of the doorway and its wearer stood surveying the scene.

The thought briefly crossed my mind that it was unlike Amnon to use ritual to flaunt himself in such a manner, but I knew the piece of fabric only too well. I had spent so long bent over it that when I closed them I still saw the pattern imprinted on my eyelids in red on white instead of white on red. I fancy other eyes dreamed of it that night. Every soul from Abiathar at the altar to four-year-old Ithream on his mother's knee caught his breath and stared.

The coat made twice the impact I'd expected it to, and I blushed for Amnon's sake. I knew and understood his modesty and was sorry I'd betrayed it. The coat did seem a bit longer and hence more pretentious than I had meant it to be. I'd thought him taller. Amnon would never wear such a thing for his own sake. Was it for my sake, then, that he was wearing it?

Then I saw that it was not so much the coat that caused the sensation as how the wearer wore it. Just so does a young concubine flaunt her first pregnancy. So do male hierodules dandy their earrings before the worshipers. Just so had Mother carried Absalom when he had been the gem of the harem's crown.

And then I saw only too plainly that the face below the broad headband tied with showy tails had more flesh than Amnon's sparse and carefully, almost timidly molded features. It was Absalom, not Amnon, in that coat. Because my feelings for the two of them were so different, I had not noticed until now how alike two sons of the same father could be. Amnon would probably always be taller and thinner. And Absalom had been endowed with that extra bit of devious, disarming, contentious charm that he wore over the basic mold like he did the coat, like a city wears great high walls that gleam from a distance, but that hide smelly back streets and congested courtyards on closer acquaintance. Contrastingly, Amnon lay like a border village, fresh and pure and open to rapine. Still, the selfsame mountains, as it were, formed the outline of their horizons.

Absalom made himself look like the firstborn son that night, just as a hunter may make himself look like a tree—or a Netherworld spirit may camouflage itself as anything from a bird to a wild camel for its devious purposes. Absalom made himself such that foreign dignitaries nodded to one another and whispered, "David's heir."

I whirled around to find the maid who'd delivered the coat. She was standing mouth agape, assuring me that the confusion had only come after her part. Not that she was as innocent in mind as she was in deed. From one limp hand she trailed Mother's wrap on the ground. I forced her hand up to serving position.

"Oh, no, mistress," she protested, but I knew the look in her eyes and let her go no further. She was watching Absalom with the look of a serving girl who fancies her sons dressed in purple.

"By fair Goddess," I wanted to shout at her. "The boy is not yet thirteen years old. And you would get sons from him?"

But a voice came from above the folds I had so carefully embroidered for another that made him seem twice that age. "Proceed," Absalom said with a wave of his hand to Abiathar as if he were the god himself.

The blade flashed and the animal was taken to the god so violently that a child could read ill from it. But the seer's glance was still fixed toward the doorway. He smiled and clapped his hands and prophesied great good for David and for Absalom. Well, the old man was paid to say such things.

⊡ XXVII ⊡

DAVID HAD TO be the first to make much over his third-born son, but with the certain skill Absalom knew from his first cry, he gave his father only enough of his presence to keep him craving more. With a great show of formal manners, he rose from David's feet and went to greet his mother. As he strode toward us between trellises of hands reaching out to offer him dainties or, most abjectly, themselves, my heart stumbled and I could only think—What have you done to Amnon? I remember a story they tell of one of David's ancestors whose brothers sold him as a slave for the sake of a coat.

"Son of Belial," I hissed at him through the screening, more as a spell of defense against evil than as a curse. "Why are you wearing that coat?"

"It has the star of Geshur on it," he said with even rhythm as he bent to kiss his mother's hand. "It was worked by the hand of the Princess of Geshur. I am the Prince of Geshur. Why shouldn't I, the princess's brother, be the one to wear it?"

The way he said *brother* made me draw back from the

screening in alarm. He said it as we say it in the temple, to mean lover, and I realized for the first time in my life, though I had long understood the theory, that if we had lived in Mother's kingdom, it would not have been unheard of for the king's son to marry the king's daughter because it was through her and through her alone that the royal blood was passed. Yes, I had known since first I learned to know anything that through my womb would pass the future rulers of Mother's kingdom. There is a certain term in Geshuri for this part of our natures, which translates as "the goblet." For, like a libation goblet, women of the divine blood exist perpetually at the sanctuary, and son after father, lord rising after fallen lord, must come and bow to us to drink the full cup of kingship. He takes a portion of divinity from us, whoever sips, and the gift of Geshur's palaces and fruitful hills with it. So it had been with my mother, so it must be with me.

What I had not seen until that moment was how a rough and conquering hand could snatch me from the altar and use me for a perversion, a mockery of my sacred station. In Geshur it was common for sister to wish to endow a dear brother with the kingdom she alone carries. But this was not Geshur and in Geshur I should never have had a brother like this one. He would have been taken to the brazier on the high place and burned before he'd ever learned to snatch for things that can only be given, or to tell with a fiendish accuracy what was worth the snatching from that which merely glittered like gold.

Absalom was now whispering to my mother words that caressed her like her maidservant's rubbing ointment into her aching limbs, and she sighed as he spoke as a lovesick concubine might. "See, you, daughters of Jerusalem," she longed to say aloud. "This one is mine. He comes to honor me and to kiss my hand. This one like unto an angel of the god is mine."

"What have you done with Amnon?" I hissed at him again.

"Is Amnon a string of pearls that my sister might accuse me of misplacing him?" He lightly tossed the question back to me without losing his smile, so utterly disarming. He did not even appear to stop speaking to our mother, so it seemed to me that he was capable of speaking two contrary streams at once. "Amnon is a prince and the firstborn of my father. He has legs—legs like a fig tree, as you so aptly put it, Sister, in your little poem—and he can walk wherever he chooses. I am not my brother's keeper."

"I made that coat for Amnon."

My voice could no longer be kept at a whisper. Absalom was in complete control of everything, including my emotions, which I could not even fumble for. He nodded in the direction of Ahinoam down at the head of the screen as he said, "It seems Amnon wanted to wear something else on this occasion. I only get my brother's castoffs."

Down the row of women I could see Ahinoam bent forward to the screen and, if I shifted angle, I could catch a glimpse of blue on the other side of her that told me her son was likewise paying his respects to his family behind the screen. When had he come in, then? In Absalom's shadow? Before that, with some prince or dignitary, and I had glanced over him, not seeing because I was looking for red? The blue coat he wore had served at a dozen functions before and was common and familiar, perhaps too familiar. Amnon that evening, as at any other time, was avoiding attention.

"One does better not to even speak to you," I told Absalom as I got up and began to pick my way to where Ahinoam sat and where Amnon was, speaking with her. But even of these words, I felt, my brother had complete control and was hearing just what he wanted to hear.

Absalom smiled and said, "Fare you well, Sister." My flesh crawled at that "Sister" as if he'd already reached out a hand to possess me. I rarely agree with David's policies as opposed to those of Geshur, but as I walked toward Ahinoam and her son, I sent a quick prayer of thanks to David's god for having made it a capital crime in Israel for children of the same mother to marry. Otherwise I would have been completely without defense.

"Why, Tamar," Ahinoam greeted me and slid over on her couch to make room for me to sit.

"Lady Ahinoam. A blessed feast to you," I replied, sitting, and then I turned at once to the screen.

"Tamar . . ." Amnon said, his breath blowing the scent of cedarwood through the screen upon my face. But he never finished the thought he had clearly begun. He turned and moved down along the screen to where Hannah was holding up her little son to greet "brave uncle Amnon."

But I cannot say that Amnon left ignoring me. Such a look shot from his eyes to the very center of my mind that it was as if we'd spoken deeply for an hour. As what he told me was not in words, it is difficult for me now to put words on it. An apology came through, and more than an apology. It was a sense of shame heightened by his feelings of helplessness. He would have spared me this hurt if he could have, I was told, but he could not. I saw in his eyes that he was forced to give up more vital things in the boys' hall that just a rag of coat to keep the peace with Absalom.

If he moved on now without saying anything else, it was not that he cared less, but that he cared for me more than the bounds and screens of propriety could bear. All who went to the screen, of course, were carefully watched from the other side. Even if they could not be seen, it was well known where each woman sat, and if a man talked to some gap longer or with more fervor than his mother or his sister deserved, then there was reason for suspicion. And suspicion could be more than humiliating. It could be dangerous.

Ahinoam's maid brought a platter of the meat of the earlier sacrifices now, seasoned and roasted, and David's wife gestured that if I would join her, she would be honored.

"Amnon tells me you worked a fine new coat for him," she said, making conversation until I should reach out my hand and take the first bite.

"Yes," I said.

"That was kind of you."

"It was wickedly cruel."

"Whatever do you mean?" She laughed.

I look the bite to avoid having to think of some response to that.

"Absalom! Adonijah!" David called. "Come, my sons. Come and feast beside me."

Ahinoam's sigh was audible. "Of course, they are the youngest of his sons on that side of the screen," she apologized for Amnon's not being chosen.

But all could sense there was more symbolism to the setting of Absalom on the king's left hand than that he was second youngest. David had lost the hearing in his right ear by a blow in battle and, though right was still for honor, left was for true hearing.

They spoke together all evening, David and Absalom. I confess I am at a loss to imagine what they talked about, but then I cannot speak of war for more than ten responses—and if it's Absalom I'm talking to, the number dwindles to two. David could not even begin to be distracted from his son—not with musicians, dancers, or priests—until the sudden and unexpected arrival of the man of god, the prophet Nathan, and his entourage. Of course Nathan had been invited to the feast. It was dangerous ever to slight him. But, as his name and title suggest, and as opposed to Gad, David's seer, he was known as his own man, belonging to no one but the god. He came if he pleased and asked no one's leave to depart. He also never did anything for either gold or honor, or even for entertainment. His coming could only be on an earnest mission from his god and, knowing this as well or better than anyone, David moved Adonijah back among the princes and sat Nathan in his place.

"See now." David spoke almost apologetically, trying to justify himself in advance for any criticism the man of god might have. "I dwell in a house of cedar, but the Ark of God dwells within the curtains of a tent. I make a covenant before you that I shall build a house for God as much greater than this palace as His Kingdom is above mine."

Nathan smiled indulgently.

David waved a servant carrying a platter to him. Into the hairless head of the lamb resplendent on it he worked thumb and forefinger and plucked out an eyeball, the choicest portion. He held it, like a peeled grape, to the newly arrived guest. "Do me the honor, O Man of God," he said.

"Thank you, no," the prophet replied, superior even to the eyes of young lambs. "The God of Isaac and Jacob calls me to a fast today."

"The Lord has set apart him that is godly for Himself." David resorted to psalmody. "O Lord, rebuke me not in Your hot displeasure."

I saw Absalom watching the man of the god closely over his father's knees. There was a look of scorn in his eyes toward David's confusion and humility and the look toward Nathan was—well, it was dangerous. "I could wrap you around my little finger, O pompous Man of God," it seemed to say.

Nathan studiously avoided looking anywhere but constantly into the heart of the god. At length he indicated that he would now perform the task he had been sent to do. He would prophesy.

For the first time that evening, I found ease for the drumming of "coat, coat" in my brain. Men of David's god prophesy differently than we of the Serpents do, of course, but as a novice struggling without a tutor, I was interested in the technique all the same. What I saw was, in the end, more instructive as a bad example than as a good one.

Nathan rose to begin and as he did, his farseeing eye fell for the first time on a thing very close at hand. His eye met the red-and-white glory of Absalom, and Nathan, the man of the god, did as any mortal did when they first saw the sparkle in my brother's eyes. As if some obscenity were scratched there, Nathan blushed and looked away and down.

Still, being the man that he was, the prophet regathered control of himself in an instant, nodded, and murmured, "Blessings on the king's son," toward Absalom. Then he proceeded with dignity to the space the congregation had cleared for him. But the damage was already done.

Nathan the prophet had many fewer years than the awe in which he was universally held would warrant. He was a frighteningly large man with a body the architects and foremen in the audience might covet for their building crews. "A few weeks on construction rations would fill him out and straighten up that self-effacing slouch, and then he could do the work of three," you could almost hear them say aloud.

His parchment-thin flesh on those huge bones became even more apparent when he removed the untanned gazelle skin he wore as a cloak and stood naked but for his loincloth and the prophet's mark upon his forehead. A prophet's loincloth is made of leather, too, unlike the priests', which are linen. This shows quite graphically the difference between a priest who is cultivated by the traditions and a prophet who, in a pristine and vulnerable state, waits to receive the touch of his god's hand. Leather is much more like flesh than linen is and so the brown leather strip hung on thongs from Nathan's hips accentuated more than concealed his nakedness. As he waited for his entourage to begin the trance music, he smoothed his hand again and again over the uncured leather as if realizing for the first time in his career how insufficient the garment was, how exposed his parts and power were to the eye and criticism of all—especially to those of the king's third son.

Nathan's disciples set to playing their drums and flutes, for theirs was a task that required no calculation. The wail and thump-thump that, if heard in the city streets, drew crowds like flies to a carcass, floated up to the diamond-studded ears of a nighttime heaven. Taking a deep breath, Nathan began to follow their lead, to do his automated part, his prophetic dance that always began the same, with the music, slowly. It would grow faster and faster and more and more erratic until he would lose all control of his steps and his mind and then the god would come and take over.

Nathan was a man of the god. He had trained as such from his childhood and had received a sure and definite call from Heaven. And yet there was nothing short of amputation that could rid his wrist of the mark of Judah—the same mark David wore, the same mark as Absalom. He was a man living in a land with a king and king's sons. He was a man with a wife and children—souls that could suffer harm. One glance from Absalom had recalled this to his mind.

And all the contention Absalom was capable of coaxing had risen in the prophet's heart, come like a thick black cloud of smoke between his mind and the mind of his god. I could see the struggle as he stood there, vulnerable and exposed, trying to decide between flattery and truth, the blessings of Earth and the blessings of Heaven. It is fatal for a prophet to entertain such considerations.

Four times the music began. Four times the man of the god began his steps, the long, powerful limbs claiming all space around him. And four times I saw it: how just as the god reached down to take possession of his man, the man thrashed wildly and flung the hand of the god away, as a prisoner might thrash against the hand of his keeper. Every time he began, it was with less and less confidence, a lack of faith the god cannot help but notice and condemn. I could see, as it were, bits of shattered prophecy hanging like dust just over the heads of the company and none could tell how to reach up and grab them.

Nathan collapsed full-length on the floor. His naked body ran with sweat and his limbs twitched with the effort. Then, after what seemed like a breathless eternity, he rose to his knees. "Go," he said, panting and unable to look the king or any other man in the eye. "Go and do whatever is in your heart and the Lord go with you."

"Ah." The congregation let out its breath and turned to one another and to the king in congratulations. When they turned again to the prophet, he had gone, and all his entourage—without a word, for shame.

That night after he had gone, after the effects of Absalom in the red coat had worn off, Nathan was given a dream from his god that drove him to return to the king in the morning and say what he should have said the night before. I was not present at this later audience and I know it only the way hearsay has glorified it. Nathan spoke glowing words of promise for the house of David. But I also know that there were words of warning that Heaven was close to being offended and turning the house upside down upon itself. I would not be surprised if, in so many words, David was told to beware of his own flesh and blood in Absalom.

But David, not quite the man of his god that Nathan was, could only bring himself to act upon the warning not to build the temple. It is easier not to do some task than it is to act against an evil that has such fetching eyes.

• XXVIII •

THE DEDICATION FEAST, the New Year, and the Feast of Booths came and went with no general premonition of drought. The cisterns had been filled that spring and so the autumn fronds were rattled as usual, in a more festive than an earnest vein. Thunder knew its business, they thought. A week, perhaps two, and it would answer the love song of the barren earth and bring the rains of winter.

Then the rains were called "late." There was still no cause for alarm in Jerusalem. The cisterns stood half full at least. It was the bitter, stagnant half, granted, but men would live very well for a month, perhaps two, on stagnant water and never be the worse for it. There was some more fervor in some few prayers, but not much.

Even the first few raids by the Amalekites upon the southern borders were ignored because men of the desert are always raiding, if not one another, then any outlying village they fancy. David's scribes looked among their scrolls and tablets and protested that the sons of Amalek had covenants with the villagers made by exchange of wives and sacrifices whereby they might drive their flocks in to feed off the harvest stubble and, in return, manure the ground. But everyone, even the villagers, understood that such covenants may break down to petty pillaging even in good years. Such is the disagreeable nature of the desert and of the men who make it their home.

Men of the desert always know first of all when water is scarce. A week or two waiting to plant the grain means little to a farmer sitting by his well in the shade. A week or two without water in the desert, and the herds and flocks are dead. Another week and men die, too. In the desert is freedom, but it is from the settled places that life must be wrested when desert freedom also means death.

David was patient with these men of the southland even when they joined with their kinsmen of Kedar, Moab, and all of Ishmael and invaded Beersheva, putting half the town to the torch, including the sacred tamarisks. David brushed his scribes aside, accusing them of being tree-worshipers that they fussed so over it. And the Beershevites, when they came to protest in torn garments and ashes, he accused of being more pathetic excuses for men than his weak-eyed scribes. David had been, after all, a pillager himself in earlier years, before he needed scribes. The courage of the Amalekites won his admiration, albeit he could not see the difference between the courage of foolhardy youth and that of droughted desperation.

David's careless attitude and easy, jesting manner kept most people in Jerusalem likewise unconcerned. The first serious murmuring did not come until Bethlehem began to feel the effects of the drought. Shimeah, David's second brother, now in charge of the family lands since the eldest had died, sent word of parched ground, sickly flocks, drooping orchards and vineyards, and of one or two Amalekite raids even so far north. But what he sent that really made an impression was his youngest son, a child of his old age, spoiled like fruit with much fondling. This young cousin of mine was named Jonadab; I had not seen him since our confrontation in Bethlehem as young children when David was moving us to Jerusalem and Jonadab had insisted his vision of the town in ruins was more correct than the opinion of a "mere girl" that there was beauty there. We had both grown since then, but changed little.

Shimeah should have given his son a plot of land, a few goats, and a wife long ago during a good year. At first it was parental indulgence that kept the boy irresponsible. But since the coming of the drought, David's brother found himself no longer able to afford the sort of girl he felt his son deserved. And it had become too expensive to keep the boy at home unwed, for Jonadab had discovered his sex without the price of ceremony and Bethlehem, the city of David, had no hierodules.

A certain Bethlehemite followed Jonadab's train all the way to Jerusalem. He dragged his daughter after him, then propped her up outside the gates for days, her clothes torn, her hair unbound and caked with ash. She was far gone with child.

"O men of Jerusalem, O sons of Jesse," he cried day and night. "Hear my plight! Here is my daughter, my shame, as you see. She was a virgin, as God is my witness, until enticed by Jonadab the son of Shimeah. What is the law of our Fathers, men? By the law, he who seduced her should take her to wife. Or if he will not, he must give me the price of a virgin in my hand so I can give her in honor to another."

Day and night this display continued, the girl looking as miserable as one might whose life depends on her father's satisfied honor and a sideways glance from a young and flighty lover. Poor pretty fool, I thought and might have dismissed her at that. But her appearance made quite an impression on me, as a moral well told, as a lesson beaten home with the rod. Just so, I thought, should one who has been wronged by men appear. I studied the sag of her head and stored the image in my mind as one may store a piece of cloth past all use but as future reference for how the pattern should be worked upon the loom.

I'm not sure what happened to that father and daughter. One day they were no longer at the gates. Either David paid them or he did not. If he did not, I suppose they were driven home again and there the girl must have been stoned. There was no other way, at seven months, to cover up her dishonor in a town without hierodules.

I do not mean to say that Jonadab, left to his own devices, was an intrinsically evil man. He does not deserve such credit. He was evil only as a lack of good can make a soul. He had but one desire in life and that was to be loved. Had it been a flood and not a year of drought that brought him to us, I would have called him a river leech. He stood gaping open, pliable, yearning for nothing but to suck the emotion out of any who would bare him the breast of friendship. His liver, his own seat of emotion, was an empty jug, waiting to be filled with whatever one cared to pour into it: wine or water or poison.

When Jonadab first arrived as one of the oldest in the boys' hall, I heard Amnon attempt to befriend him, cheering the fellow who might feel lonely and homesick. But Amnon's way to build a friendship was to ask after the other's wishes and Jonadab had no wish but to be molded. So it was Absalom who soon caught and broke into Jonadab's hollow shell. Once he had the fellow won (never wise enough to realize that he was being won), Absalom gave Jonadab full rein to do as he pleased as long as he stood always within call, to say the right word, to do the right deed, at just the right time.

The things Jonadab said when left untutored were things to ingratiate himself to a hall full of untried young men. He spoke in graphic terms of his experience in the beds and grainfields of Bethlehem, things the rest of the boys loved to hear and then repeat, thinking that mimicking that same emptiness, that same shallow leer, made men of them. Had he had more wit, a little mystery might have mellowed Cousin Jonadab's coarseness into dash. But his god did not see fit to give him any such gifts.

One afternoon when Jerusalem sighed for the freshness of a dew, Jonadab and Amnon found themselves alone in the boys' hall together. They could not know that I could overhear them, sitting in my mother's rooms with my sewing. I heard then how poison was spilled from the newly readied jug.

"I saw your sister today," Jonadab began his gossip.

"Which one?" Amnon asked. "You know I have many."

"Why, whichever one you like. We'll discuss her."

There was no response to this, so Jonadab continued. "Frankly, I like them all."

Although he tried not to, Amnon could not keep a grunt of disgust from escaping his throat.

"There's absolutely nothing wrong with my taking a liking to your sisters," Jonadab said. "They are all my father's brother's daughters and so, by ancient custom, I may have my pick. Like Isaac got Rebecca, Israel his Rachel and his Leah. I may take my . . ."

"There is one you have no claim of blood upon then, thank God." I knew Amnon spoke of me, and I grew warm and stabbed with distraction at my handiwork as if I had been in the same room and within sight of them and had to pretend I had heard nothing.

"And who might that be?" After a moment's pause without answer, "Ah. Her. Maacah's daughter. Well, I can do without the burned scrapings in the bottom of the pan." Another very taut pause. "Tell me, son of David, who's going to be your first? Who's going to claim your blushing virginity?" Yet another pause. "Who are you going to *marry,* then, if we must speak in courtly terms to keep your face from bursting into flames? I'm afraid all my sisters are already wives and mothers, else we could arrange some sort of exchange here, sister for sister. It is cheaper that way."

I held my breath. In his distress Amnon wasn't going to tell how he had promised to marry me, was he?

"Well," Amnon replied with scarcely concealed derision, "one who is the crown prince can hardly be expected to take a bride from a shepherd village like Bethlehem, even if they are cousins. Kingship has more important considerations than bride-price."

I breathed easily again. I knew he could not betray me.

Jonadab found himself soundly beaten in that exchange. But soon he was able to come back with, "Well, perhaps they'll marry you to some lousy Amalekite princess with bony hips like a starved camel's. To keep peace on the border, that's an honorable, kingly reason for a match. You'd have to get special dispensation, of course. Spending your seed on such a one would be like spilling it on stones and dead things, and that, as we all know, is a sin."

Amnon was silent. I could not see, but I had no doubt that he was doing his business—searching for a misplaced scroll, perhaps, or a thong to mend a broken sandal—as quickly and with as much concentration as he could so he might soon escape the room and his cousin's tongue.

"Well, something must be done to keep those bastards of Amalek quiet," Jonadab said, exasperated more by Amnon's silence than by the raiders. "I'd say it's your duty as firstborn."

"The Amalekites are hungry. It's the drought."

"Oh, yes. Of course. You would come to their defense. You like the Amalekites, don't you?"

There was such an insinuating tone to Jonadab's last remark that I expected Amnon to fling back at him, "And just what is that supposed to mean?" I know that is what I would have done. I all but shouted it down through the air vent at him.

But Amnon was silent. He knew only too well what Jonadab meant.

The silence was precarious, balanced, as it were, on the edge of an abyss by the anarchy Absalom kept as a pet. For all that my brother was not in the room, his hand and teaching goaded Jonadab's every word. And Jonadab was so much the creature, rough cut and amorphous without his trainer's hand, that he did not see the abyss below the silence. Or, if he did, he thought it was only part of his joke.

"That must be why David prefers Absalom to you," Jonadab prodded the silence further. "Absalom is his first real son. Abigail's Daniel is a thing bewitched by some jealous spirit and you— Well, David can't be sure you won't run off into the desert and join the sons of Amalek, your brothers, as your mother did."

"My mother—"

"Well I remember when the news was brought to us in Bethlehem." Jonadab would not be silent. "I was only five at the time, but we watched David's exploits in Ziklag and the wilderness with interest. We were his kin, after all.

"Word came to us," Jonadab continued, "that while Uncle David campaigned with his lords the Philistines, the Amalekites—it was a year of drought, just as this—came out of the south and raided the coast of Judah and the south of Kaleb. Ziklag they burned with fire and they took booty. All David's household they captured as slaves: Abigail, your mother Ahinoam, and your sister Hannah, who was but a baby."

Now I remembered having heard the tale, too, but never before in such a light. It was only three days until David caught up with the raiders, recovered his losses sevenfold, and smote the sons of Amalek. "And there was nothing lacking to them, neither small nor great" I had always been told—not even so much as a wife's honor. I had to admit those words had the patent ring of myth. Three days was plenty of time. There are those who think a wife must be stoned if she spends a single night alone in the wilderness and cannot produce witnesses to vouch for her virtue. One must worry about the lechery of desert spirits, even if one has no need to consider what treatment Amalekites are known to give their female slaves. Abigail was there, too. Abigail must have stood as witness to her co-wife's unravished state. Unless she herself had been ravished . . . I'd never stopped to think. And what this might mean for Absalom's hopes to the throne, if it were generally supposed . . .

"Is it a wonder that you were born at the new moon of Ab, nine months after your mother was taken captive?" Jonadab asked with gall bursting green-black upon his words as he drew them out, as when one cleans fowl carelessly.

"David loved my mother as soon as he redeemed her and lifted the ban on women from his troops." The tang in Amnon's voice was tasting the gall that had embittered the whole bird. Pretense for policy's sake was no longer possible. There was nothing to it but to spit the offensive flesh out and throw it to the dogs.

"You are so certain of that because you were already conceived at the time, a mite some two or three nights old, squirming like a fry in your mother's ravaged womb. Is it any wonder that you are the shame of the sons at slinging? David had no part in the making of your right arm."

There was a crash—crockery, a platter, a jug—something hit the ground and was shattered. When the reverberation up to my little air vent had faded, Jonadab was laughing to clear his tension and I knew Amnon had stormed from the room. Well the proverb says:

> The words of a talebearer are as wounds,
> and they go down into the innermost parts of the
> belly.

I tossed aside my work (it did not crash) and likewise left the room I was in. I was driven by a similar rage and also by a pummeled softness inside of me that wanted to act as a poultice to my stepbrother's bruises.

But I must admit I had other reasons for seeking out Amnon's face. This was the first I had heard of such a vicious rumor circulating the palace. It was so unfounded that it never passed Abigail's doorway and entered the harem. The Amalekites were causing problems on the borders and so one remembered other years when they had done likewise to find precedence for how to deal with them. That was much more a task for the soldiers and makers of policy than for women. That was all it was, I said, that and Absalom's ambition. Still, my heart faltered and I needed reassuring as much as Amnon must have. I wanted to see his face, to assure myself that the spot of hot pink in his cheeks was like David's and not like any desert man's.

Though Mother's room and the boys' hall shared a common wall, there was a maze to negotiate to get physically from one door to the other. By the time I reached the hall through which Amnon must have bolted (I knew because a slave was picking up the pieces of a broken vase), only Jonadab was there.

Jonadab was leaning against the brass rivets in the door, cleaning his nails with his dagger.

"Here, you forgot this piece here," Jonadab said to the slave, picking his foot up off a shard he'd ground to slivers. "By God, the land you come from must be a land of pigs if that's all the better they taught you to clean up after yourselves."

What effort that man went through just to feel superior to a slave! Cousin Jonadab looked nothing so much as like a figure of clay, all material and no light or life of soul beneath. I tried to stop short, but there was no turning or escape.

Jonadab pushed himself from the door with a thrust of his buttocks. Upon sight of me he was able to ignore the slave to such a degree that the man had to move his hand quickly so as not to get it caught between Jonadab's foot and the splinters of pottery on the floor. Lording himself over me would take more effort than over a slave, perhaps, but he would find it much more self-flattering.

"Well, Cousin," he said, choosing the form of address that indicated that he had traditional rights over me according to the law of David's god. "This is an honor. Absalom tells me that your hair unbound is a rope by which one may draw up refreshment from your well, and that you will be the deep source of princes."

I did not stay to hear what more my brother might have to say of me by the mouth of his creature. I quickly retreated, but still I was obliged to hear more as I fled: "What a damned unfriendly bitch. Too good for your cousin Jonadab, eh?"

Back through the gates where only women and children were allowed, I was glad for the pair of dour matrons keeping their own sort of gossipy guard at the door.

▣ XXIX ▣

EVER SINCE THE evening of the palace dedication, Ahinoam, the mother of Amnon the firstborn, had shown a certain interest in me. It was a timid sort of interest, such as an old warrior may show toward the youth of promise he is training: an admiration and a desire for intimacy tempered by an awareness that his own best days are passed and that the youth might well outstrip him in deeds of glory. Ahinoam was a grandmother and I imagined I was to her a young woman in whom all the fond dreams of her girlhood might at last be fulfilled, seeing that her own daughters were already placed with men and that there the romance had ended. I must admit that sometimes when she would glance at me, I would find myself thinking: "I will do better than the daughters of Ahinoam and she will be unspeakably jealous."

I put off intimacy with her whenever possible, for I felt I was a young woman who would inspire jealousy only when viewed from a distance and that, unless I was given more time to prepare myself, her too-close, too-soon acquaintance would destroy the picture. She never forced herself on me, and her quiet, patient goodness soon taught me how childish such thinking was.

Having come to this realization, my thoughts went to the other extreme and I wondered why it was she found anything of interest in me at all—she never had before—and, thinking it charity, I avoided her all the more.

Nevertheless, Ahinoam persisted, steadily, but not at all forcibly, until I could no longer be cold. And one day when neither Mother nor Michal nor Zipporah could offer me any excuse, I consented to go with her down toward Anaiah to visit the black tents of Kedar.

Whole pedigrees of these tents perched like black carrion birds, low and long, about the House of Anaiah at the eastern foot of the Mount of Olives. The people in these tents were proud, but of desperate circumstances because of the drought that had beaten them from desert to steppe, from steppe to the hills. One could buy anything from them—to the very poles of the tents—for a cup of water and a loaf of bread. Their daughters and even their wives were going that year to anyone who could feed them. Many of the best houses still have two or three of this generation of desert women grown old in the strange settled lands and slavery because of this time of great drought.

In the harem they told tales of the dwellers in tents. It was said how they spirited off young girls for their beastly pleasure and boys like Joseph of old to be slaves. I remembered what Jonadab had said of Ahinoam, the very woman who was my guide out there, and I looked sidelong at her thin and yet-shapely body for assurance as I walked beside her. It was also said that the people of the desert knew black secrets, communed with spirits, and could tell the future. Even if these tales were true, Ahinoam had greater magic. And the drought had parched all image of evil from the tents. I felt no fear.

Indeed, as we passed between the stone vineyard walls on our way out, I felt more hostility from the Jebusite peasants than I ever did in the wilderness. The peasants were laboring like senseless beasts in the very heat of the day, carrying up leathern buckets from the dwindling spring in a vain attempt to keep their vines from withering. The grapes hung in ones and twos, the rest having turned to dust at the blossom stage. The peasants could picture themselves very shortly descending to the straits of the desert people—to begging, ransoming their lives at the dear price of freedom and pride. They faced the prospect much more bitterly than those for whom the prospect had been a reality for a year and who had found that life was still worth living, nonetheless. The drought, like some great whirlwind, grew and grew from its eye in the desert. And those who sat in its eye felt the calm "God willing" more strongly than those who were feeling the lash of sand at its edges for the first time.

"I've come to see about certain spices and fragrances they have for sale among the tents," Ahinoam told me.

"They have such things in such times as these?"

"Even in the worst of droughts there are invisible networks across the desert whereby from clan to clan are passed the priceless commodities that grow beyond the southern desert in Sheba and nowhere else in the world."

"You must have good friends in these tents."

Ahinoam glanced at me as if to determine if I believed the rumors. "I have friends," she said.

"It must be nice to have such friends."

"Yes." My words seemed to assure her that I was not one who suspected her virtue, for she continued, her eyes looking ahead in unconcern. "In these trying times I like to be the wife who knows how to get such niceties to throw in David's braziers, strew upon his bed, or fold into his ointments to soothe him."

"He likes it?"

" 'I am a warrior,' " Ahinoam said, mimicking her husband perfectly and yet without guile as only a longtime wife can. " 'As a boy I tended the sheep and slept night after night on stones in the fields. What need have I for herbs and spices?'

"Still," Ahinoam continued with a gentle, knowing smile, "he appreciates it."

"I'll bet he sometimes slept on wild thyme or onions when he was a shepherd."

"Yes." Ahinoam laughed. "He and I slept on wild thyme together once. That first night after Ziklag, the night my son— Well, others, younger than I, they enjoy that privilege now."

The servant who accompanied us carried a great sack of flour pendant from a band across his forehead and Ahinoam herself carried a jar of olives on one hip. I carried nothing and kept my arms folded severely in front of me, gripping my forelimbs to hide their emptiness. It is a stance of defense as well, defense against cold, for example, although cold was certainly the last thing I felt as we arrived among the tents. They were like black lungs gone flaccid for want of a breath to lift them, and between them were the bare stones which the sun's torture seemed to have exploded to twice their normal size.

"Forgive us, Lady," said the tent dweller who came out to greet us. "The reports you heard were false. We have long since traded away the last of our frankincense and myrrh and, not being in our traditional pastures, we have had no chance to trade for more."

Ahinoam motioned for the servant to set the sack of flour down anyway. I began to suspect it was more charity that had brought her on this venture and that all the talk of herb-strewn beds had been to deflect me. Her greatest frustration was that the tent dwellers insisted on baking the flour then and there into bread and gruel to give variety to our feast and forcing it upon us until we honestly could eat no more. Only then did they hand it out to their own children, hovering about and staring with starved eyes at every mouthful.

Our host's tent was pitched at the top of a rise. Bedding was airing—not drying, as there was no water for washing— on the guy ropes. The lads set to shepherding what scrawny flocks were left to their families, tossed stones in front of those that were getting too far away to spare themselves the running and yelling. The blessed afternoon breeze came over the hill from the west, and the dwellers rolled up the tent sides to catch it, but all the same they insisted that the main opening face the desert to the east. Subtly but defi-

nitely they spoke the language of the black-hair houses.
They turned their backs on the low clay houses of Anaiah,
on the glory of Jerusalem; and, under the most crushing
blows the desert can deliver, they nonetheless faced that
desert head on. The tents, like the people's hollow, sunken
eyes, yearned across the desert to the wilderness they loved.

"We welcome your charity," our host said. "It is necessary. But the charity we long most for, pray to our dusty
Gods for, is the shadow of clouds across the eastern horizon
that will let us know there is rain."

As I sat beneath the tightly woven shade, the sea-wind at
my back, my anticipation could not help but be turned by
the situation of the tent and by the sigh-length glances of the
people eastward. Equally with them I began to look for
some joy, some relief from the desert, from the Way to
Jericho.

We sat with our host in the dark shadow of his men's
section, rather than being regulated with his women. To be
deprived of my sex in order to accept a place as David's
emissary was a dubious honor. But our host was gracious
and clearly was doing the best that form allowed him to. It
was part of the testy ambivalence that continued throughout our meeting.

He was a thin man, our host, wasted by the famine and
a care for his people. He had not let these troubles make him
despondent, however, nor lacking in pride, for pride was the
breath of life to him. Long, lanky bones started from his
flesh and the flesh seemed so tough that a day of boiling
would not be enough to soften it. Poor diet had made his
beard sparse and of a coarse texture and much riding in the
sun made his naturally dark face indistinguishable from the
charcoal color of his beard. In the midst of all that darkness,
the crumbling cairn of his mouth—teeth gone and half gone
to enemies' blows and to stones passed off as grain—seemed
clean and white, and the whites of his eyes were clear and
piercing. He entertained us with what men of the desert have
in abundance even when they have nothing else—their lush
words and poetry:

Tell me, O you whom my soul loves,
where you make your flock to rest at noon.
If you know not, O fairest among women,
go your way forth by the footsteps of the flock,
and feed your kids beside the shepherd's tents.

Being one who loves the fruit of the tongue, I drank my fill until I doubted my ability to walk a straight line in the sober world of everyday.

"I am neither Amalekite nor sheikh of Kedar nor petty prince of Moab," said my host in one of his poems. "I am Nahash the son of Nahash, king of the Ammonites." This poem had the ring of personal memoir in it.

"Lady Ahinoam," I chided, "you knew this all along and didn't tell me." I bent and kissed the man's woolen hem in due reverence. "But what is the king of the Ammonites doing in the tents of Kedar in the fields of Judah rather than sitting in the luxury of his great towers on the other side of Jordan?"

"Indeed," the king replied, setting his voice to a pitch that could maintain a long tale, "since the days of Saul of Israel, since he came up against us at Jabesh-gilead, and my father, rest his soul, made treaty with him, we have kept the terms of that treaty and stayed within our ancient borders. Also as terms of that treaty, we have sent a portion of the grain grown in our God-blessed fields as a tribute to Israel every year, to Saul or David as the case happened to be. I know well where the grain is stored: the granaries of Jericho, within sight of our own shores. The dishonor of tribute I can bear, but I cannot bear that David should go against his god and our treaty."

"Has he done so?" I asked.

"We pay tribute, we expect protection in return. Our fields have been fruitful for many years, but this year Milcom, our God, is angry. There is drought and our people have nothing to eat."

"Many gods are angry this year," I interjected.

"True. Time and time again I have sent to David, 'Give us a fair portion of that surplus you keep in Jericho, for we are not able to store as much as you, seeing that we pay you tribute. Our hunger eats away our marrow and there will be none to till the fields of Ammon when, if Milcom wills it, the rains should fall again.' "

"Surely David can not refuse such a plea."

"My messengers brought only evasion in reply. So now I have come in person to plead with David."

"And has he been so low as to refuse you place in the palace?"

The old king smiled. "I am a son of Ammon," he said. Among Israelites, the term is one of abuse. To this man, it was the greatest honor to which he could aspire. "My fathers were men of the desert. Every summer I move from the stifle of my clay walls and go out and watch the grain ripen from my tents as my fathers did before me. This tent is my own, made sacred by generations and by the presence of the palanquin of my God. Shall I leave it to go and plead with Ira the Jairite, David's hireling, that I be given an apartment equal to that of the Moabite ambassador? Shall I jostle for position at his right hand as I eat his food? Here I am my own man, even in the face of famine. The Amalekites and the men of Kedar who camp about me, we are brothers from ancient times. I am honored to be counted among them, even in their suffering."

I nodded with grave respect.

Nahash lightened the conversation as a good host must with the recitation of a proverb: " 'Drink waters out of your own cistern and rejoice with the wife of your youth.' " Then he turned to me with warm dark eyes and said, "I have a daughter complected just so." He smiled and teased me as a father would, "Are you perhaps a child of Ammon run away to the city and to David's court?"

I told him my parentage. "I am a Geshurite of the royal house and through me Geshur's heirs will come."

"Ah, Geshur," he said, stroking a smile above his beard. "Geshur in Aram."

"But we are not Aramaeans," I protested.

"Nor are you Israelites. Yet you give wives to David."

"And we have, at times, taken husbands from Ammon."

"Yes. Such exchanges are in the memories of our old men."

The king spoke with smiling diplomacy as a foreign ambassador might speak to David. It was the first time I had ever felt myself treated as an emissary of the land where I'd been born, as a person whose opinion could make national policy and was therefore worth exploring. It was, indeed, the first time I had heard of Geshur from any perspective other than my mother's sighs of homesickness and David's lists of tribute. I spoke carefully so as not to betray either confidences or my own ignorance. The king spoke carefully, too. That is the way with heads of state and, though my stomach knotted throughout the interview, the tension of the politics exhilarated me as does brisk exercise. It was, I realized, my long-denied birthright.

"How can I speak ill of my brother David?" the king asked rhetorically and not without bitterness. "All my people have eaten like birds from his hands this year and six months." The quick black eyes shot a grateful glance in Ahinoam's direction. "But even slaves are fed.

"It is of no concern to me who sits within the walls of Jerusalem," he continued, "Jebusite or Israelite. Or Aramaean, for that matter. Let them fight it out among themselves. But now I hear rumors from Jerusalem. 'There is copper in the land of Ammon. Copper for weapons, salt for our meat, grain for our bread. All that is in Ammon. What more do we need?' Then my heart grows anxious. David is no fool. He will not always send to the Philistines for bronze and iron weapons. Nor will he wait to win a battle with slings and stones and then take the pickings from the fallen enemy. When I hear rumors of copper in my barren hills, my heart grows anxious within me and I wonder, Even when the rains do come, Milcom willing, will our pastures be the same? Will they be ours to return to, Milcom willing? Rumors make me worry that they may not be.

"Ah!" Nahash threw up his hands in a helpless gesture. "I am a man," he said. "A man who pecks from another's hand and has neither flocks nor wool to trade these two years. Milcom knows best."

Ahinoam and I murmured an "Amen" to his pious fatality. The king stretched a sinewy hand toward me and held it out until I took it in my own. If I had been a man, I might have taken it as a gesture of friendship. As I am a woman, and as he held it as a comfort during all the conversation that ambled on throughout the afternoon, I knew it was a hand stretched toward the divine Woman in me, the source of eternal solace, even to those who call upon a god.

"My heart goes out to the son of Ammon," I said, and I was impressed that even in such dire circumstances, he faced the world as a man. As something more than a man, though that little bit more be only the wind of poetry. Poetry is prophecy and prophecy is fact, more certain than myth, more certain than memory.

The king smiled his crumbly white smile at me. He opened his mouth to speak more, but what he said had nothing to do with the drought. "Ah," he said, "here come my sons now," and he rose to greet the newcomers.

◉ XXX ◉

MY LIVER STIRRED within me when I saw who it was Nahash greeted. Then was there something to the rumors Jonadab spread?

Ammon, Amnon, I thought. How like Ammon is the name your mother gave you. Is it true, my stepbrother? Are you in truth not David's son at all? Does this explain why you and he have souls of such a different cast?

Last year at the season of first fruits, Amnon, you faltered on the blessing "A wandering Aramaean ready to perish was my father." You stumbled on these words as you brought the first offerings to David's god and then you turned from the altar and saw the faces looking up at you, the desert faces full of hunger that might well be the faces of your kin, and yet you dared not claim them. Some said that slip was because you feared the famine in the very heart of Israel. You feared that next year there might be no first fruits. Some, Jonadab tutored by Absalom among them, said more seditious things.

It was indeed Amnon my brother that the son of Ammon rose to greet. I looked to Ahinoam's face to see if she would betray herself, but I was already so confused, thinking of my Geshuri home, thinking of love, thinking of Amnon, that I gave up my puzzling, trusted to the poetry of Heaven, and put on a smile. That is often the best thing to do in the face of great and unanswerable mysteries.

We stepped out of the tent's shadow to greet the new arrivals, and then I could not sanction the suspicions of the jealous any further in this matter. Who could not see David in the high pink color a day in the sun had given to my stepbrother's cheeks and nose? As for Nahash's speech, do not men of the desert call any man they would honor with familiarity either "son" or "brother"? And if that were not enough, behind Amnon came Hanun, the Ammonite king's son and heir, and also Shobi, his second son by a favorite younger wife.

Amnon greeted his mother with affection and, it seemed, thanksgiving. Perhaps he had been suffering from some homesickness on this journey. Some secret sign passed between them. Then Amnon laid a hand upon my shoulder, too. I had been taller than him the last time we'd stood side by side. I was startled to see that—in just the past week?—he had caught up with me.

"My son and his companions have been this week in Jericho," Ahinoam said proudly.

"My father is too occupied to go himself," Amnon said.

"But he sent you, his hope and his heir, as second best only to himself, to assure the people along the Jordan that he was mindful of their plight in this drought."

"Thank you, Mother." Amnon took his turn to refresh himself from the jug of water at the rear of the tent. He looked like he wanted to dump the whole thing over his head, but in consideration of the land's curse, he only refreshened his tongue. Then he passed the jug to the youngest. "Hanun and Shobi came along to see to their father's own interests in the granaries of the City of the Palms."

Ahinoam asked, "Did it go well?"

"There is nothing like a drought to uncover graft and rumors of graft where wheat is concerned," Hanun replied.

"The caretaker in Jericho has been removing unauthorized quantities of grain under the pretext of mold," said Amnon.

"Mold! In this dryness!" exclaimed Shobi.

"He was growing fat on it himself and selling it at a profit," said Hanun with anger.

"Rather than distributing it to the needy whose loyalty is worth buying, as my father instructed," said Amnon.

"As you, my son, suggested to him," said Ahinoam.

"The granary will have to be rebuilt," said Amnon, trying to see both sides of the subject. "Moisture can get in."

"But the caretaker is obviously a thief." Shobi took the other side.

"And I even dropped a word at the local inn that we sons of Ammon would not look at all askance if he should suffer a fatal accident on his way home one evening," Hanun continued with discomforting earnestness. He received nods of confirmation from his brother and his father.

"As long as they send his buxom daughter to me when they're through with him, I shall say nothing," Shobi said, laughed out loud, and then, at a quick glance from Amnon, just as quickly apologized to Ahinoam and me.

"There is grain enough in Jericho that my father should fulfill his obligations to the sons of Ammon," Amnon admitted. "I shall tell him so."

In this manner the returned embassy made their preliminary reports to Nahash as they gratefully spread themselves out on the king's shaded rugs. Outside, their little donkeys panted, but could be spared no water until returned to David's stables. The Ammonite and Amalekite children, bored with grown-up talk, moved from the edges of the tent to the donkeys where they rifled the packs for food and presents and begged from the grooms.

Once business was over, the three young men determined to entertain themselves. Shobi brought out a flute over which he puckered his fleshy lips and to which Hanun kept time, clapping in an intricate and varying rhythm.

"Come, let's dance," Amnon said to his friends.

"Oh, it's too hot," complained Hanun.

"Just a little," begged Amnon.

"He knows how well he looks when he dances," Ahinoam whispered to me. "He wants to show off." ·

Indeed, Amnon wouldn't take no for an answer until Hanun rose, grasped his shoulders, and danced the leaping, stamping steps of the desert. They shook their locks like lions and roared and shouted their exhilaration and defiance.

Then Hanun sank laughing to the rug. "Really, no more. I must have another drink now as it is. Perhaps some curdled milk, if there is any."

But Amnon, better fed than his friends, had energy to spare. He called for another sword and clashed it over his head with his own.

"Now he will really show off," confided his mother.

And he did. By the time he was finished, my hands were at my mouth, my heart in my throat. I'd flinched any number of times and actually screamed out loud once or twice as the blades flashed over his head, whirled around a wrist, juggled in the air, and come within a finger's breadth of a nose or an ear or a toe, all this in perfect time to the wild screeches of Shobi's flute, the double time of Hanun's hands. Amnon finished with a grand flourish of a leap, twirl, and collapse. Then he sat panting beside his mother and accepted a bowl of curdled goat's milk from her hand. Over the rim of the bowl he caught my eye. Had I enjoyed it?

Well, enjoyment was not exactly the word. But I guess some people get nervous watching us dance with Snakes. Amnon had certainly enjoyed it. What confidence was in that body! I took my hands from my mouth, smiled, and looked down. Let him know I was impressed, anyway.

"Perhaps your sister will dance for us now," Shobi suggested as he tapped spit from the hollow of his flute and wet his tongue with precious water.

I looked away in confusion. I was ashamed to dance here and after such a display the shuffling, tiny, earthbound steps of a woman. My hips were always too rigid, anyway—they all said so at Abigail's parties—and my movements too clumsy. I needed a Snake.

"My sister doesn't dance." Amnon came to my rescue,

still panting, and I looked at him gratefully. "But she does sing."

So I sang. Shobi hung his flute by its red goat-hair tassels, and the whole tent clapped while I sang the popular songs of watering flocks and driving them home as the shadows grew long in a world we had almost forgotten, a world of lush pastures, oases, and tinkling bracelets on the ankles of barefoot girls.

By the time I finished, the moon had risen in a dull brassy twilight. We wished we could stay in the tent all night and enjoy the tranquil coolness just before dawn. But Amnon still had to report on his mission to his father that night. A runner had gone on ahead to warn the gatekeepers that we were coming and not to lock us out. So we said our good-byes and Amnon lifted me on what had been Shobi's mare. He lingered a moment before me, his fingers lightly on my waist as if for balance, but I had no more need of that than I had of help to mount a donkey. It is the unnecessary things in life that are important.

Then Ahinoam walked up to us from the gathering darkness. "Look," she said, but her eyes avoided looking directly toward us. She held out a bit of dried shrubbery. "I found some wild thyme."

"That's nice," Amnon said, turning from me in confusion.

"It's quite dead with the drought, but it still has a strong scent. Perhaps it will do for your father better than frankincense and myrrh. Like the time after Ziklag when you, Son—"

"What's that you're saying, Mama?" Amnon said as he handed the reins of my beast to a groom and sent us on ahead while he went to show his mother the same careful help in mounting.

"Here, smell."

"That's nice, Mama."

"I only like to think that sometimes the smell, as smells do, may sometimes remind him—for a moment—"

"Uh-oh, Mama. It looks like this poor old creature's gone lame."

"Come help me down, Amnon. I must have broken his back."

"Not your featherweight, Mama, I'm sure. It's Hanun. Riding like a desert fiend."

"I guess I must walk."

"Don't think of it, Mama. Come, let me help you onto my trusty Smoke."

"Will you ride mine then, Prince Amnon?" offered one of his men.

"Thanks, Isaac, no. Keep an eye on my lady mother. I'll walk."

Up through the invigorating darkness he strode and reclaimed the reins of my donkey for himself. He kept the lead short and walked nearly beside me. If I should drowse, I thought, I can rest my head upon his shoulder.

But for the present there was no thought of drowsing. There was not much to see, as the moon was but a slip and the hillsides only dark silhouettes like sleeping giants. One was thereby spared the depressing sight of the wilting countryside that was inescapable by day. But the air was rousing with scents. The rue, the Jericho rose, the mustard, the acacia, Ahinoam's wild thyme that grew in these wild places were mustied and concentrated as if one had spread them on the roof to dry. They had been culled during the day by the poor to thicken their soup pots, and the smell of the bruised plants thickened our lungs as we passed.

Night birds hallooed news of their hunt from ridge to ridge. And Shobi's melody kept rippling through my mind like a pebble thrown into water. There was a shooting star, a south wind, and suddenly, it all came to my lips in poetry:

> Who is this that comes
> out of the wilderness
> like pillars of smoke
> perfumed with myrrh and frankincense,
> with all powders of the merchants?

And again:

Awake, O north wind;
and come, you hidden one of the south;
blow upon my garden
that the spices thereof may flow out.
Let my beloved come into his garden,
and eat his pleasant fruits.

Amnon had me recite the verses over and over and he
murmured along like the purl of a hidden brook until he had
them memorized, too. With rhythm in his head, he made
verses of his own, of stock phrases at first, but gaining
courage and originality as we went.

Who is she that looks forth as the red of morning,
fair as the white of moon,
clear as the sun . . .

"Amnon, have you got a girlfriend?"
No answer.
"You'll make me jealous. 'White as the moon.' I know
that can't be me."
"That's a common saying."
"Is it? Among those young men of David's in the hall?"
"But it is. 'White as the moon.' You are, tonight. You
catch the gleam of moonlight on your skin."
"Go on," I told him. "What's your next line?"
" 'And . . . and . . . And terrible as an army with ban-
ners.' "
"Terrible!"
"Yes. Terrible."
"Am I—I mean your girl—is she supposed to be flattered
by that?"
"I hope so. Terrible because there is that in you—in her—
that calls for surrender, that is unafraid and courageous and
a conqueror."
"The lover and the warrior maid at one and the same
time."
"Yes."

"Now I'm not so jealous. It is Goddess you speak of."

"Perhaps."

I studied his face as well as I might, but we were already shadowed by Jerusalem's walls and it grew darker still.

" 'Turn away your eyes from me,' " he said in verse again, " 'for they have overcome me.' "

The guards, disgruntled and bored with waiting, had fed their watch fire with little care for the lack of fuel caused by the drought; it was not their backs that had to bend to gather it. The fire roared into the already-hot night, prying like an incorrigible cat into the business of others. By its light I could see that more than just the guard attended us. Absalom and Jonadab were there.

"Been out sporting with the Amalekites, brother Amnon?" Absalom asked. I cringed at the flawless tone of his voice and feared, even when it spoke subtle ill of him, that it had powers to convert Amnon along with everyone else.

"Out sporting with your sister, Absalom, or so it seems to me," Jonadab answered with a wry twist to his smile.

Amnon handed the reins of my mount to the groom at once and went on ahead to join those two to go in to David and to speak in prose of droughts and armies once more. He gave me not a backward glance.

I suddenly felt the weight of all the happy hours of that day. Or perhaps it was the weight of Jerusalem's walls. Now I longed for a shoulder alongside me, but the groom went dutifully ahead and had no words but a singsong of profanity to keep the donkey moving.

I was so tired, I could hardly find the strength to say a polite "Thank you" to Ahinoam as we parted.

"Don't thank me," she said. "Thank my son. It was he who told me to bring you out to the tents of his friends for his homecoming from Jericho."

"So he could make a fool of me in front of Absalom and our cousin."

"My child," she said, scolding gently. "He loves you."

Ahinoam looked at me, joy battling with jealousy. These

things a mother feels when she sees the woman her son has admitted plainly has replaced her as the lodestone of his life, the bosom he will run to for comfort from then on. Then she buried her face in her sprig of wild thyme.

◉ XXXI ◉

As ONE PUTS new wine away in jugs after the vintage tasting and is content to let time do its work of sweet fermentation, so I was obliged to put Amnon out of my mind for several months. He had his work and I had mine, at opposite ends of the palace.

And there was much to occupy us. Nahash, the aged king of Ammon, had taken ill—poison, it was rumored, in some food sent him from David's kitchen—and his sons, in anger and fear, had packed up their tents and moved back to their ancestral lands across the Jordan. On the journey, the old man died and Hanun, who rose to rule in his father's stead, swore revenge.

David sent emissaries to proclaim peace and goodwill toward the new sovereign, but no member of the royal house was sent as token of special trust. Amnon pleaded to go, but, "I don't want you poisoned" had been the less-than-innocent answer.

The emissaries spoke too much of copper, too little of Jericho's grain, and so, drought or no, Hanun maintained his pride and did an act that was tantamount to declaring war. He plucked out the emissaries' beards, cut off their garments in the middle, leaving them exposed in their loin-cloths, and sent them back across the Jordan in shame.

And suddenly we women were weaving blankets and cloaks for soldiers. The grain we had been grinding to feed the hungry was now mess for the army, though the poor and the new recruits were one and the same thing. It is always politic to make charity fight for you.

It was in connection with these duties that I was sum-moned one morning to David's throne room. At least, I supposed that must be the reason, though what I had such authority over I couldn't imagine.

The kingly figure at the end of the hall seemed an echo, a reflection, a desert mirage, of the great pillars he stood between. His core substance, like theirs, seemed to be of native limestone, firm and earthy. But for all the dry, baking heat of the drought, the pillars, like his flesh, maintained cool tints of olive green. As the natural stone of the pillars was sheathed in bands of hammered copper and friezes of geometric patterns in reds and blues and purples, so the figure added grace and modesty to his body by a multicol-ored robe of Tyrian make, well trimmed with bronze and copper ornaments.

This man was more slender, firmer, more youthful and vigorous than I remembered the king, who was struggling with a paunch in his growing age. He was more command-ing of respect as he stood among his counselors, too, obvi-ously their superior, so I felt some constraint to bow to the ground. This was the custom in other courts, as ambassa-dors to Egypt and Tyre reported, and which David from time to time declared he would adopt. But David was as forgetful on the point as his ministers were and so the effect was usually what the priests and prophets, who did not forget such things, preached so vehemently for: bowing only before the god enthroned upon the ark. This left only the overawed peasant, those pleading for their lives, or those who flattered themselves with worldly ways and were mocked for it, to kiss the carpets in the throne room.

The messenger was hesitant to announce me and thereby

interrupt the counsel. And I did not fall immediately to the ground for fear the effect might be wasted as long as I was ignored. I was looking down, straightening the hang of my gown, when a voice said, "Tamar." David never called me Tamar—he could never remember my name—only "daughter."

It was the firstborn prince who was reigning that morning in the throne room. It was Amnon. Those who now still believe the rumors that he was not the king's son should have seen him as I did that day, come to the perfection of young manhood, born to inherit his father's kingdom.

The counselors were stopped in mid-sentence and all things seemed suspended between

A time to embrace
and a time to refrain from embracing

as the preachers say. At last Amnon seemed to remember that he was in the king's place that day, that it was up to him to indicate to us all how we were to react. One of the counselors was told to fluff the cushions for me on the divan for honored guests and another to bring wine. Then, grumbling that they had work to do and was it not such duties that one bought slaves for? they were dismissed and we were alone. The last look they gave me reminded me of Ahinoam's words, "He loves you." Was I being seduced? Here in the throne room, of all things?

"Wine?" Amnon offered.

"No, thanks," I said.

He helped himself. I saw, for all the early hour, he was drinking it neat. There are those who gossip that Amnon drank more than was good for him. Well, on this day it was not to get drunk that he did without water, but because his fierce conscience would not allow him that luxury when there were animals dying for want of water in the wells. He was taking the drought personally, I saw, even before he spoke of it. This concern, weighing down the flesh of his face, was part of the reason he had seemed so old when I first entered, so old that I mistook him for his father. The drink was not helping him to relax, however.

"You might as well know at the start," he said after a heavy drink, "that my father has forbidden your spring rites."

"He has no care for his people or his land." My hackles were raised. This did not sound like I was being seduced. It didn't even sound like I was cared for very much.

"He has a great care for his people."

"As long as he and his are drinking sweet wine, he has no care."

Amnon put his bowl down firmly and repeated, "He has a great care for this land and this people. That's why he wants no . . . no abominations."

"Abominations! I'll tell you what's an abomination—"

"We are all praying for the Lord to bless the land. When our prayers are not single-minded, how can we expect them to be answered?"

"Prayers to Goddess are not the reason the heavens withhold their moisture. It is because two years ago at this time, Her High Priestess was murdered, even as she was sanctified and portraying the Queen of Heaven."

"My father told me to tell you." Amnon was almost shouting now, high pink in his cheeks. "There will be no rites."

"Fine. You've told me."

"Will you swear?"

"Swear?"

"He wanted me to get you to swear to it."

"How can I swear by Goddess not to honor Her?"

"Swear by God then."

"On my tongue, an oath to David's god is meaningless."

"I want to do what my father wants me to do. My father is a great man. He killed a giant when he was younger than I am, he's made this empire—"

"If it makes you feel any better, I wouldn't swear if the Goliath-killer were here on his throne in person. He could kill me with his slingshot, too. I wouldn't swear."

Amnon sighed, nodded, and seemed content.

"Well?"

"Well?"

"Is that the end of your orders?"

"Yes."

"May I go?"

To my surprise, I was not dismissed. He said nothing. I wondered if I should just leave. I didn't like this Amnon, heir to the throne. I was just a pawn to take his orders, as to his father. But still there was something behind that harsh exterior that almost begged me to stay and set it free. I stayed.

"Do you remember the Ammonites?" he asked at last.

"King Nahash and his sons in the tents on the Mount of Olives?"

"You remember." He looked at me hopefully for the first time that day.

"I remember David has declared war on them."

"He has."

"For a trifle."

"That's . . . that's a matter of opinion."

"He covets their copper."

" 'You shall not covet your neighbor's—' "

"What's that?"

"Nothing."

Amnon stretched out deliberately on the divan across from me. He rested his head sometimes on his fist, sometimes back against the wall, always with his eyes weighted shut. It was not a comfortable pose in any case, not for me, not for him.

"Would you care to know what the ministers had been flailing me with this morning?"

"I think things are more pleasant in the harem."

He didn't take my hint. "The sons of Ammon have sent to the Aramaeans of Zoba, Maacah, and Ishtob."

I pretended disinterest, but I was listening for mention of neighboring Geshur. Obviously my grandfather was trying to remain neutral, with his daughter and granddaughter in David's court.

"Among these tribes, Ammon has found allies to increase

their numbers for the conflict. The army that gathers now in Ammon is so numerous that Israel and Judah will be as chaff before a whirlwind. Yet our cousin Joab insists on crossing the Jordan to meet them anyway. My father insists that I insist that he insist."

"That is how David has made an empire."

"The Aramaeans with seven hundred chariots and cavalry beyond number, the army of Joab made hungry and disorderly by the drought—one can almost smell the rank blood of Israel's defeat. In the south, more Amalekite raids and, of course, from every corner that fears no war come cries for wheat, pulse, even a cupped hand of water . . ."

"Now you know, this doesn't sound at all like the Ammonites I met. They hardly had their own donkeys, yet chariots? Amnon," I leaned forward to him, truly interested at last, "Amnon, do the ministers and chroniclers tell one thing, do I—and you—know another?"

Amnon committed nothing.

"And where is your father in all of this?" I asked the obvious question.

"My father?" Amnon said. He opened his eyes to look at me, then closed them again. "My father has escaped to the arms of his new love and is not to be disturbed with the troubles of the kingdom."

"And who might his new love be?" I couldn't remember having seem David in the harem for a while.

I remembered as soon as Amnon said it. "Bathsheba." It was a name that could hardly be said without a sigh, but my stepbrother seemed to give it more sigh than it warranted.

"Now that you mention it, I have heard the gossip, although I usually try to ignore it. Isn't she the daughter of Eliam and granddaughter of Ahithophel, David's head counselor?"

"Such a liaison can't help but attract attention, I suppose."

"David hasn't married her yet, or brought her to the palace. She's still living at home. How serious can the infatuation be?"

"If an oracle had numbered my father's days on one hand, he couldn't be more reckless."

"Well, David's been infatuated before."

"It's not infatuation."

"We've always managed to live through it. Isn't that what makes a king, in his eyes, anyway?"

But now I could see this was more than an ordinary infatuation in Amnon's eyes. "Amnon, don't tell me you're infatuated with her, too?"

The high pink color rose in Amnon's cheeks and he blurted: "It's not infatuation. Besides, I saw her first. From the parapet. I saw her bathing on the roof."

"An older woman."

"She's not so much older. And she's—she's very beautiful."

"Bathing on the roof. Pretty shameless, wouldn't you say?"

"No more shameless—no more shameless than the rites of your demon goddess."

"Oh, Amnon. You would have gone to her?"

He softened a bit. "She had all these signals, where I was to meet her, when her husband was at home. A red cloth on the line meant the coast was clear."

"Did you go?"

"I thought about it all the time. I even set out once or twice. But always I thought, What would my father say? Well, now I know what he would say. She grew tired of waiting for a prince when she could have the king himself. By the God of my Fathers! He flings all righteousness in Heaven's face. Bathsheba is a married woman!"

"You didn't seem to mind."

"It's different for a prince."

"How is it different?"

"Besides, I just—thought about it."

"David's never let a previous marriage stand in his way before, either."

"What do you mean?"

"I mean my mother."

"Yes, but he always took care that the man be treatied with first."

"What about Michal?"

"Or—or conquered."

"And Abigail?"

"Abigail's first husband died."

"Yes, Nabal died."

"A natural death."

"Very natural. When David and his band of runaways tried to extort ransom from him and he refused. When David and his band surrounded Nabal's house like a pack of bandits and threatened to kill everything within the walls if Nabal didn't pay. And when Abigail went out unbeknownst to her husband to bribe David with two hundred of those crispy loaves only she knows how to bake and those sheep dressed with thyme and all of that. And with her plump little cheeks like apples and her plump little bottom bouncing up and down on her donkey, knowing all the while that David had been out there in the wilderness, celibate, ever since he fled from Saul."

"My father was God's anointed."

"Well, after that, 'God's anointed' swore he'd only kill the things in the compound that 'pissed against the wall'; everything else he'd take for himself. And when Abigail shamelessly went back and told her husband *that*—yes, I'd say it was a natural death."

"God struck Nabal and turned him to stone."

"She knew perfectly well he had a weak heart."

"It was the Hand of God."

"Conquered or treatied or god-disposed of—very god-fearing of your father. And of Abigail."

"Oh, you are infuriating. What do you know about these things? Packed away in the harem as you are."

"May I please be excused to return to my harem?"

I was not excused. "Uriah is a nothing," Amnon said.

I took a breath before I could bring myself to give him another chance. "Who's Uriah?"

"Bathsheba's husband. He is . . . was . . . a Hittite mercenary in Father's army."

"You speak in the past tense."

"Father's sent Uriah to the front."

"That's where mercenaries belong."

"He's told Joab to see that he doesn't return. If he's not dead now he soon will be. Bathsheba's with child. Uriah was such a good man he couldn't even be talked into breaking the soldier's ban on being with women to make it look like his."

"Well. So now Bathsheba is free."

"Tamar, are you heartless?"

"She's as free—as Michal, then, shall we say?"

"There's a world of difference between Michal and Bathsheba."

"What's that?"

"Bathsheba is happy with my father. Michal is not."

"So that makes what he's done with Bathsheba worse?"

"Yes."

"I should think having made someone happy at least had merit."

"Michal is the daughter of the king."

"So her misery is all right?"

"To be expected, anyway, and endured."

"Your oracle for me is not good."

"Among royalty things are done as they—must be done."

"Just among royal women."

"No, I mean for myself, too. And my father. We must do our duties. But Bathsheba was the only bright light in Uriah's life."

"It sounds like she was sorely lacking in duty when she stepped out on her roof to seduce an unsuspecting prince."

"I was not seduced, that's the point."

"I must congratulate you."

"My father was. She brings no lands with her, no wealth, no jewels. It's my father who breaks the coffers to adorn her. We have a war to be fought, whether we like it or not, mercenaries to be paid—not bumped off like Uriah. Can you imagine what this will mean among the troops? What if the word gets around? They all start to worry about their wives at home? They all start to worry that that man at their

back has been hired to see that they don't come home instead of protecting them from sniper shot? A man anointed
to be king has a greater responsibility than the average man.
He must live by a higher law. By no means should he plun-
der his subjects."

"Other kings, however—"

"Yes, if he can get away with it. But not people who've
sworn fealty to him. It wreaks havoc on morale. It's as if a
man with large flocks and herds killed another for a single
lamb, his only lamb, which slept all night in his breast.
Sometimes—sometimes I see Bathsheba. Sometimes she
stands on her roof with these sleepy doe eyes and one thigh
bent like this and bare and I—"

"Amnon, it sounds like she's still trying to seduce you."

"She is just—very beautiful. She can't help it."

"She could cover her leg. That she could help." I was
surprised at myself. My heart was beating more than it
should. Before this time, I'd considered Amnon's attention
to me cute, or to be taken for granted. Was I jealous?

"She cannot seduce me," Amnon said, as if he hardly
believed himself. "She cannot. That would be civil war.
Even she must see that."

"I don't think civil war would faze her. Women like Bathsheba are like men like Absalom. Goddess would have recommended they pass through the fire at their births."

"How can you say such things? Killing babies, that's an
abomination."

"Or at least turn their energies to other uses." Why was
I trying to placate Amnon? It was already clear which side
he was on.

"I—I would always put the welfare of my land and people
above my—my pleasures. If anything is causing God to
curse this land, it's my father's behavior."

"Do you think so?"

"Certainly. God has made my father powerful. He
should act so as to be worthy of that power. By God, I will
not act so when, by Heaven's grace, I am king. He should
act . . ." He opened his hands helplessly on his knees.

Those are nice, strong knots of knees, I thought. Why was

I thinking so? "He should act so a son can be proud of him,"
I said, to be saying something in the breach.

"That's right," Amnon said firmly, but I saw him blink
tears from the corners of his eyes.

"We all can hardly wait until you're king." Come, there
was no need to be so sarcastic. The boy is almost in tears.
More gently I said, "Are you charged with the kingdom,
then?"

"By default. The petitioners come, wait a few days, are
given this or that excuse, told that their plight is under
consideration. They have desperate cases that call for immediate attention, and all the time my father is toying with his
darling in the gardens and not to be disturbed. So they come
to me."

"And what do you do?"

"All within my power. I try to present a calm and controlled face, first of all, but when I'm alone, I throw up my
hands in despair. It is not so much that I am young. There
have been younger men come to a kingdom before me. But
then their fathers were dead and not tempting God in the
wings. Not able to come out at any minute and say: 'Fool!
What have you done?' Younger men than I have been duly
anointed and crowned. But I have no true power. If I could
have true power, the first thing I'd do is call Joab back until
more men can be recruited from the northern tribes at least.
No, I'd call them back and send them to their parched fields
so we could all worry about this drought with a single mind.
But letting Joab cross the Jordan was one decision my father
roused himself from his love-drunk stupor long enough to
make, and I am stuck with trying to make my decisions—on
supply lines and weaponry and recruitment—to match that
first mistake. Well, I cannot do it."

⊡ XXXII ⊡

AMNON DRANK DEEPLY of his neat wine, realized its strength, put his bowl aside, then felt a thirst again and had to drink more. I was pained and silent.

"Ah," he sighed, having swallowed. "Why do I bother you with all this? I have my reasons. If I am to have some semblance of power, at least I can choose who I want for my counselors, not Ahithophel, who has come to hate David's house because of what we—what my father—has done to his granddaughter. Not Ira, who can't even . . ."

"I know nothing of war and care to know less."

"Tamar, don't," he said with a touch of anger. "Don't be falsely modest like everyone else around here. I need words of faith and courage."

"Well, what shall I say? That it would be better to call Joab back, yes, I agree with your policy there, your majesty. But as for the courage to do such a thing—"

"You do remember Hanun and Shobi, the sons of Ammon?"

I remember our time there as one of the best of my life. And the consideration you showed to me that night— "They did seem like good men," was all I said.

"That is more than all the fearful bigots I'm surrounded by will admit. That is enough to recommend your counsel. And it is enough that you, at least, confirm my feelings. I would not ask you whether I should deploy the archers here or there; Joab knows that business better than you—or I, for that matter—could ever hope to. But there is something you are an authority on and it's on that subject that I ask your counsel."

I could not think what that subject might be, unless it were grinding wheat, and I told him so.

"The drought," Amnon said.

"The drought?"

"I have carefully considered and it is clear to me that the drought is the basic cause of all the difficulties that plague us: the war with Ammon, the unrest in Dan, the raids by the Amalekites in the south. If the drought would end, these others would settle of their own accord."

I shook my head. "The drought is in Heaven's hands."

"Precisely."

"You've already told me the royal ruling on the drought. We're to pray to your god."

"Which means to you—?"

"We will all perish of this drought."

Amnon nodded at my counsel. What is he dancing around now? I thought. Something more deadly than a sword blade?

"What I told you," he said carefully, "was David's ruling on the subject. I told you what he had me swear to tell you. I'm a man of my word. I told you."

"You did, indeed. You are getting good at giving orders."

"But you no better at taking them."

"You want me to swear?"

He made no comment.

"I'll swear if you'd like."

"Tamar, you will?" There was a strange sadness in his voice.

"Yes, I'll swear by Goddess that I will do everything in my power to see the rites performed. As Goddess is my witness, the land will perish without them. But as She is my

witness, I am almost powerless to see them done. I would die
to see them done, I swear it. But without a miracle from Her
hand, I swear—"

"So. I've heard your vow. That gives me courage."

"Courage?"

"Snakesleeper, what are we to do?"

He called me Snakesleeper, my ritual name. "I—I don't
know what you mean."

"You said you are powerless. I am not so powerless.
What do you need to keep the rites?"

"I don't— I mean, David has forbidden them."

"And David has ordered the army to cross the Jordan.
That I can't counter. This, perhaps I can."

"You would allow us to return to Topheth?"

"Let's just say David would never notice in his bedroom
and I—I will look the other way. That I can swear to. I can
order the guards to stay clear of the place. I can—well, I
don't know. What's needed?"

I found myself laughing and crying at once. I wanted to
hug my stepbrother, but that didn't seem correct. "You
would really do this?"

"You have my word."

"But what about—what about your god?"

"Yes, what about Him? I don't know. Perhaps I'll stand
condemned. Well, so be it. All I can say is, He seems to be
looking the other way while my father dallies with Bathsheba and kills her husband. I want to be virtuous. Being
virtuous means honoring your parents. But if virtue means
honoring my father while he does this—well, I can't believe
it. Is it virtue to stand by and say nothing, do nothing? No!
And how can being passive and compliant to evil accomplish anything? There must be something to stand opposed
to this, to give virtue other options. Your goddess is all I've
thought of. All my life I've been taught about 'abominations,' but yours is the first counsel I've thought was truly
honest in all this mess. And it does seem to make sense, in
a way. Your priestess and her—consort? Is that what you
call him? Father killed them at your spring festival and—

and we haven't had a drop of rain since. There seems no other answer to this simple sum."

"Yes," was all I could say to all of this.

"So? What do you need to set it right?"

"I—I— Well, but the shrine in Topheth is desecrated."

"Surely it can be reconsecrated?"

"That would take great numbers of offerings: burnt and sin offerings . . ."

"I have the powers of a king—nearly. It can be done. Besides, the people are desperate. They come pleading to me every day to do something. They will help us—you."

"The priestesses and hierodules will have to be gathered, the Snake pit replenished."

"I'm sure you can do that."

Why was I the one doing the arguing against this? But suddenly where it had been only one insurmountable barrier, there were now scores of little details, likewise insurmountable. "The images must be replaced."

"They are still in the storehouses. I know where. They haven't been melted down. Father could find no Hebrew who knew the skill and no Jebusite who dared such sacrilege."

"Goddess cakes must be baked."

"Michal and Zipporah can help you there."

"But—but we need the Holy Couple." Ah, that was the main obstacle, wasn't it?

"You may have anyone in the kingdom."

"Not too many people in the kingdom are willing to face the possibility of dying like the last Couple."

"Haven't I given my word? I will not interfere."

"Still, as long as you aren't king—"

He looked truly hurt.

"All right, yes, the odds are better. Yes, thank you. But it's more than just this fear of death. It can't be just anyone. The Son must be a ruler of land where the rite is performed. Araunah king of the Jebusites is old and feeble and he has no sons left to him in his old age."

"Araunah is no longer ruler of Jerusalem anyway," Amnon said with a fit of family pride. "We are."

"You think David would appear in Topheth?" I asked sarcastically.

"He's too busy with Uriah's wife." Amnon spoke bitterly, got to his feet, and walked away from me. Then he turned with the violence of his decision. "But David's firstborn son offers himself."

The western sun poured through the window at his back and he stood in that light like a secret revealed. His cheeks were the color of apricots stewed in wine, but I knew he was earnest. "Of course," I said, almost smothered by the awe of the revelation. "Who else?"

"Who else?" He smiled as if giving me courage for a dreadful leap and shrugged his shoulders to fit them to the mantle he had just assumed.

"But who—who will be High Priestess? She lies under a pile of stones outside the gate."

"Why you, of course." He said it just like that, as if I were a dog tossed a bone.

"What am I? Your wife?" I exploded. "A woman who has asked her husband, 'Who's to clean up this mess you've made?' and he replies, 'Why you, of course.'"

My anger truly took him by surprise. He came to me and put his arm about my shoulders. "Tamar, what's wrong? I'm trying to help."

Of course I knew that was what he was trying to do, but still there was some catch, even in the lay of his arm, that made me angry. "Of course, you'd rather it were Bathsheba." There was no call for me to say it. But—there it was.

"Yes—all right, fine." He jumped up away from me again. "Yes, I'd rather it were Bathsheba. I'm laying my life on the line and you—you're not Bathsheba, Sister. But I've said I'd do it. Isn't that enough? It's more than my father's done. My father—? My father may never speak to me again. He may disown me. He may kill me. Isn't that enough?"

I stepped to him and gently took his hand. "Yes, Amnon, yes. Forgive me. I've been foolish. It is enough. More than enough."

Pressure was returned on my hand. Then his hot pink

cheek was pressed to mine, then his lips. My heart raced. There was no taste of Bathsheba there.

"So we do it, you and I?"

"It cannot be me," I whispered.

"For the love of God, why not?"

I smiled gently at his Israelite's view of the rite; their view of the world that thinks one rite can serve all places. "If this were the temple of Aphek in Geshur, yes, then, that would be my calling. This is Topheth in Jerusalem."

"But I don't understand. You are the Snakesleeper."

"Yes. I will have other vital duties. But, Brother, my good, honest brother, I am not of the blood of the High Priestesses of Jerusalem. It must be the blood of Jerusalem, or the land and air of Jerusalem cannot respond. This duty I cannot perform."

"I had hoped, Tamar, that you and I— I mean, it would be easier if it weren't a stranger— I mean, I was beginning to—"

"I, too, Brother—" I let him take my hand and kiss the palm. "But it cannot be. It will not work. Perhaps someday—"

Amnon left me and walked to where drapes of Egyptian linen were struggling to keep out the western sun but not any blessed breeze caught in passing. How limp and lifeless they hung at that moment! Amnon stood framed against them like an ancient monolith against the pale, dead sands of the desert valley it marks with hope of life.

When he turned to me again, he was as assured as I was of the path we had to take. Later, Goddess willing, there might be time for us, just as the preacher says: "A time to embrace . . ." But now we could not carelessly sink into individual personality as David was allowing himself to do. There was Heaven to propitiate and the land to save.

· XXXIII ·

THE SUN WAS unrelenting on the irregular pounded clay of the roof of the grain merchant's house. The roofs of Jerusalem are like roofs everywhere, with their slight refuges of grape arbors, their cats, their corners full of garbage, their laundry, their sticklike plants trying to grow in broken crockery, and their children, everywhere, sliding down the domes and squabbling.

Here at the grain merchant's they were shelling dried lentils. The merchant's wife and daughters were doing most of the work themselves, for the drought had seriously affected the merchant's business and they had not been able to hire the hands they were used to. Even some of their slaves had had to be sold to travelers going south to Egypt where the Nile counteracted drought and where slaves from Israel were going quickly and cheaply. Those who could not be sold were given their freedom to fend for themselves, which meant they either were honest and starved to death or stole and were executed.

I knew at once who the merchant's wife must be. She had the air of mistress, the pursed lips of one responsible to see

that whatever her husband brought home was made to feed
the entire clan. I also noticed something about her forehead
and eyes that reminded me of another. They were light eyes
with thin lashes, transparent and unshaded as if they saw
much that other mortals missed. I remembered such eyes
closing as they bent to kiss my Snake skin at the threshold
of the sanctuary. I remembered them wrinkling, clutching
like fists as the ecstasy of the Great Mystery tightened every
muscle. The eyes were startling because I had thought them
long shut in death. In all other aspects, this was a woman
one felt comfortable with, motherly and unthreatening.

A timid, everyday version of the sublime chaos, swirling
pain, astonishment and enraptured frenzy all together, entered this pair of eyes as I explained to her why I had come.
For this wife of the grain merchant, this sober Jebusite
matron, was of Goddess's house of the shrine of Topheth.

"You want me to rise to the position of High Priestess?"
she asked dumbfounded. "And enact the ritual this year?"

"Someone must. The land—"

"You don't need to tell me about the land," she said.
"Just look at us! The family of a grain merchant making its
bread with lentils! And look what shriveled little things they
are."

"You'll do it then?"

"She was my sister."

"I know."

"She they stoned two years ago. She was my sister."

"I know. I'm sorry. That's why I came to you. I didn't
know where else to turn. If it's too much to ask, if you are
afraid, I don't blame you, but—"

"I'm not afraid. If someone doesn't undertake it this year,
I fear, we'll all be dead come the next time of mourning."

"Goddess forbid."

"Goddess forbid, but the god seems to will it."

"I have the Groom."

"Oh, he's a brave man. After what they did to the last
one."

"Yes, he's brave. His name's Amnon."

"David's son?"

"Yes. But it mustn't be commonly known."

"No, of course not. Amnon the son of David. Well, there's hope for the land yet."

"You'll do it then?" I still read hesitation in her face. "Or lead me to someone who will?"

"My family has never known any greater honor than to live and die as representatives of Goddess."

"You will do it."

"I hesitate only that I am not worthy of such an honor."

"She whom Goddess calls—"

"Yes, but you see, I have been secularly married and made a mother and generally steeped in the mundane for the past fifteen years."

"These are hard times for piety—for all of us."

"I have a daughter," she suddenly suggested, though I could tell the thought had been growing in her mind since I first mentioned my errand. "She is not yet initiate, but had there been the Mysteries last year, she would have been. She is of age."

"Let me see the girl," I asked, and the woman called her daughter's name.

The girl arose from her crouch before the lentil shells and walked toward us. She was of startling beauty, all the more startling because her slight, tenuous figure was repeated nowhere else in the courtyard, not in any of her younger sisters, solid and big-boned, nor in her round-kneed little brothers who seemed to have baby fat even at seven or eight.

The mother seemed to sense my start. "She is a Goddess child," she explained. And there was pride in her voice.

So I understood that the girl had been gotten by her mother on the altar when in her youth she had served as hierodule in the shrine. Who the father was, was fogged in incense and divine intoxication. Obviously he was not the grain merchant, who was like a round, doughy loaf, dusty with flour and just waiting to be patted into the oven. Even the mother would have thought it impious to make inquiries as to who it might have been to come to her that night. She only counted herself blessed to have brought forth such Goddess fruit. Such children, they say, take the mother's beauty (and every woman is more beautiful when she performs the rites), lithify it in youth, and chisel it even finer with the tools of Heaven. Women tell of the delightful feelings they experience while this forging is going on within their wombs, while the Heaven-got child is still unborn, and of the blessings of miraculous good fortune that follow such a birth.

The unearthly beauty of the girl was proof of the legend. And she knew it. One hated to burden her small, uninitiated parts with the name of "breasts," yet the way she carried her shoulders, the way they in turn carried the drape of a wide, low neckline, was a certain sign that she knew. She knew she was meant to be adored. She knew that even when times were hard and her sisters would have to content themselves with hand-me-downs, she would be indulged with new lengths of wool, new bangles and beads. She knew that with every step she took, no matter how mundane, with every swing of her thick black braids against the narrow band at her waist, she recalled the temple dances to one who knew them or aroused the desire for the Mystery in those who did not. Her knowledge of her sublime power caused her no blush of shame as she steadily met my eyes throughout our introduction.

And I knew that she knew the moment the sudden convulsion passed over me. She was used to seeing it in others. She had learned to live with it as others must with the reaction to a limp or a twitch or a birthmark. They know the world thinks of nothing else when it sees them, and yet the world politely ignores the topic as if it were the mention of death itself. The girl smiled in a way that seemed calmly, comfortably intoxicated. She was seeking to put me at ease before what she might consider her handicap to a normal life "like other girls.' " But the sensation her beauty caused was new to me, new and terrible and frustrating and inhibiting. I was jealous and selfish and threatened, and so I was defensive.

I know what I felt was silly. Worse than that: in this case it was wicked. One who has been initiated, one who has a knowledge of the Mysteries as I had should fear no loss by those same Mysteries. There can only be gain when Goddess is served. You may want to shout this at me, but I knew it already. I was shouting it loudly myself into my pounding mind that morning on the merchant's roof. You are acting like a child who hasn't learned to share, like Mother toward Bathsheba (like yourself toward Bathsheba!) or whomever else may be new and favored in the harem. Have you no trust? Can it be that you are afraid of losing Amnon? How can you be afraid of losing that which you're in no way assured of ever getting? Is he even worth getting, worth more than saving the land? Certainly not! And how can you feel jealousy over what is a rite for the good of the whole land—like drawing water for the fields or spreading manure?

Granted, mortals can have no control over the outcome of the spring rite. "When two maidenheads meet . . ." they say. But if Goddess should choose to ignite an enduring flame beneath this couple I was forming—and I saw no reason why She should not take pleasure in such an act, bless it with children, bind it with Her girdle of stars—that was Her will, was it not? I should rejoice. The drought would end. The earth would glow with Her choicest blessings. Yet my mind turned from any consideration of this as one flees, shawl over mouth and nose, and arm over eyes, from a desert sandstorm, running blindly, anywhere but into the heart of the storm.

"She is uninitiated," I said gravely. I found it a good measure of self-defense to treat the girl as an object, or perhaps as a ewe we were haggling over in the market. The girl seemed used to this sort of treatment, this sort of reaction to the Goddess power in her face.

"It's not like it hasn't happened before," the High Priestess said, "that a woman has risen from the bed of initiation and gone directly to the Great Bed of the Gods. My sister, Goddess rest her, she did it."

"We will have more than the usual difficulties this season," I urged.

"Two years of drought, yes."

"Not just the drought. We must consider that these years

were preceded by five years of weakening and neglect of the shrine under David." I was grasping at straws. "Even those who've been full participants for years will have had all this time in which to forget."

"We've all been trying to forget, haven't we, the horror with which the last ceremonies were aborted?"

"What else might be forgotten with it?"

The girl's stepfather, the doughy, placid little man, came up from his accounting room to join us. Into what he'd been overhearing, he interjected: "Excuse me, Wife. Perhaps it's none of my business—"

"Yes, Husband?"

"I pray for an end to the drought as much as the next man," he said, "don't misunderstand me. But if both options are equally proper, then I would prefer you, my wife, should undertake this calling, not the girl."

"Why is that?" asked the High Priestess, unable to look him in the eye. Did even she struggle with jealousy, at her age and with her experience? Did it hurt her that her husband could give her up to Goddess more readily than the girl?

"Forgive me, but in times like these— What I mean to say is, the girl's great beauty has given me hopes for a good marriage for her."

"Marriage?"

"Yes, do you remember that man Dan?"

"What? That pious Israelite?"

"Pious he may be, but he owns such large grainfields in Jezreel. I've said nothing of it to you because Dan's finances are not of the best in this drought, either. But if the rains can be brought, our daughter's marriage to him may be a way to repair our losses to some degree. It would be a great comfort, wouldn't it, to have her so well established in these uncertain times? I only fear her chances might be marred if it were discovered she had participated as Goddess's proxy. It would be difficult enough to explain how she came to the marriage bed without blood to be spilled if you insist on initiating her."

"She is Goddess's child."

"I know, dear. And I've been proud to raise her as such. Forgive my material concerns, but if it can be bought, I will sway Goddess's favor in this direction with the gift of an ox for this year's celebration and a bushel of wheat for every child the girl might bear—once the rains come."

Those who are third- or fourth-generation Goddess-children are just so much more distilled of beauty, rare buds at the most succulent, but even the first and second generations are so entrancing, so divinely graceful, that men are rarely content to allow it to go further. They must set their claim on it, mingle their blood with the divine, and snatch Heaven down to their own lowly dust.

I felt a twinge of guilt, yet I said, "Thank you, sir, for your concern and your tempting offer. Priestess, it is a generous offer."

"Yes. How welcome the gift of the ox will be now, when people are so poor and fearful. And . . . and I must confess I've been thinking it over ever since you brought it up. There are several large chunks of the liturgy I can't seem to remember."

"Perhaps if you think about it for a while."

"No, I'm quite sure they're gone."

"You can't remember—?"

"No. Can you, Snakesleeper?"

"I? I was only initiated at that last season. I only heard them once."

"Well, perhaps I'll ask Deborah or one of the older women. At any rate, I'm feeling a little daunted myself at the mass of words I must somehow commit to memory before the Time. At least I have a feel for what must come where. My daughter would have to start from scratch. Yes, I think it would be best if I undertook it this year."

"Mama—!" The girl wailed with disappointment.

"Never you mind," the High Priestess said. "Your turn will come soon enough."

"But Mama, I don't want to marry any pious old Israelite."

"You go on back to your lentils. You will have your

initiation this year, I promise, blood on Dan's sheets or not."

"But Mama—!"

"We'll discuss it later."

So the girl returned to her lentils disappointed, but her father and I both returned to our places relieved.

I was very young, please remember, insecure, and had grown suddenly very possessive of my stepbrother. But I knew what I should have done and I did not do it. I can only say that I learned from it, learned better that Goddess-madness is not to be controlled by mortals and that it is meant for all, to be given freely as She decrees. I thank the Almighty One that She blessed us in spite of my weakness.

And I can't help but think that Goddess is in jealousy as much as She is in love. When springtime loosens the bonds of love under which we labor the rest of the year, then to be jealous is counterproductive. So in spring one may go so far as to feel guilty for allowing jealousy to strike, as one may feel guilty during the rest of the year when an unlawful love is imagined and burns in the heart. To deny the existence of the one emotion is as foolish as to deny the other. Accrediting both to Goddess helps me to understand and accept these emotions that one cannot control. We should not add guilt to the sufferings of either love denied or jealousy that lingers and should use them both to best advantage as the seasons allow.

The reason we are blessed (or cursed) with love is obvious: there must be children brought into the world. People (especially men) then tend to forget that the creation of a child does not end at coitus when Goddess lifts the heavy burden of love from one's loins and one can turn over and sleep. Goddess, Who is first of all a Mother, and only secondly a Lover, knows that the time of bearing cannot really be said to be over until the child is grown and come of age. Jealousy may be said to be the drive that brings the child to its delivery as a self-sufficient adult, that drives us to cleave to one we love for longer than just the divine moment—lingering into many divine moments—so that families, the creators of adults, may endure.

I thought of how farmers press their seals into their mounds of grain (like pregnant bellies) left on the threshing floor so that none will disturb what is necessary to their lives. It was with these thoughts that I was later to add this verse to my Song of Songs:

> Set me as a seal upon your heart,
> as a seal upon your arm;
> for love is as strong as death,
> jealousy is as cruel as the grave.
> Its flashes are flashes of fire,
> a most vehement flame.

◉ XXXIV ◉

IT WAS A problem I had not considered until then, but it became the greatest one of that year. The liturgy was lost, completely disappeared in those two years without its use as if it had been some physical thing, an altar cloth or holy vessel that could be set to the torch or ground into sand by David's zeal, not a free and living song that, even if it were tortured from them, could still live on in the original, safe in people's minds.

I went throughout the town, from wineseller's to weaver's shop to farmer's hovel, wherever I heard of women who might still know the words. From these places I drew the necessary ranks of attendants from the scattered remnant of the once-great shrine: sacrificers who were butchers' wives, incensors who were perfumers, chorus members whose only exercise of voice in recent months had been lullabying their children.

Many knew parts of the liturgy, the choruses, the responses. From my one time in the most holy place, even I remembered the much repeated "My beloved is mine and I am his," and then the vow of love, the "I adjure you, daughters of Jerusalem . . ." But everyone who remembered the answers Goddess gave to these choruses—to praise the Son's fair color or his beauty as a shepherd among the lilies or the strength of his love in the garden—could not remember the order they came in, or if they thought they did, they contradicted each one her sister.

There were some who remembered a couplet or two for personal reasons: an affinity for this phrase, or "One year the high priestess forgot the line and none of us forgot it since." One supple, long- and dark-limbed beauty who still danced for wages and love in a wineseller's house remembered the entire song of the dance: "How beautiful are your steps in sandals, O nobleman's daughter . . ." She had profaned it in her art.

But no one, I was finally forced to confront the fact, had had the will—or the courage, perhaps—to keep the song alive in its entirety. The former High Priestess had been the last to study it seriously. If she had had an understudy, a niece or a cousin somewhere, the woman was nowhere to be found. And so the secret had died and been buried with her under the pile of stones without Jerusalem's wall.

"So we must do the best we can with what is left," the new High Priestess said when we met again to discuss the state of affairs. Amnon was with us and he agreed there was little else we could do.

"Unless . . ." I said.

"Unless what?" Amnon asked, taking his gaze from the other woman for a moment to look at me.

"Nothing," I said, sorry that I had disturbed his devotions, as it were. Those two had enough to worry about without stopping to wonder where their speeches would come from. They must perform perfectly, something I could not teach them. That was the most important thing.

But to myself I finished my thought: "Unless— Unless Goddess Herself chooses to speak and inspire us. If it is Her will we are undertaking, surely She should condescend to help us and teach us words pleasing to Her as She must have taught the first Woman who bowed in the first year of drought and asked for Her help."

How *had* mortals first learned the divine words? I wondered. And then I answered myself—or perhaps was given the answer—the Serpent, of course, the Giver of all Wisdom.

The evening before the last phase of the moon of Sivan, I left the palace and went down to the shrine alone. Mother's advice never to be the first because one would thereby miss the effect of community had to be set aside this time. There was work to be done that I alone could do and that I must do alone. I trusted Amnon and the High Priestess to see to the final preparations: the last seams in the holy robes, the final gathering of fragrances and flowers and musical instruments—though if my plan failed, all of this would be like a filigree-gold setting for a lump of dried-mud liturgy.

I carried Father of Shadows on my head in his hamper. I could feel the curl of his coils about my head like a cooling wreath of freshly plucked grape leaves. He lay still in spite of my motion, his body rigid in anticipation.

Spilling over the hillside and into rich dark pools at my very feet in the little-used path, the anemones were blooming, rich and red, the dear Son's life blood, but I alone as yet was dressed in mourning. Spires of white lilies and the musk of asphodel and, in the distance, poppies in the corn, were few and far between and served as but brief refreshment from the everywhere-sticky warmth of those god flowers. Drought had not stayed their coming from their deep and ancient tubers. Like us, I thought, like the return of the rites. They were sparse and dark and hard against the lifeless ground like dried bloodstains on linen bandages in need of changing. I remembered an old, old hymn where Our Lady is described marching across the battlefield "her head crowned with severed hands, her waist belted with bleeding heads." With a great fear of Heaven, with a pain to feel my own blood coursing still and yet so tenuously at my wrists, I stopped a moment to pick some of those flowers seeping up from the Netherworld. I found their stalks brittle and their blooms already half wilted. Perhaps it was in vain I hoped they would last, so parched, until we could call down the water the whole world so desperately needed.

Earlier in the month, about the time of the fullness, I had come with Amnon and the High Priestess and a few others to clean and purify the site, to set the images on their pedestals, and to dig the sand out of the spring. At that time, by day, I had scrubbed the walls of the Snake pit with rose water and lime and laid new fig leaves on the litter of gold and jewels on the floor. Then I had loosed three female snakes donated by some who had been keeping them for the prosperity (and mouselessness) of their storerooms. I looked to my Father of Shadows to give us good increase by next year.

Now when I arrived I found two more house-snake caskets before the door to the sanctuary and felt the living weight of their occupants when I lifted them. I released these together with Father of Shadows into the pit, promising to return shortly. Then I went up and started the fire that would not die until life was restored to the Earth. I kneaded meal and oil together and gave it all to the fire, feeling in myself the need to fast for the request I was about to make of Heaven.

Night fell at once, but the cool breeze of evening never stirred the air within the shrine, where it was always cool and breathless. The stars, having but the last slip of moon to contend with, were large and full of luster. They seemed to throb closer and closer to Earth. I sat down where I could see them in one of the chambers where people come to sleep hoping for dreams of inspiration to visit them through the open roofs. But I was not planning to sleep; the dream I hoped for was too urgent.

I prayed and sang and watched the stars 'til they and my weariness tranced me. Over and over again I rehearsed all the liturgy I had been able to gather, feeling its timeless force and its direction. I filled my head with the symbols and rites of the season. Times of hunger I thought I could not endure faded into times when my weariness was the only thing I could think of. But these in turn faded with more and more frequency into a panic that the task was beyond me, that I should fail miserably and be condemned forever.

There is nothing like fear to thwart the entrance of inspi-

ration and these feelings only fed upon themselves. Once or
twice I thought spirits skirted the edge of my vision and I
heard their voices like the call of satisfied night birds come
home from the hunt. But mostly the spiritual evaded me,
and altogether the night passed most mundanely, most dis-
couragingly.

How slowly the time dawdled. And yet, how quickly, how
quickly it flew! I spent endless moments trying to stop its
hurtling onward. It seemed I had not breathed more than
once or twice before Her sacred turtledoves, newly migrated
back to their nests beneath Her eaves, began to ruffle themselves and coo one another awake to greet the dawn. I have
failed then, I thought, my liver sinking as if it would pass
from me. Am I not Snakesleeper? Am I not? Then, Goddess,
why do You not come to me? I closed my eyes to spare that
one sense, at least, confrontation with the defeat and harsh
reality of the day.

There came a noise outside, a sound of stumbling on the
hillside facing the shrine. Mourners? was my first thought.
Has the day passed, too, and is it evening already and are
the mourners beginning to gather and to wait expectantly
for our liturgy to work miracles?

I continued to sit with eyes closed at the defeat but when,
after a while, the High Priestess had not arrived to second
me, I ventured to hope that there might still be some time,
that the whole day might still lie before me full of promise
and of Goddess. I opened my eyes. I stood and peered out
of the sleeping chamber into the forecourt. It was not even
dawn, and the person scrambling about in the darkness was
my stepbrother.

Amnon was wearing the red and white cloak I had made
for him. Had I known so long ago that this was to be his
destiny that I should think to clothe him in the colors of the
Son? He walked about there, ignorant of how splendidly,
even in the half-dark, those divine colors became him in a
more subtle, organic way than they had done the usurper
Absalom. He had gathered and crowned himself with anemones as thick and lush upon his head as about a spring. He
was regal, come to survey his domain before it should be

sanctified to women alone. His step was sure and defiant of
all gossip but that whispered by star to star on a moonless
night. Sent by Goddess to remind me of the promise I had
made so long ago to sing a song for him. Come to be the
True Beloved.

> Who is this that comes
> out of the wilderness
> like pillars of smoke?

I recited to myself the verse I had composed for him. And
suddenly dawn broke over the Mount of Olives. The direct
rays would not penetrate Topheth until midmorning and
they would never enter the shrine proper. But there was no
denying it had dawned with the sudden rush of a million
birds, the sudden drawing off of every last pool of dark, the
sudden explosion of precise and brilliant color.

The vision faded. Dawn wandered off westward and became another hot, dry day. With it Amnon, too, had vanished. But I remained light-headed and pliable. I felt myself
as empty and will-less as a new jug that has as yet contained
no oil or wine or even water so every pore was open—no
prejudice or previous flavor lingering there. I waited for
whatever the Mistress, my Purchaser, my Redeemer, cared
to fill me with.

I was so light and empty that the flap of a returning
turtledove created enough wind to carry me to the door of
the Snake pit and halfway down the stairs. There I stopped
and sang, and almost without coaxing Father of Shadows
crawled up to my feet.

Firmly and with passion I kissed the Bringer of Her Word
upon his raised head. I grasped him behind the jaws and let
his full great black length curl and slither across the Serpent
skin I wore as a girdle, across my own flesh gone prickly
with rigor. His tail thrashed between my legs. My heart
pounded and the blood throbbed in my ears. I undid the
clasp at my throat and bared him my breast to the waist. My
song dropped from high, clear syllables to low, guttural
sibilations. I pulled in a deep breath of anticipation—

Father of Shadows struck, as startled by his destructive reflexes as I was by the sudden jab of pain, the pumping of the poison that burned like fire as it entered my body. In my hollow veins, poison coiled, clotted with my blood, and began to swell and fill me. The Snake fled back into his shadows when I gasped and dropped him. Already my head was pounding with the meter of verse when I reached the top of the stairs.

> Rise up my love, my fair one, and come away.
> For lo, the winter is past,
> The time of late rains is over and gone.
> The flowers appear on the earth.
> The time of the singing of birds is come
> And the voice of the turtledove is heard in our land.
> The fig puts forth her green figs
> And the vines with the tender grape give a good
>   smell.
> Arise, my love, my fair one, and come away.

There were only pinpricks of blood on my breast. How was it, then, that I was so weak? Wonderful and stirring as the words of my song were, I could not follow their plea and arise. I sank against the door to the pit to close it and collapsed there on the flagstones, the song, the rhythm, the words, swelling to become my whole being.

I remember nothing of this world at all for an entire day and a night. Then, "Tamar! Snakesleeper!" It was the High Priestess, who had found me when she led in the initiates and neophytes.

For one who had been long absent, this world is bewildering at first glance. I tried to speak, telling them to go away. I was in a panic lest in this mundane blur I should lose the priceless gift with which I'd been entrusted. But my tongue was huge and swollen and I couldn't seem to open my mouth around it.

"Water. Bring water," the High Priestess said and she lifted my head to take it.

I wanted nothing of this world to contaminate my mouth

until I had said it all. I turned my head away from the bowl
she offered. But she forced me like one would a petulant
child. A trickle went into the back of my throat and allowed
me to pull my tongue like dried plaster from the roof of my
mouth. I bent forward of my own strength and spat the
water out. I turned to the priestess and grasped her hands
for support and so she wouldn't try to force more on me.

"The Song—" I said.

"A song?" she encouraged gently.

> The Song—the Song of Songs which is Shulamite's,
>   Our Lady's.
> Let him kiss me with the kisses of his mouth:
> for his love is better than wine . . .

I could not recite it fast enough, spilling from the abundance of my great hoard into all ears. And there was plenty
for all. When I had given the High Priestess all she could
contain, I turned to the choruses, the musicians, and then
back to the Priestess again.

When I reached the end, I was hoarse and could only
croak the words:

> Make haste, my beloved,
> and be like a roe
> or a young hart upon the mountain of spices.

It should be a finale, with all singing and playing and weaving the words in and out of one another, repeating and
harmonizing and building, building to the climax. Though
I couldn't give details, my hearers understood, each her
part.

"Thank Goddess," they said, looking with wonder from
one to another. "We have heard a miracle."

"Snakesleeper," said one shyly, hating to interrupt. "Can
you come to the grille? Your brother the prince is there,
worried sick. He has heard you are Snake-killed and will not
have peace until he sees you."

I nodded. "I can come."

Not Snake-killed, but more alive than I have ever been
before or since, I appeared at the lattice that had to stand
between us until Amnon's entrance for the greatest of Mysteries. Behind him was the newly weeded and planted sacred
garden in a glory of sunlight that made me blink.

"Thank God, thank God you're alive," he said, reaching
a hand to touch me through the grille.

I moved out of reach and held up a hand for him to listen.
"Listen!" I filled his ears with the words he was to speak. He
was learning them this time for another, but both of us
spoke them back and forth with a deep awe and reverence,
for we realized at every word how personal the miracle was.

I have no doubt that you will know my verses, no matter
who you are. They are the greatest songs of love ever composed. Greater than the previous liturgy it is admitted by all
who recall it, fresher from the Source and without age's
perversion. No singer of love in ages yet to come will be able
to sing without my images and my phrases. No, I will not
play a humility here, for it would be false. I would be dis-
crediting the Greatest of All in Her pearl-strings of words.
That I was called to be the one to open Her deep, dark
oysters and find them is my only honor, which I gratefully,
meekly, return to Her.

You may not even realize as you sing them by your winter
fires or on your wedding days or as you work in the harvest
fields or draw your water, for what occasion they were first
sung and to what holy and needful purpose first applied.
Though generation after generation will take these verses to
themselves, translate, interpret them this way and that according to how their lives do flow, set them to a thousand
different tunes that Goddess never gave them, still they were
first and best for us, without ritual and additions, Amnon
"showing himself through the lattice," and for me, "his
sister, his spouse," Snakesleeper.

> My beloved is white and ruddy,
> The chiefest among ten thousand.
> His head is as the most fine gold.
> His eyes are as the eyes of doves

By the rivers of waters.
Washed with milk and fitly set.
His cheeks are as a bed of spices,
As sweet flowers.
His lips like lilies,
Dropping sweet-smelling myrrh.
His hands are as gold rings set with beryl.
His belly is as bright ivory
Overlaid with lapis lazuli.
His legs are as pillars of marble,
Set upon sockets of fine gold.
His countenance is as Lebanon,
Excellent as the cedars.
His mouth is most sweet.
Yea, he is altogether lovely.

Naturally Goddess gave the work to me not to keep between ourselves, but to give in turn to every lover, to every bride and groom, to every young man who wakes on a spring morning, to every maid who plucks a flower of the Sivan hillside. But never will a voice exult more than mine as I joined with the chorus, as Amnon appeared "white and ruddy" before the Great Bed in the cloak my hands had made for him. Some singers were unsure of the tune, cautious, but that made the words all the more tender, like a new bride, yet all the more triumphant, like the Groom.

This is my beloved,
And this is my friend,
O daughters of Jerusalem.

When he threw aside the cloak and sanctified the earth and the year with Ritual, I felt no hesitation in inviting all Jerusalem to join me in adoring him with my divine-gotten words.

And outside, above our song, we heard the low distant rumble of thunder.

 XXXV

Since you may hear the Song of Songs, profaned and yet somehow still sanctified, on any street corner, I will bore you no more with the words that I shall ever find joy in, that follow one another in my mind unbidden in their cycle like lovers year after year to the hills. These words will never let me be lonely until the day I die. Only this last little bit, which, for its sacred nature, may still be known only to the initiate few, this will I include:

> I am one who has no mother; you are my mother.
> I am one who has no father; you are my father.
> You have taken my seed into the womb;
> Have given birth to me in the shrine.

This has always been most dear to me, for besides referring to the events in the Great Bed, it best describes what happened to me there in the shrine of Topheth, in the pit of the Serpents. There I was, not conceived, perhaps, but first truly born unto myself, born in the poem that was born of me, poor weak vessel of Eternal Heaven that I am.

Vessels of Heaven? By Goddess, they all cracked that spring like a storehouse in an earthquake.

"What's that sound?" I asked those who attended me in my weakness, and they laughed.

"Have you forgotten, Snakesleeper, what rain sounds like?"

They carried my cot to the grille so I could watch the wonder of it, and I'm certain it got me to my feet sooner than otherwise. We all went out into it, every man, woman, and child in the land. I shall never forget that first cool, wet touch on the dry heat of my Serpent-poisoned skin.

The first showers vanished quickly into the soil. But they kept coming. Stampede after stampede of bull-god clouds thundered in from the west and stockaded over our land. Better than a rich manure was what they dropped in sheets, in buckets, in cartloads. It was the former and the latter rains together. There were even squalls of hail. Everywhere, everywhere, it worked on the chapped land like a healing balm. The cisterns and the springs filled and gurgled into overflow. The Kidron was a river again, a torrent. The farmers' plows could pierce the soil again. They worked in the rain, which was like swimming, to get a crop in. There was no time now for barley and wheat, but every pea, bean, or handful of pulse that had not gone into the supper pot was sown, for they could yield before the height of summer, even if this was all the rain there was.

But that wasn't all the rain. For two full weeks, it poured. There was half a day of sunshine after that, when the moisture rose from the earth in visible mist. After that, for the rest of the holy month, it continued to rain on and off until people, with the short memories they have, began to complain that the crops would be washed away, that there would be flood; they spoke the name of Noah. It rained continuously until, as the preacher might say, its sound was like a contentious woman in a closed house.

It was more than enough, but not too much. And how could anyone dare to be ungrateful? And how could anyone forget those first blessed days when we danced with open arms trying to embrace it, when we first washed the grime of drought and mourning from our hands and faces, when we drank it straight from the sky, when we sang and shouted against its wonderful noise, when we went about hugging one another—even strangers—for joy.

And I shall never forget the sight of the hierodules, standing and sitting, chatting and laughing together as they waited for the men to come to them to serve Goddess. Crackles of lightning echoed their laughter and illuminated them, then plunged them into damp shadows again. Their clothes were so wet they clung to their bodies, revealing every curve, every crease, every nipple as if they'd been naked statuettes in the inner sanctum. Only their face veils remained opaque.

The first week or so after the enactment of the Great Mystery is always the greatest demand on the hierodules. The men, having seen the procession, are pricked in their hearts. This particular year, what with the rain as a perfect *responsa,* men were stirred with wonder and fear in their souls. They kept the women busy day and night. As soon as I could get off my cot for longer periods, I asked the High Priestess if she wouldn't consecrate me to the work so I might bear some of the burden. With a face gone expressionless with exhaustion, neutral in the battle between gratitude and Goddess-fury, she consented and made short work of it.

Yet I might have spared her the trouble then. We never stopped to think that men, never very secure in such a situation, might absolutely refuse from deadly fear to touch one who had slept with the Serpents, much less let themselves enter her body, which they were certain would eat their parts away with the bane. But it was so. I passed my time reading fortunes, bringing the folk messages from my Snakes, interpreting their dreams, and preparing the food and unguents the women needed to sustain themselves. For, though I offered myself and stood fully consecrated for the work and in holy veils, I was not approached.

This was just as well, for, though I suffered no serious effects from Father of Shadow's bite, it did leave me weak and light-headed and prone to falling into secondary trances from time to time. This did much in its own way to encour-

age the work. People would gather and watch for signs when
the fit came upon me. They collected my frothy saliva in
vials to use as cures and begged a hair or two of my head,
"little snakes" they called them, to promote fertility.

It was not until the time of the full moon, when I had not
fallen for several days, that I felt more solidly planted on the
earth, clear-headed and yet, alas, more mundane than I had
since I could remember. Our ranks were depleted. Some
women had pleaded that their husbands would allow no
more this year, some had pleaded that Goddess had taken
them unto Herself with Blood Mystery for these few days of
the month. Demand had fallen off, but as the number in
service had, too, it was thus that I was called to duty that
evening for the first time. The evening was cool, the earth
around me still damp and smelling like Heaven with the
blessed rain. There I sat, the only unoccupied woman on the
sacred stone benches, waiting. Peering at the world through
my holy veils, I saw a man approach. I suppose all other
liturgies may pass away and be forgotten before men forget
how to begin this little exchange that leads to the sacrifice of
self upon Her altar.

"Lordly Queen," he said,

". . . the cultivated flax, luxuriant,
Goddess, the cultivated flax, luxuriant . . ."

He was a stranger to me, as is most apt to please Goddess
with the anonymity, a pure and selfless offering, of the task.

The grain luxuriating in the furrow—
Sister, who have your fill of lofty trees,
Lordly Queen, who have your fill of lofty trees—"

He was perhaps just thirty years old, but of course, from
my place at eighteen, he seemed ancient. He was not un-
comely, with straight dark hair, brows, and beard, and tiny
eyes set in skin brown and already wrinkled by the sun as if
he were much older. So much I learned by studying him. As
he tried, in return, to pierce the veils and study me, could he
tell? Could he tell I'd never done this before?

I will hoe for you, will give the plant to you,
Sister mine, I will bring you the cultivated flax.
Goddess, I will bring you the cultivated flax.

Nothing about his appearance, but something about the
invisible air he exuded, came to my senses next and un-
nerved me. At first I thought it was rising from the court
below where the hierodules were working, the wild, musky
odor of sweat and drunkenness and rough passion. Then I
realized that he was the source of all that filled my nostrils
now, pungent, like the lash of a whip through the air. Full
of wine and of his own importance, this man was come to
me unsatisfied after many others, more wise in the Mysteries
than I.

The burden of his sex and of his little scraped-together
wealth lay heavily upon him. His wealth, a measure of flour,
he tossed into the bowl at my side. He could not rest until
he'd done the same with his sex as well. A mindless stone
rolling down the hillside cannot stop until the bottom is
reached; so it is with such men. Let them be paid their bread
and their pallet, a change of clothing once a year, but no
more, for the rest they waste with neither piety nor even a
sense of good for themselves or for anyone else. Such men
would do well to be unsexed, for how they abuse it. But I
could not say such things aloud. A servant of Goddess must
not question whom She brings to Her service. I had to
respond:

Brother, after you have brought me the cultivated
flax,
Who will comb it for me? Who will comb it for me?
The flax, who will comb it for me?

My heart fluttered wildly. Every time I wished it to settle,
it found the perch too insecure, too full of fear. It would not
refuse, yet it could not accept. Perhaps it was so with the
dove sent forth by Noah our ancestor, which flew here and
there and returned to the ark with mud on its feet, having
found no solid and safe ground on which to perch. As I

refused to let it sink into the mire of terror, my unsettled heart provoked an anxious and uncontrollable trembling in my extremities.

> Sister mine, I will bring it to you combed,
> Goddess, I will bring it to you combed.

> Brother, after you have brought it to me combed,
>   Who will spin it for me? Who will spin it for me?
>   The flax, who will spin it for me?

I smiled and laughed nervously as I finished that speech. Too fast, I thought. I know the words too well and they are passing too quickly from my lips. Dear Goddess, give me time to think, to prepare for this.

> Sister mine, I will bring it to you spun,
> Goddess, I will bring it to you spun.

The man was taking my trepidation as a flattering response to his lust. I must admit the two are very close together, fear and lust, and I, too, as if in answer to my prayer, was beginning to find in my uncontrollable quivering a desperate need for climax and satisfaction.

> Brother, after you have brought it to me spun,
>   Who will braid it for me? Who will braid it for me?
>   The flax, who will braid it for me?

"Sister mine, I will bring it to you braided . . ." Another figure was standing before me now. Was it Snake Vision again? No, there were two voices giving the responses. As if lifting a very heavy, burdensome veil, I looked up at the newcomer. It was Amnon.

"Brother," I recited with belief and true meaning, "after you have brought it to me braided . . ."

As the little dove's muddy feet must have come to the railing of the ark upon her return, so my eyes fastened onto his in weary gratitude. Henceforth it was to him I gave answer and not to the other.

You have captivated me, let me stand trembling
  before you
Bridegroom, I would be taken by you to the bed-
  chamber . . .

And when they both thrust their gifts at me with the fierceness of their rivalry, it was the string of carnelian—warm
from Amnon's hand—I took and not the other's measure of
flour. Though one could not say in true sincerity that the
will of Goddess alone dictated my decision, I doubt it ever
does. Is not the older, poorer man always left standing?

The stranger grumbled something about David's house
getting everything these days and sat down in the dust where
he was with a jug of wine until another woman should be
unoccupied.

Truly, it was not to Goddess but to me that this string of
beads had been given. I held it fast as I moved toward the
altar to present it to Her, hoping that if I pricked my hands
on the sharp edges in enough places its image in drops of
blood at least might remain with me.

My heart stayed yet in suspension as my hand stayed over
the altar, as I let the chain fall with a prayer. I seemed to
float slowly and steadily over the ground to the first empty
platform and Amnon, following me, seemed to stay suspended, distant, at the very edge of my sight.

I leaned back against the platform as I had seen the other
women do and when he made no move, I held my hand out
across the great distance that separated us, inviting him, if
he would, to set his hand to lift my veils, to unclasp the
brooch at my throat.

"Sister," Amnon mumbled. "May we not go elsewhere?"

"If you wish."

Again I began to lead the way, never looking back, as if
I feared he might disappear as we passed through the court
where so many anonymous mortals were struggling, groan-
ing, writhing, twisting in the throes of Goddess-possession.
Overwhelmed by that heavy, smoky musk, might he not become one of them, phantomlike, nameless, not my brother
at all? Might he not easily turn into that same man whose

measure of flour I had rejected, come for me again with a vengeance?

It is considered a good deed to perform the rite outside the sanctuary as well as in. Outside, the fields and flocks can more intimately benefit from the transference of fertility. Where the full moon explored the breast of an anemone-covered hillock, here at last I turned to face him. "Here?" I asked, uneasy to break the silence.

Amnon made no reply but to finish the climb up to where I was, and there, deliberately, firmly, but without passion, he fumbled in the night and took my hand.

▫ XXXVI ▫

WE STOOD THUS for a very long time in silence. I came to feel it must be marble I was holding, it was so still and engendered no sweat.

"Amnon," I said to the darkness at last, dropping his hand and then my veil. "I did not realize you were still in Topheth with us. Were you waiting for me? Did you not recognize me till I spoke because of the veils—?"

"Would you have gone with him?" was his reply.

"Amnon, what . . . ?"

"That drunken farmer who needed no oil to his meal because there was plenty oozing from his hands."

"Amnon, be charitable. The fellow was being pious."

"Piety, I'll be damned. What about you? Would you have gone with him?"

"You wanted to go with Bathsheba."

"Yes, but I didn't. Besides, I'm over that. I was stupid. I see what a silly, ambitious woman she is."

It was some little triumph to hear him say that, but a bitter one. "You went with the High Priestess."

"That's different. That was necessary."

"So now that it's rained we can stop doing Her great service? Forget Her as She was forgotten for two full years? You're as bad as Joab, who wouldn't even let his concubine come and mourn with us."

"Joab, fie!" Amnon said and made a sign against evil into the darkness as if he half expected our speaking of David's general would conjure up his presence. "But Tamar, Tamar, my sister, my love, I cannot bear to share you with any others."

"Have you endless carnelian chains, then, that you may always be the highest bidder?"

"I do not want to have to buy you like a length of cloth," he said, without hiding his anger. "The God of my Fathers finds it an abomination."

I smiled gently, but only to myself, for my back was to the moon and he could not have seen it. To encourage a Goddess-openness in his heart, I said, "You know the High Priestess has a daughter."

"She was initiated this year."

"Yes. Don't you find her beautiful?"

Amnon shrugged.

"She is. She's a Goddess child. Her mother got her on a night such as tonight. We considered having her act as High Priestess at first. But I was jealous. Jealous of you in a most guilty jealousy. With her mother, that is one thing, but with a beautiful young Goddess child . . . Next year I will be stronger and do what must be done. You should have her."

"How can you think I would want her over you?" he asked, hurt in his voice.

"You have not seen her except as a face in the crowd of neophytes," I said, allowing neither of us any delusion. "The fact is, Amnon, we all have a share in Goddess-given life. Even your father, for all his talk of abominations. As we all have a share, we must all do Her service when we are called, otherwise Her power becomes perverted and causes—"

"Causes what? Abominations?"

"Causes little things like Bathsheba, which can disrupt the very fabric of life. We must share our best beloved with the demands of time and ritual and eventually, even with, spare us, great God Death. I have sworn to you my faith by entering into the Serpent's pit and bringing forth my Song of all Songs for you. By a labor as if I had sealed our marriage with the birth of a child—nay, of twins. And yet that Song must go out to all the world. I know it must, in snatches a wandering minstrel can earn his crumbs of supper with. Do not begrudge the weary world a share in the Mystery we have created—for surely I conceived this poem of you. You would not deny our child the freedom to go out and seek his own destiny, pain you as it might? Then do not let jealousy make you a tyrant."

"Was it very painful?" Amnon asked.

"What? When I gave my girlhood to Goddess at initiation?"

"When you let the—Father of Shadows bite you."

"I have forgotten the pain, remembering only the thrill that came after. In both cases."

I took his hand once more and found it now alive and damp with sweat. I brought it to the clasp at my throat, which he fumbled with until it fell open and one could see what was left of the Serpent-swelling and the points of penetration: red pinpricks like two anemones on the moonlit hillside.

"Compose me no more poems," Amnon said, touching the mark gently.

"No?"

"You have fulfilled that promise. I am satisfied. And I would not have you suffer that again."

"You have yet to fulfill your promise."

"What is that?"

"You must marry me."

"I have been your husband longer than you know."

"Then make me your wife."

The touch of his lips on mine was without pressure, but incredibly full of sensation. If nettles gave supreme pleasure instead of pain, we would all brush them lightly against our faces as he brushed his lips from my hair to my throat and we would not clamp down upon those leaves to break and

crush their stinging spines. As one sips hesitantly at a scalding bowl of broth until either it should be cooled enough to
take into one's earthly parts or one's mouth should rise in
heat to meet the glowing fervor, so did Amnon kiss me, over
and over, quickly, lightly, sweetly as a springtime breeze. I
hardly dared to breathe lest his lips should be but a feather
fallen from the great tick of night sky and by breathing I
should blow it away. But I am not Goddess. I must breathe
the used air out. And so I did in a little, high-pitched groan
of delight.

> This, your stature, is like to a palm tree
> And your breasts to clusters of dates.
> I said, I will go up to the palm tree,
> I will take hold of the boughs thereof.

He had seen it, then, seen how I had worked my own
name into the song as a potter may scratch his mark into the
base of his finished jar so that others may think it only
decoration, but he knows his work. Tamar, "the palm tree."

Now he began to strive for more sensation, and when next
our lips met, his tongue plunged in to meet mine, curling
about it as if it were a sweet, cooling yogurt to be sucked
into himself with the firm yet innocent pressure of an infant's mouth at breast. He let me gently down into a bed of
anemones and asphodel.

As one peels off a pomegranate skin to expose the sweet
and glistening fruit inside, so did I lift the red cloak from my
beloved's shoulders and found them sweet and glistening
with unguents in the moonlight. I closed my eyes against the
overwhelming clarity and power of my vision of Goddess
there within and all around our love. And I held my
breath—indeed, I was required to from time to time from
exertion. But came times when I had to breathe and then the
smells that filled my lungs and rose into my head stung the
very edges of my brain. I wondered, I prayed, that I could
be strong enough to accept all that must be accepted by my
nostrils, by my brain, by all my being.

Was it the smells of Amnon's shoulders that were so

overpowering, of his hair, of his loins? Was it my own body, sweat slipping out over the oils and perfumes? Was it the bruised asphodel, so much stronger since the miraculous rain? Does Goddess Herself wear divine scent when she condescends to mortals, when, through us, Her magic curls out and into the growing things spreading their leaves and petals all about us? It was a combination of all these things.

Watching us, unknown to us, silent and thick like a wall that would not let the scent we engendered expand, dispense, and waft through the world as it was meant to do, were perhaps a dozen men. May Goddess send Her black curse upon their souls.

We were blissful fools one moment. The next, there was a deafening crash of crockery. A group of about a dozen men had crept upon us, encircling us, carrying torches concealed in jugs. Then at one signal, like Gideon and his small band before the hosts of Midian, they cracked their jugs and the lights blazed. We could be fools no longer.

The sudden sound wasted divine silence, deafened me; the glare blinded. I floundered in confusion, clung to my love for security, hardly knowing whether it was part of love they never told me of or whether the sky itself was raining fire. I was certain of nothing for several endless moments, neither of my own existence—much less of Amnon's—nor even of Heaven above and Earth below. And then I began to comprehend.

"Say, Cousin Amnon," was the first thing I came to hear clearly, though it had to throb there in my mind with several heartbeats before I could attach sense to it. "How do you find that goddess's womb? Lush as a harlot's?"

"Ho, stand back, my friends," mocked another. "Just see how the grass springs up beneath our feet."

"No doubt about it, it's a damned powerful magic we have come upon."

That last voice I knew was Absalom's and suddenly, though I could not pierce the confusion with my understanding, I could step back from it and hence come to see. Absalom and Jonadab with all their men stood about us with their torches and grins like barren mountain cliffs. My brother's companions were older and more experienced than he, but I could tell his mind was nonetheless behind this act. Absalom and chaos, they were partners. Absalom appeared, and all life gave itself up as a cloud of smoke given up by his burning lust for power.

"Sweet Lady of Heaven," was all I could find to say as a defense.

Amnon said nothing. Anything he might have said would only add fuel to the bitter sarcasm and deep-throated obscenities that were blazing all around us. Without a word, he got to his feet, threw his robe over his naked shoulders, passed beyond the circle of light back into the sanctuary of darkness, and was gone. He did not reward his adversaries with so much as a backward glance.

"Amnon!" I cried and scrambled to follow him.

"Hold her!" Absalom said. I was caught and held by Jonadab's great manacle-like hands, the span of which reached nearly from my shoulder to my elbow, and in which I felt anything but the coolness of Goddess's absence that he professed.

"Clasp up your gown, Sister," Absalom said, grinning. "You are a disgrace."

There was neither disgrace nor disgust in my brother's voice. He was full of triumph and enjoying it as if he'd brought an entire kingdom low. And indeed, that seemed to be exactly what was on his mind, not only in his reply to Jonadab's statement "The maidenhead of Geshur is still intact, Cousin," but also in the way he looked after Amnon and fingered the purple border on his own robe.

I have never grown used to the notion of my younger brother as a man. In my mind he is always the helpless infant held above the brazier in Topheth. That was part of the power to confuse and catch me off guard that he held. He could sneak up on me in the dark and whisper grown-up obscenities with a knowing wink, this creature whose dirtied swaddling bands I'd once helped to change. This voice it took a conscious effort on his part now to keep in order-giving range had, at one time that I recalled so clearly, yelled with cheeks so round and brown and dry, as yet unable to

call forth tears at his command. His chin was still beardless
on that night, but it was hard and firm and would not be so
naked for long. And the words that passed through his
full-grown teeth (I remembered only toothless gums or the
jagged mouth of a six-year-old) were the orders of a man
with a man's deep and well-thought plots beneath them.

Jonadab, who knew Absalom only as a forceful, self-
assured young man, suffered no confusion in his presence.
As if he stood at the calm center of a whirlwind, Jonadab
could only marvel at the destroying effect the flying sand
had upon those of us who must brush against the outer edge
of that great storm. He bowed and made of it a god.

"God send me only sons," Absalom said. "There's too
much trouble in womenfolk.

"Look, Sister," he continued, moving close to me, stepping with heavy and profane feet over the spot where the
wildflowers were crushed by our love.

Sister? I thought. I cannot be this grown man's, this
demon's sister.

"If you don't bloody your bridegroom's sheets," he continued, "I will see that the blood of Geshur's women ends its
course splattered outside Jerusalem's walls."

I didn't have the courage at that time to flaunt him with
the fact that Goddess already had my girlhood. Grant me
this courage later, I prayed.

"And let me tell you now," he said, "that son of a Jezreelitess Amnon will not be the one you honor, Sister. Not with
my kingdom. Not with my Geshur. I swear this, by the God
of my Fathers. Bring her home, Jonadab."

It was days, weeks, past the end of the holy month before
I could feel anything but a shudder when I thought that I
was already initiate, though I knew I should be proud and
reverent of the women's Mysteries.

⊚ XXXVII ⊚

THAT DAVID'S SON—his firstborn son—had performed the forbidden rite could not have been kept from the king for long. Yet he had guilt enough of his own with the ill-gotten child of Bathsheba and the murder of her cuckolded Uriah preying on him. The prophet Nathan foretold all sorts of doom upon the household for this betrayal of its inviolate nature and that gave David, always a believer in prophets, some sense of his own limitations. Then, too, he could not deny that even as the triumphant procession of Goddess and Son made its way through Jerusalem's streets, that the rain had begun to fall from a sky that had been perfectly clear at dawn. Other than sighing with relief, I doubt David attempted any reaction to the happenings at Topheth at all. I know for certain that he never scolded Amnon, or even sent a minister—dotty old Ira, maybe—to do the scolding for him.

There was, of course, the matter of Baal-Hazor on Mount Ephraim where Baal possessed a high and ancient court. At about the time we were renewing the rites in Jerusalem, David overthrew the old god's priests and thereby came to inherit a fine estate. How tongues wagged in the harem, how Mother blushed with pleasure, when word came that David had bequeathed this property to his third son, Absalom, as his inheritance. Some gossiped that this oversight of Amnon was no oversight at all but punishment for dealing with Canaanite demons. At the time I thought the whole affair a bit exaggerated by rumor. Amnon already had estates, David's own family estates in Bethlehem. Daniel, the second son, could not even be trusted to keep his clothes clean, so childish was his mind. Absalom was the next son to provide for. It was as simple as that. And yet Baal-Hazor was to prove more fateful to all of our lives than anyone, even the fiercest gossips, suspected.

Fear of Nathan's curse upon the ill-gotten fruit of Bathsheba's womb occupied the rest of David's attention clear until the vinedresser's festival when the child, never healthy enough to circumcise, finally did die and cut the ropes of hope the king had clung to his merciless god with. All hope gone, things could begin afresh and unfettered from the beginning again. While David waited with renewed piety for the time of Bathsheba's impurity to pass, he found energy and care to see that his other dependents did more than simply eat and sleep.

"Buy yourself a house in town," David told Amnon his firstborn, "and prepare to take a wife."

I went with Amnon to make his decision about the house. To others he explained my presence as a need to know if it was as suitable for a woman as it was for a man. I was to check on the arrangement of the inner rooms, the lining of the oven, and so on. And to see if I would like to be mistress of the place, as he told me.

It was a lovely house, old and in the lower part of town; one could tell that it had been loved. Even the sparrows had found it homey and built their nests in the walls; lizards slithered out of our way and capers, too, grew in the crumbling clay. Life in the kitchen, being so much more productive than life elsewhere, had caused the pounded dirt kitchen floor to rise on its debris much faster than its neighboring rooms. How long this life had been accumulating was seen in what had once been a doorway between the kitchen and another room. The kitchen rafters had had to be raised several times. We had to stoop in the kitchen now to peer through the arch, stand on tiptoe in the other room to see into the kitchen.

"This disqualifies the house, I should think," Amnon said to me.

"Not at all," I replied. "It's nice to be able to keep an eye on other parts of the house while you're baking."

"But a child—" Amnon said, keeping his voice impersonal and looking away, "a child could tumble through that old doorway and hurt himself."

"Yes, perhaps it would be wise to set a grille across the window. But it's still nice to have a window like that."

"Have you had a problem with children falling—?" Amnon turned and asked the old man who had let us in and was acting as our guide.

"For forty generations," the old man said, not really addressing the question. But we had to agree when he continued, "It is an accursed generation that after forty lifetimes produces no heir.

"Houses were neither bought nor sold under the Jebusite kings," our host said further on, too old and full of grief to worry that his words might give offense. "Only under David."

The oven and the arrangement of the rooms were fine, rooted to the spot with age until one could no more argue with them than with the lay of mountain ranges. But what I liked most of all was the garden. There was an ancient olive there, gaped and gnarled by its many years. I imagined the half-legendary hands of the old patriarch who must have planted it, his son who grafted, his son who dug and dunged, his son who took the first-fruits. The earth at its roots was barren of what small garden crops might be planted there, but across the yard, against a rising slope and a darker wall, a pair of almonds was in bloom like great spindles of newly carded wool. The way the old man looked within the blooms, wondering at their capacity to bear when he remained childless, the way he leaned his hand against their trunks and sighed, these things told me that he had been the one to plant them with hope in his early youth.

Amnon and I felt obliged to look away as he performed this private devotion. And that gave us a moment of our own to press hands in a deliciously cool shiver of a breeze beneath the ancient olive. We felt wafted by that breeze to a space of our own hopes, unassailable by time or worldly necessity. It was a space, a deep and dark holy of holies forgotten by all but the drowsing, hoary god whose dwelling it was.

"I asked Father," Amnon said.

I looked up at him and realized by the look in his eyes that it was of our marriage he spoke. I could see what supreme effort it must have taken to approach David on this matter. What internal struggles had gone into this presentation! Amnon idolized his father and feared him (as one does a god, but one cannot love this sort of god as one can Mother Goddess). To speak to such an object of reverence and awe—one's creator—of ambitions of one's own creation— there was sacrilege indeed, and an act of greatest daring. I pressed Amnon's hand in acknowledgement and thanks.

"What did he say?" I asked.

Amnon gently smiled encouragement to my hoping- against-hope whisper. "He likes the idea," he said.

"He's said we may marry?"

"Not exactly. The thought was new to him, and he said he must take time to consider it. What appeals to him, of course, is that it takes care of you. He can marry you off and yet still keep the blood of Geshur in his control. That you might marry some foreign prince and take Geshur with you has stopped more than a few matches, as you are aware. Israelites, of course, accept a daughter's claim to inheritance only rarely—only when there are no sons. They call Absa- lom heir to your land by the Sea of the Lyre. But Father is not such a fool that he thinks he's convinced Geshur to follow what the Hebrews in Jerusalem say. So, he is in favor of our marrying. But—"

"But what?" I asked. There was something ominous in his voice.

"He takes over Canaanite lands, yet he cannot bring himself to take over practices that have maintained the people here since time began. He cannot be convinced that our marriage would not be an abomination in the sight of God. You and I are not even of the same loins and yet he feels the force of his roof must make it a sin, an 'uncovering of the father's nakedness,' as the priests would say."

"Are there no counselors to speak in our behalf?"

"Many, and Father hears them with favor. But he must also lend an ear to the priests and seers who are merciless when it comes to obedience to the God of my Fathers."

"Then he will refuse?"

"It hangs in the balance," Amnon replied. "One more voice speaking for either side will make the decision final. I have pleaded all I dare without it becoming unmanly and turning him completely away."

"Shall I plead before him?"

"He would find that undignified and in this decision, he must think himself more a king than he ever has, for he fears weakness of purpose above anything. I have offered a calf to the Lord. If you but pray earnestly in Topheth, that will be all that we can do. Then we must leave it in Heaven's hands."

I nodded and heard our host prattling something as he shuffled over from his almonds to where we stood. I could not understand his words, for I was thinking on another level, and I was slightly annoyed with him for disturbing us. But there was little more that Amnon and I could say to one another at the time beyond sighs and "I wishes," which only increased our discontent and our anxiety.

Amnon gave the old man a ring as bond of payment in full to come. Then we left, walking through the streets toward the palace and our necessary separation as slowly as our feet and city sights would allow. Little boys trotted their donkeys on tiptoe to and fro through the narrow, rising streets. An Aramaean picking his great nose scurried by carrying a pile of rugs. A tailor was at work in a little hole lined with his rubbish like a winter-ruined nest and with no more room than he needed for his needles and himself. He fluffed around in there, shifting like a partridge on her egg.

Then we stopped in front of a spice vendor's shop. Or perhaps it was an inn where the spitted lamb was being basted with a pungent sauce. I don't remember exactly where we stopped, but I am certain there was a heavy smell of cumin in the air, for I would never smell that spice again without the scene we witnessed there being recalled vividly to my mind. I can pour dead seeds out into the mortar with my mind worlds away. But when the first pound of the pestle crushes out the fragrance, I am immediately brought back to a sober consideration of the thoughts that briefly and ominously crossed my mind that day so long ago. How desperate is life! How beastlike in its drives! And how helplessly we are chained by the demands of blood to submit to that violent desperation! Even when our love is so strong, crossed my mind, how can it hope to prevail against such power?

A man of Judah had struck a man of Benjamin in the camp of the united army over against Ammon. There were always tensions between David's tribe and the tribe of Saul: can fire and water dwell together in the same vessel? But this time the consequences were more serious than usual. The Benjaminite died of his wounds and his murderer was forced to flee the camp to avoid vengeful kinsmen. He fled to Hebron, the city of Judah that David had set up as a place of asylum. As you might well imagine, the sons of Benjamin did not have the patience to endure the blood of their fathers throbbing unatoned in their veins. They decided to defy the Judahite king and take justice into their own hands.

"What shall become of my authority if every man can set up justice to his own liking?" David did well to ask himself. He had the offender hidden away before the angry sons of Benjamin surrounded Hebron's gates. But David forgot to consider one thing—under his own law, the life of the high priest could serve as a substitute for the malefactor's. When the Levite came out to speak peace to the multitude, he was taken captive instead.

Then every Levite priest in the land threatened to leave his post for want of proper protection. That would leave David in an untenable position without any signs of his god's support. Besides, the whole episode was proving a serious detriment to the war against the Ammonites. With half of Benjamin gone from the field to satisfy their blood-thirst and half of the other tribes refusing orders in sympathy, something had to be done at once. If the act could not be particularly strong and decisive, it had to be at least compromising before Ammon culminated its chain of victories by crossing the Jordan and sacking Jericho itself. David was forced to give in to the Benjaminites and turn his own kinsman over to the wrath of blood.

The only part of all this I saw was the great procession of Benjaminites marching and flaunting their victory through Jerusalem right under David's turned-the-other-way nose. The hapless Judahite, more miserable than the average condemned man because he had found his last place of trust betrayed, marched in their midst led on a rope like an ox-for-sin-offering by the little ten- or twelve-year-old son of the man he had slain. The death agony was being postponed—or perhaps prolonged—until the man of Judah could be brought with proper ceremony to the great altar where his blood would have the most cleansing effect—namely the very spot where he had slain the other man. There, under the eyes and jeers and pity and showers of dust of the camp of all Israel, the stain of blood would be washed out with blood. Then peace in Israel (if it did not erupt into a full-scale feud in the meantime) could be bound and turned as a single arrow against the Ammonites once more.

Cumin smell makes me think so clearly of his face. No, not the condemned man's face, which was as if shrouded already, but that of the young Benjaminite who led him. How firmly it was set, for all his ten or so years! How ancient the line of his jaw, how steady and ageless—as stone—the forward stare of his eyes. Ah, Goddess, when he came at last to draw his sword, his father's sword and his father's father's before him, how eternal and omnipresent would the revenge of his young arm be! For it would not move with just a personal, limited hatred, but with every drop of blood that every lust of Benjaminite for woman had engendered, moving as unbidden as it courses now through all those million million veins. The boy could not help what he had to do any more than his victim could help what he had done. Or than David, decisive and in control as he liked to think himself, could help committing the dishonorable betrayal he had done.

And if David could not help it, how could we? I felt the helpless weight of our births and of our destinies that afternoon as I do again every time I smell cumin. I looked up to Amnon to see if he felt it, too. Did he share this sense of entrapment—trapped as the manslayer of Judah was—by the fact that he had been born David's first son? I, by that same perverse fortune, had been thrust beneath his father's roof, "his father's nakedness," with just such a younger brother. Didn't my stepbrother feel it? For all the sharing and love we two could build with words and hopes, for all our prayers, for all our sighs, for all our powers, both Heaven- and man-given, neither of us was magician enough to escape. I have Snake Sight; I could see—

But one cannot live with such desperation. If Amnon felt this premonition, too, he did not share it. It was too everlastingly awful, too ruinous of the day of bright hope we were spending. And so we passed on to more cheerful sights with only the sweet-grass smell of cumin lingering in our nostrils.

· XXXVIII ·

"YOU WILL COME with me today for an audience with the king my father."

I had been expecting such a summons for some time, ever since my afternoon with Amnon in his new house. But somehow I had expected a messenger other than this grown-up and grinning Absalom who leaned with self-assurance against the jamb of our apartment door and held the hanging up with one casual yet keenly discovering hand. I got up and went wordlessly with him, praying in my heart.

I didn't care for the music David had playing. He rarely played himself anymore, as if it were beneath his maturing dignity. But is it dignified and masterful to let someone else make your music for you and thereby decree what mood you will be sung into at every moment? Whether they had come prepared for it or not, the music turned every man present into a soldier with his hand tapping the lively rhythm upon his dagger hilt. It recalled to my mind the fact that Joab, after a long siege, had finally reversed Ammon's earlier successes and captured the fortified water supply of Rabbath-Ammon.

"Come now, my king and my uncle," Joab had sent by swift messenger, "and lead us in the final storming of the town lest the men say it was my hand alone that took it and call this citadel forever after my name and not yours."

So every man of Jerusalem who could carry a sword would march with their king to Ammon tomorrow. Taking booty was easier gain, even, than sitting and counting jars in a storehouse. Perhaps it was by David's command that these musicians played as he commanded the ram's horn blown during the heat of battle to inspire the soldiers to more bloodthirsty deeds. But perhaps no musicians were really needed to inspire such deeds at all.

I fought against the attacking march the music prodded my heart to until I was exhausted. I had come hoping to become a cherished bride, not the object of spoils and pillage. I saw Amnon as I entered the bustling throne room (all David's now). He was wearing the golden circlet and anklets as the crown prince does upon the battlefield, never under the marriage tent. He was going to cross the Jordan, too. Rumor had told me so. It was to be his first campaign. I worried. Would we be allowed a night as man and wife before he went?

My heart beat its way through the distraction of music and many soldier-voiced conversations and tried to link with his, but failed. How could he not know I was there? I was the only woman in the room, like a single mourner at a great festivity. (Women mourn at the sound of armies coming or going.) And Absalom who led me, his presence my stepbrother had learned to sense from sheer need for survival. I could only think that Amnon ignored me on purpose and that it was with studied calm and self-preserving disinterest that he bowed to his father and left the king's side and hall as if on urgent business just before Absalom and I were presented.

"Ah, Tamar, my daughter." David remembered my name; Ahilud the recorder must have briefed him carefully on the business of the day beforehand.

I allowed myself to be given a hearty kiss on either cheek. A man who has fathered twenty-five children and known three times that number of women dispenses kisses as freely and with the same sticky, heavy sweetness as he might hand-fuls of dates. He made no pretense to hide the force of his lust, even for incest's sake. But I felt pity more than disgust when at last he released his grasp on my shoulders. I had smelled the sour smell of age on his breath and heavy henna on his graying beard. Try as he might, a licentious manner cannot feign youth and deathlessness forever.

"It has been brought to our attention that we have been very negligent in our duty as a father toward you," David said. "You ought to have been making me a grandfather long before now. How old are you?"

"Nineteen, my lord."

"Nineteen, my God! And I remember when you first came here, just so high, clinging to your mother's skirts and scared to death of us. Ah, well. If we have been negligent in our duty, it is only because of the love we tender toward you and your beautiful mother. And her land of Geshur, of course. We could not bear the thought of losing either. But now an arrangement has been brought to our attention whereby we need lose none of these things that are so dear to us."

I wondered again where Amnon had gone. He should be there and we should be sending silent messages of joy and triumph back and forth to one another across the common, insensitive multitude. The only one whose temper I was sensing was Absalom. My brother stood now, just out of my sight on the right side. Having a prince's prerogative to stand how and where he would, he had taken a position against one of the pillars, where he could fold his arms across his chest and watch the proceedings with the cool regard of a stone god surveying his creation. Immovable and idle as he appeared, I was acutely aware of the driving intensity of his ambition. What has he to grin about? I asked myself. Surely there is nothing here for him.

". . . So she said, 'Shocking! Why, that's never happened before, that a bride passed gas in her husband's arms.' "

David was chatting cheerily on, attempting humor on the subject of marriage and women. Those with the most to lose or gain laughed the loudest and most forcedly. Cousin Jonadab, I noticed, was laughing loudest of all.

Now David grew serious. ". . . Our reverend ancestors, Isaac and Jacob, both went to first cousins for their brides. It is a good and honored practice, full of tradition and a source of solidarity, and we might do well to follow their ancient example in this present day of faction.

"So, keeping this in mind, we have decided to give you, Tamar, to the son of our elder brother whom we love and tender as our own. Tamar, daughter of Maacah, we will give your hand in marriage to Jonadab your cousin, the son of Shimeah."

My opinion was not being asked, of course. I was simply being told what had been decided on my behalf. I gave my opinion anyway. All Earth could not have kept it from bursting from me. "No!" and again, with more energy, for no one had listened the first time, "No!"

"Hmm. That's what comes of leaving them 'til they're nineteen," David said.

I said, "No!"

"They think they can think for themselves." He tried to make a joke.

"No!" I said again.

Absalom was by my side. "Quiet, bitch!" he hissed in my ear.

"No!"

"Well," said David, smiling apologetically to the foreign dignitaries present who might think he could not run his own household, much less the great expanse of his united kingdom. "You have till we return from taking Rabbath-Ammon to get used to the idea—"

"No!"

"—and to like it. I've already put the host of Israel under ban. That includes you, Jonadab. We cannot expect our Lord of Hosts to march with us if you go into battle reeking of the weakness of women and of the marriage bed—"

"No!"

"—especially not that contrary one. By the God of my

Fathers, I hope you can knock some obedience into her, Nephew—"

"No!"

"By your leave, Uncle," said Jonadab, laughing.

"Maacah and the other women will prepare everything it is that women prepare for such occasions and you'll have a grand and triumphant homecoming. Perhaps you, Jonadab, will even capture an Ammonite slave or two to bring home as a gift for your bride—"

"No!"

"Take her out, Absalom, take her out. There is a war to discuss right now."

Still I held up my solitary word, my little "No," against the all-contrary jarring caving in about me. I did not stop saying it until Absalom had me out in the privacy of the corridor, where he slapped me three times, hard, until my teeth went through my gums and the blood came.

"You will marry Jonadab," my brother said, "and you will like it."

"That's what I think of Jonadab." I spat a wad of blood into a gap between my brother's sandals. "He has little to do with the matter anyway. He's only a convenient and obliging wallet you've decided to deposit me in for safekeeping, may Goddess damn you."

Absalom hit me again, to the floor. I couldn't even muster a "No!" after that.

◎ XXXIX ◎

I DID NOT see Amnon at all after this audience but for the distant glimpse as he rode out of Jerusalem with his father at the head of a grand parade to go and take Rabbath-Ammon. And of course I was not there on the other side of the Jordan when all of the things that I will now describe took place. But the news was daily shouted from the roof-tops and reviewed in detail in this version and then that in the harem courtyard. And, too, I later heard the whole tale from Amnon's own lips, so I may be allowed a personal recounting.

All the land of Ammon from the Jordan eastward was completely devastated, for General Joab and the forces of Israel, not to mention the army of the sons of Ammon, had been advancing and retreating over it for more than a year. Towns fallen and recaptured were burned and then burned again. Every man had taken his provisions where he found them, for an army moves faster and in greater secret if it does not have to have flocks and grain wagons bringing up the rear. Besides that, soldiers are no farmers and when they have swept a field like a cloud of locusts, they do not bother to stay and carefully renew and dung the land so that it may produce another year. Indeed, in the case of the Israelites, when they had the time, they strewed the fields they passed with stones, cut down the fruit trees, and filled in the wells so that years would have to pass before Ammon's fields and orchards and wells could produce enough to send to Jericho again. All this upon the face of a land that Heaven had already seriously scarred with drought.

Above this desolation rose Rabbath-Ammon, the age-old city, like a great chameleon basking on the hillside and taking as its colors whatever the rising or setting sun on natural stone beneath it gave. Her towers were round and of stones so big that one had to attribute their building to the giants that had once lived in the land. In the battle before these walls, Bathsheba's Uriah had met his doom, sent headlong down the ravenous parapet, along with many another man of valor more honestly mourned at home. A psalm had been composed to encourage the fainthearted Israelites in those early and trying days of the siege:

Who will bring me into the strong city?
Will not You, our God?
Through God we shall do valiantly,
For He it is that shall tread down our enemies.

And the rousing chorus:

Moab is my washpot.
Over Edom will I empty my shoe.
Over Philistia will I shout in victory.

Now that the lower city and the streams had been taken, it was all Joab could do to keep his men from rushing to scale the final fortifications that contained the palace and temple before David's arrival, so addicted had their blood become to the driving momentum of conquest and pillage.

The walls, the giant-raised stones, the steep and treacherous parapet might have been no more hindrance now than gullies and ruts cut in the streets during a heavy rain. Nothing but the mighty hand of Milcom could have saved the sons and daughters of Ammon in this position and he did not see fit to do so at this time. Two days after his arrival in their land, David stood as conqueror within the very shrine of that god.

Joab and Abishai climbed upon the giant god figure three times the size of a man and took off the famous crown of divinity. It took the two of them to carry it down and to present it to their victorious king, so heavy was it with gold and precious stones. David had the greatest of the stones knocked from its setting then and there and ordered it set in his own crown. The rest of David's bodyguard appropriated for themselves what they wanted of Milcom's offerings (and they were great and rich, for the people of Ammon had set their all upon this figure of stone, who in the past had often saved their fathers).

Then the leaders and generals of Israel and Judah went out into the courtyard of the citadel where the members of Ammon's royal house were being held prisoner. Godforsaken as their futures appeared, the captives still lifted up their voices in prayer. Amnon told me again and again how this struck him, that though prayer had proven vain, it was one with breath and one must continue as long as the other did.

The pandemonium of directing the common citizens of Ammon to their posts of enslavement was going on apace in the lower city overseen by the captains of hundreds and fifties. Most, what able-bodied men and boys there were left after two years of a losing war, were to be sent to the pits and smelters of the new copper mines. Those of weaker, less rebellious constitution would be set as brick molders and lumber hewers for David's new building projects in Jerusalem. And right then and there in Rabbath-Ammon, the womenfolk were called upon to begin their duties. With their men as yet present, milling useless and helpless as dumb oxen when the rains are late and the plowing postponed, the daughters of Ammon were used as soldiers always use conquered women to make their victory complete. One never hears the details of such things, even when the harems and slave quarters are suddenly filled with all these newcomers. But I have seen one of them sitting sometimes, alone, exhausted at the end of a day, staring at her hands as if to assure herself that something was still there with a thin layer of skin that differentiated it from the rest of the world. I could not bear to look at that daughter of Ammon for long. I would always quickly turn to look away to the walls of Jerusalem, to the guards who stood upon them to protect us, and I would always try to comfort myself with this flattery. But Jerusalem's walls had been overcome in my own lifetime and the guards, often as not, would not be standing, watching the horizon with care, but squatting down to their games of knucklebones. My security was false, I knew in my heart. Rape can come from inside as well as from out. And yet I had to trust in our security as we all must trust in the final triumph of our individuality or we should never have the peace of mind to continue, to ever do more than sit and stare in fear, mistrusting the existence of even our own hands.

The women gave us few details of the conflict. Even fewer did we hear from our men when they returned. Victors, the survivors, are afraid of the soulless creatures they were driven to become by war, afraid of a creature without fear. At home again, with his family and those who know him, who know that he is afraid of dogs and that he weeps when his children die, a man must forget that he faced the nameless horror all as coolly and with as little involvement as the open expanse of Heaven does.

"One cannot listen to it," was all Amnon ever told me, "or watch oneself participate in it or remember any of it afterward. I made my heart as stone. For the moment I let the sounds in the background—the weeping, the screams— become more than just an annoyance, I should have been overcome with horror and with pity and I could not have continued to stand there—as I had to stand there—silent by my father's side."

The kings and princes, those the annals a thousand years from now will remember by name, had to stand aloof both in body and in spirit above the bestial anonymity that was taking place in the common streets below. David treated the royal women with personal concern and respect, as if they'd been his own.

"You'll be a wife again," he promised the dowager queen, "in my bed."

Hanun's eldest sister, Ruth, a beautiful girl, stood clinging to her mother, ash and dirt weighing down a head of already heavy thick black curls. "And this one, too— No . . ." David gave Ruth reprieve as he fondly wiped her cheeks of tears, leaving tracks of clean wheat-colored flesh in the gray ash. "You are too young and beautiful for an old man like me," he said with a smile and in the same breath. "I give you to Amnon, my firstborn."

Amnon was walking just behind his father. He nodded when his father gestured to him, but said nothing.

David went thus on down the line of girls in size and the list of his own sons by age: "This one for Daniel, this pretty one named Baraa for Absalom . . ." The littlest one, a mere toddler named Naamah, Hanun's own child, was promised the care and keeping that a bride for his as-yet-unborn son by Bathsheba should have.

David turned next to the young Ammonite princes. "We will bring them to Jerusalem with us—as hostages and dependents, it is true—but to be raised along with my own sons and nephews in the great boys' hall. What is the name of that one?"

"Shobi," answered Joab of the one whose bright good looks and the meticulous manner of his married-for-love mother had won especial favor in David's eye.

"Let him remain in Ammon with the entourage he needs."

"You will risk another Ammonite king, my uncle and my king?"

"We will have our troops here, too, never fear. Let the young man act as overseer where his father was once king."

"What shall be done with Hanun?"

"Ah," said David, "my rival king. The cause of all this long and bloody war. You know, Joab, I haven't quite decided yet."

Considering, David stepped now to where Hanun was being held separate from his family. The task of Ammon's king's particular guard was one of honor, and David had given it to his nephew Jonadab, for whom there were no Ammonite princesses but who had already been honored with a betrothal just recently at home in Jerusalem. Jonadab had relieved Hanun of his broad sword and battle ax and held them, one at either side, as he made the bow to his king.

David stepped past him to meet his foe. Hanun, too, put a hand to his bosom as if to make a sign of submission. But in his bosom he had concealed a dagger that Jonadab had failed to find. Before anyone even saw the weapon, the leap was made.

Now when Amnon saw death a span's length from his father, he saw the crown just that far from his own head. There was hardly time for anything more than a reflex of self-preservation, like the blinking of the eye at bright light, and perhaps Amnon did move as much to save himself as to save the man he stepped in front of.

Hanun's dagger did not touch David at all, but Amnon was caught under the arm and opened nearly to the waist.

"The Ammonite bastard's death!" David found voice to spit out these words. "Immediately! Quartered. With a dull saw. Nail the pieces to the temple of their alien god to defile it."

Then King David waved all others from his son's head and stooped himself to bear the body out of the sun.

Hanun's death order had been clear enough—one could hear it already being fulfilled in the courtyard. But what David said, or tried to say, of thanks, of apology, of prayer, of disbelief to his firstborn son was garbled and incoherent. Most of what was understood was the dirge: "Amnon, Amnon! Oh, my son Amnon, my son, my son Amnon! Would God I had died for you, O Amnon my son, my son!"

The physician came panting in, knelt and ripped away the fine purple wool of Amnon's robes as if it had been sackcloth. The full extent of the damage struck David and he hid his face in his hands. The blood was still coiling, forming a dark pool on the ground beneath his son's chest.

"By the God of my Fathers, Amnon, speak if you have breath."

"Father . . ."

David uncovered his eyes and grasped his son's hand, getting in the way of the physician, who was frantically trying to staunch the blood with wads of torn purple wool. "Amnon!"

"Swear . . ."

"Swear? Anything. Anything, by the God of my Fathers. Ask any wish, even if it seems impossible to mortals, and I swear by God I shall fulfill it."

"Don't . . ." Amnon gasped, "don't give Tamar to Jonadab." And then mercifully he passed from consciousness.

The king stepped out of the shadows to give the physician and priests room and to spare himself the undiluted source of his grief. With tears fogging his eyes, he found Jonadab there in the courtyard, Jonadab whose carelessness had given the Ammonite opportunity to strike. Jonadab was on his knees, his arms stretched forward asking for forgiveness.

"You!" The king's voice was ugly and shrill. "You are unworthy of your bread, much less of a royal wife."

Then the king of Judah, Israel, Moab, and now of Ammon sank into the arms of his attendants and was helped to a chair. And he who slew Goliath and bought Saul's daughter for two hundred Philistine foreskins began to be old.

◉ XL ◉

HANUN'S DAGGER WOULD have sunk deep between David's ribs. It entered Amnon's body at such an angle that it ran along the ribs as if flaying, as a stick is played by small boys along a lattice, so that, thanks be to Goddess, no organs were damaged. This no doubt saved his life. Nonetheless, the wound was grievous enough that for two weeks after runners first brought the news to Jerusalem, they could only shrug their shoulders and shake their heads and murmur "infection," "loss of blood," and that his life was in the god's hands.

At the end of the month Amnon was carried on a litter and by slow stages at last into the best care the palace and his mother could give him. I was not allowed a visit, but sending maids with numerous gifts and hovering myself around Ahinoam's doors informed and comforted me with slowly improving reports.

There were graver things to worry about, perhaps, but I could not help but be concerned about whom we should have play the Groom that year in Topheth. The season of the Mysteries was rapidly approaching, much more rapidly than Amnon seemed to be recovering.

I took my concern to Father of Shadows and counseled with him. *Wait,* he told me with a calm no amount of anxiety on my part could disturb. I had no choice but to believe him, but it was one thing to believe and quite another to express that belief in definite words to convince the others concerned.

The retiring High Priestess finally grew exasperated with my hesitation and went out herself and found a second cousin to Araunah to match her beautiful daughter, who had blossomed to Goddess-perfection during the year like a perfect bud come to a perfect and full-blown rose. I drove the man away when I found them, all three together, rehearsing the poetry one afternoon in the shrine. But to the anger only half camouflaged by looks of bewilderment that mother and daughter silently fixed on me, I could say nothing but, "I will ask Father of Shadows again." I knew, but was bewildered and even frightened myself, that the answer would be the same. *Wait. Have patience.*

The holy evening came like the slow closing of a great eye in tear-dampened sleep. The mourners began to gather as do the edges of a healing wound, dark and dry, to the center of Mystery. The new young High Priestess, blooming in new Goddess robes, waited by my side, peeking out at the gathering congregation, then nervously pacing across the chamber to the inner altar, setting the sacred emblems in position for the fortieth time, then pacing back to the grille again. Her white hands, hennaed until they appeared like doves that had fallen into a paint pot, fluttered at her hair, her veil, her throat, her skirts, then were firmly forced to settle in a folded, prayerful attitude. Then they escaped to peck at her necklace again.

"What was that?" She started at every sound, every shift of the Serpents in the pit, every whisper of wind through the valley.

And when I replied, "Old Rivke has come and is telling them the sorry tales of mourning time. They have begun to weep," she herself burst into tears, like a bride repudiated on her wedding day, or perhaps from a longing to be nameless and secure in the crowd on the hillside as once in her childhood.

"Very well!" I cried. "We'll send for Araunah's cousin."

But I immediately condemned my lack of faith, for just as I spoke, the answer appeared.

Like a welcome rain cloud, it moved down into the valley. We watched full of wonder, as the "rain" came, for clouds have no legs. Serpents are known as Goddess's Messengers because of the disembodied spirit of their movement. Thunderclouds are thought to bring the word of certain other gods; even so did the answer come.

The litter, for such it was, moved in the twilight as if without bearers until it stopped before the garden lattice. The wonder, more awesome still because it combined elements of fear and mystery with those of the marvelous, like lightning or the strike of Serpent venom, appeared in the form of Amnon the son of David.

"Forgive me for being late," he greeted me with teasing in his voice as I ran to meet him. "I had to avoid Father's guards, for they never would have let me pass."

The young High Priestess quickly brushed away her tears until the kohl was smeared from her eyes down to her chin. Then she laughed so brightly with relief that I had to hush her lest the congregation, which must still think the Bridegroom was counted with the dead, realize that there was already great reason to rejoice.

Amnon, of course, was very weak and had to lie down and be alternately nursed, scolded for his foolishness, then blessed for his devotion and bravery during most of the preparations. During the deed itself, I kept my eyes fixed to his face. I saw the glaze of swoon, escape from the pain, sweep briefly over his eyes. But he arose smiling and triumphant from the Great Bed, and I think I was the only one who bothered to notice that he had broken open the wound and set it bleeding once more. Though such a thing rarely ever happens, it is not ill omen when blood is left upon the Bed, only seed. And, indeed, it only seemed to give more fervor to our voices as we all joined in the final Hosiana of the rite:

May the lord whom You have called to Your heart
The prince, the king, Your beloved husband, enjoy
    long days at your lap, the sweet.
Give him a reign goodly and glorious.
Give him the throne of kingship on an enduring
    foundation.
Give him the people-directing scepter, the staff and
    the crook.

From where the sun rises to where the sun sets
From south to north,
As the farmer, may he make productive the fields,
As the shepherd, may he multiply sheepfolds.

Under his reign may there be plants, may there be
    grain.
In the steppe may the acacia grow high,
May the orchards produce honey and wine,
In the garden beds may the lettuce grow plump and
    the cucumbers long.
In the palace may there be long life.
May the holy Queen of vegetation pile high the grain
    in heaps and mounds.
May he enjoy long days and nights at your holy lap.

Dear Amnon. How faithful he was! How brave, how
dutiful! How he brought joy to us all that day, even to those
of us who had to let it sift down upon us vicariously. At
what personal cost was this sacrifice made! He deserved
every bit of this blessing and more. He is in no wise to blame
that it could not be fulfilled upon him. Nor is he to blame
that the land never came to benefit by his reign thus foretold.

Amnon did not return to the shrine after the triumphant
procession. He had gone home to rest, they said, and that
was understandable. Nevertheless, it was with joy caught
from him, from seeing him able to walk again, from sharing
in his courage and his victory, that I knelt to be sanctified

before the new High Priestess and to take on the hierodule's veil.

I stood by the altar and remembered my little goat named Sage from all those years past. Running my fingers along the grooves that were still damp with the blood of more recent sacrifices, I remembered what his little life and little death had taught me. I likened it to Amnon's sacrifice, what he had risked and laid down for the good of all upon the white sheets and sweet-scented reeds of the Great Bed. Here was a worthy Son indeed. The pain of that time was past now as was the pain I had endured to bring forth my Song of Songs. We could step back from both deeds and only wonder as one does at the child of one's womb, forgetting all but the supreme joy in this something that is newer and purer than oneself and therefore a touch of the eternal.

Exulting thus in my beloved, I came to love all things, even pain and death, and that is love indeed. And I went forth with this same love to stand in my place among the hierodules. I had as yet known no man, I recalled, and though I was no longer a maid, I might well have had fears as I met this unknown. Yet I rejoiced and trusted perfectly that whatever petty vows, uninspired prayers, or stinking battlefield-like lust these men might bring with them, with Goddess between us, we could make it as divine as a sunset, though it last no longer.

▣ XLI ▣

A FOURTEEN-YEAR-OLD SHADOW hovered just over my shoulder as I stepped out to take my place among the hierodules. As if it were only just happening, I remembered how the solemnity of my infant brother's presentation on the brazier had been interrupted. Now again there was the rumor in Topheth, "David. David's men," blowing like a wind through the sacred trees. And it was not my imagination. My veiled companions were clustered like purple grapes and whispering, pointing.

I stepped to the edge of the clearing and confronted the group of armed men there. They had not stepped into the sacred precinct, where it is forbidden to bring weapons and wear shoes. But they hadn't abandoned their weapons in preparation for meeting Goddess in the person of one of Her veiled servants, either. And as long as they stood there, no other man dared to come forward to make an offering.

"If you've come to solemnize the season with us," I said, "please, welcome."

Their torches roared like a smelter in the wind and facing them I spoke with less certainty than I would have liked.

The weapons bristling beneath their cloaks caught the torchlight like leopard's eyes in the darkness and assured me that nothing we boasted could keep them from breaking the taboo when they decided to take that step. Still, I saw interest in some of the men's faces.

"May the God of my Fathers curse these vile and pagan rites and all who practice them," Joab spat, for it was the general himself who stood at the head of the men and torches of this foray.

"If not, then I adjure you in the holy Name of Goddess to be off and to leave us in peace."

"Is that you, Cousin Tamar?"

I said nothing. It is forbidden to acknowledge such discoveries when made.

"Well, you've made it easy for us. Save us having to go through the lines ripping veils off. That could get messy. You're the only one we're after."

"If I come with you, will you leave these other women alone to continue their holy work?"

My words "holy work" drew hearty laughter from the men.

"There's nothing I'd like more than to turn my fellows lose in this place for a little romp," said Joab. "But—those are not my orders. Just take off that silly veil so I can be sure I've got the right one and let's go before my men are beyond the constraint of any order."

That order was hardly necessary. In the dull and common air beyond the sanctuary the veil seemed like a coating of sweet wine left in the mouth overnight. The unsanctified air was too thin for me to fill my lungs with through a layer of cloth. I folded the veil over my arm and so walked with a sigh in the midst of the soldiers up the hill to Jerusalem. Again it would not be Goddess's will that I unify with Her in the anonymity of spring.

At the gate we passed Absalom with the watch. Joab and his men nodded their respect to him and Absalom returned the nod, but then he turned from us to a blank wall.

"Is this your idea again, Brother?" I snapped.

There was no answer, only a quivering anger in my brother's back.

A soldier nudged me on and I found myself led not to the palace, but to Amnon's house in town. A doorkeeper opened for me, but Joab and his men did not follow. David alone stood waiting in the garden. I bent to kiss his hem.

"Thank God you're here," he said. "He has exerted himself too much. He has taken a turn for the worse. No one but you could pacify him."

The house was as silent as death and I thought what I had not allowed myself to think until then: Amnon is dying and I have been sent for in his last hour.

"Is he—?" I began.

But David had already joined his men in the street and I stood by myself in the garden. It was the end of my being led. What I did now inside the house was my business.

The trees in the garden were no more than shadows against the last of the light. They were past their bloom and no scent was there. But the tiny fruits, green and hard, were full of promise, the fruitful promise of Our Lady of Harvest. I tiptoed on through the court to the rooms that were familiar to me because I had helped to choose them over a year ago. I remembered speaking of "your great chest here" and "your armor there." There, indeed, everything was.

I found the sickroom by the heady smell of camphor and myrrh.

"A good plan, don't you think?" Amnon's voice greeted me from the dim light. He chuckled shallowly for the sake of his wounds, but with no less spirit he continued: "I must only endure the sour looks of the physician and a lecture from Father on the debasement of Goddess rites and I am pampered with whatever I wish."

"And what did you wish for?" I asked him.

"I wished to spend the holy days with you. Father has agreed. And my man at the gate will make certain Absalom and Jonadab do not come upon us with torches in their jugs again."

He reached his hand to me. I took it and let him draw me to a seat upon his bed. It was the arm on his good side he used and I noticed he favored the side where fresh blood had seeped through new white linen.

"You're in no condition for celebrating," I scolded him gently.

"Be with me a while and we shall see."

I bent and kissed my brother lightly on the forehead and then on the mouth as I recited:

Let him kiss me with the kisses of his mouth
for his love is better than wine.
Because of the savor of your good ointments
your name is as ointment poured forth.
Therefore do the virgins love you.

We laughed together because his ointments this festival were those prescribed by physicians.

"Well, come now. If I can do nothing else, I can still eat," Amnon said.

"If you can eat, you're not that sick," I teased.

"The women are preparing a feast for us to break the mourning fast with, but I want you to make the Goddess cake with your own hand." He pulled that hand to him and kissed it.

I rose to make my way to the kitchen, following the sound and light, but Amnon kept hold of my hand and stopped me. He called for a maid instead and sent her to bring flour, oil, honey, raisins, and more light for me to work by. Then I set up my baking board in the doorway to the sickroom and we chatted and laughed pleasantly as I mixed the dough. Amnon had not thought to equip his kitchen with an Ashtoreth-cake form, so I had to mold Her by hand, holding the figure up from time to time for his comments—"No, your bosom is more ample than that. Your legs are longer and more slender"—until we were both satisfied with the work.

"It's not supposed to be me," I insisted. "It's supposed to be Goddess."

"And how are we poor mortals to know what things in

Heaven look like unless we go by their reflection here on Earth?"

"As long as you realize I am only Her imperfect copy."

"And the cake is an imperfect copy of you."

"She made me, I made it."

"Send it off quickly now to be baked before I perish of hunger. And tell the girls it must be right well browned to match the color of your skin."

"They would have to let it burn to match me."

"Don't worry. They will. They are a pack of careless gossips."

"Then I should go and oversee them."

"No. Stay." Amnon's voice was suddenly serious, almost frightened, as that of a child left in the dark.

"What is it, Brother?"

"If you were my wife before all Israel, if I could be assured that I may have you with me all the rest of my days, then I would let you go. But now—no. Not during this brief and stolen time."

"Even man and wife have the insecurity of death between them."

"Please, Tamar. Do not say such things. Not tonight."

So I sent the girl off with the cake and returned to his side on the bed.

"Do you know who that was?" he asked.

"Who?"

"The slave who took the cake from your hands just now." He was smoothing my hands across his cheek and seemed only vaguely interested in the topic he had introduced.

"No. I've never seen her before."

"That is the Ammonitess, Hanun's sister. The one I'm supposed to marry. Indeed, all I have to do is find the strength for consummation and it is done."

"What is her name?" I asked.

"Ruth," Amnon said and moved my hands to his mouth to kiss.

Ruth returned just then, having discharged the cake to someone else in the kitchen. She squatted down in a far corner with a bit of needlework and fell silently back to her vigil. She had been there all evening but I looked at her now with interest and curiosity. And her presence now, where before it had been no more than that of a chest or a stool, caused us to fall into long lapses of nervous silence and to guard our words.

At least, there was caution on my part. Amnon continued to behave as he had done before, as if she were a piece of furniture. "Ignore her," he told me, "or I'll send her away."

The Ammonite tongue is only a different dialect of the Hebrew, with the variations only twenty or so generations of separation can cause, so she understood very well what we said. I saw her haunches grow tense beneath the fine wool of her skirt. She was preparing to be shooed away at any moment.

She was a very pretty girl, I thought. Give her the clothing and makeup and she would be regal as well as attractive. I saw now the family resemblance, attributes of Nahash, Hanun, and Shobi blended together and tempered with the soft, almost liquid qualities of the mother I had seen once or twice in David's harem. She was small and dainty, rather too thin, but that, no doubt, along with the shabbiness of her hair and the scabs upon her face, would disappear when her grief was eased, when the position of prince's wife should bring her new honor as a diversion.

"Marry her, Amnon," I said under my breath, hoping she would not hear.

"What did you say?" He spoke as loudly as ever, calling Ruth's attention to our conversation.

I was spared other reply than "Nothing," by the announcement that the meal was ready to be served.

Five royal guests could have feasted on what had been prepared for the two of us. There were great platters of steamed barley flavored with onions and garlic, vegetables—chickpeas, spinach, and fava beans—dried apricot pudding and stuffed dates and figs, and the sacrifices—a white young kid, heavily gravied with its own grease, and a fat-tailed sheep, the tail prepared with scallions and herbs, the body stuffed with prunes and almonds.

I had broken my three-days' fast earlier, but only with a

swallow of yogurt and honey for strength as I prepared to
serve as hierodule. I did not tell Amnon this, lest I offend
him by mixing flesh and milk in my stomach, which was
distasteful to him. Still, I could not eat my share of the
spread, for my stomach was shrunken and weak. Amnon
himself could eat even less because of his wound—nothing
heating or too thick and heavy. Our picking at the two
sacrifices, served whole, did not disturb their still-alive look
much at all, and even the Goddess cake lost nothing more
than breasts and hair.

With the wine, however, we were more than liberal.

"The physician allows me all I want," Amnon said, "to
ease the pain." And he laughed freely to prove its effect as
he sent Ruth out for another jug.

There had been an awful lot of cumin on the cucumbers
and I could still smell it on my breath. It reminded me once
again of the sight of the man of Judah being dragged off in
triumph by the vengeance of Benjamin. I remembered my
feeling of hopelessness, of the brevity and vanity of life from
that time, and it was heightened by the wine I'd drunk.
We're condemned to lose this, I thought. With Ruth gone
from the room in a slow and sorry obedience, I said again,
with more earnestness this time, "Marry her, Amnon."

"Marry whom, for God's sake?"

"Hanun's sister, Ruth."

"You're not serious."

"I am. Oh, Amnon, how can you be so heartless?"

"Me? Heartless? What are you asking me to do to you?"

"In this case I don't mind."

"You don't mind. Are you telling me you don't care
about me?"

"Oh, no, my brother. Not at all. I love you more than I
can say."

"And I love you. So let's hear no more about taking
anybody else to my bed but you."

"And the High Priestess."

"That is duty."

"This is duty," I insisted.

"I feed her, I clothe her, I give her a roof over her head.

And it wasn't I who murdered her brother and destroyed her homeland. Just look at this well I have in my side from all that."

"Do you hate Hanun now?" I asked.

"By the God of my Fathers, no. The man is dead—he died horribly—and I am alive. He was my friend. All he did I understand. He had to do it. And I do not hate him."

"Then, for his sake, marry his sister. Take the shame and grief away from her. Help her to forget. Make her beautiful and a royal princess again. Implant in her a new life to replace that dead and gone. Otherwise I fear, my love, that she and all of Hanun's house will fade out of this life forever for grief."

"No, by God, I have sworn I will marry you."

"Marry us both, then," I said, and rose from his side.

"Father frowns on princes having more than one wife. He would see it as a threat to his sovereignty. Concubines he doesn't care, but wives . . ."

"Then make her your beloved concubine, at least."

"No. I will have you and you alone." He lifted himself on his elbows after me and then fell back on the cushions. As the blush of wine was seeping up to his cheeks, so the blush of new blood seeped through the old and the linen on his side with the effort.

"My love, my love," I soothed him. "Peace. Do you forget what we learned of the Mysteries in the shrine? The flicking tongue of the Serpent? Remember how the blessings of Goddess, the blessings of life and love, come to us all, generally and namelessly."

"I forget nothing," Amnon said. "I will tell you what I know of lust and love and namelessness. I will tell you what I saw and heard in the streets of Rabbath-Ammon while our soldiers celebrated victory. I will tell you of the girls—eight, ten years old, held, raped by one after the other until life slipped from them as grease from the side of a spitted roast. I will tell you of the wives, widows, grandmothers, the women great with child bent over the walls about the public cistern, mounted as if they were stupid ewes and shoved in when they expired or merely fainted and no longer gave the proper struggle. I will tell you of the . . ."

"No more, no more," I pleaded, beginning to weep for his agony as much as for pity toward those he spoke of. I understood that it was the wickedness of the world he was angry at, not me, but it was hard to teach my emotions that.

"I did not want to mention it tonight," he said, speaking relentlessly against me and against himself, by which he meant to be relentless against the relentless world. "I did not want to spoil this evening, which indeed belongs to Her and wherein we should find joy. But, by God, it is too much for me that you should put on the veil of a hierodule and voluntarily submit to such use. It makes me ashamed and hateful of all my sex. And it makes me hope the jealous God of my Fathers does take over every nook and cranny of this land. You cannot convince me there is any difference between what is happening in Topheth right this moment and what I saw in Rabbath-Ammon."

"Nobody dies in Topheth," I wanted to argue, "nobody is forced," and "We—Goddess is paid for it and we serve Her. There is honor and ritual. There is joy. There is such a vast difference as there is between killing in war and holy sacrifice." But Ruth approached out of the darkness with more wine.

"Speak no more of this, beloved," Amnon said to me as his slave entered. Perhaps he said it because he saw some flicker of hope in her eyes as she silently observed our division and he wanted it drowned at once. "Come, let us not spoil this precious time we have together. Father may come tomorrow and find me all too healed by your soothing presence and your Goddess cake. He may, God forbid, send you away again."

I wonder what Ruth the Ammonitess might say of me if she should ever lift herself far enough above her grief and shame to tell her story. I truly felt compassion for her and wanted her to be allowed some joy. I saw a shadow of concern cross her face. She had seen new blood on her master's bandages and thought the physician ought to be sent for.

But peace had been declared between my beloved and me. I let him draw me down to sit upon the bed again and looked steadfastly into his face and not at hers as he waved the maid out of the room and had her drop the hanging behind her. Ruth could only obey.

I slipped off my sandals and drew my legs up onto the bed. Amnon then caught me gently by the nape of the neck and drew my head down to rest on the good side of his chest. The sweetness of that night's reality slowly faded with kisses, caresses, giggles, and murmurs of endearment into the sweetness of dreams.

> Last night as I, the Queen, was shining bright,
> Last night as I, the Queen of Heaven, was shining
>   bright,
> Was shining bright, was dancing about,
> Was uttering a chant at the brightening of the
>   oncoming light,
> He met me, he met me,
> The lord of my heart met me,
> The lord put his hand into my hand,
> The lord of my heart embraced me.

Only just as sleep overwhelmed me did a belch of contentment bring the taste and smell of cumin up through the taste of too much wine and kisses to cast an unnameable shadow on the brightness of the night.

◙ XLII ◙

AMNON WAS IN no condition that night to repeat the feat he had accomplished already once in that cycle of the sun. I did not mind, of course. The Mystery is only a very small portion of the divinity we could share. There would be other days and nights, I assured both of us. But this must now confuse my readers, for certainly they are expecting to be told the tale they know so well—that I left Amnon's house come morning, running through the streets of Jerusalem, my virgin's garments torn, my hair and face smeared with ash and wailing for my maidenhood. A dramatic picture, no doubt, and good material for storytellers. But there isn't a bit of truth in it.

Let me ask, you who insist I must be avoiding the issue, are you a Jerusalemite? Were you in the streets that day? If so, answer truly, did you yourself see me, Tamar, David's daughter, in such a dismal state? "No, but someone said that someone else . . ." Trace back that someone else to his source and I promise you'll find Absalom there in every case. The tale you know, the tale that minstrels sing and priests recite in heavy moral tones was fabricated and

spread by my brother, my mother's son. You can see I had
nothing to bewail at this time, but only to rejoice in. The tale
that I was "fair" and of some remarkable beauty is a similar
fabrication, but one readily believed by those who know, or
think they know, what happened. They cannot imagine that
"such things" can happen to women of plain looks and
quiet ways. They are confused and think Goddess must play
some magical part in "such things," for otherwise they are
incomprehensible.

The day, you see, had only just begun.

I did leave Amnon's house. That much is true. He begged
me not to, begged me to disappear only into the kitchen
while he entertained his father and the physician on their
morning visit with the leftovers of last night's feast. But I
pleaded that I had to go to the palace for a change of
clothes—something other than the sacred hierodule robes I
had come in. I should look in on the shrine, too, give a few
oracles and assure them I had not deserted them or even
wished to avoid my duties for that month. But I promised
Amnon I would not myself participate, however much they
might need me. As the representative of the Son, he had the
right to ask for that.

"At least take a maid," he said, "a guardian."

But I protested I would get my own girl from the palace
and not leave him shorthanded. That is how full of trust,
confidence, and good humor I was that morning. Amnon
was more cautious, less full of dreams, as a man and a prince
of David must learn to be.

So I left my stepbrother's house. And I found my brother
Absalom waiting outside.

The sunlight was cruel and merciless that morning, the
more so since the worst of the summer was still before us
and Jerusalem's stones had yet to grow callused to so much
liquefying light.

"Good morning, Sister," Absalom said. There was music
in his voice, but I didn't care for the tune.

"Good morning," I replied.

"Where have you been all this night?"

I did not reply, for it was obvious he already knew. He fell into step beside me. He was not waiting for David or for anyone else. He and his men—there were four of them, but I noticed at once that Jonadab was not among them—had been waiting for me and for me alone to appear. I was too proud to let them intimidate me back into the shelter of Amnon's garden.

"Have you been with Amnon, our dear brother?" He was as persistent as flies at a wound.

"He is sick," I replied, more apology forced from me than I felt.

"So they tell me. But expected to live."

"Wounded protecting his king."

"Such a brave soul." Absalom's sarcasm was unabashed.

"Ask the soldiers if you don't believe it, you who are still too young for war. Ask your friend Jonadab. I'm certain he appreciates our brother's bravery. Much to his own shame."

"Why don't you ask him yourself?"

Absalom had stopped me before the cavernlike opening of a wineseller's. He did it very subtly so I was only half aware that my further progress toward the palace was blocked by the thick and grinning bodies of his men. I was too dazed with surprise at the moment to see beyond the glowing pit where half a lamb was spitted, for certainly no greater soul than Jonadab was drinking away the morning within. Indeed, save a witless beggar boy clapping his hands for coins in the doorway and the proprietor, who grinned his teeth quite dry before the spit and bowed again and again at Absalom, the shop was deserted but for this cousin of mine. The girls who usually served in the establishment were all in Topheth now. If one wanted to make use of the back rooms, he had to bring his own.

"Off with you!" The proprietor beat the beggar off with the end of last night's torch. The boy took his beating as if he were as senseless in body as in mind, yet he was not so stupid as to go any further off than a drunkard could throw a crust. There the proprietor let him be in order to turn with grand style to Absalom. "Come in, son of David, come in. You do me and mine great honor."

Absalom did not immediately answer the invitation.

"Come in, Sister." He gestured to me as the host had done to him.

"I've no desire to visit a wineseller's," I scoffed, but I was beginning to get uneasy.

"We, however, desire you."

"Come on, Absalom, tell your men to let me by. I have to go home to the palace."

"You should have gone there last night. It's too late now."

One of the men nudged me one way, one the other. Their nudges became shoves and I found myself actually inside the inn. And when the bulk of their bodies blocked any view of the street from me, the only place I could step to get away from their shoves was into Jonadab's arms.

"Please . . . stop . . . please . . ."

Those were the last words I said. I thought: I must scream. The law says, if it's in the city and nobody hears you scream, it's not rape; the law of David's god considers that you were consenting. But Jonadab had caught both of my arms and held them tight behind me. In this position, any movement just a finger's breadth different from the one he wanted me to make shot pain through my arm from wrist to shoulder. In this position, he dragged me, stumbling, trying desperately to keep my feet, through the inn's back rooms and then up a narrow flight of stairs to the second floor. All this time, though my mind kept saying, "Scream, scream," I could only make little sobbing animal sounds. At one point, I caught the eye of the wineseller and made some of those little sounds in his direction. But he had eyes only toward Absalom. Toward Absalom he continued to bow, wring his hands ingratiatingly, and say, "Welcome, welcome, son of David."

Negotiating the tight top of the stairs made Jonadab loosen his grip on me. I managed to wriggle free and take two or three steps down and away from him. But there on the steps I ran into Absalom, and Absalom had a dagger drawn.

"You do everything our cousin says, Sister. Be real nice to him"—my brother smiled dangerously—"or else—"

He slipped the dagger up under my Serpent belt. He's going to cut the Snakeskin, I thought, and he did give the blade a twist. But Jonadab had caught up with me by this time and, by both aching arms, he yanked me to him again. It was my own living skin, not the Serpent's, that was cut in the process.

"If you need any help, Cousin—" Absalom smiled again.

"I do not need help—Cousin!" Jonadab shouted. There was fury in his actions now, and when he tossed me into a little room at the top of the stairs, fury gave him the strength to fling me against the far wall. Gray, then black, closed in on the edges of my sight. I was conscious enough to feel I had not hit the floor as well as the wall, but fallen across a rough, narrow bed strung with raveling ropes, enough to hear another, "Damn you, Absalom, I don't need any help," and a parting "Enjoy yourselves" snorted from the rest of the men. Then my senses cleared unmercifully and I felt the full impact of Jonadab's next pair of blows, the smothering well of blood in my nose augmented by the choking weight of my cousin on my chest.

"You little bitch! You cursed little bitch!" he spat, punctuating his phrases with more blows. "I'll teach you to tease and then try to get away. Cursed little tease. What are you? Too good for me? Good enough for any drunkard that stumbles into the Goddess's brothel, good enough for that pathetic first son, but not good enough for me?"

There was hardly time for a breath before he began again. "By God, I love you, Tamar. I am sick for wanting you." Then with the very next breath: "Lie still, you daughter of Belial, and don't scream again or I'll cut your throat. Just see if I don't."

He said his lines—and it seemed his acquaintance with love knew no others—automatically, as one says "High!" or "Ghee!" to a donkey, expecting the dumb creature to be capable of either going or stopping but nothing in between.

I tried to wrap one leg around the other, but was not strong enough to keep it there against the assault of Jonadab's knees. Single minute details latched onto my mind: a filthy wad of blankets that the small of my back rocked over

and over, the fraying hem at the neck of Jonadab's tunic.
Then my cousin tore at the vent started by Absalom's knife
in my hierodule's robes, and through it my Serpent skin
touched my bare flesh. It brought to my mind a sudden
vision of my holy initiation, that which was being so horribly defiled. My mind clung to that holiness, reciting the
Mysteries, singing the songs, recalling the pain and smell but
also the kind and reassuring faces that had surrounded me
then, the promises of power I had been given. Goddess help
me, help me survive this blasphemy. For a very long time I
managed to give these memories more reality than what was
really happening. They pulled my spirit and my body after
it out of the morass and helped them survive.

This vision buffered me so well that Jonadab had finished
his worst before I was aware of it. He was shaking me gently
and offering me wine and bread with yogurt from a tray. I
couldn't believe it. He was smiling.

"Come, drink a little. You'll feel better."

His smile, not the wine, made me nauseated.

Then he began to kiss me. Not again, I prayed. These
were kisses trying to be gentle.

"Come, be happy. We're to be married now, you see," he
said.

I shook my head weakly.

There was another flash of the terrifying fury in his face,
and I steeled myself for another blow. But it was another
kiss I got and I couldn't decide at that moment which was
worse. I raised a weak hand to shield me from more attempts at affection, and my hand reached a sticky wetness
in my snarled hair instead. His seed—

"Now some wine—"

I vomited all over the goblet and his hand.

"Bitch!" he screamed, throwing the bowl and wine in my
face. It was a slight improvement over what was there.

A dirty rag followed. "Here, clean yourself up," Jonadab
said between clenched teeth. "I'll be back. And you'd better
be a bit more charming next time or you may not live to
enjoy having this relationship legalized."

Jonadab spat as he left, loathing me in my ruin as much

as ever he had lusted. He hated me to avoid having to hate himself to death for the act. In this hatred, he might have murdered me as easily as one crushes a bothersome fly to remind himself of his manhood and his ability to subdue the earth.

And I was left alone with my thoughts.

I feel like the rung on a ladder, I thought. To Jonadab, I am a rung on the ladder he must climb, a stepping stone back into the good graces of David, something to kiss like the edge of a rug to win a half smile from Absalom. And Absalom—Absalom had plans to put my broken pieces to further use; shards are at least useful for scraping boils.

Absalom went now to climb upon his father's knees and whisper his fabricated tale with sweet chords into David's ear. And David was caught in the web. The law required him to give me to Jonadab for the loss of my maidenhood. So either he must go back on his word to Amnon, his word given in exchange for his life and by his god, or he must agree to say publicly that Amnon had done the deed. Although David knew this story Absalom proposed to spread was an unabashed lie, for he himself had been with his ailing firstborn son at the time, if put thus, the deed could be forgiven in Amnon as exuberance, youth, and (miraculous) health and, in myself, with death by stoning. Surely that would be the easiest way for all but me to save face.

David did as Absalom hoped he would, though any of the alternatives could have been made to fit my brother's plans. David wrung his hands, tore his hair, and made a show of weeping. But Absalom had trapped him and the only decision he found himself capable of was no decision at all. This left the people open to the version of the tale Absalom cared to spread. And the people began to murmur among themselves saying, "If the king cannot bring discipline among his own family, how can he discipline us? Is Absalom the power in that house? May we look to him for just revenge?" Absalom's name began to be said as one full of hope and promise to come.

I was left in the inn all that day with nowhere to go but the room of my disgrace, outside of which Absalom's four men idled, and the roof above which one could reach by a ladder. The way the soldiers looked up from their game of knucklebones to watch me let me know I only had to give them half an excuse to lay hands on me and they would help themselves to their superior's entertainment and blame it on my own uncooperation. So I went up on the roof and stayed there instead.

The good wives of Jerusalem came up to hang their laundry, air their bedding, beat their rugs, scrub their children, turn their drying herbs, wash their hair, comb it, and gossip in the sun. And then, at length, they gathered up the wash again and retreated below from the heat of the day. I envied them their work. If my hands had not been quite so useless, so helpless, I might have endured the time better.

Women could understand and help me, I was certain, if only there were some way I could tell them. But my plight was not something I could shout across the rooftops, contrary to what the law of men assumes. All women can appreciate the terror of rape, but it is something that for the sake of the listening men must be whispered about, as private yet as common a terror as turning one's damp hair to the sun to dry is a private yet a common joy, not to be divulged to the insensitive. Besides, my shouting would bring the soldiers up, and then the possibility of women's help would be past.

No woman appeared on either of the two roofs that communicated with the inn. I think the houses must have been deserted; their doors were locked; Absalom thought of everything. So after I had been all around the perimeter of this block, I found the narrowest space I would have to jump to escape was over an alleyway nearly four spans wide. Tottering on one narrow railing, I could not hope to land firmly on another. The alleyway itself, two stories below, seemed to offer the most comfort and the best escape, and I hovered there between existence and nonexistence for a very long time.

"Who are you? What are you?" I asked myself over and over again. The shadows grew from the nothing of noon to life-sized as I could find no better answer than, "If you are, as all the world seems to be telling you, only dirt, the rib bone of a man who is only a lump of clay, then the alleyway is the best place for you. Cast the filth out to be eaten by the wild pi-dogs and be done with it."

But then, at length, the true, Goddess-given responses arrived and saved me. They came in fits and starts, for even She is weak against the blackness when She has been violated.

"I am . . ."

"Who? What? A nothing."

"No. I am she . . ."

"What is she? Weak, stupid, groveling."

"I am . . . I am Snakesleeper. Yes. I am." I sighed with grateful relief and sank down on the safe side of the railing. I took good, clean breaths into my lungs and smiled to find them my own. Then I shouted with all my strength to all who cared to hear. "I am Snakesleeper!"

A soldier came up from below to see what the matter was. I turned my face from his toward Topheth with a firm purpose. And I began to sing the solemn, sacred words that must have sounded just nonsense to him. The soldier laughed loudly and waved a hand of dismissal at me as the proprietor below was probably doing to the beggar boy at that moment, leaving him to entertain himself with his witless clapping.

So I was left. I laughed to myself, though quietly and without bravado. And I continued to sing the Song of the Snakes.

◉ XLIII ◉

WHEN JONADAB RETURNED after sunset, he found me still sitting and crooning softly alongside the rooftop's railing where the soldiers told him I had been all day. By this time his loathing—again of me, but only because he was not man enough (or perhaps, by other definitions, too much a man) to direct it where it by rights belonged—against himself—had so intensified that I suspect he did not really want to come and face me once again. But Absalom had promised his cousin that we would be man and wife and, by their god, he had better husband me, even if an entire Netherworld of emotion should stand in the way.

I remembered when Jonadab had first come to us in Jerusalem. I remembered the girl, misused by him, who had sat at the gates with her father crying for justice. I remembered the helpless pleading, wounded look on her face, the slope of her shoulders, and I tried to copy them in me for, though I was not yet myself—it would be months before I would recover that fully—I could not expose my true thoughts to him in any way. But all the while I continued to sing my Song.

"Oh, God, don't look at me like that, Tamar," Jonadab said as if all the sins of his life were passing before his eyes. That happens, so they say, when a man looks into the face of his death.

"Come on, come down and come inside," Jonadab continued. "The proprietor has set us out a supper and I know you've eaten nothing all day long."

I said nothing but continued to sing, accompanied by a slow, rhythmic rocking. He had come to me, my pet, my Messenger, answered my Song from deep in the pit of Topheth, moving like a spirit in the shadows of the alleyways and the cracks of walls as only a Serpent can. Entwined with the dead skin of my calling's sash I cradled the live body of Father of Shadows so that even in full light it would have been difficult to tell one from the other. I kept his body warm against my own when the chill of nightfall might have made him sluggish. I held his head up to my cheek, caressed the smooth, black scales, and let him lick my ear clean with quick flashes of his tongue to fill them then with wonderful words of power. So I said nothing to my enemy, but sat and sang and watched and waited.

"Oh, for God's sake," Jonadab said, striding across the roof to me. "Stop being such a bitch about the whole thing. Weren't you at Topheth just yesterday? You're still in your whoring robes." He grabbed me by the arm so fiercely I had to hold my breath to keep from screaming with pain. "Whore a little more for me, or I'll give you a slap around that'll make you forget all about your sweet whore of a goddess."

"Strike," I hissed my breath out. "Strike."

And before Jonadab realized that it was not he I commanded, Father of Shadows came to life and struck like lightning near the groin.

Jonadab drew his dagger and thrashed into the air to defend himself, but the living, thinking, poisoned knife stabbed with all the advantage of surprise, concealing darkness, deep, eternal wisdom, and bewildering swiftness. When my cousin instinctively raised his arm to turn a gash in the face into a harmless flesh wound, he found his arm burning with venom every bit as deadly in the finger as in the heart. Father of Shadows struck so quickly, even I could not keep track of the number that found their mark, but it was certainly more than five before Jonadab regathered his wits enough to turn and flee back down the stairs flinging curses black with terror as a dog tries to shake himself of muddy, leech-filled water.

I had to sit perfectly still for many deep and even breaths after that, for the striking had become compulsive, a nervous, uncontrollable tick in my friend and deliverer, and I had to sing soothingly all this time until he coiled with exhaustion. Then I quickly scooped him up to hide in a water jug and sat back down with the jug between my knees to see what would happen next.

The moon rose above the rooftops. It was very thin and small. As soon as it did, I saw the curve of a drawn bow rise up to the roof from the rooms below. It was very moonlike in its shape and in its cold, tense glow. My heart beat rapidly, for I knew that with a bow, Father of Shadows and I were outdistanced. I took what courage I could from the knowledge that the moon was as yet so small that it would give very little vision to my enemy and that quickness and terror of the unknown were still on our side. Beneath the bow followed Absalom's head.

"Tamar?"

I did not reply, but his eyes grew used to the night and finally found me where I sat.

"All right, Sister," he said. "What do you want?"

"What do *you* want?"

"To talk."

"Then talk. I hear you."

"You won't set your beasts at me?"

I smiled to myself. Jonadab must have told them in his fright that there were more than just the one. I could hear him saying with the wounded soldier's exaggeration: "I killed ten or twenty of them, but there were twenty, twenty times twenty more."

"That depends," I said.

"I will kill them."

"They, will kill you. Very miserably."

Absalom was silent. He reached the top of the ladder, then very cautiously stepped out onto the roof. He sat down where he was, slowly untensed the bow, and laid it down before him as a gesture of treaty. I have heard tales from the fields of battle, how entire armies have been put to flight without a blow being exchanged if the first few slings volleyed live Serpents instead of stones. Such is the fear of fully armored men for these swift Messengers of Heaven.

I imagined further all that had happened below when Jonadab had stumbled down the ladder and into his comrade's arms: how Absalom had ordered man after man up the ladder and all had refused, even on threat of shame or death. So, rather than defile the inn with a massacre, my brother had finally taken the challenge himself. "I will show you cowards," he might have said aloud, while thinking to himself, "my life is charmed. Before I was a week old, Heaven willed that I should escape the ravenous jaws of this ravenous bitch from Gehenna. I have power over her, that damned goddess of my mother and of my sister. I shall come out the victor in this confrontation as well."

"Your husband lies dying," Absalom said to me gravely.

"My husband?" I laughed.. "I have no husband."

"Our cousin Jonadab, then. But you must claim him as your husband or you will suffer death by stoning."

"I fear no stones." I laughed tauntingly to hide a laughter of nervousness that would have said that I lied. "Serpents are swifter than stones and ten times more deadly."

Absalom was silent and his silence admitted to me that he, too, had heard tales from the battlefields of the terrible routs effected by Serpents.

"Well, let him die," I said. "I would much rather be his widow than his wife."

"It is not a pleasant thing, to watch a man die from snakebite." My brother spoke quickly now, and I knew he was speaking in earnest. Fear had humbled him. Yet I must be cautious not to let his voice strike that piercing, whining tone it could take and win over dumb stones to tears.

"It is not pleasant to suffer what I have suffered this day."

"Forgive me. It was necessary."

"Then this death is necessary. Yours, too, eventually. I do not forgive you. I cannot. Goddess would not allow it."

Absalom cleared his throat to stifle his usually scoffing reaction to any pious mention of Goddess. "I have come to treaty," he said.

"What are your terms?" I asked.

"You can heal the victims of serpent bite?"

"That depends," I said.

"You cured Michal, Saul's daughter," he said. "I remember that. I know you can do it."

"It still depends."

"On what?"

"On whether I want the person to live or not."

"Let Jonadab live."

"I hate his life, his every breath, more than I have words to say. I spit on his suffering."

"I will make it worth your while." Jonadab's suffering, I could see, had affected Absalom deeply. "If you cure our cousin," he said, taking deep breaths between phrases, "I will publicly announce that Amnon had nothing to do with this, that all hint of disgrace should be removed from him. And I will set you free."

"Free to go back to him?"

Absalom breathed again. "Free to go wherever you wish."

"I cannot promise a certain cure." This admission of my limitations suddenly led me to another idea so pleasant in its prospect that I might have agreed to come down without further enticement.

"My word is certain if you will but try."

I did not believe him for an instant. And even if I had, there would have been much, much more I would have demanded in retaliation. But since I had already decided upon my immediate course of action, I had to appear trusting. "Swear it," I said, just to make sure I didn't appear the fool.

Absalom swore by his god and may that god, if he is any god, exact the punishment of broken vows a thousand times

upon my brother's head in the life to come. I nodded, then
slowly got to my feet. Absalom picked up his bow and I
picked up the jug where Father of Shadows coiled. "The
Snakes are in here," I said, and I was glad it was a very large
and imposing jug. "Don't make me drop it."

Absalom lent a polite, steadying hand to me as we descended into the room where the soldiers sat, cowering, at
the edge of the lamplight. Jonadab himself lay on the very
bed of my outrage, his left arm, both legs, and his belly quite
swollen and discolored with blood and bruises beneath the
skin until they appeared to have taken on the markings of
Father of Shadows' scales. I walked over to him, enjoying
how he cringed as if he were trying to sink away from me
and my jug into the bed.

"She's promised to cure you," Absalom said.

"I have promised to try," I said calmly and coolly, pre-
tending, making a survey of the case, poking him where I
knew it would hurt. "Even I cannot always guarantee success." I could readily see that Jonadab was so frightened, his
heart pumping the poison at twice the normal rate, that it
would be a job just to keep him from dying of fear.

"Bless you," Jonadab said with lips gone numb with poison.

"We shall see," I repeated. I then turned to the rest of the
room. "I must be left alone with him," I said.

Absalom's four men were only too glad to hear those
words and they jammed armored shoulders trying to get out
of the doorway at once. Absalom was more hesitant.

"You, too," I insisted. He rose to go. I thought of asking
him to fetch a maid to help, someone, any woman would do,
to share the work. It was a pity my triumph should be taken
alone. But I resisted. I only stopped my brother at the door
to ask, "A dagger. I will need a dagger. Good and sharp."

Absalom looked at me with a piercing distrust, but I took
that look with a calm and placid face and innocently held
out my hand for the weapon.

Absalom looked from me down on Jonadab. "For God's
sake," the stricken man said with all the force he could
muster, "give her the dagger, Absalom."

"Yes," I said, forever calm. "We haven't a moment to lose."

Absalom drew his dagger from its sheath and slapped the hilt of it into my open palm. Then he stepped out and slowly pulled the door to. His eyes with their piercing glance, their ever-present shade of cunning duplicity, lingered last of all.

"Bless you, Tamar, daughter of David," Jonadab said to call my attention to himself.

I slowly turned from the doorway, from mulling over the magnitude of evil in my brother, to my lesser but present opponent. With equal slowness and detachment I began to speak. "Do you understand, O son of Shimeah, what you have done?"

"You've let your accursed Serpents bite me, that's what I understand."

"No, no," I corrected slowly. "I am talking about before that. Can you remember back before that to what you did to me?"

"Oh, that."

"Yes, that."

"Well . . . ?"

"Well?"

"What does that have to do with getting this poison out of me?"

"Everything in the world. It is how you got it in you in the first place. Putting your poison in me."

The poison flushed in his face slightly and he said, "Very well. I'm sorry, Tamar. All right? I'm sorry. But I was in love with you, you see. David said I couldn't marry you. I am in love with you now. Dear God, you're beautiful, Tamar. Can't you see I'm madly in love with you?"

His words were as tedious as a daily liturgy. Bad liturgy, uninspired and in clumsy verse to anyone who had heard the Song of Songs. "And how many times have you said that?" I stopped his singsong wearily. "To how many scores of girls and women?"

"I don't know. But Tamar, it's you . . ."

"You see," I interrupted him again, "it was not just me

you abused. Many of my sisters before me. And—if I let you live—I have no doubt there will be many after me."

"No, Tamar. I swear it. I'll be yours forever. I swear it before God."

"Don't call your god into this. This is not a task for gods."

"Sorry."

"How many, then? How many in Bethlehem? How many in the Land of Ammon when you were at war? How many here in Jerusalem? How many have you raped? Or half raped? Or raped in their minds with lies and sweet words and disparagement and forced dependence and acts of violence and mindless power until they gave their bodies willingly but were no longer themselves in spirit?"

"I don't know how many. But I'm sorry for all those, too."

"Do you remember one day in the boys' hall in the palace?"

"For God's sake, I'm a dying man. I can't remember everything."

"A vase had been broken and a slave was trying to clean it up. But you were tormenting him, grinding the shards to slivers. Do you remember?"

"No." Jonadab whimpered helplessly.

"How many slaves, then, have you treated likewise? Slaves, male and female, who happened by the will of Heaven to be set in lower stations in this life. To be womanized, one may say . . ."

"All right, all right, I'm sorry for every wrong I ever did any living soul."

"They are not just crimes against humanity, which would be bad enough. But they are desecrations of the divine Womanhood in us, in all of us, gotten from our mothers and their mothers, back to the greatest Mother Who created us all. Male and female. It is Her forgiveness you must seek."

"What must I do?" Jonadab asked wearily and painfully.

"Give up your manhood."

"What?"

"Give up your manhood to Goddess. Become as a

woman, gentle, humble, peaceful. All mortals must be as women before Her."

"Oh . . ." Jonadab whispered.

"When I was four years old," I said, "my father castrated himself. He ran naked from the temple after he'd done the deed—"

"Not David . . ." Jonadab nearly laughed in disbelief.

"No. Not David. My real father. In Geshur. He submitted himself completely to Goddess. As you must do."

"No! No! As God is my witness, I will not."

I smiled. "Then, as Goddess is my witness, you shall die of Snakebite."

"But . . . but such butchery would kill me anyway."

"No, it wouldn't. Not if you submit to it with a heart of total contrition. I know how to use the dagger with skill. And your parts, I know them—"

"Fiend. You daughter of Belial! You bitch from Gehenna!"

"Now, now. The more excited you become, the faster your heart beats the poison to every part of your body. You'll be dead before midnight at this rate. You will be the one in the Netherworld, Gehenna, as you call it. Then even I will have no power to bring you back."

"Those are your terms?"

"Those are my terms."

"And you could cure me then? Of the snakebites, I mean?"

"Yes. It will be easily and quickly done. Father of Shadows is my intimate. We know each other's ways. You'll live, childless, true, but to a high, gray-haired age."

"Let me think about it."

"As you wish. But there is not much time, you understand. Is your vision blurring?"

"Quite badly."

"Yes. Not much time at all."

"All right, all right. Go ahead. Do it," he blurted.

"I have your permission, then? Your humble submission to Goddess?"

"Yes, yes."

"Let me hear you swear it."

He mumbled some god-formula vow with the proper sex of divinity substituted.

"May She smile on this proceeding," I said. Then I offered him a jug of wine from which the soldiers had been drinking. "To help deaden the pain," I said. He took it and drank it all. I went to the door and called for more. He drank that down as well, all but a little bit I poured as a libation on the dagger to cleanse it. Then I had him hitch up the skirt of his tunic and undo his loincloth while I brought the lamp close and warmed the dagger in the flame. I brought the point to touch his naked flesh.

"No, no! By the God of my Fathers, bitch of Gehenna!" he cried out, knocking away the blade. "Let me die a man!"

I stood up, retrieved the dagger, and slowly slipped it into my belt of Snakeskin. Then I picked up the jug with my Serpent in it and left Jonadab on the bed without a word.

Absalom set a stool for me in the main part of the inn and I sat down, cradling my pet gingerly in my lap. Food was brought before me, and I blessed it and began to eat, for I was very hungry.

"Well?" Absalom asked at last, and his men echoed him. "Well?"

"He will die," I said, licking my fingers. "I am sorry."

FOUR

▫ XLIV ▫

I HAVE SAID I was not myself at this time and you have seen that it was true. But I am hardly to be blamed for that, having had another will forced upon my own with such brutality. So it was with gratitude as much as with any other emotion that I reacted to Absalom's breaking of his vow. As soon as Jonadab had died, I was taken under guard and by night away from Jerusalem.

"Where are you taking me?" I demanded.

"You let me worry about that," Absalom replied.

Gingerly, I shifted the jug that held Father of Shadows in my lap. Absalom looked gravely at the jug, cleared his throat, and said: "I'm taking you where you'll be safe."

"Where?"

"Baal-Hazor."

"Your country estate?"

"That's right."

"That's days from anything."

"That's right."

"All alone?"

"Don't worry, I'll post guards. Besides, you have your snakes, don't you?"

I hugged the jug closer to me, feeling him better company than any guard. I should crack the jug right then, make an escape. But I knew it would take Father of Shadows a week or two to build up his poison again. There might be enough left for one man, but I couldn't guarantee it would be Absalom. There was certainly not enough for all five of my escorts. It was best to go along for the moment. It was best not to let them know the limits of my power. It was best to keep it in potential.

From the whisperings of Father of Shadows I came to realize on that journey that I would never see my mother in this life again. Then it was that I tried to think back to the very last time I'd seen her (for so much had happened in between) and to remember her like that.

It was on my way down the hill to Topheth to begin the mourning that I chanced to look back and see her watching me go from the parapet of the palace. I have made excuses for her all the other years she didn't come with me to the divine service, but I can't even remember what the excuse was this year. Perhaps there wasn't one at all and her staying away had simply fallen into habit as it does with so many others.

Absalom was standing with her that evening, perhaps already plotting how he would get me to the inn and how he would assure that it was empty so that all could be done according to his will. He leaned forward over the wall, the intensity of his thought turning into an intense yet strangely unseeing stare he shot in my direction.

But Mother had stopped looking at me. She considered me already gone and beyond the use of her looking. She stood straight and tall and with as much dignity and beauty as ever she had. But the hand she stretched out now with the finely shaped and painted nails was in Absalom's direction. She reached toward him tentatively, as one does to test an oven one fears might already be too hot.

The sun was setting behind me and it seemed, as I watched, that the David-tint of red in my brother's mass of remarkable hair turned to a living flame. Mother continued to reach out her hand to that head on fire, slowly and deliberately, as if she were fully aware of the danger involved to her person but as if, through repeated contact like some fire-swallower in the market, she had grown numb and careless of the pain. Her hand lighted on his hair with an awe-filled caress and then, even as I watched, it seemed as if she, too, beginning with the red tips of her fingernails, caught fire and, like dry kindling, was taken into the glowing heart of Absalom's being. But though Absalom's hair was like old Moses's bush that burned and yet was not consumed, in a moment, twilight had turned my mother to ash and I could distinguish her individual features no more.

I turned my back against the scene and went on down the path that I had chosen and on which I knew now Mother would never again join me. It touched me with melancholy, but I knew there was nothing I could do. She had made herself what she had become. And perhaps it was for just such an advancement, to go on and do the things she could never do herself, that she had made me as well.

Now you may question how it is that I found Baal-Hazor pleasant, or at least not objectionable, when it is true that I was taken there as Absalom's captive and held there against my will for the better part of two years. But you must understand that Absalom himself only rarely stopped in at his country estate. I was obliged to confront him and the work of his hands much less frequently there, where all was simple, pious labor, than I would have been in Jerusalem, where intrigue was ever thick and smoky.

Baal-Hazor, as the name indicates, had a court, a high place thick with oaks and dedicated to the worship of the great god Baal, which David had overturned. The fire-blackened clay heaps of its ruins were the first thing that greeted the new arrival, that greeted me anytime I stepped through the single, narrow doorway of the estate's main house, once the priests' house, where I lived. But I soon learned to ignore the sight, for Baal-Hazor was also blessed by a cave and a silent grove to Goddess hidden at the foot of the hill, which David had not touched because they were unannounced by outward signs.

It was here that Father of Shadows did his part to revitalize their Snake pit and I performed mine as oracle and Snakesleeper whenever such skills were needed. But, you know, that was not very often. The people of Baal-Hazor already knew what was required of them and they never attempted any movement under Heaven that had not been proved by their mothers and fathers before them. They were already so close to the Great Mother that they could tell most everything they needed to know for their lives for themselves, merely by standing in their open fields and sniffing at the wind, or by observing clouds and the flight of birds at sunset, by watching the way sheep stood in the fold. And sometimes they needed no more omen than the feel of air before the fires were stirred on a morning. I learned much from them that has been a help to me in my omen-taking all my life.

And I learned these things not by asking and being told, but by doing. Baal-Hazor was no place for a lady of leisure supported by her slaves. There was always more to do than every hand working with all its might could possibly accomplish. We never fetched in every single apricot, never shooed off all the ravens. And yet there was no pressure in the work and the pace was never as intense as in a town. What could not be done one day could keep, if necessary, until a sound and deep sleep had returned one's strength to start afresh. And if all the apricots were not taken in before they fell, well, they rotted and composted their strength for next year's harvest. I helped with the lambing and the sacrifice of those lambs, the pruning, the harvest, the milling, the baking, and finally, of course, the eating itself, to which all things led but which was an integral part of every action. We ate to get strength to work, we worked all day with what we were to eat that evening.

I remember one day when an order came from Absalom that he wanted more chickpeas this year than last. Because my brother had little understanding of the times of plantings and only thought of eating the things when he saw them already blooming in the fields, the order came too late.

"Just do as you're told," the deliverer of the message said. He was also my guard, who considered it enough of a service to life at Baal-Hazor that he kept me in sight at all times. He never did any other sort of work.

So the High Priestess, who was also the local midwife, mother of half the village's children, and head woman in the village, shrugged and caught her husband's eye. Then with no debate, the two swung their tools—he his plowshare, she her hoe—onto their shoulders and marched out to the field they'd left fallow but which could be planted to chick-peas without damage. The High Priestess dug her hoe in the soil some, nodded to her man, and then, again without debate, hoisted up her skirts and the pair made a quick but lusty bit of love while their children tumbled about and mimicked their actions beside them. The woman gave a shout of triumph in her ecstasy that cleared the earth of its ban of fallow, then they stood up at once and began to break the land; one deed was neither more nor less important for the planting of chickpeas than the other.

She was still panting from love when she strode over to me and handed me a hoe to help, and as we walked together to the place where the work was to begin, I felt her arm about my shoulder. I had told her about Jonadab; everything comes out like no more than asking for a drink of water when you work long enough beside another. She knew I sometimes still had to turn away when the rites were performed, and that was what she was sensing in me just now.

"Consider the ripening grapes," she said, waving her hand in the direction of the next field as we set our hoes to the soil. "Slowly, carefully, over all the summer, they store up the strength of the sun and the moon, the power of thunder-driven rain, the force of rocks from the soil. And when they are pressed and fermented, see, they have the power to knock down a full-grown man."

She winked at me as if at a private joke and smiled with a mouth full of bad teeth.

"Praise be to Goddess," was all I could think to say, but I knew at that moment, through the slow action of sun and moon and rain, I was healed of my pain and my sorrow and come to myself once more.

In Baal-Hazor, the joy of the time of the Great Marriage was always compounded by the festivities of sheepshearing. Indeed, to these people, the terms were interchangeable. The green almonds and the apricots had been gathered, the anemones come to the fields, and one could see to the end of the wheat harvest. It was my second such season on the land and I knew, without help of priests or their calendars, that as soon as the gleaners had passed, the sheep would be driven onto the stubble and then it would be time.

I straightened my back from the binding and looked about me. I counted off the time not in sunrises and sunsets, but in sheaves bound. Time moved thus in a slow, marked pace from stand to stubble across the land. We were preparing the Earth Herself, shaving in Her private, sacred parts, as a bride is for Her wedding day. I surveyed the land and the work, as much a part of Her face as birds or stones, and I saw that it was beautiful and infinitely good.

But the world and its way of marking time was bound to catch up with me. And one evening as the maids and I entered the compound from the fields, speaking slowly and softly among ourselves but almost too tired for speech, it descended upon me indeed. For there stood Absalom watching us from the torch-filled doorway.

"By God, you've become a peasant." Absalom greeted me with a wry smile of only half-tamed fierceness. He managed to tell me from the others only when they bowed deeply to their returned lord and I did not.

"By Goddess, you've become a man," I replied with equal wryness. It was an interesting bit of irony that both of us spoke what was meant as an insult and it was taken as lavish flattery by the other.

My brother had indeed grown up. Or shall we say his body had finally caught up with his mind. With him, baby fat had gone immediately to hard muscle and he always managed to keep a shape that women found irresistible, to cuddle as their infant or love as their man. Perhaps because he was not large, he gave them the feeling that they did not need to fear him. But I knew that feeling was false.

Absalom's beard had come in, too, full and black. I sometimes had the impression that the bloody blackness of his inside, stunted with his growth and not finding enough outlet even in his heavy hair, was forced out in the fierce growth on his chin and lip. And yet, at other times, perhaps because I remembered his younger face, I felt it was a mask such as thieves wear to give their victims no precise, substantial details of their evil, not even so much as a clear view of their features as a defense.

The chief shepherd, the High Priestess's husband, and the overseer arrived then, bowing and grinning stupidly to hide their nervousness. Absalom went in with them and said no more to me. I should have gone to help fix the supper, but it was suddenly necessary to call a maid to wait on me in my room as I washed and changed into more courtly robes. They were wrinkled with storage.

In time I descended to do some of the serving and to hear Absalom fume at the poor quality of the apricots that we had in apricot stuffing for the sacrifice, apricot stew, apricot pudding, and apricot paste pounded with almonds. Even I did not dare to add an explanation to the humble apologies, for the simple fact that the need to eat apricots in every and all possible ways was obvious to us. The best had been donkey-backed to the master—he had enjoyed them himself in Jerusalem weeks before—and the only ones left, those there was no space for on the drying mats, were rotting before our eyes under clouds of flies in the courtyard.

I waited in the kitchen with the other harvest-hungry women for the platters to be returned half-emptied to us. Yet I was too anxious to join in their speculative whispers in the corner. The decisions made in the great room would only indirectly affect their permanence on the soil of Baal-Hazor and offered in the meantime a momentary diversion. I could be disturbed forever. I thought of going out into the night and singing my Snake to me, just in case, but there wasn't time.

Absalom dismissed the men, all but the overseer, who stood by to fill my brother's bowl with wine when it was dry. Absalom ate on alone, for he did not want dining companions, only fulfillers of his orders who could be placated by a lump or two of mutton leg as were the hounds at his feet. I stood in the shadows and watched him eat as one watches kites perched on the backbone of a donkey's carcass—with a sober fascination for the destiny of one's own flesh and whether it will be kites or worms that will make a meal of all one's many and varied meals in the end.

When he had satisfied the hunger of the road and he began to eat slower and with more pleasure, Absalom looked up and saw me standing there. He gestured in my direction. At first I withdrew, for I thought he was calling for more service. But then I saw it was company he demanded, so I went.

"Now that's better," he said, appreciating the change in my appearance a few hours had made. "I suppose you'll be presentable in two weeks."

He gestured that I should join him on the divan. After I had, yet allowing myself no comfort there, a lengthy silence passed, which I was finally forced to break myself. "And what will be in two weeks?"

"Why sheepshearing, of course," Absalom replied. He finished his meal, belched contentedly, and gestured for the platters to be removed. Then he continued to speak. All the while he looked not at me but at the women as they came and went with the trays. People wear blue beads against the sort of evil-eyed possession he fixed them with.

"It will be," he said, "the greatest sheepshearing Baal-Hazor has ever seen. I have spoken to the men and arrangements are already under way. You will help, too, I trust."

"Do you plan to put in an appearance?"

"Yes. I will stay here until then. To watch the work. But I won't be the only one here for the festivities, of course."

"Of course?" As if those of us who were always here did not count.

"All of David's sons have been invited down to celebrate with me."

"All?"

"From Amnon down to little Solomon."

"And are they coming?"

"Solomon is not, damn him."

"And why not Solomon?"

"Ah. I forget. You have not been in Jerusalem since Solomon was born. Well, I will tell you. Solomon is too precious." He said it with sarcasm and violence so sharp that the edge crumbled and became dull and conversational. "Would that his nurse were more corruptible and she would long ago have painted her teat with henbane. Sometimes I feel I must deal with that toddler first before full-grown men. But Solomon can wait. It is the other sons I will deal with right now."

"And you do intend to deal with them."

He smiled with what could only be called kindness. "Yes."

Shivers ran up my back. "David will kill you first."

Absalom shrugged at my trustingness. "He's ordered them to come. Only a serious matter with the Tyrians keeps him from joining them himself."

"They won't obey that order. Not to come here, not to Baal-Hazor where you forge every sword. Not after . . . not after what you've done to me."

"They will come. Oh, I suppose that here in Baal-Hazor with nothing but the blooming of the peas to think about, what happened two years ago may still feed your fancy. But things are different in Jerusalem. So many other catastrophes have come and gone in those two years. Something of equal magnitude crops up every week to occupy the gossip."

"Catastrophes of your making?"

"Oh, some of them, yes." My brother smiled again. "But there are plenty of other men with ambition. And the women, if possible, are more ambitious than any man and they clog the harem with their plots. For example, somebody in some harem couldn't leave well enough alone and had to turn up a concubine of old king Saul's who had seven sons to her name, each one claiming the right to his father's throne."

"What became of them?"

"David had them executed, of course—or *sacrificed* is the politic term—to the sun in Gibeon. And Jonathan's son, the cripple, he has been put in protective—but firm—custody in

the boys' hall. Farther afield, we have soundly beaten the
Amorites for their aid to Ammon, taking thousands of
horses and chariots. Father has taken their city of Damas-
cus and garrisoned it. Well, you may imagine what sort of
intrigue such a great expanse of territory stirs up. My dear,
all but the most scrupulous of chroniclers has long ago
forgotten any little inconvenience to you. The rest of the
world hasn't time to care."

"Amnon would not forget," I insisted.

"Amnon is damned sentimental."

"Amnon won't come to your little festival."

"Amnon will come, at the head of the line. My dear, you
are here. As I said, our brother is a sentimental fool."

Having had his fill of food and of after-dinner talk, Absalom ended our interview, rose, and stretched himself. As an
afterthought he returned and said, "Oh, Tamar. Do you
know my wife?"

"No," I replied, taken aback. That was the last thing in
the world he had prepared me to hear.

He pointed her out to me, a figure sitting in the corner of
the room. I had not noticed her until then. She was still
bundled in her traveling veils, as patient as a merchant's
wares, waiting for his pleasure to be unpacked.

"Take care of her, will you, Sister?" Absalom said.
"When she comes to her time, it may well be the heir to the
heir of the empire that stretches from the River of Egypt to
the River Euphrates that she bears."

Then he went off to take his fill not of his wife, but of the
serving maid who had caught his fancy as the platters were
cleared. I could not prevent a groanlike sigh from escaping
as I saw that the one he chose to take to his bed was none
other than the eldest daughter of the High Priestess of the
grove of Baal-Hazor.

▫ XLV ▫

MY SISTER-IN-LAW WAS more familiar to me than I had at first suspected. When I offered a hand to take her veils, it was an Ammonite face I saw. I learned her name was Baraa and that she was sister to both Hanun and Amnon's Ruth—Absalom's spoil from the sack of Rabbath-Ammon. She was with child—far gone. She bore the condition not as the tree does figs or the goat her kids, with a natural grace, but as if she were a Goddess figure made of clay upon which strangers in a strange land had decided to slap the burden of more prominent, more obscene breasts and belly in some clay gritty with foreign matter and impurities and quite unfired.

"My brother is a fool as well as a demon" were my first words to her. "To bring you down from Jerusalem in your condition."

"He wants me with him," Baraa replied simply, clutching at what small favors a strange princess who cannot run home to her powerful father can.

I wanted to laugh at her innocence. "Didn't we just see him leave the room with another?"

Then I saw in her eyes that what I was for Geshur, she was for Ammon.

"He gathers us as bees do honey." I nodded.

"And from our soft honeycomb he will make an impenetrable claim to his father's empire."

Baraa's voice told me something more, and something of more immediate concern. The day's ride had done its worst, and Absalom's hopes would be somewhat premature. She was already gritting her teeth with labor.

"By Goddess," I said to her. "Would you have sat there in the corner 'til the child was born?"

"He was busy with the men," she said, but she grasped the hand I gave her as if, having heard my oath, she knew she could at last give full expression to her divine and fearful calling as a woman.

After many hours of long and difficult labor, Baraa's hands yearned past her now empty belly and between her legs. "My child, my child," she begged weakly.

I refreshed the cooling cloth on her forehead. "I'm sorry, Baraa. What can we do? Three months before the time. The child is dead."

She screamed in her grief louder than she had in the labor. And now I did not try to calm her, but hoped Absalom would be disturbed in his rest. The High Priestess quickly caught up the small bundle, wrapped it in rags, and carried it out so we could bury it later where its stillborn life would best call down the blessings of Goddess.

When Baraa finally slept, the High Priestess shook her head and whispered, "We did the best we could, but I fear it may be Goddess's will that she have no more."

I nodded. It did not look good.

"Never have I seen such an ill-omened child. What a strange, blue-black color! Perhaps she bruised it on the ride down."

"I think rather it is my brother's evil seed that rotted the fruit in the womb."

The High Priestess wrung her hands longer than necessary as she dried them, roving her eyes up through the low

lamp-lit rafters of the room to where she imagined even now
her daughter must be taking that seed into herself. "Snakesleeper, I think you are right. Like vinegar poured into
milk."

"I wish there were something we could do for your daughter."

"We'll just make certain she flushes it out with henbane
in the morning."

In the morning, while the High Priestess scurried her
daughter off to her medication, Absalom stormed about
outside the birthing room.

"The bitch, the stupid bitch! Can't even birth a baby
right."

"Yes, master. I am. I have failed," Baraa wept.

Then I dared to step in front of Absalom's pacing. "I
won't let you blame her," I said. "I won't. Isn't it enough
that you drag her all the way down here in such a condition,
but you must blame her for your impatience?"

I knew the power of his arm and closed my eyes, expecting
to feel it again. Instead, my brother's raised arm met the
other across his chest and he set his lips into a thin line.

"Everything does not come at once, even with force," I
said. "Some things are destroyed when forced."

Absalom could not deny that I spoke truth. Without a
glance back at his wife, he turned and strode from the room.

I waited on Baraa throughout her recovery, during the
next two weeks while the sheepshearing was being prepared.
One day when she was looking better, I broached a subject
I had heard nothing of for two years.

"How fares your sister Ruth?" I asked, leading into it that
way.

"Fine, fine."

"Is she—is she still in my brother Amnon's house?"

"Oh, yes, she is mistress there."

"Mistress?"

"By default, I guess you could say. For Prince Amnon
still refuses to make her—or anyone else—his bride."

"Oh, Amnon—"

"Don't fault him, Snakesleeper. Every other privilege of

matron is hers. Ruth has even been allowed to give these nice little parties at which we exiled Ammonites could gather on an evening, or on a day sacred to our God Milcom, and sing the songs of our homeland. Only—only we don't do it anymore."

A few days later I tried the subject again: "Why does your sister no longer have her little parties?"

"There was a man. A young man of our country. Once he was the son of a governor under my father. Now he is a foreman on David's building works. But he is young and kind and my sister is young and . . ."

"And Goddess moved between them," I translated her shrug.

She nodded.

"Did Amnon forbid them to ever meet again?" Did this mean he was finally taking an interest in Ruth? I asked myself. That was what I wanted, but now I suffered a flash of jealousy at the prospect. I held my breath for the answer.

"No," Baraa said. "No, he has never mentioned it. I think perhaps he has noticed nothing. But Ruth says, 'He knows, he knows.' She fought love and fear within herself for a long time and, after many tears and prayers, finally fear won out."

"Oh, Amnon!" I exclaimed. "I love him dearly and that makes me overrate his ability to be kind."

"Lady Tamar, the Hope of Israel and Judah is never unkind to my sister. I envy her lot."

"Neglect, I suppose, is better than what you have endured," I murmured to myself, but loud enough so that she could hear it if she chose.

"Ruth says what she fears is not his wrath as much as his hurt. He would not beat her, but she fears to betray him. He has been such a good master to her. She fears to be an unworthy servant. She fears he might . . . Ah, but who can say what David's firstborn thinks? He is intimate with no one. It is a mystery even to himself.

"Since my people were defeated at Rabbath-Ammon," Baraa continued, "Prince Amnon has never once been to train for war with the other sons of Israel—even since he

has, thanks be to Milcom, been healed of his wound. Nor
will he have the weapons of war in his house. He drinks
rather too much—at least, that is Ruth's opinion—even
now that his wound is but a scar as clean as you could wish
and must trouble him only when it rains. And it is his
practice usually to drink alone, which—I mean, to us of
Ammon—is an unhealthy practice."

"How fare the rites in Topheth?" I asked, the thoughts of
one mystery leading to another.

"I am not allowed to go," Baraa said with an unconscious
glance to the doorway lest we be overheard. "But they say,
since you are gone, it has lost some of its energy."

"Surely they will not forget the liturgy again."

"Goddess forbid! I pray there may be one among the
scribes so busy copying laws and histories that can be moved
by Heaven to include the Song of Songs in his book as well.
Ruth tells me only twenty or so came last year to speak the
liturgy in the shrine. The others, the rest of us, we recite the
blessed songs at home before our teraphim that we must
keep hidden behind curtains."

"But my brother Amnon went down, didn't he?"

"Of course. He and all his household, they made up half
the congregation. And my sister wept when she told me how
well he plays the part of the Bridegroom."

"Does he mention me?" I asked. "Does he say anything?"

"Ruth says when he first heard of . . . of what my husband
and your cousin had done, that he forswore you—forgive
me, Lady—for a deceitful whore. His wound infected with
his anger and they feared for his life. Then he was told of
how horribly Jonadab died and how you had been forced
against your will. Then he grieved and repented his mistrust.
He cried out blasphemy and prayed that his wound might
kill him quickly, that he might descend to give battle to
Jonadab in the Netherworld. But it did not. His tears
washed away the infection, cleaned the wound with their
salt, and one day he did rise from his bed again. Ruth says
he might have risen before—but that he drinks too much."

"Because he lacks vision," I made excuse for him. "There
is no Snakesleeper now in Topheth and the people perish

without vision. Amnon seeks to gain by wine what only women by the grace of Goddess can be given in the form of intuition. I wish he would marry your sister. Then he might have some little vision at least."

I mused on. "And he sorely needs it, for Goddess, blessed be Her Name, saw fit to send him against not the coward Jonadab, whom I, a woman and alone, could defeat, but against Absalom, who I sorely fear may be an evil against which there is no defense."

I said this then and in all the two weeks of our preparations at Baal-Hazor it proved so that, though I prayed and fasted and made offerings and read omens, I was given no helpful clue as to how to forewarn Amnon before his arrival put him wholly into Absalom's hands. Only that very first day, when I went down to the grove with the High Priestess to bury the little mite of blue-black flesh, Absalom's son, was I able to do anything. And that was only to sing in a whisper to Father of Shadows of my plight and to beg him somehow to get the message to Jerusalem. But there was one of Absalom's men standing to one side to guard us, as there was all the rest of those two weeks, and so I could not even wait for my Serpent's answer.

· XLVI ·

THE BANNERS AND the curtained sides of the pavilions were drifting gently in the hot south wind. The cook pits and ovens smoked and groaned with the feast for the king's sons, and everywhere sheep and goats numbed the mind with clouds of dust and their pitiful bleating. The shepherds sang like mothers lullabying to their flocks and the women sang the songs of woe, the songs they have always sung at this season of mourning when the Earth shows signs of Her painful vulnerability. And they all sang new verses, age old in their feeling, from the Song of Songs:

> Where has your beloved gone,
> O most beautiful of women?
> Where has your beloved turned aside,
> that we may seek him with you?

Runners came early that morning with the news that, having overnighted in Michmash, David's sons would be in Baal-Hazor before noon. They were traveling slowly for the sake of the younger ones and their nurses and had taken the opportunity to indoctrinate the folk of Michmash with a sense of their father's power by the way.

"All of them?"

"Amnon the son of Ahinoam the Jezreelitess leads all the rest."

Having received that reply, Absalom grew as confident as running water that has no fear of even fire. His movements and his laughter became that of a spring stream and, liberal to me as to mossy banks, he allowed me to go down to the grove unattended.

The Sacred Grove, as if it had been a fruit orchard, bloomed with the color of bunting and the offered ribbons and beads of generations. Three-footed braziers of incense had been set at the four cardinal points, and they filled the hollow as if it were winter with sweet-smelling mists. Boulders were set here and there by the Hand of Goddess Herself as seats for participants. They were of the limestone of the region which, when freshly cracked, reveals a reddish heart. Goddess Blood it's called, and special sacrifice must be made if one accidentally wounds Her so. These boulders made a stern, silent presence, as did the call of lonely doves and the dapple of sun through the oaks, for there were so few celebrants that year. So few celebrants, so much Goddess. The cleavage where the grove lies narrows at the farthest end to the Holy of Holies, which in this sanctuary is a natural cave in that limestone. I had been in the sanctum only once, at the rites the previous year, but I saw that the lamps there were already burning for this year. It was irreverent to look deeper at this time.

I did think, however, as I passed as deep as I dared into the cleavage, how Nature was fulfilling the image of the Song on a grand scale:

A bundle of myrrh is my well-beloved unto me;
He shall lie all night between my breasts.

"Ah, Goddess, could it but be true!" I prayed and then instantly refuted it, realizing that if Amnon were to come to me in Baal-Hazor, that night would be his last.

"Your will. Your will, O Goddess, Your will," I prayed as part of my mourning as I went down to the Grove. I wished there were some rites I could follow to conform Her will to mine. I knew how to call rain and Serpents and healing, but not this. I saw the problem plainly: I could sustain no conceivable future with my will. And so I prayed only that She give me the strength to conform my will and to learn to submit it to what Hers would bring, whatever the prayers of mortals might be.

Though Absalom allowed me, finally, permission to go to the Grove this last day of the traditional mourning for the dead Son, I was not allowed to appear to mourn—I must keep my garments fresh and unrent, my face and hair clean, painted and of fashionable set. A hunter tries to keep the bait in his trap alive and, if its death has been unavoidable, he still tries to keep the wounds hidden and the look of life about the corpse. So did Absalom for the fox he hunted, Amnon.

Yet, as most of the women were called for in the great house, at the ovens or bundling fleeces, I did not feel out of place or disrespectful descending to the shrine in such dress. It was as if I had come too early rather than too late, as if the ceremonies had yet to begin. What chanting and rites had to be performed were carried out whenever there was a free moment by whomever could be spared from my brother's competing rituals. I joined but a handful in the shrine, and mostly the blind, the old, and the lame, of little use elsewhere. We still hadn't even recognized a couple for the Great Bed. It was impossible that Absalom would spare the usual Groom, the High Priestess's husband. The High Priestess herself felt she shouldn't take the part when her daughter was active in Absalom's bed; there are sanctions against this in Baal-Hazor.

"A curse on Absalom!" the High Priestess said.

"Maybe we should count Prince Absalom as the Lord and make his the Great Bed this year," suggested another woman.

"That's a pretty bit of blasphemy if you ask me," the High Priestess said. Still, she had to admit, "We've a quandary here. Which lord, that of Earth or of Heaven, will make life in Baal-Hazor more miserable if he is displeased?"

"Heaven has mercy and can forgive." Baraa added her wisdom. After that it was generally concluded that none of us could say the same of this ruler of Earth.

I sang in the Grove for Father of Shadows, but I received not a whisper in reply. Momentarily I flushed with hope that there might be something my Messenger could do to answer my prayer and preserve the well-beloved of my heart. But it was time for mourning and for general despair. I dared not lighten my heart until I saw clearly the consummation of the year. In the meantime, the High Priestess was gone, her consort was gone, the Son languished in the Netherworld, and we had to wait on Heaven to grant us joy.

I was tempted to call up another of the Snakes so I could lose myself in some Goddess vision until all the horror had passed, or at least until all that was left was the horror of everything having been shaken down to its lowest point. At least then there would be something for me to do, some stone to pick up and place upon another to begin the process of rebuilding, something to lift the idle and helpless weight from my hands. But who could say when my help would be needed? And on that day I dared not trust my bared breast to a Serpent as yet a stranger to me. And so, as Father of Shadows still failed to appear, I sat down on a stone and tried to learn its patient submissiveness as I waited.

I sought retreat and seclusion in the grove, but my escape was not complete. From the height of the great house at the top of Baal-Hazor, which is the height of Mount Ephraim, one can see the entire length of the way to Ophrah from Michmash. By descending into the grove, I avoided seeing the train from Jerusalem when it was tiny and helpless and impersonal as a line of ants. But I could not avoid the sight of it when, life-sized and brimming with faces I knew, it rounded the last bend, shouted its welcome to echo against the faces of exposed limestone that make up Mount Ephraim, and entered its doom.

Abigail's witless Daniel, Haggith's Adonijah, Sephatiah and Ithream, Shammuah and Shobab, and that little one, grown up so and swaggering as if he were four times his age and had just killed his first man, that must be little Nathan. So I picked the royal princes out from the company of their retainers by their lively mounts, their purple robes and their faces, half David's ruddiness and half their various mothers.

I counted them. And then named and counted them again. Then, rising to my feet, I made review of every retainer. Even the women I carefully scrutinized as if by some miracle of transformation, some total submission to Goddess, Amnon might have hidden himself in traveling veils. But every time I reached the same conclusion. Wherever he was, the son of Ahinoam was not to be counted among the sons of David that day.

I strained to hear what might filter down into the grove of Absalom's greeting, but the wind and the shield of trees thwarted me. Even when I stepped out into the open, I could see no more than Adonijah's explaining gestures, which were wide and vague as if he said, "Our brother has gone with all four winds."

Absalom shot a fierce glance in my direction, which made me retreat back into the Grove. Later I saw a company of scouts trot off to Adonijah's "four winds" and I feared as only the ignorant can fear. Yet I did not want to trade the hope of my ignorance for a more fearful certainty. So I sat back down on my stone and waited once more. And all my thoughts, my hopes, my fears, epitomized and made real by the tale of the Man-God doomed to the Netherworld, brought me alone to a mourning deeper than I had ever felt in a full congregation at Topheth. None but Goddess and Her power could bring a light into that darkness.

"Woman, why are you weeping?"

It was a liturgical question and as soon as I caught my breath, I responded as Goddess is said to have, as one must always do at this season in similitude of Her, " 'Because my Lord, the joy of my eye, is gone and I know not where.' "

"Woman, why are you weeping?"

" 'If you have any news of him that brightens my eye, tell me and I . . .' "

But I never said what it was that Goddess vowed to do in

times long passed because in that instant, Her will became mine at last and I responded with words and gestures all my own. The Man-God that stood before me, having defied the chains of death, was none other than my own brother, Amnon the son of David.

"Peace, Sister, peace," Amnon said with a finger held up before his gentle smile. Otherwise I might have betrayed his presence to the great house with the exuberance of my greeting.

"Where have you been, beloved?" I asked with a lightness in my voice that spared us both from the strain of the moment's true import.

"Gathering mandrakes for you," Amnon replied with equal lightness and verified it by dumping a load of the roots with the fresh earth still clinging to them into my lifted skirt.

When that laughter of surprise and delight was past, I allowed myself slightly more earnestness as I asked, "How is it, beloved, that you do not come to Baal-Hazor in the company of David's other sons?"

"You don't know?"

"No," I admitted.

"It was your doing."

"I can't have had anything to do with it. I've been here in the Grove all day—"

"Oh, but you did, Sister."

Gathering my mandrake-filled skirt with one hand, I took him by the other and led him to my stone. "You must tell me this story from the beginning."

"I was in rank at the foremost of the party riding out of Ophrah. My mount, a pretty, light gray little she—"

"Is it old Smoke?"

"No, Smoke died last year. I called this one Terebinth, an intelligent beast who, having no cause to fear this morning, stepped lively through the blooming and peaceful countryside. She did not notice the Serpent, lying nothing so much as like a shadowy crack across the stones in the path, until it was too late. She had stepped too close to the black head and been struck."

"Father of Shadows!"

"I'm certain of it."

"I'm sorry about Terebinth. But her life was in vain! Why didn't you heed the Serpent's message?" I pleaded. "Why didn't you turn back? That was what he meant to tell you. Can't you see? Absalom has invited you here only to kill you."

"I know that, Sister," Amnon said. "I knew that before I ever left Jerusalem."

"Then why did you ever come?"

"Because you are here."

He sounded too frustratingly like Absalom. "Curse that I am here. Oh, Amnon, you've walked into the very jaws of the trap, for all of Father of Shadows' poison!" I turned from him to hide my grief.

"Don't you remember, Tamar, what you told me once about death? When I shied from feeding the dormouse to your snake and you told me about the goat you had once been asked to sacrifice. His name was Sage. I still remember. Don't you?"

"Of course."

"All things die. I have accepted that. Even for myself."

"But . . ." In this case I found it impossible to accept my own wisdom.

"Two years is too long, Tamar," Amnon said. "Too long to sit all but prisoner in Jerusalem, having to call a bodyguard every time I wanted to walk from my house to the palace. Too long to live in fear of Absalom's assassins behind every post, his poison in everything I eat. Most of the men in Jerusalem would not even spit if his dagger found my heart on their very doorstep, for they believe the lies he's spread. His lies—saying I defiled you instead of Jonadab—they've become as good as truth. I almost believe it myself."

"What?"

"Not the part about you, of course, but that he has cause of revenge against me because of you."

"It's you who have cause of revenge against him."

"Peace, love. Two years is too long a time to pass without your touch, without so much as the sound of your voice. Let us speak only of peace."

"But, beloved, the grave is eternal."

"Love, I have been dead—as good as dead—the past two years. I didn't dare go to the practice field—weapons all around—I didn't dare let myself get to know the men I would someday have to rule or sit in with my father at his counsels. Nothing. Today—even if it is just today—I have life again. If I had continued to sit around in Jerusalem, sooner or later Absalom would have found a way to become firstborn son even while I sat cowering within my walls. Then it would have been eternally too late for us indeed. This way at least I may see you once again before I die.

"I have made my final peace with Jerusalem," he continued, "bid farewell to Mother and to my sisters."

"What about our house?" I asked. "And what about your Ammonitess? What is to become of her? You never married her, did you?"

"Before I left, I thought perhaps I should husband her, as you suggested. It seemed the least I could do, in memory of my dear friend Hanun and in gratitude for the service she has given me so faithfully. But then I thought of her, left my widow, carrying my son, perhaps. And I thought how Absalom would eye that son. Ruth has suffered enough in this life. I did not wish her to live after me a widow as well as an orphan. And then, perhaps, to suffer the sight of our son spitted alive on Absalom's sword. Or if I left no son, to be forced to marry that demon brother of ours because the law requires him to raise up sons to me when I am gone."

"So you did nothing. You simply left her."

"There was a certain son of Ammon," Amnon said, "a young man of her country working as a foreman in Father's building crews. He had come once or twice to call on Ruth—with others, true, but it was he who attracted my attention. Just before I left I bought the man his freedom and, for a length of cloth (which I myself gave him as a manumission gift), sold him the house and everything in it. Our little house in lower Jerusalem with the fig and almond trees in the garden. I hope you don't mind. Not too much."

"I'm sorry it was destined to be ours only that one single night when you lay languishing on your sickbed. But since it is destined so, I am pleased . . . But tell me, do Ruth and this son of Ammon . . . ?''

Amnon smiled. "I suppose they will marry. I have seen it coming.''

I began to weep then, whether for joy or sorrow I couldn't tell. "Ah, beloved,'' was all I could find to say.

"Don't curse me for coming, love,'' Amnon said. "Rejoice with me. What a day I have had! Praise Goddess for that Snake of yours that gave me the excuse I needed to dismount—I was thrown off, actually—see the graze on my arm? We had to put an arrow through the poor donkey's brain so it wouldn't linger in pain, and then there was no reason at all why I shouldn't leave the party and the trail and make my way to Baal-Hazor by the wildest, freest way I could find.

"By the God of my Fathers, Tamar, and by Goddess, too. Didn't you see the day today? The polished turquoise of the sky, flawless but for the kites come to feed on poor old Terebinth. And even they were beautiful as they hung in the air like bated breath. The wildflowers, Tamar! I made wreath after wreath, each one, I thought, more perfect than the last. But then I left them all, for I realized that the most perfect flowers were always those still in the ground, those still in touch with Mother Earth. I followed bees from those flowers to the stump where their hive was. See? I only got stung once, and then I feasted royally on honey and bits of broken comb warm as mother's milk from the sun. And with my bare hands I dug these mandrakes when I found them, got the good Earth under my nails and drew the very deepest of its smell up into my nostrils. Tamar, no day to come, even should a miracle spare me, could match this day. Then what further reason have I to live? Only this night, which you must share with me, and then I am complete. Then old Amnon returns to Mother Earth who first created, then sustained him. He returns quite satisfied and convinced his was the best of lives that any child of Earth may know, strive as and for what he will.''

He drew me sobbing into his arms, but now I knew it was for joy that I wept, as my earlier weeping had been for

misery and helplessness. For now I saw that this was Goddess's will. It had come by Her Messenger, Father of Shadows, come by Her all-powerful Hand moving even in such
a being as Absalom.

Amnon took me by the arm and led me gently into the
Holy of Holies. There in that Womb of the Earth, lamps
gave a pinkish glow to the limestone, natural save where in
an ancient age someone had carved several images of Goddess—eyes, breasts, buttocks, vulva—with a liberal hand.
Here the Great Bed was spread. There wasn't room for
much more than that, just cushions and rugs on the ground,
strewn with sweet-smelling lilies of the field and fogged with
incense.

"My beloved is a shepherd among the lilies . . ."

And there were two attendants. Aged crones heavy with
signs of their former fertility, their initiation robes seeming
as old and of the same cast as the limestone. One was deaf,
the other almost blind, and between them I doubt they could
boast a full set of teeth; they were the only Faithful Absalom
didn't demand for himself. They had set out a tray with
wine, Ashtoreth cakes with ponderous thighs, and sweet
early figs. They gestured us toward them, but suddenly I
balked.

A tray of wine—I remembered the tray of bread and wine
Jonadab had offered me, and my stomach lurched. Though
two years dead, he still had the power to haunt me, and
Absalom, his driving force, was still very close, very much
alive. I dropped Amnon's hand as if it had stung me and
hugged myself, suddenly as cold as death. My teeth, chatter-
ing, brought tears of helpless panic to my eyes. Amnon, too,
was helpless. He tried to touch me, but I shook his hand off
my shoulder as if it had been Jonadab's.

The attendants knew drastic measures were called for.
Fortunately, their wisdom taught them just the magic they
needed to work. Although she was deaf, the one of them had
a sure and nimble hand. She rolled a large drum to her lap
and touched its skin. It was goatskin, the hair left on and
ragged where it was tied to the body. The hair was worn in
spots from much use. These spots the old woman knew like

her own body, and she found them with an uncanny rhythm that seemed to give the instrument a voice. This was the signal—I knew it well—the Bride should begin to dance:

"Turn, turn, O Shulamite, turn . . ."

A voice within me said, "I can't," and veered away. But those two old faces watching me were so full of wisdom, so understanding, even without words, because they had been there once, like the faces I'd seen around me at initiation. A voice said, "You're a singer, not a dancer." But the drumming, the drumming, *tink thunk-a thunk thunk tink,* was more compelling than any voice in me.

The drummer's hand rocked and thunked from high tone to low, and my fingers in spite of themselves twitched in imitation. The drummer saw and smiled her guileless, gapped grin and nodded in time to her drumming. My head began to nod as well.

"Turn, O Shulamite, that we may look upon you."

Now the blind woman began to sing. Her voice was deep and resonant, given divine overtones by the hollow of her mouth, then by the cave.

"How beautiful are your steps in sandals, o nobleman's daughter."

She sang the words I knew so well because I had introduced them to Baal-Hazor. But on her tongue they were as ageless as the Goddess figures on the wall.

How we gaze upon the Shulamite,
As upon a dance before two armies!

Then I felt the possession, first in my breasts, then in my pelvis, and both moved without command, without thought, with a life of their own. They struggled to be free of my clothes.

My hips moved, as the head does in the Serpent Charm, and like the Serpent Charm, I saw it called, it compelled Amnon to life. He had the same gentle brown eyes he had always had, the same brown hair with highlights of David's copper. But he was like the sacred statue behind Michal's curtains, something more. And I was no longer the same. I

was something to be worshiped. Amnon began to worship
me, and as he did, each part was transformed. And from me,
the power emanated out beyond the shrine to the waiting
land:

> Your hair is a flock of goats
> That descend from Mount Gilead.
> Your eyes like the fishpools in Heshbon.
> Your lips are like a thread of scarlet,
> Your teeth like a flock of sheep just shorn,
> Which come up from the washing,
> Whereof every one bears twins,
> And none is barren among them.
> Your neck is a tower of ivory.
> Your stature is like to a palm tree,
> And your breasts to clusters of dates.
> I said, I will go to the palm tree.
> I will take hold of the boughs;
> Your belly is a heap of wheat
> Set about with lilies,
> And below that, a goblet,
> Not lacking in liquor . . .

The dance continued in me, even as he spread me out in
all my parts across the Great Bed. Through his worship, I
became divine. I knew the great shout of triumph and joy as
Goddess took me to Her and I became Her.

The drummer echoed the shout with great rolls on her
instrument. She and her crony murmured something together, helped themselves to some of the figs and cakes, then
helped each other to their feet, up and out of the grove, to
spread the news that fertility was Baal-Hazor's for yet another year.

After that, Amnon and I were on our own, and what we
did was for ourselves and ourselves alone. We made each
other divine again and again and again.

The dew still glittered on the grass of the Grove, the doves
were beginning to murmur, when we heard them. Their
profanely shod feet sent the doves up in a flutter.

"Stay, love," I pleaded.

"I can't, my love and my life, I can't." He was dressing quickly. "I don't want their feet to defile this place."

I didn't dare peek after him but lay where I was, prostrate at Her feet in the smoke of the burned-out lamps. But I couldn't close my ears.

"Brother"—Absalom's voice—"we missed you at the festivities last night."

"I'm sorry, but I had a little accident."

"So I heard."

"I'm sorry I was detained. I'm here now."

"Please, do me the honor of riding my best mount."

"Thank you, I will," Amnon said to Absalom, "but you and I both know I'm not here for your honor."

I think Absalom was a little taken aback. He'd been convinced his evil was invisible. I had to sit up and look now, just to see the expression on his face. He fought the expression as only Absalom could, and as long as I watched, he continued to treat our stepbrother as a welcome guest. Absalom hated to have his little dramas interrupted.

And Amnon rode away from me with his head held high, as if he guided the donkey beneath waving palm branches and over people's cast-down cloaks in the triumphant procession, out of the grove, between two rows of Absalom's men.

I stayed on in the grove and breathed the morning air. I had always assumed that death came when you had finished all the work you had to do on Earth: life at the end of a full and busy day when there is no longer light to see by or strength to do more of the chores that can be done with but little sight. Then you could go with gratitude to your cot and lie down and welcome the rest. So I thought. But now I know that rarely is this ever so, certainly not with the greatest souls. You are taken when you are busiest, when the most depends on you, when the world, it seems, cannot go on without your one soul. Perhaps this is to teach us to savor life more, to miss the loved ones more when they go. Or to teach us that the world can indeed go on because there is no choice: it must. And so, I told myself in the grove, must I.

Father of Shadows, I found, had returned, and I gave him milk. His steady, unblinking eyes offered no sympathy, only strength and the knowledge that there must be no more mourning. The time for that was past. Goddess had worked Her resurrection power once again. She had descended into the Netherworld and broken its bands. Singing Her songs, I used the mandrakes Amnon had brought me to work a magic to be certain I could snatch an ember of life from this, his last glow, to carry on with me to warm myself by in the cold days to come.

▣ XLVII ▣

I UNDERSTAND IT is commonly reported that Jonadab was the one who calmed David in Jerusalem and told him that only Amnon was dead when false and panicky reports led the king to believe that Absalom had murdered every single one of his sons in Baal-Hazor. You have seen that Jonadab was dead before this time and could not possibly have been the one standing there by David's throne. Who it was I cannot say, but such details can little concern me. I was, at the time, in my brother's custody, heading even farther north.

This journey can hardly be called anything but a flight, for Absalom dared not stay within Israel's boundaries with Amnon's blood on his hands. He dared not even fly to the altar of Shechem as a man does who seeks refuge from the lawless in the law. For anyone's justice, even David's, would demand Absalom's death if it were allowed to have its sway. And so Absalom fled to wait and plot until the next move could be taken with safety.

Yet I am mistaken if I accuse Absalom of cowardice. Daring or not daring hardly seems appropriate when discussing my brother's motivations. He did as he pleased, feared nothing, and never considered what the effect of his actions on anything but his own gain might be. Other men who dare to flaunt much before the world have limits of the fear of Heaven that were quite foreign to my brother.

There were other purposes this move of caution only camouflaged. We traveled by night as a rule because the heat of the summer was upon us and moonlight was less wearing than the sun. The souls we met by moonlight when we stopped to sleep or for water and food were the restless souls, the souls who for blood and crime upon their minds, if not their hands, could not keep to their beds. They were souls that listened with sympathy to Absalom's version of David's aborted justice, souls that would keep the name of Absalom alive throughout his banishment and nurture their own grudges mixed with his until he should return again.

No, Absalom "dared" nothing. Everything he did was according to plan.

I was my brother's prisoner, but our destination seemed to me no prison, but a land of glowing promise. The place where Absalom would seek asylum was in the court of our grandfather, Talmai the son of Ammihud, in Geshur, the land of my birth.

That my brother's plans concurred with mine should perhaps have given me pause to reevaluate my longings. But I was slowly learning the peace in allowing Goddess's will— things She allowed and which I had no power to change—to become my own. Besides, longings for Geshur were too much a part of me, imbued since earliest childhood.

Grandfather, warned by runners of our coming, met us on the western shore of the Sea in the fishing hamlet of Hammath.

"The boats are ready here," he said, gesturing to the little wooden craft that dared to stand with their noses to the great expanse of Sea.

"We—we intended to cross on foot, farther south, across the River Jordan," Absalom protested.

Grandfather smiled indulgently, but some of the sailors actually guffawed out loud. Absalom had used the Geshuri form of "we" that means more than one woman. Naturally, what he did know of the language (for he would never allow that Mother and I should have secrets he did not understand) was all women's talk, the certain forms, almost a dialect in themselves, that are reserved for women. On a woman's tongue they signify, "I am a partaker of the Mystery of Goddess." On a man's, they are baby talk, a holdover from his toddling days in the harem. Absalom flushed but didn't have the vocabulary either to make his argument more forceful or to correct himself.

"A river crossing is impossible," my grandfather said. "Untoward currents there caused several deaths this spring and the purification of the ford is not yet complete."

Absalom said nothing, but language or no I could tell he did not like the looks of those boats. He was an inland man, a man of the Judean hills. He liked to have the ground beneath his feet.

"By all means we must cross by boat." I concurred with my grandfather. I turned my back on Absalom to let him struggle alone with whichever he feared most, impurity, restless water spirits, or the open sea.

"I thought we could load the baggage in this boat, but I see you haven't much."

"We did leave in something of a hurry."

"Yes," Grandfather said with a twinkle in his eye that said further, "Let this Absalom find Geshuri words to explain all *that*." "So maybe you should ride in this one, as it's the largest and sturdiest, if that's all right with you, Granddaughter—"

Though Goddess had willed him the main labor of ruling our land for many years, Geshuri etiquette demanded that he defer to me, and Grandfather was nothing if not a prince of politeness. This was the second step in effectively cutting Absalom out of discussion.

My grandfather did have a commanding voice, deep and full of the gutturals he loved best of all and always emphasized for effect. I did not remember him from my childhood and was shy at first. But it was the good sort of shyness, closer to blushing joy, that must have subconsciously remembered his voice calling me his "Little Brown Eyes" as he tossed me in the air. My love for him grew from a duty and a fearing to a true and easy pleasure almost immediately.

I had imagined—hoped—that my grandfather would be dark like me, but he was not. His eyes were blue-gray, the color of iron, the color of the Sea when the mists rise on a winter's morning. And his skin, naturally light, had been kept pale by his life as one of David's tributary princes with little but the hunt to keep him out of doors and active. He was a good huntsman, however, and must have been a good soldier once.

"But I don't even do that much anymore," he said. "I am the first to admit that a show of force against dumb animals, unless from need, is a vacant and inane substitute for the real power men long for. Alas that I allowed my real power, your mother, to go south to David's harem so long ago."

Light flesh, though it wrinkles and ages slower than the dark, does so, I feel, with much less grace, especially on a man. Dark skin shrivels and dries; the white merely rots. I am sorry I don't remember my grandfather before the spots appeared, the irregular veins and old scars bulged, which his color could not hide or dignify with mellowness. Yet there was much of the younger man still intact in his thoughtful, deliberate movements, the strong, firm lips of ample proportions, the high brow that plunged straight to a nose that was regal and that, with its wide base and high bridge, dominated all the rest of his face. I felt a moment of jealousy for my grandmother. Though she had died before I was born, she had known and loved my grandfather in his prime, and that was something to envy.

"Come," Grandfather said, leading us up the pebbly shingle to a fire struggling to life from a few sticks. "My men have caught these *mousht* fish, and while they load the boats, I hope you will break the fast of your journey. They say if you take longer to cook and eat a fish than it took to catch it, you will have indigestion."

I laughed out loud with pleasure at my grandfather's folk wisdom. "What else do they say of fishes here?"

"They say: 'We feed on the fish that fed on the worm that fed on the king.' That's enough to keep a king humble, wouldn't you say?"

I laughed heartily with my grandfather throughout the meal as I had not been inclined to laugh for months—no, for over two years. Absalom, it was clear to me, did not care for fresh-caught fish and was struggling to keep enough of it down to be polite. In Jerusalem, our fish had always come from either the Jordan or the Great Sea, a distance that meant, if it were not salted and brined beyond distinction, it smelled foully and was highly suspect. Absalom's face as he put the white flakes of fish in his mouth was the true cause of my mirth, and yet I did not dare to laugh openly at him until we should reach the other shore. And so I let my grandfather give me any number of other, silly, wine-induced excuses to let it come forth in other directions.

But the bubble of well-being within me was only just beginning to swell and rise. When we pushed off into the Sea at last, then my feelings truly soared.

I have always felt the Sea of the Lyre might be better named the Sea of the Looking Glass. For so it seems to be—the mirror of Goddess Herself to peer down into, whether one imagines Her perch to be in the cliff-top temple at Aphek or in the ever-changing vault of Heaven. Our Lady's mirror is of iron, or polished bronze, or, at night, shimmering black onyx to glimpse the moon in. Sometimes the Sea reflects a face of polished alabaster with lush, dark curls on the horizons. Sometimes She will see Herself in nothing but silver or, on occasions of highest state—at sunset or at dawn—the purest gold.

Because I imagined thus, I knew no uneasiness as the rowers pulled us farther and farther from shore and into the midst of the water's insubstantiality. Indeed, I felt so light and the water seemed so good and true that had my grandfather in the next boat called for me to come, I am quite convinced I could have walked to him upon it. And yet the solidarity I felt in the water was not that of ground my feet had known beneath them before. I can best explain what I felt from the moment we pushed off from Hammath by saying that I felt myself escaped to a world where the laws were much more favorable to the spirit than the one I had just left. It was the world from which the Song of Songs had come, for now I found my very blood coursing in meter. It was a life of more true living, or rather, life more conscious of its Source and of Her divine Breath in everything.

The air was filled with life exhaled by the great palms and impassable jungles at the Sea's edge. The area teemed with wild boar, leopard, nameless myriads of birds; they breathed a surfeit of life. The jungles hung like veils about the Sea and, like veils, were heavier still with sweat on that summer afternoon.

And yet, within the trickery of this mirror world, things that should have been weighted down flew. There is a bird in these parts called the eagle gull because it is much bigger than a regular gull. For the sound of its cry and for its size, the natives call it the donkey of the Sea; they, too, though they were born here, sense the magic of the place where things that but plod elsewhere can soar through the air.

But the wonder of wonders came as the sun set behind the western hills of Naphtali. A breeze came up, as it will at that time of day, tantalizing us with a nip of the mountains in the midst of the stifling heat. The boatmen could then unfurl their sails. Baraa beside me squealed, half with fear, half with excitement and I, too, caught my breath as we began to skim across the water. On the rim of the next boat, Absalom's knuckles were white with clutching. I threw back my head and laughed with pure delight.

And then, all fell silent with a blow, for the last of the sun caught the eastern ridges, the wall of black basalt that is Geshur. The naked rock was heavily swathed in trees—not the palm and cane of the lowlands, but oleander, pine, cedar, and balsam as sweet smelling as any Gilead can boast. In many places Geshur's soil was black or blood red like the stone from which it eroded. And, as if the soil were the blood of life, it was everywhere pulsed up into foliage so that green became a lame and stumbling word for the colors we saw. They were much richer, much deeper than what one usually associates with that word, for everywhere rich black and red were undertones.

Ah, Goddess! And to think David's god would cut down all those trees! "Divinity does not dwell in a dumb stick of wood," he rationalizes. Very well, be blind to the undertones. But don't let your blindness make you stupid.

I fear such stupidity might well be inevitable; it was Absalom's last order as we rode out of Baal-Hazor. "Cut down the cursed grove," he shouted. "Yes, to the very last tree. By the God of my Fathers, I mean it." And then defile it with Amnon's poor body left unburied there for the jackals and kites. Such a deed accomplishes its purpose. 'Til the end of the Earth no one will ever worship there again as Amnon and I did on that final perfect night. The very first winter rain will wash away all the soil that once made Baal-Hazor fertile. In simple terms, there will be no trees to stop it. In loftier terms, the Mysteries will have ceased and Goddess will no longer haunt the place. Ah, Goddess! I pray it never happens here in Geshur.

The last light played now upon the high ledge of rock where Aphek stands to overlook the Sea. The ancient and hallowed temple to Goddess, built of native basalt, shone like an obsidian blade, and little blinkings of the houses, Her little children, lit their night fires and nestled at Her feet. I knew I was meant to be in Geshur and that only human folly had kept me away before. I have been in many other places and felt comfortable in them all, with time and patience. Yet Geshur was like the very bands of my infant swaddling. I could grow and leave them behind. But they were empty, useless, lifeless without me. Geshur is not Geshur without the women of the sacred lineage to rule her, and I was the last of that line.

I was the last, but not for long. When we arrived on the shores of the Sea of the Lyre, I had already missed one time of Blood Mystery. The mandrakes had worked their magic and I knew that new Goddess-blessed life was clotted within me. I tried to convey this to my grandfather from the moment I saw him by the beaming in my face, that he might know that not only had his seed been returned to him, but that it had come to multiply his joy in his old age. I don't think he saw it quite then. His eyesight was failing and he was weeping. But I had come at last.

Ah, Goddess, I've come home at last! Ah, Goddess! I bent over and hugged the jug with Father of Shadows in it to my heart. I closed my eyes tightly, for the dream could not become any more real or I should swoon.

◉ XLVIII ◉

MY WONDER AND love of Geshur has never faded, even in all the years it has been since that first view. That first year I often had to pinch myself to be certain I was not dreaming. Each season, each day of weather, light and dark, rolled up across the Sea. Watching it from the parapet of the temple, I could not help but think each moment more wonderful than the last. I stood amazed at the changes, always the same and yet always new and different. And most amazing of all was the miracle happening within my own body.

I remember one day very early in my pregnancy when I had only told Baraa, Grandfather, and the priestess who had helped me perform the necessary sacrifices. I sat cleaning wheat in the courtyard. At Aphek we always try to sift through every measure twice, for it would be a great shame to offer cakes made of any particle of ground stone or other impurity on the high altar. It is a tedious task, even if there is only one sifting to do, and even if the courtyard is filled with women and girls to chatter away the time. But this day I was left alone and I drowsed over my work in the heat of the afternoon.

All at once my mind came to my body again as I found cradled in my palm two grains or, rather, one grain and one very grainlike pebble. I tossed the pebble across the court, but only after I had studied the contrast between the two—one contained the miracle of life and the other did not. Though the mere existence of a stone is a miracle, it is a miracle past in its long-ago creation and not present and yet to come. The tiny grain had the power to swell and grow and burst—as there was within me—into a stalk, a patch, in patient time, into an entire rich, white field of ripened grain. And it held the promise, the hope, of the smell and taste of fresh-baked bread on a famished stomach, a symbol of life to lay on the altar.

When others came to the court later to lend a hand, they found me not dozing, but with my eyes closed and my arms opened to Heaven in prayer, letting the warmth of the sun down to swell and enrich the still tight, hard grain of my belly, to enliven the already-planted seed, the miracle within me. It is with the greatest reverence that I have ever after cleaned the wheat and taken honor in all similar tasks. I love to handle the tiny flecks of life as I loved to feel my body then, rising like yeasted dough beneath the cloth by the oven.

I came to my time on a winter's day, on a day called one-eyed, for it was dark on one side and bright on the other. A black mass of clouds licked with lightning lay upon the western and southern hills and the edge of the Sea, resting, panting, as if exhausted from a forced march up the Arabah. The northern part of the Sea remained carelessly at play in the sun all the time I watched. But I did not heed the childishness of the sunlight. I, like the great, swollen clouds, panted under my load come to maturity. My temples, my armpits, my thighs, were seeping sweat as the storm seeped rain. My sweat caught the chill of a gust of wind and I shivered. The girls inside the temple screamed and giggled at the deep rumbles of thunder. Earth shook to the very core to bring forth new, bursting flowers on the hillside, blossoms in the almond orchards; Earth echoed the wrenching, thunderlike rumble of life inside me.

Once upon a time Goddess stood at the door of the Netherworld and shuddered to descend. Just so did I prepare to enter my own Valley of the Shadow of Death to rescue from oblivion the breath of life of my long-dead love. In the end, they say, She had no choice but to descend. Earth would languish and die if She did not rescue it from sterility.

I panicked for a moment. The first drops of deathly rigid rain fell, the wrenches of thunder, of labor, came in evermore-rapid succession and I knew I must go in, as Goddess had gone in, perhaps to return when the storm had passed and washed all new and fresh, perhaps to go down to darkness forever and not have the strength to return. I prayed for a breath, a pause to think, to rationalize, to separate myself from it, to better withstand it. But life gives no pause from one breath to the next. A storm cannot be reasoned away. And so, like some lightning-startled animal, I withdrew inside the temple gasping Baraa's name.

It was not an easy labor. A night, a day, and yet another night passed before I was delivered. All strength and sense failed me more often than I can remember and both our lives were feared for. And yet, I would rather have a child bought dearly than as cheaply as they come to some of these big-hipped hierodules who have one a year, as regular as summer, and in any corner as easily as a cat has kittens. It is too easy for them to shrug at the value of life. Goddess, it is said, is pleased with the sacrifice, similar to Her great sorrow, of pain and blood offered in Her Name in the birthing room.

As I had helped her, so Baraa was the main attendant at my delivery. But Baraa herself was five months gone with new seed of Absalom's and she had not the strength to maintain me long after the stamina in my legs had sweated away and they were useless to hold me. I reduced two other women to fearful, pitying tears as well during that endless, swimming, drowning pain. They despaired and I, I longed for the end, any end at all.

But then, at last, the blur of my vision, smarting with salt, told me that someone new had been brought into the room. With a curious roughness trying clumsily to be gentle, a fresh pair of arms like bands of new-forged iron caught me out of my heap on the floor.

"Scream for Goddess. Scream," the new voice ordered. "Submit yourself to Her entirely, Tamar, my daughter."

And I did scream, startled away from my misery and total exhaustion to press once, twice, and the third time with a superhuman power behind me. I went blank then and praise Goddess that this time they could leave me in oblivion and did not have to revive me again with rosewater and balm, for my work was finished.

I awoke after sunrise. The storm was past, and the Sea and every green thing was steaming in the new sun. From inside, from the room where I lay, came the only sound: the tearless, healthy yell of a newborn child whose mother has been neglecting it. Any number of women and girls were fussing around the infant, vying for the honor of simply looking and ah-ing and holding out a hand to touch the wonder of wonders, defier of all knowledge, the tiny new world I had brought from nothing.

A single figure sat still beside me, watching with a humility and concern for when my eyes should open. When they did, she replied with a smile, gestured toward me with a bowl of broth, then helped me to rise to an elbow when I nodded yes, I was famished.

The arm that held me was as firm as iron, and when I grasped the wrist that brought the bowl to my lips, I noticed how strong it was, how heavily haired.

"It was you who supported me at the last," I said with gratitude after I had drunk my fill.

The figure nodded modestly. Such creatures do not like to speak much. They are ashamed of the deep bass of their voices in the midst of all our women's piping. For my attendant was one of the sexless ones. Usually they do not come into the birthing rooms. They are kept busy with those tasks that take their once-upon-a-time male strength. That is if they do not let themselves grow too fat, in which case they are not much good for anything but rolling the distaff over their great fat thighs in the spinning room.

I knew this one by face, by a middle-aged yet strong and

supple form. I knew her name, too, though I don't think we had ever spoken to one another before. I had caught her eyes watching me intently as our various duties made our paths cross from time to time. The intense longing I had seen in those eyes I had always attributed to the sort of jealousy for all born girls and initiated women that such born boys, grown men, and women only by violence must feel. Nevertheless, I had bothered once to ask after a name for those eyes and, curiously, I remembered it. She was known as Gomer, and I called her by that name when I thanked her for all her services.

She smiled gently. "Lady, it was a pleasure and a privilege for me," seemed to be the words behind this smile.

Gomer gestured with her hand in the direction of the baby, and I nodded and smiled, but I did not understand. So at length she was required to speak. "Would Snakesleeper see her creation?" she asked, approaching each word as lightly and cautiously as possible so as not to startle me with her male tones. I realized another reason for the sexless ones' lack of chatter: they must, at the time of their change, go from the male dialect completely to the female and so, as the stranger does, they tended to silence, hoping most of the talking would be done for them.

I studied Gomer's face as she rose from my side and went to comply with my nod. Her features were quite fine and strangely beautiful, especially for one who, busy caring for me, had not yet had time to perform her necessary and daily ritual of shaving. Her entire face, it seemed, from a short and heavily veiled forehead and deep black eyes, yearned down a long, thin, finely chiseled nose to a mouth big with sound, white teeth and bordered by lush, full lips of a very feminine curvature.

But one thing stood out above all else and that was the deep, rich, loam-colored cast of Gomer's skin. The sexless ones are usually darker than whole women because of their duties and their past histories. But Gomer's skin was the darkest, the richest I had seen. Gomer was darker, even, than me. Gomer was . . . And I caught my breath and stared until tears came.

Gomer led the way for Baraa carrying my baby and all the other women trailing after in triumphant procession. But at the moment, I had eyes only for Gomer, and I caught her great wrist in both hands when she reached the edge of my bed.

"Gomer, Gomer," I whispered earnestly before the others should come and interrupt me. "Are you—were you my father?"

It was foolish of me to ask, of course. The sexless ones are not allowed to speak of such things. They are not supposed to show any signs of remembering or of hearing any mention of their past lives. But Gomer betrayed for a brief instant that she had heard, that she knew, that she was.

Then I was obliged to let go the wrist of my past and to accept in my hands my tiny little future.

"Praise Goddess, what a lovely daughter you have brought forth." Baraa burst with joy and a pride I caught immediately when I saw my little one, whole and naked, at my breast. She had something of the darker skin in her, too.

I also noticed a bit of envy in my sister-in-law's voice. Not that Baraa meant any harm. She could not help herself. I thought it wise, however, to take a charm from my neck and hang it about my daughter's right away, just as a precaution.

Then there came the general marvel at the nourishment the baby's quick, firm tugs brought forth from my flesh. The milk was really no milk yet, watery and thin, but at present it was all she asked for. As her stomach grew stronger, so would my milk. And when she later proved the good health of her insides and her individuality by wetting herself and most of the bed, that was a further great and marvelous wonder.

Gomer faded out of the room. I don't remember when or how she went, and I did not see her again for several weeks. When the chance did occur, neither of us dared to speak— we hardly dared to let eyes meet. But I knew she knew, she knew I knew, and that was all that was possible. That was sufficient. She had lived to see the posterity she thought cut off from her forever bringing forth another generation of fruit for her long-dead loins. That is all the eternity a man— or a woman—asks for.

◉ IL ◉

WITHIN A WEEK, I presented my daughter before Goddess with proper sacrifice and she was greeted with glowing promises of long life and beauty, children to rise up and rule in her stead and in mine. What a pleasure it is for a Snake-sleeper to prophesy for her own daughter!

I was briefly tempted to give her the name Gomer, but I knew that was no inspiration from Goddess. It would never do to name a daughter of promise after a sexless one. I dared not ask after my father's old male name, either, that I might feminize it for her, for it had undoubtedly been forgotten. This is what I would be told, even if it were not forgotten in fact. I had no desire to name her after my mother, who these days, alas, seemed more gone from me than my father, lost in the tragedy of life. And so at length I decided to call her after the Sea. Kinnereth she became.

And here my story might have ended, turning from tale to poetry. But I cannot drift into a sublime Goddess-willed-ever-after as yet, for my brother Absalom was still in Geshur with us, and that was in defiance of all Her commands.

The way he looked at my Kinnereth from the first made

me load her little neck with several other amulets. He saw Amnon in her, ghostly before him, and cursed the day he had taken asylum in a land where he did not have the right as a brother to stone me and my infant for my choice of lovers. His looks grew even fiercer when Baraa again failed to carry her full term and brought forth in her seventh month another blue-black dead male child.

At the end of another year, when Kinnereth was toddling all about and into everything, Baraa at last, sustained by innumerable prayers and offerings at Goddess's altar, was able to carry the full term and gave birth to a sickly but living son. At first I feared I had misjudged my brother's powers of creation, but when the child was brought before Goddess, he was found to be, like his father, too full of evil to be allowed to live. Aphek is not Topheth. Absalom could not interrupt the sacred proceedings as his father had done before him. The little boy was passed through the flame and so died.

Now Baraa came to me, a thin, tearful, desperate shadow, and pleaded, "As you are a woman, won't you use anything in your power to give me a child I can keep? Absalom," she continued, "has endured all he's going to of his powerlessness in Geshur and of Geshuri ways. He's sent to Jerusalem to Joab."

"What does Joab say?"

"David needs but the flimsiest excuse and he will forgive my husband and restore him as heir to the throne."

"I can't believe even David's justice can be so changeable. Amnon—Goddess rest him—was his son."

But as Baraa assured me again and again with panic that it was so, I took her words on a sort of blind faith before this male enigma. I was far from Jerusalem, of course, and could not know all the aspects of the case that moved the king of Israel. But beyond that was the fact that I had given up trying to understand such men. People simply assume that David's one goal in life should be empire, and that any man in his position who did not have the desire to gain ever more and more despotic power was seriously deficient. Very well, I will accept that as granted, a male mystery I have no hope or desire of initiation into. What confounds me is that those who are so wise in such mysteries could be so blind to the obvious effects of allowing a second such driven and positioned man, Absalom, son like father, into the same land.

"If we return to Jerusalem," Baraa concluded her plea, "who then shall hear my prayers?"

"I agree you can hope for little help from Goddess in Jerusalem. But Baraa, I must tell you this frankly—"

"Yes?"

"I doubt very much whether any seed of Absalom's can be brought to fruition. The High Priestess of Baal-Hazor thought the same."

"How can this be?"

"My brother's very life from infancy has been an offense to Goddess," and I explained the circumstances of this fact.

Baraa shivered at this news that, though she was not happy in her marriage, she had never suspected. Now she could see that it must be true.

"Then what am I to do?" she wept.

I thought and then I said, "How long will you stay here still? Until the coming of the Great Mystery?"

"I don't know. I don't think so. Joab the son of Zeruiah has already formed a plan whereby he will get David to give his word that my husband may return without persecution. Joab is fond of his cousin, my husband."

"I think rather that they share a similar self-serving nature. It would serve Joab's purposes to have an heir as cunning and reckless as he is to pull at David's heartstrings. Joab must be having a terrible time getting complacent Adonijah to speak on his side in anything. But once Absalom is back in Jerusalem, our cousin will learn that a similarity in natures rarely means less conflict. Indeed, seeing as it's Joab and Absalom we're discussing, it will probably mean more conflict."

I stopped musing aloud and, in consideration of her sorrow, turned to Baraa once again. "Yes, we cannot hope to keep you with us until the time of general love. I don't suppose you could get Absalom to let you serve as a hierodule before then?"

Baraa laughed through her tears at the absurdity of the idea.

"Not even if you told him it would give him a son? No, I suppose not. Not this one. Not Absalom."

Impossible as such thoughts were, they nonetheless steered us in the right direction until at last we determined on a plot. The next time Baraa came under the blood possession of Goddess, she pretended to her husband that she spotted a few more days than she actually did. This gave her a longer week of impurity afterward when she could avoid him, a few precious days of fertility of her own with which to work. It so happened that during those few days, Grandfather was entertaining Uriel, a governor of Gibeah, in his court. Well-magicked with mandrakes and secreted in hierodules' veils, we sent Baraa to him for his comfort and ease for the two or three nights of his stay. When the time came for my brother and sister-in-law to leave Geshur, when Absalom sat impatient upon his donkey while Baraa and I bade farewell, she was able to embrace me and whisper in my ear that she knew she had conceived by Uriel and that Absalom would never be the wiser.

"It will be a girl," I told her with Serpent Sight. And although I wept as that same Sight told me I would never see her again, it could not promise me the same for my brother. Geshur was too important for him to leave it forever.

After their departure, however, there was a fertile, uneventful peace in Geshur for over six years. The stanzas of the seasons that always end in rhyme passed one after another with their refrains of holy days and hosiana. Kinnereth grew without threat or care. I grew, too, twice as fast as I had ever grown in the spirit before, because I had her growing to add to my own.

How like her father she is! I am often startled into remarking to myself. More like him than she is like me. How can she thus have his very turn of the head, the very grace of his slender body? How can this be when she never saw him? I smile and shake my head at the wonder of the ways of Goddess, how the gleaned stubble is plowed under in the fall and proves a fertilizer to the next crop. I praise Her that

I could be trusted with a part in this, that I could carry a particle of my beloved's soul here to this land of Geshur where it might grow to greater fulfillment than it had been allowed in Jerusalem. From the time she could walk, all Geshur could see that Kinnereth, blessed with long, fine limbs that Jerusalem never appreciated in her father, was meant to be a dancer. She trained and then served as such in the sacred ritual. I was the only one who ever imagined her struggling to balance a spear, grace struggling against a demand for violence and success.

Yet ever and again we received news from Israel to remind us that there were those who insisted on making a story of life and who were not content to sit and listen to its poetry. It must, for such people, have a beginning, middle, and end rather than turn in a cycle. And more than that, the end must be better than the beginning. By this they understand that it must be of their own making, which to my mind only tends to make it worse.

We learned of the death of several of my old friends: Ahinoam and Zipporah of fever, Michal of mad grief at the loss of her faithful old maid all in one winter. Abigail died of old age next summer. For me this meant that I punctuated the wheels of my days with brief spokes of mourning, with fond memories and honor to these women. For Absalom their passing could only mean that our mother was the woman of highest standing in David's harem, an implement my brother could make use of at every turn.

We in Geshur who remembered Baraa fondly were happy to learn of the birth of a healthy daughter. She had rejoiced and insisted that the child be called after me; as an Ammonitess she understood no harm to name after the living and so was not offended. Absalom preferred the name Maacah, not after Mother who was still alive, but to flatter the emissaries from the kingdom of that name just north of us whose interest he was courting at the time. The poor girl has suffered all her life from that difference between her parents and is still called sometimes by one name, sometimes by the other.

Though David did allow Absalom to return to Jerusalem,

he at first kept up the form that was substitute for the execution justice demanded. He refused to see my brother in court for two full years, which, though he had every other liberty, must have been very hampering to Absalom's ambitions. But after Ahinoam had died, it didn't take Absalom long to risk the insolence and rage to be fully recognized. It seemed that here in Geshur where Amnon had never set foot but where his image sang and played clapping games in the courtyard every day, David's firstborn was better remembered than in Jerusalem, where he had lived all his life.

Like the ill-tempered child he was, my brother set fire to Joab's barley fields to get his attention. And Joab, fearing this wantonness, which he saw was greater, even than his own, went to David again with his words of a shuddering philosophy: "For we must needs die and are as water spilt on the ground, which cannot be gathered up again. Forget Amnon your son, therefore, and remember Absalom."

So Absalom was returned to favor once again, without a clue of discipline. He expanded his new prerogatives to their limits at once. He built up barracks and stables full of men, horses, chariots, weaponry that answered only to him and followed him with pomp and intimidations through the streets. He sat in the gates, a perfect example of justice perverted, then self-righted. Many were the hearts he stole by showing that David was distanced from their griefs by too many officers and scribes, and that the bribe a man had to pay to get his case heard directly before the throne was exorbitant and, under a quick, brief justice handed down by Absalom, unnecessary.

It did not take my brother long to reach the limits of growth that even a well-favored heir-apparent must suffer and to feel stifled by them. For instance, it became obvious that Baraa would bear no more than that one daughter. A daughter is not enough for a man with ambitions like Absalom, but as long as he was only a prince there were but two things he could do about it. He could take concubines, but that was not what Absalom wanted. He was not after the satisfaction of his groin, for he was not natural in that respect. All his lusts were focused in one direction only. As

Baraa once whispered to me, "It's like being ravished by the whole faceless land of Israel, trees and springs and mountains—things with no consciousness of love." He wanted wives, not concubines. But men of account did not give their daughters to be concubines.

Or Absalom could, secondly, according to the rites of David's god, erect a pillar in the valley near the spring Gihon, an act whose symbolism must be plain even to a very simpleminded Heaven. This Absalom did to make his chafing public, but that Baraa have twenty sons by this magic was not what he really wanted, either. However, alliances with foreign powers, sealed on the marriage bed, are for a king to make, not the prince, who must be satisfied with one wife until his father dies, at which time he inherits all his father's alliances—all his father's wives. To expand one's harem before is an act of treason.

And that treason began to sound most beckoning to Absalom.

We heard in Geshur how Absalom went with all his chariots and men to Hebron—to make sacrifice, he said. Hebron was where David had first been anointed king while the house of Saul was yet in power. The very name of Hebron rings with the sound of a kingdom on the make. We heard the sound of a trumpet saying, "Absalom reigns in Hebron. Absalom is king."

And now the news came much more rapidly, and yet in a confused and jumbled state out of which it was difficult to sort an order of events.

"All Israel has answered Absalom's call," announced one runner.

"But most of Judah keeps faith with David," gasped the next one, hot on his heels.

"David has fled Jerusalem."

"Absalom took the city without a blow."

"Absalom has laid claim to all his father's wives who were left behind in the flight."

"All except Maacah, the head queen, who has gone with David."

"It sounds like David is managing to keep from Absalom

the one thing he wants most," commented my grandfather, "claim to our Geshur."

"Absalom made the alliances of the rest of the queens his own under a canopy in public view."

Grandfather chuckled. "And he always thought the Great Bed was an abomination."

"David has fled across the Jordan, up the King's Highway."

"He is hindered by the Benjaminites."

"They still remember their King Saul," I commented.

"He is helped by Shobi in the land of Ammon."

"David has halted and turned at Mahanaim."

"How ironic," I said. "That's where Ishbaal, Saul's son, made his final stand against David."

"Your brother, Lady, has made a false start leaving Jerusalem, brought on by his counselors."

"My brother always did do better when left to his own cunning."

"Absalom now pursues his father's limping forces."

"Absalom has all of Israel under his banner, all of Israel in neat and massive ranks behind him."

"See that the good messenger has drink and food. And a place to sleep for the night," my grandfather ordered. Then he turned back to me. "They are moving so close to us," he said. "We won't be able to stay neutral for long."

I nodded.

But when he continued to express his concerns by saying, "David will send for us to make good the promises of treaty we made when we sent your mother to him," I shook my head.

"David doesn't think as a Geshurite does," I told him. "To him, it is clear that a grandson is of more account than a daughter. He already assumes we will help Absalom and that he must look elsewhere for his allies."

"Even though David has your mother with him?"

"Even so. It is Absalom who will expect us to join him."

That night, my words proved true.

◙ L ◙

IT WAS ABSALOM himself and no mere messenger who rode into Aphek under the cover of night. With him was but a handful of chosen men. He was nearly twenty-seven years old—but then, Absalom had been a man since he was born, merely waiting for his body to catch up with him. He was not changed.

After I had seen this from my darkened balcony, how his face above the shielding blackness of his cloak burned with a greater fierceness than any of the torches his men held high, and after I had fortified my soul against it, I went down and greeted him at the gate myself.

"Good evening, Sister," he replied, kissing me on the cheek, very close to the mouth, with an ardor that made me shiver with its warmth. The chill in the courtyard was bone deep, and it was not just the wind rising from the Sea. I wished I had wrapped another blanket around my shoulders to spare me from the confusing cold-hot pierce of his eyes.

"Can I see our grandfather?" he asked, speaking Hebrew.

I nodded and without a word led him to the counsel room

to wait. Then I nodded again and smiled as I left him there, with the slaves only just coming in with torches.

Grandfather was in his room belting on his robe of state with the deep purple fringe. I kissed him lightly.

"Dressed already, Grandfather?"

"Old men sleep shallowly," he said. "Is that Absalom who made such a commotion?"

"Yes, he's come."

"Your Serpent Sight is with you again, praise Goddess."

"He's asking for you."

"Your brother doesn't know that you've been making all of Geshur's decisions for the past six years."

"And I didn't bother to tell him. Do you mind so very much breaking your comfortable retirement to entertain him a little?"

"Let David have every advantage of time."

"I hoped you'd see it that way. In this matter I feel, for the first time in my life, that David the son of Jesse is the lesser of two evils."

"See, I'm dressed already."

"And a reverend sight you are. Give me plenty of time to dress, won't you, before you call me in to the counsel?"

I kissed him again, then left him while I returned to my own rooms. There I took the careful time to put on my finest purple robes of state, trimmed in gold at the deep armscyes, bound at the waist with my Serpent skin. I had a maid comb out my hair and arrange it from the first braid anew. It took her a savoringly long time, for there was still great sleep to be rubbed from her eyes. Atop the braids we placed the royal crown of Geshur, set with star diamonds, from the forehead of which a Serpent rises. I even allowed myself the slow, whiling pleasure of looking in on Kinnereth sleeping soundly in the next room before I was ready to answer the summons that had been growing more insistent for over an hour. Let my brother know that Geshur was no minor governorship that he could order around as he pleased.

Absalom was pacing the floor outside the counsel chamber and, when I arrived, he stopped short and swore, "By the God of my Fathers, I wish a curse upon this land of

Geshur where one must wait for a woman to do her hair
before one can get anything done."

I nodded at him with a smile and held up the hem of my
robes for him to kiss, which he did. The wait had at least
taught him that I was recognized head of a kingdom while
he was just battling for his. Then I went in to see my grandfather.

The sudden weight of responsibility had crushed my
grandfather. He was suddenly a very old man, sitting weakly
in his chair. I refused to let him stand when I came in, but
went to him at once, knelt at his feet, and held his hands.

"Ah, dear child. My Little Brown Eyes," he sighed, ad-
mitting to his frailty as readily as I saw it. "How often I have
thought you should take a husband, if only to get up in the
middle of the night to see to war counsels for you. I am too
old and there are so many more important things that one
of Goddess's blood such as yourself must be concerned
with. Ah, but you would not marry. You take all the responsibility on yourself. Sometimes I wonder if that is wise. It
will put you in an early grave, my dear."

"On a night such as tonight, I am inclined to agree with
you, Grandfather," I said. "We'll think about a husband in
the morning. But come, tell me now what it is my mother's
son asks of us tonight."

"You speak as if you doubt David's fatherhood."

"Absalom camps on the plains of Mahanaim against
David as if he doubts it, too. Come, what does he want?"

I was expecting any answer—two thousand men-at-arms,
five hundred chariots, provisions for all Israel, swords,
shields, hounds to guard his encampment at night—
anything but what my grandfather replied. "Absalom asked
me for your hand in marriage."

"He asked what?" I made Grandfather repeat himself
apologetically before I could say, "Yes, yes, I heard you the
first time. I only couldn't believe it, that's all."

"That's what he wants." Grandfather held open his hands
in a gesture of similar amazement.

"What did you tell him?"

"I told him, 'Here in Geshur one must ask the bride first.' "

"Here in Geshur, it is the bride who does the asking," I corrected.

"I don't think Absalom would appreciate that if I'd told him."

"Well, you might have saved us all some sleep by telling him 'No' right away. Oh, no, no, dear," I said, gathering up my grandfather's shaking hands once more. "It is not you I am angry with. It is best that I know all the depth of his schemes, and he would not have come out and told me this. You have been of great service to me tonight, bless you. It is he who boils my blood. The arrogance of that man!"

"It would be quite in accordance with Geshurite practice to marry your brother," Grandfather reminded me with what sounded like hopefulness. "Your grandmother and I were brother and sister. Bless her soul, she married me so that I might share in our mother's legacy."

"The difference between you and Grandmother and me and Absalom is that she loved her brother and was certain he would make a good and just ruler for Geshur. The one thing I am certain of is that I shall die before I let my mother's son touch the throne of this land."

"Consider now, Brown Eyes, before you speak so rashly." My grandfather hushed me, certain that we could be heard out in the hall. "We—*you*—must now make a choice in this matter between David and Absalom. Geshur can no longer be an aloof aerie where we watch in safe neutrality while Israel and Judah tear at each other's throats. Absalom has thrown the challenge at our feet and we must take it up or else."

"Or else what?"

"Don't you see, Brown Eyes? His armies vastly outnumber those of David. David's are hungry and hunted out in the wilderness. If we refuse Absalom, he will go away quietly tonight, yes, but when he is through with Judah on the fields of Mahanaim, he will stop over once in Geshur. He lived here two years. He knows all of our defenses. We would be conquered in a week. He would show more mercy to our land if we submitted to marriage rather than the sword. Even if we threw all our goods and souls to David's side, I see no chance that he could carry the day."

"Grandfather," I asked quietly, "was it just such fear in numbers added up that made you send Mother down to David when I was but a child?"

My grandfather did not speak, but let the tears in his eyes answer for him. I could almost see them, Grandfather and my mother, in those tears, in the very room where he and I now sat as he tried to convince her of much the same thing he was now trying to convince me. But I am made of sterner stuff than Mother.

"All those years, Grandfather," I whispered, "all those years wasted in Jerusalem when I could have spent them here, on your knee. My brother—I mean Amnon, my beloved, my only true brother—is the only man I shall ever consider for my bed. Of course, as High Priestess here in Geshur, I fulfill the rite of the Great Bed once a year, but I have produced an heir and that is all my duty. Amnon never saw Goddess face to face and yet he taught me much of Her wisdom. It is better, Grandfather, to live a painfully short life with virtue on the bosom of the Earth than to live out a century having raped Her. I shall die, if needs be, protecting Aphek's honor. I trust that you are ready to do the same."

Grandfather nodded and sighed. Then he said very slowly, wiping his eyes with a shaking hand, "Absalom said this is how you would respond. 'Damn the ways of Geshur,' he said, 'a land that makes sniveling women of all her men. By God, Grandfather,' he said, 'if you do not make that lioness of a granddaughter of yours see reason, you are no better than those pitiful lumps of castrated flesh you allow to live around in the name of a man-eating Goddess.' That's what your brother said, Tamar."

"And you believed him?"

Grandfather shrugged. "Perhaps — new ways — who knows?"

"As my subject, I order you to sustain me in this decision," I said harshly as I got to my feet. But such harshness was how Absalom got his obedience, something I was trying to spare my homeland. I repented at once, though there wasn't time for full amends. I bent and kissed the balded spot on the top of Grandfather's head and did what I could with some few words of tenderness to ease the suffering of a once-powerful man in the weakness of his old age. "Let us trust to Goddess," I said, "to Her Messengers and to. Her shield in battle. Surely She will not let us fail. And, Grandfather, I love you. Remember that if nothing else." I kissed him once again and left the room.

Absalom was not pacing the floor outside the chamber. It surprised me a little not to find him there. But no doubt he had overheard our conversation, at least the most emphatic parts of it, the parts that most concerned him. It was just as well he had heard my answer. It spared me having to tell him word for word, face to face. Although I felt strong enough that night for such a confrontation, I had more important things on which to spend my energy.

◦ LI ◦

THE TEMPLE OF Aphek is built high on a hill and not in a valley as is generally considered most becoming to the sex of Goddess; high places are as a rule for the male gods. But the temple marks and guards a complex of ancient and most sacred caves deep in its bowels. One of these serves as the Serpent pit, my domain, though as High Priestess and as heiress here in Geshur, I have many, many other responsibilities.

The Serpent pit is contrived so that it has a little antechamber where I can sit and listen to the sound of scale on scale. By means of a narrow crack, this chamber communicates with another, larger cave that is open to the public. The crack is concealed from general view by cleverly arranged stones, and it is only at one certain angle that one can know that it is there. Folk coming to ask Goddess's advice by means of Her Messengers can be heard in the antechamber where I sit. They hear, in turn, the voice of Snakesleeper, the sacred words of oracle, boom like all eternity in their greater cavern though I but whisper. I do not think I offend by revealing this secret of the Serpent pit.

Even if you know how the magic works, it is still wondrous and it in no way discourages the divine power of the messages themselves.

But it was not for any public illusion that I descended into the caves that night. I went to consult Father of Shadows for my own sake and I went alone. At least, I meant to go alone. But I was not alone. Somebody followed me down to the cavern of the Snakes.

I did not realize this until I was far past all the sleeping palace and past the general parts of the temple where the priestesses who must keep the incense burning and the prayers droning all night were yawning over the holy words. There, in the tunnel that allowed no turnoff—one could go either down or up—there I heard the sound of someone else's feet behind me in a place no other soul should have been at that hour of the night. And they were not the bare feet of anyone who came to the place respecting Goddess. They wore the heavy, leathern high-topped sandals of a soldier. Though I traveled in darkness, having the way memorized with long familiarity, the man behind me carried a torch. Sometimes I could see the yellow stain of it bouncing on the walls beyond the last curve.

Most frightening of all was the fact that these footsteps were coming at a much faster pace than my own. I forsook my slow, reverent step and matched the time of my pursuer. Then I recalled that he was a man and took more distance with every step. I began to run.

The way to the Serpent rooms seemed endless that night, but at last I reached the public room, felt for the familiar crack in the wall, and pressed my way through to my own antechamber, just licked by the torchlight that rushed into the room after me.

A Hebrew soldier's voice swore by David's god as he was confronted by the blank walls of the room I'd just left. But he was confounded only for a moment. Then I could tell by the waving of the light through the crack that he was searching the walls for just such a secret exit.

I was helpless to think of what I should do. If he were a small man, he might very well be able to press through the crack after me once he saw past its camouflage. If he were a large man, he could still pass his arm and either a sword or the torch in and that could prove my undoing just as well. The anteroom where I hid was very small, and one false step to escape a waving sword or torch would send me tumbling into the midst of the Serpent pit. Granted, I am Snake-sleeper, but that made me know with all the more surety that such a jump, without the proper songs, protected by only a few crushed fig leaves on my hands, with the Serpents angry and frightened, could prove fatal to me as well as to any other mortal.

I should begin to sing, I thought. I must call Father of Shadows up to me, send him through the crack against my pursuer. And yet I dared not. My heart was beating too wildly to set the proper tone. And though I knew full well that the magic of the rooms with their crack made the voice seem to come from everywhere and though I might have said something in a loud, Goddesslike voice, I could not be sure that this would unnerve him, a man with the heat of pursuit and murder driving through his veins. I dared not even breathe my panting, heavy breath, much less sing or call down Heaven's curses on him.

There came another oath to David's god. It was one of triumph, for the soldier had found the crack. But after that I did not know what happened. There were sounds of struggling, grunts like animals fighting, a sigh as one expired, the drop of a heavy body on the floor. Still I dared not breathe as deeply as my lungs cried out for. I waited and waited until at last the cool crystal silence on either side of the crack was broken by a familiar voice.

"Snakesleeper? Lady? It's all right. You can come out now. Danger is past."

It was Gomer's voice, and I stepped out, laughing without control in relief. "Ah, Gomer. What are you doing down here with the Serpents this time of night? What—?"

But then I noticed, by the light of the torch she held high, that she was barefoot, proper for the sanctuary, in her great padded feet that could move across the stones without a sound. As my eyes crossed the floor, I saw a black shadow lying prone against one wall.

"Who is that?" I demanded.

"Do not profane your eyes, Lady," Gomer said.

But I insisted and drew her hand until it fell upon a man of Absalom's, dead, with the sword meant for my heart still in his hand, with the eyes nearly popping from his skull and with a sickly blue tint to his face.

"How did you do it?" I whispered in awe up to my bene-factress.

Gomer, ever loath to use her deep voice much, answered by simply holding out the great, manacle-like expanse of one hand. She had strangled a fully armed man to death with no more than that. And yet she had not escaped completely unscathed. Thrashing wildly with his sword at what he couldn't see behind him (alas that he never knew it was one of the sexless ones that soldiers scorn with so much vanity), the soldier had cut a great gash in Gomer's arm that was bleeding heavily.

"Here, let me take that." I gestured for the torch so she might have a free hand to try and stop the bleeding on the other. "Let's get you to the physician."

But Gomer would not relinquish the light. "There is something else, Lady," she said.

"What is it, Gomer?"

"Your daughter."

"Kinnereth? What about Kinnereth? Oh, Goddess, did he set out to assassinate her as well?"

"No, Lady. Rest assured the child still lives. But—"

Goddess, but a lack of practice makes the sexless ones slow and clumsy in their speech! "But what, Gomer?" I prodded. "Do not hesitate to tell me."

"The handmaidens let him in. They are weeping, begging your pardon, and fear you might have their heads for this."

"I will punish no one who does not deserve it."

"I was sent to tell you . . ."

"So tell me."

"They thought he was only a doting uncle come to look in on his sleeping niece."

"Absalom. Where is he?"

"He has escaped Aphek, Lady. We have all his men—this one here is the last. But your brother has escaped. With little Kinnereth."

"Ah, Goddess," I moaned.

I could see his plot at last. Absalom never expected me to say yes to his proposal. Although it would have made things easier and not so costly in men, he did not really expect Grandfather to talk me into it. All he wanted was to get me away from my sleeping child and unawares. If he could not grapple Geshur to him by the mother, he knew there was enough sacred blood in seven-year-old Kinnereth that, brided and bedded, could make him king in Geshur sooner or later, even if his heavy-booted man failed to assassinate me.

"Ah, Goddess," I whimpered again, unable to say more.

And Gomer held out her bleeding hand to stay me. Sometimes we consider that because they are of indefinite sex that their emotions are likewise indefinite and unreal. We expect the sexless ones to be our stays and to require no support beyond bread and meat in return. But Kinnereth was her granddaughter, I realized, and, as her very daughter, my suffering was hers as well. Her concern had to look down two generations while mine went only one. I looked up the generation to her, she who was losing blood and yet still offering me her strength. I took the torch with firmness now and Gomer did not protest.

"Grandfather was right," I said as we made our way out of the cave. "Absalom leaves us no choice. The men of Geshur must go down to the plain of Mahanaim. But they shall go down on David's side, by Goddess, not on Absalom's."

"But the men—" Gomer said briefly, allowing me to fill in the rest of her thought.

"Yes, you are right. Even if all our men join him, even if he does have the loyalty of all the priests of his god, I fear the odds are still too much against David and his cause."

"Goddess—" Gomer said.

"Yes, Gomer. You are wise in your silence. As soon as

I've got someone to look at your arm, I must go back into the pit. I must ask Her will. But already I know a part of that great will. I must sing Father of Shadows into his jug and then we, Snakesleeper and Snake, must go down to the plains of Mahanaim. And you, Gomer, you must come with us as well."

Gomer's eyes glimmered with a truly masculine response to the scent of war. But womanlike, she said nothing.

"But pray Goddess," I entreated. "Pray to Her this battle takes place in a terrain that She can dominate or we are lost indeed. Little Kinnereth, Geshur, all. Goddess must be able to dominate the terrain."

◉ LII ◉

THE WOOD OF Ephraim is the only spot on all the plains of
Mahanaim that the impious hand of men, either in the name
of their god or in the name of expanding wheat fields (which
often amounts to the same thing), has not pruned and axed.
It is a rough bit of land, cut clean across by a deep gorge in
which there is always water, even in times of drought, but
which holds hidden patches of treacherous marsh. Perhaps
this is the reason it has been spared.

The Wood received its name from the defeat of the
Ephraimites at the hand of Jephthah and the Gileadites
when, it is said, forty-two thousand lost their lives and were
thwarted in their purpose of expanding across the Jordan.
But the Wood was sacred long before forty-two thousand
men fertilized it with their blood and made it a spot of
pilgrimage, a place where even the most stone-hearted must
pause and grow weak-bellied at the briefness of life and
hang a scrap of his hem in the branches as a token of
remembrance.

There were Goddess trees in profusion: tamarisks, oaks,
wild figs, growing thick at the bottom of the gorge where

anything could grow and did. There were other trees, too, whose very names are wilderness: thorn and bramble underfoot so one could not walk at times, and everywhere the savage species of acacia from which, if a man but carelessly brush against, he may spend an hour extracting himself.

The moment we came upon it, I knew it was a place ordained. Father of Shadows knew it, too, and stirred in his jug to sense so many of his kind. I had a very strong impression of the sort of living power one might draw from the stillness of the Wood's branches. I determined that Gomer and I should spend the night there in the heart of the Woods, offering sacrifice and prayer, while our men-at-arms marched on to reach David's camp before sunset. Dawn the next day would see the two armies engaged in the battle that would decide all our fates.

"We fear for you, Lady, at night in this place," protested my captain of thousands.

"Do not fear for me," I said. "I have Gomer with me. Gomer has killed a man with her bare hands.

"Only tell David," I continued, "that as he loves his life and his kingdom, he must drive Absalom and the forces of Israel in this direction. If they begin to lose and must flee, let them flee to this ground, bringing the enemy in hot pursuit after them."

"David will not hear us," the captain protested again.

"As Goddess lives and grants us all life, he must hear you," I insisted. "Tell him it is I, Snakesleeper, High Priestess of Geshur, who orders it and who will help him to carry the day if he but hear me."

"Suppose, with his singleminded god, that he still won't hear us."

"Tell him your service under him is contingent upon his use of this strategy."

My men nodded, saluted, and rode off toward Mahanaim, giving the Wood wide girth as they passed in the awe even they, hardened and banned from women in preparation for war as they were, felt for the place. When the last of my troops had marched on, fading into dust across the denuded plains, Gomer and I left our mounts hobbled in a bit of pasture, removed our shoes, and proceeded to pick our way down the slope of the gorge.

Branch grew into branch and our descent was a continuous prayer that Goddess, Her attendant spirits, and Her Messengers that dwelt in that place might forgive our trespass, for we came prayerfully and with humble hearts.

Everywhere life teemed, shot up, scampered, cascaded, swelled before us. The roar of insects was deafening. We saw any number and variety of birds—crow, heron, and stealthy partridge—which vanished like spirits through the knotted thorns and grass that we found all but impassable and vicious to our bare feet. There was the snort of wild boar, the sound of playing otter, the purr of a well-fed leopard basking in the sun. There was so little to do with death that I momentarily doubted how our prayers for a carnage of the evil could be brought to pass. Where would all the jackals and kites come from? And yet I believe that when particles of life are so thick in one spot, they have that power: they can take on any shape that will best use the gifts Goddess offers them.

It was nearly sunset (and sunset came early down in the gorge) before Gomer and I came to what we knew must be the very heart of the Wood. Others before us had sensed the same thing, for there was an unhewn stone covered with ancient lichens erected there to serve as an altar. It was in a clearing, but clearing only in that a great terebinth, the greatest terebinth in the Wood or that I had ever seen, was so thick with its circle of foliage overhead that nothing at all could grow green in the faint wisps of sunlight at its feet. I knew that in Hebrew, terebinth and goddess are the same word.

Even to we who had lived long among the pines and balsam and fat, docile cattle of Geshur, the surfeit of undisturbed life here in the Wood of Ephraim was intoxicating. Gomer broke into spontaneous song, the sacred words bursting from her lungs as green bursts from the hard, dry hull of a seed. I joined her firm, melodious bass in a descant as we went about our work.

Gomer carried smoldering in a box of ivory at her belt a

spark of the sacred fire from Aphek's altar. With this she turned the life force of a bundle of thistles and fall wood into a fire upon the altar. Then Goddess provided the sacrifice: a gazelle that bounded into the clearing and froze there with large, unblinking eyes, offering no resistance at all when Gomer drew her flint knife and splashed the leaping blood of the Wood—fire—with the throbbing blood of the animal. She cut the heart out and, having shared a morsel of the still-warm and sticky organ with me as a symbol of our enemy, she buried it beneath the great terebinth. This was meant to give the tree roots like veins and the power of motion the animal had had for all the next day until the heart should grow cold and stop pumping.

I searched among the trees of the Wood until I found one of divine knowledge, a fig. Because of the lateness of the season, many of the leaves had already fallen, baring the tree limbs like a mass of tangled, knotted ropes, with only the very bitter end of fleshy winter figs at the tips. But enough foliage remained to provide me with aprons for Gomer and myself and fruit to make a meal, insipid and pasty on the tongue, but divine when mixed with venom in my veins.

Father of Shadows had seemed listless, lying like death in his jug, and I feared he might have sensed something in the air that made him want to retreat into his yearly two-month's sleep. I had kept him unfed and painted an invigorating sign on the side of the jug in henna, but beyond that I could only hope. Things would go very ill if he were slow-witted, even worse if I had to call up a new, strange Serpent at this critical time.

At last all was prepared and I could lift the lid from the jug. I began to sing the ancient, inborn words to call Father of Shadows forth:

> For you are that mysterious and shapeless
>   thing, of whom the gods foretold
> that you should have neither arms nor legs
>   on which to go following your brother gods.

Imagine my joy as I realized that his sluggishness had been only due to his languishing in the deathlike stage through which Serpents must pass as part of their immortality. It had been the secret time of his Mystery, likened by some to the once-a-month sloughing of women, whereby the old skin and life are shed for a new. I took my Snake's old life, light and fragile as air, and handed it to Gomer to intensify the magic she must work with her quietly gathered herbs and greens.

I did not cease to sing and dance, even while rejoicing in Father of Shadow's rebirth. His scales were glossy and jewel-like, supple with youth and vigor, virgin-ideal, wet from the womb, and his eyes glowed, unblinking, eternal, all seeing, all knowing, as he tasted my song and my essence with his tongue.

Because I was without fear, his bite was quick and more titillating than painful. I began to trance almost at once.

Serpent trancing is a curious thing and difficult to describe to someone who has never experienced it. The first time I attempted it, you will recall, the inspiration I received came in words. Indeed, I remember seeing nothing except perhaps what the Song of Songs by sheer power of its words extracted in images upon the blackness of my mind until Topheth's High Priestess roused me.

But this time I saw much more than I was given to hear. I had a vision of my daughter and how she fared, bewildered and frightened in Absalom's camp for all that he had ordered her treated with honor and care as a valuable bit of booty and as his bride-to-be. But none there spoke the only language she knew, and the food, the people, the god seemed strange and soulless. I stood by her little cot much of that night to dry her tears and let her sleep in my arms to gain the strength she would need for the day of war ahead.

I saw many other times and places in the journey of the mind that night: the grove of Baal-Hazor that had produced my child, Topheth when David had refused to give Heaven the son that was its due and who now, in gratitude of a black sort, was tearing up his kingdom in civil war.

I continued to trance even when my mind returned to the

Wood, where Gomer tended the fire and me in strong and silent vigil. What Gomer and I had sensed upon our arrival—the Wood's quivering life—was but a pale shadow of what the venom made me see. I actually saw life, a slow, curling, vibrating force not unlike animated bitumen that swelled up from Mother Earth and was sparked into fire whenever sunlight touched it on the fringes of leaves, on the blades of grass.

But even on the ground, where a heap of fallen cane or leaves or broken vines lay seeming lifeless to untouched eyes, I could see it, rich and moldering. Her steaming, dancing, glowing presence in everything that was. Even death seemed alive then and swarming. It was like what pure music would look like if it could be seen, undulating from flute across the floor to dancer.

It was at times too much for me to endure. Gomer would catch me as I moaned and swooned, drunken on the vision.

Priests and seers of the god put up their petitions that night as well: Ahimaaz the son of Zadok and Jonathan the son of Abiathar in the camp of David, and with Absalom, Uzza and Elisha, also the sons of Zadok and Abiathar respectively. One might assume that both camps were equal in fervor, in gestures or prayer, in modes of sacrifice, in the poetry of their curses. And the god must have been divided and confused in his affection.

So it was Goddess Who made the difference on the battlefield that day. David, for pride, had had no thought of driving his enemy toward the Wood. Besides, his men, in fear for the safety of the god's anointed, insisted that he stay with the priests behind the walls of Mahanaim. He had but little influence on the outcome. It was She Who had to do it in the end, putting some thought of brilliant maneuver into Absalom's head right when he seemed about to win the battle, throwing him and his army into the terebinthine arms of the Wood of Ephraim.

They say, "The Wood devoured more people that day than the sword devoured." They mean by that that it was Goddess Who devoured. They could only see the tangle of branches and blades of thorns and prefer to think of them

as inanimate. I saw Her moving in them, reaching out a
thorn to catch a fleeing hem, giving the animals, leopard,
boar, and Serpent, the instinct to pounce and gore and strike
rather than flee when they were startled. What had been just
a tactical maneuver became a rout.

Absalom made his way into the very center of the Wood
by sheer demonic contrariness, hacking the living limbs
before him without mercy and driving his beast until its
flanks were flayed raw and bleeding. His helmet hung down
his back to let the sweat flow freely and his hair, always as
thick and unruly as his spirit, had fallen loose and halfway
down his back from its soldier's knot. Had only the god
been directing affairs, my brother would have escaped
cleanly and without harm to gather yet another army to
fight another day. But Goddess drove him so he rode beneath the terebinth, his red-black hair just passing beneath
the branches of the tree as beneath the teeth of a lover's
comb.

I was seeing in slow motion so it was easy to speak his
name at the precise, inspired moment. He turned, startled,
unthinking, for a fatal instant reacting to a Goddess-given
emotion rather than to cold, hard calculation. The ass gal-
loped on, braying with gratitude to suddenly have its burden
lifted, yet ever-mindful of the bite of the whip. But Absalom
stayed behind, his hair, the glory of his head, helplessly,
painfully tangled in the Goddess-finger branches of the tree.

It was highly unlikely that he would have hung there for
long if left to his own devices. Indeed, the strain of his
weight would have brought an end to a brief captivity in
moments, even if he had not still been in possession of his
sword, which he began to thrash over his head to hack either
branches or hair or both.

But I stepped into the clearing through the smoke of the
ancient altar and I spoke his name 'again. His arms went
limp at his sides to see me, wild in fig leaves and the Serpent
skin crossed between my fang-marked breasts.

How pale he looked then, and how young. He's twenty-
six years old, I thought. This rite comes twenty-six years too

late. But twenty-six years is but the time of a sigh to Goddess. She will take Her due.

Absalom seemed to me to be even younger than that other time when I had seen him caught between Heaven and Earth in the High Priestess's arms over the brazier in Topheth. In all his leathern armor and purple and gold, he seemed more exposed than he had been then, unswaddled in her hands.

"By order of the Queen of Heaven," I said, "I, Snakesleeper, have come to claim your life."

Absalom said nothing. Even as an infant he had had the will to yell. I hesitated.

Gomer did not hesitate. She gave a deep-throated battle cry and lunged like an infantryman at her foe. I waved her back in time. No mortal should do this deed, especially no mortal of such masculine movement.

I broke my hesitation then with my song that the Woman in the Garden was the first to hear. And the Serpents remembered and responded, not only Father of Shadows, but all the great Messengers of the Wood: those with spikes of horn above their eyes, those short, stubby, and ghostly gray, those great yellow Serpents, regal, beautifully patterned, and deadly, those black asps that the Egyptians especially revere for their ability to raise their hoods. As if from nowhere they crawled, gliding from the earth, the living essence of the offended soil.

I closed my eyes with the effort of bearing up all that creeping, writhing, sharp-fanged power with nothing more than my voice. Sometimes my mind grew foggy with exertion and with the poison in my veins. Sometimes I thought I dreamed. Absalom must have thought that he, too, dreamed, for I heard not a whimper from him as the Messengers curled up his legs, across the branches of the tree down through his hair, even beneath his armor and pricked his skin in every part. But of course I was too much concerned with my visions to be listening.

Joab the son of Zeruiah, general over a third of David's host, was under strict orders from his uncle and his master to "deal gently with the young man Absalom for my sake."

David was ever a father, proud when his sons showed initiative and manhood, very susceptible to Absalom's spell. And Joab had no personal grudge against his rebellious cousin. Indeed he admired the skill and determination with which Absalom had carried off the hearts of all Israel. Such a man was worthy of his devotion, not his grudge, and there had been times during that day when Joab had been on the verge of betraying David and throwing in his lot with the young and vigorous upstart.

But when David's general and his close guard came upon Absalom hanging in the center of the Wood of Ephraim, Joab's heart grew watery within him. What he did, though he was afterward sorely blamed for it, he did indeed do out of compassion for "the young man." His men, who shrank from the divine horror of the scene, were greater cowards.

"Shoot, Cousin, shoot," Absalom cried with poison-swollen lips. "I am a dead man."

The first of Joab's darts frightened away the last of the Serpents. The other darts ended what would have otherwise been a very prolonged and ugly death. And there in the center of the Wood, Joab and his men cut down the body and honored it by building a heap of stones in the spot already much honored by lives and by deaths.

▣ LIII ▣

Now I FEEL myself constrained to write but little more, and that in brief and simple terms. Kinnereth was rescued unharmed from Absalom's camp in the midst of the confusion of defeat, fleeing, and pillaging. Gomer carried her out in her great arms, and we returned to our home in Geshur.

Our homecoming was not without sadness: my grandfather had died while we were gone. The end came, I was told, when he had decided to take the knife and join himself completely to Her will, to become female before Her as my father had done at the very edge of my memory. But his age and his lifelong masculinity had not been able to endure it, and he had died but two steps from the altar. He was returned with every honor of both king and sexless one to the arms of his sister and wife and to the Womb of his Great Mother.

I have ruled alone since then. But this year Kinnereth had her first Visitation and she will become a woman and initiate when next we mourn the few months out of every year when Goddess must absent Herself from our fields. My daughter will be able to help then. I think I shall let her take my place in the Great Bed in two or three years' time. She takes a lively, youthful interest in men, as any child likes to toy with what is new and different. So great is her interest that sometimes she even thinks like a man. I must hope and pray that this is only a phase.

Kinnereth carries the sacred blood in her veins, spills it every month as sacrifice and Mystery of eternal life, and is well worthy to replace me as High Priestess on the hill of Aphek that overlooks Goddess's mirror. But she is not Snakesleeper. I alone am that source of power and it is not a gift I can pass on, even to my daughter. I hope Goddess will see fit to call another to this post before I die. I would hate to have the pit in which every shadow can be called by name be first neglected, then deserted altogether as I have seen happen elsewhere. Unfortunately, that is not a position I can create a replacement for. Goddess Herself must call the Snakesleeper in her youth.

And I can see only too well with Serpent Sight that such old ways are passing. Absalom's death did not bring peace between Judah and Israel. There are too many other men who share David's lust for power. There was Sheba next who tried to have his way, and now David brings it on himself by flattering Haggith's Adonijah and yet making every foolish promise to young, spoiled Solomon. He will make men of his sons yet.

Men have learned to melt Goddess's mountains and to put them on the ends of arrows. They have learned to put them as spikes in the wheels of their chariots and to fly across the plains of their enemies. Thus clad in iron, they fancy themselves invincible, like gods themselves. Sharp, pointed things, they begin to feel, by right and might shall rule the earth. If they do not question all divinity together, it must be a god they worship, for the blast of war horns deafens them to the quiet strength that can be gained from resting but a moment on the gently sighing bosom of the Earth, feeling Her even, steady heartbeat and hearing the low, storyless syllables of her lullabies.

But I have chosen to live in the past, to cleave to old

values and to try to instill them in my daughter. There are those—many (Mother has written to admit she is one of them)—who despair for me—for both of us, Kinnereth and me—in the days to come. We will be crushed beneath the spiked wheels of progress, they say. Empire and wealth will leave us behind and we will have no future.

Well, be that as it may, I choose the sanctity of the past, nonetheless. Let them shake their heads mournfully—"Poor woman! Freedom is offered her and she is too ignorant, too oppressed by the fear of outmoded gods to accept it." I do not reject a vision of the future because I fear it. You've heard my story. You see I do not lack courage. I only feel that those who hope for the future to be more wonderful than today must always be sadly deluded.

I prefer life as a cycle of poems, a Song of Songs, with no real beginning and no real end, rather than a rise, decline, and fall. I prefer the veil of Goddess service that allows me to retire into spirit rather than to pant beneath the strictures of a body. I prefer a place where all people—men, women, children—are counted as female before the great force of Her power.

Do not pity me or call me downtrodden. If such as I, if such as Gomer, are permitted to be driven from the Earth, then we shall see what true downtrodden souls are like.

Blessed old Gomer. Like her, I feel myself more and more inclined to sit in the courtyard sun, nameless, unspeaking, just cleaning the wheat, fingering the eternal round of life as if numbering beads upon a string circle.

We sing to ourselves sometimes, Gomer and I, she in her deep bass and I in descant over her. We sing the greatest song this world shall ever hear:

> O my dove, that are in the clefts of the rock.
> In the secret places of the stairs,
> Let me see your countenance,
> Let me hear your voice;
> For sweet is your voice
> And your countenance is comely.

And sometimes when the sun is hot and when the mind is given up to Heaven, I reach out a hand toward her knee. "Father?" I murmur.

"Yes, daughter Tamar? I am here," she replies.

Then we look at one another, study faces growing old, but aging as the rocks do age, into solid permanence. Then we cover our faces with our veils to hide what must always remain a mystery. Neither of us minds living this ritualized lie. It is restful to the body and invigorating to the soul. And that makes it the truest of truths.

We raise our voices and sing again:

"I sleep, but my heart is awake."